CW00549471

"The definitive behind-the-scenes portrait of the show in the Eighties; densely researched, eminently readable. Marson has talked to almost every key player."
Dominic Maxwell, *The Times*

"Extraordinary. A great piece of work. I read it in two days' flat, I couldn't stop. I've never seen a biographer enter the story like that, it was brilliant and invigorating. It really is a major piece of Doctor Who history and the history of an entire industry. An entire age, really. In the end, I think the book is clear - we have to forgive JN-T. That ending - he didn't deserve that. And I think by writing about it, you have made something elegant and even beautiful out of such a wretched mess. And I think that's very kind of you indeed. This book says a lot about JN-T but it says a lot about your good and kind heart too."
Russell T.Davies (Writer/Producer)

"Deeply researched, full of surprises, turning out to be the best read of the year so far. It's a hell of an achievement, and I'm in awe of the evident work put into this. Thoughtful analysis, sober focus. A fine book. Highly recommended."
Christopher H. Bidmead (Script Editor)

"Riveting. The honesty shown throughout your assessment of his life is heart warming to those of his friends still left. I do hope that reactions after publication look at the whole rounded story which you have drawn with empathy and understanding. Ian and I are glad that we were able to contribute in a small way to a book you should be rightly proud of."
Fiona Cumming and **Ian Fraser** (Colleagues and friends)

"Wickedly funny...deliciously showbiz - it ultimately had us both crying and laughing. Utterly, utterly wonderful - one of those books where you make excuses to run off and keep reading it."
Gay Times

"Completely addictive - scurrilous, fascinating, hilarious and naughty."
Sophie Aldred (Ace)

TOTALLY TASTELESS

THE LIFE OF JOHN NATHAN-TURNER

RICHARD MARSON

Totally Tasteless: The Life of John Nathan-Turner

This edition first published December 2016 by Miwk Publishing Ltd.
Miwk Publishing, 45a Bell Street, Reigate, Surrey RH2 7AQ.

Parts of this book were originally published as **JN-T: The Life & Scandalous Times of John Nathan-Turner**

ISBN 978-1-908630-65-0

Copyright © Richard Marson 2016.

The rights of Richard Marson to be identified as the author of this work has been asserted in accordance with the Copyright, Designs and Patents Act 1988.

All rights reserved. No part of this publication may be reproduced, stored in or introduced into a retrieval system, or transmitted, in any form, or by any means (electronic, mechanical, photocopying, recording or otherwise) without the prior written permission of the publisher. Any person who does any unauthorised act in relation to this publication may be liable to criminal prosecution and civil claim for damages.

A CIP catalogue record for this book is available from the British Library.

Cover & book design by Robert Hammond. Cover illustration by Andrew Skilleter.

Typeset in Utopia and Trajan.

Printed in Great Britain by TJ International, Padstow, Cornwall.

This book is sold subject to the condition that it shall not, by way of trade or otherwise, be lent, re-sold, hired out, or otherwise circulated without the publisher's prior consent in any form of binding or cover other than that in which it is published and without a similar condition including this condition being imposed on the subsequent purchaser.

www.miwkpublishing.com
This product was lovingly Miwk made.

CONTENTS

To Patrick Mulkern
My oldest friend
"The future is in the past..."

ACKNOWLEDGEMENTS

I'd like to thank everyone who gave their time so generously to talk to me about their memories of John. They were: Sophie Aldred, Ann Arohnson, Mark Ayres, Colin Baker, Lynda Baron, Gillian Beaney, Andrew Beech, Lovett Bickford, Christopher H Bidmead, Christopher Biggins, John Black, Darrol Blake, Nicola Bryant, Andrew Cartmel, Clare Clifford, Chris Clough, Tristan Collett, Karilyn Collier, June Collins, Ben Cook, Ron Craddock, Stephen Cranford, Peter Cregeen, Peter Crocker, Fiona Cumming, Russell T Davies, Peter Davison, Shaun Dellenty, Gordon Doble, Pat Dyer, Kate Easteal (Thomson), Janet Fielding, Grahame Flynn, Ian Fraser, George Gallaccio, Anita Graham, Christopher Guard, Barry Hannam, Margot Hayhoe, Janet Hargreaves, Graeme Harper, Roy Hawkesford, Sue Hedden, Corinne Hollingsworth, Anna Home, June Hudson, David M Jackson, Harold Jessop, Mark Jones, Paul Joyce, Tony Jordan, Ron Katz, Bonnie Langford, Sarah Lee, Gary Leigh, Colin Leslie, Ian Levine, Sarah Lillywhite (Cheetham), Ronnie Marsh, Jessica Martin, Lorne Martin, Dominic May, Sylvester McCoy, Val McCrimmon, Stuart Money, Vivienne Moore, Andrew Morgan, Michael Morris, Stephen Payne, Jacqueline Pearce, John Phillips, Professor Jonathan Powell, Ed Pugh, Janet Radenkovic, David Reid, Professor Jeffrey Richards, Lynn Richards (Gray), Bob Richardson, Matthew Robinson, David Roden, John Frank Rosenblum, Liz Rowell, Norman Rubenstein, Gary Russell, David Saunders, Bill Sellars, Mark Sinclair, Carol Snook, Andrew Smith, Brian Spiby, Mark Strickson, Sarah Sutton, Paul Mark Tams, Mike Tucker, Paul Vanezis, Jan Vincent-Rudzki, Antony Wainer, Alan Wareing, Matthew Waterhouse, Joe Waters, Jane Wellesley, Marcia Wheeler, Betty Willingale, Ronald Wilson, and Ralph Wilton.

I'm grateful, too, for email contributions from Nicholas Briggs, Michael Cox, Terrance Dicks, John Finch, Sarah Hellings, Julie Jones, Alex Leger, Edward Russell and Dee Dee Wilde.

I also made use of my own archive interviews with Peter Grimwade, Robert Holmes, Peter Moffatt, John Nathan-Turner and Eric Saward. The original recordings of these are were preserved by Charles Norton and my thanks are due to him. Video archive of conventions and uncut interviews was provided by Peter Crocker, Ian Levine, Dominic May, Brendan Sheppard and Ed Stradling (who was unstinting with his time and advice).

Fiona Cumming and Ian Fraser, who were almost family to John and Gary, read the entire manuscript and made some astute observations, which I greatly appreciated.

As the guardians of much of John's photo and paper archive, Paul Vanezis and Stephen Cranford couldn't have been more helpful. Stephen also located John's original recordings of his *Cinderella* pantomimes for me. I'd also like to thank Sophie Aldred, Grahame Flynn, Barry Hannam, Dominic May, Bill Sellars and Jan Vincent-Rudzki for sending me valuable material from their private collections. Margot Hayhoe kindly lent me the programmes for John's 1973 production of *Cinderella* and the 1977 Martin Lisemore tribute show. Stephen Payne allowed me to read the unexpurgated version of the interview he conducted with Eric Saward for *Starburst* magazine in 1986. Kate Easteal (Thomson), John's secretary for nearly three years, went out of her way to help, sending me her daily desk diaries as well as a cache of photos. Of the published reference material, I'd like to give a special mention of two excellent and vivid memoirs, which bookend John's time on *Doctor Who* – Matthew Waterhouse's *Blue Box Boy* and Andrew Cartmel's *Script Doctor*.

In addition, I'd like to thank Jim Perkins, archivist for the King Edward VI Aston School, for all his help with researching John's schooldays. Richard Bignell, Richard Molesworth and Marcia Wheeler offered sound advice and vital information. Andrew Pixley and Julie Rogers were ever willing to pinpoint facts and figures and locate obscure texts. Useful contacts came courtesy of Chris Chapman, David Darlington, Kevin Davies, Dan Hall, John Kelly, Johann Knobel, Gary Leigh, Russell Minton and Jeremy Swan. I'm grateful to them all.

At the National Film Archive, I'd like to thank Jonny Davies and Carolyn Bevan for allowing me access to the John Nathan-Turner collection and at the BBC Written Archive Centre, Jessica Hogg worked tirelessly retrieving dozens of related files.

Huge thanks go to my wonderful publishers, Miwk, who took over when others fell by the wayside and did the most superb job in a tight time-frame. Matt West, Robert Hammond and Phil Ware couldn't have been more enthusiastic and supportive, as well as making the work fun – what more can you ask?

To Rupert – you are never forgotten and always with me. Happy memories of the planet of fire...

To my wife Mandy and daughter Rosy, for putting up with me as I journeyed through John's life – and regularly treated them to my impression of the man himself – thank you, I love you and *stay tuned*!

A NOTE ON JOB TITLES

Throughout the text, reference is made to the job titles that contributors had at the time they worked with or knew John. Over the years, some of these were changed and this is intended as a quick reference for the uninitiated.

Production Assistant At the time John joined the BBC (1968), this was the title given to the person who runs the studio floor or location shoot, ensuring it stays on schedule. They have a major role in planning and organising a production. This is the job that often leads to the successful incumbent becoming a director. Towards the end of the 1970s, the BBC changed the title to production manager. At the same point, director's assistants were rechristened production assistants. More recently, production managers have become first assistant directors, in line with the feature film model.

Director's Assistant This was a crucial job, which encompassed typing and timing scripts, continuity on location and in the studio, taking notes for post production and calling shots in the studio gallery, following the director's carefully marked-up camera script. For many years, the assistants were also responsible for reporting costs. The title was amended to production assistant (see above) whereas now it is often credited as script supervisor (again, bringing it in line with the world of films).

Assistant Floor Manager Responsible for the ordering, setting and striking of all a production's action props, marking up rehearsal room floors with coloured tape to indicate for cast and crew where sets will stand, running rehearsals, giving artists' call times and assisting the production in a myriad of practical ways. An important part of the role was to plot moves into the rehearsal script – some directors expected the AFM to copy these into his/her script for camera shots and cuts to be decided. On location, AFMs also had to act as floor assistant because FAs very rarely went on location. Later, as more drama was made entirely on location, a junior or trainee AFM would act as a runner.

Floor Assistant The most junior job on the production ladder. What used to be known as a call boy (urban myth has it that the BBC changed the title when women began to be employed in the role as they could hardly refer to call girls!) – responsible for ensuring that artists are in the right place at the right time in the studio, helping to cue, and doing lots of fetching and carrying.

Production Unit Manager A role created in the early 1970s. PUMs assisted producers, budgeting and taking responsibility for many practical as well as financial aspects of a production. The job, which is described in more detail in the text, later became known as production associate. The nearest modern equivalent is line producer.

Drama Department Manager The job of the manager was to run the department for the head in much the same way that production associates ran productions for producers and production managers ran them for directors. The manager also liaised with planning department, hired temporary staff, scheduled staff on to productions and coped with crises. A key aspect of the role was working with the head on "offers" for the next financial year (the wish list of productions the head wanted to make), and the subsequent negotiations with resource departments when the commissions came through. When series and serials were amalgamated, the manager was joined by a deputy.

PREFACE

THE MEMORY CHEATS

When I first started to think about writing this book, I was struck by the common ground I share with John Nathan-Turner. We were both, to some extent, frustrated performers, with an early ambition to act. We both took leading roles in school plays and revues – when we weren't directing others to do it the way we thought best, a rehearsal for our professional lives. We were both dedicated BBC men, starting with the same job in the same department. We both progressed through the system until we were running flagship BBC programmes – in John's case *Doctor Who* and in mine *Blue Peter*, shows whose fame and longevity we cherished and developed in our own way, casting actors and presenters who would become favourites for generations of viewers. We both wrote, produced and directed a string of sparkly song-and-dance-based Christmas pantomimes (his were traditional stage productions, mine lavish TV concoctions). Ultimately, we both struggled with the challenge of keeping alive a programme which, despite the affection of the British public, BBC management had ceased to value and actively undermined. Perhaps unwisely, we were both emotionally as well as professionally involved in our work and yet, years later, we are still part of the respective "families" of these uniquely British institutions.

In the spring of 1981, production had begun on John's second season as producer of *Doctor Who*. His star was in the ascendant. Meanwhile, I was 14 years old, interred at boarding school out in the country where life seemed bleak. All the usual clichés applied. It was perpetually freezing; the religion was sport, sport and more sport, and like-minded friends were thin on the ground. I watched the clock and dreamt of life beyond this stultifying place. I knew where I was heading too, having switched my allegiance from a career as an actor to a journalist and from there to the intoxicating world of television. My father, who was a lawyer, had links with London Weekend Television and had recently arranged a day-long visit to their South Bank headquarters. I was captivated by the studios, that characteristic aroma of electricity, paint and nervous adrenalin. Back behind bars, I read anything and everything to do with television and even wrote to Shaun Sutton, the BBC's head of drama, with a long list of precocious questions, which, staggeringly, he took seriously and found time to answer. The fly in the ointment was that the school regime made it nearly impossible actually to watch anything. Every night we had prep (homework) from seven to eight thirty and quite often some kind of activity or house meeting afterwards. At weekends there were film showings in the vast Victorian Grignon Hall, creaky affairs with scratchy 16mm prints of five-year-old movies that had done the rounds, projected on a battered screen. They came in reels of two or three and the boys would jeer and jostle as the reels were changed over. Films seemed to me to belong to the past and it was television that had the promise of the future and an air of magic and allure.

At this stage, I had no interest in *Doctor Who*. I hadn't really watched it since 1977. Until then, it had been a treasured part of our family ritual. I remember the thrill of the summer day in 1974 when cricket was cancelled and replaced with an omnibus repeat of *The Sea Devils*, the only time there was a benefit to my brother's obsession with bat and ball. I still carry a scar on my arm from the day he decided to impersonate one of the still-terrifying mummies from *Pyramids of Mars*. He'd stalked me through the garden until, hysterical with terror, I shut the kitchen door on him. We struggled but he had a firmer grip on the handle and was stronger than me. When he suddenly let go, my arm plunged through the glass in the window and his expression changed from the implacable mask of a robot killer to one of shock and frantic apology. I was rushed off to hospital for stitches and felt quite heroic. But then Geoff had gone away to school and *Doctor Who* had started to seem sillier and I had no time for the idiocy of an increasingly self-indulgent Tom Baker.

"Nicholson, what's that you're reading?"

A shrug and a grunt and the boy held up the cover of a magazine so that I could see. *Doctor Who Monthly*. The cover featured the cast I had loved the most – Jon Pertwee, Katy Manning, Nicholas Courtney and Roger Delgado. I felt a pang of nostalgia and curiosity. Eventually, I persuaded Nicholson (we never used first names at school – but his was Jonathan) to let me read the magazine. Then I started to interrogate him about his knowledge of *Doctor Who*. It turned out he was something of an expert. He had *Doctor Who* books too, novelisations with gaudy candy-coloured spines and agreed to let me borrow a couple. And that was it – I was hooked. I began to buy the books myself. Some of the stories I remembered vividly, some were new to me. During that summer holiday, the BBC repeated two of the recent stories: *Full Circle* and *The Keeper of Traken*. I was impressed that the silliness, which had so put me off, seemed to have been eliminated – the programme was now brighter, pacier, fresher. By now, I was buying the magazine too and it was in its pages that I first became aware of a man called John Nathan-Turner. At an age when most adults seemed ancient, this guy actually seemed quite young. I liked what he had to say in his interviews and, more importantly, I liked what he was doing with the programme. What I could see of it.

Back at school, the only time when television was an option was at the weekend and then, if there was something you wanted to see, you had to get a chit signed by a prefect, as well as by your housemaster, and pay ten pence to the house fund for the privilege. The set, perched on a high shelf, lived in the housemaster's office. *The Professionals*, shown on a Sunday night, was the only programme that everyone seemed to bother with and the room would be crammed with excited boys whooping at the car chases and cast of crude stereotypes. I was there too, because it was better than nothing. Once I did manage to convince my housemaster that *Not the Nine o'Clock News* was a serious current affairs show, worthy of my education. Grudgingly, he signed the chit. Unfortunately he then chose to walk in during the infamous *I Love Trucking* song, at the precise moment when Pamela Stephenson happened to be manually stimulating Rowan Atkinson's gear stick. I don't think he minded too much as it gave him an excuse to beat me. What hurt much more was having to miss almost all of *The Five Faces of Doctor Who* repeat season in 1981, a brilliant crowd-pleasing stunt by this Nathan-Turner man. I did take my bum in my hands every Monday, when I could be fairly sure my housemaster was occupied elsewhere, and crept into his study, leaving the lights off, gingerly switching on the set and keeping the volume at its lowest audible level.

That Christmas, an extra present came in the form of *K9 and Company*, Nathan-Turner's brainwave – to give Sarah Jane Smith her own show. He was a quarter of a century ahead of his time. Meanwhile, everything about the parent show seemed to be changing in a way I found exciting. Peter Davison had been cast as the new Doctor. I thought he was inspired casting and I liked the line-up around him, too. Unfortunately, a new school term began after the first two episodes of *Castrovalva*, so I made elaborate efforts to record the soundtracks of the others and my sister Deb filled in the gaps by describing what she'd seen by letter or during my weekly call from the payphone in the house corridor. I'll never forget the thrill when she told me about the utterly unexpected death of

Adric. The return of the Cybermen had been cool enough but this was a moment of pure soap melodrama to be relished. Silent credits – wow! Years later, I discovered Nathan-Turner had nicked that from *Coronation Street*. I nicked from him too – one of my *Blue Peter* title sequences ended with a little pinpoint of light shooting out from the back of the frame and exploding my final credit in a white-out. Pure homage.

It was the summer of 1982 when everything changed. After months of persistent nagging and negotiation, I managed to convince my parents that I would be better off elsewhere for my sixth form. I would no longer have to board. Using the same powers of persuasion, I convinced my mother that renting a video recorder was a vital necessity, and this fabulous machine arrived just in time for the summer repeat season called *Doctor Who and the Monsters*. But I wasn't content with my freedom to be a stay-at-home fan. I was determined to find a way of getting more involved. I found it quite by chance. While I was talking to a girl at my new school, she mentioned that her boyfriend was the brother of a woman who had been in *Doctor Who*. "You can meet her if you like."

The woman turned out to be Louise Jameson, who'd played Tom Baker's companion, Leela. Naturally, I was keen. But I thought it was just too much of a cringe to be introduced like someone on day release from a *Doctor Who* fan asylum. (Back then, there was absolutely no street cred to be had in being a *Doctor Who* fan.) My mother, who had been a journalist, suggested that I take my ghetto blaster (how 80s is that!) and record an interview with her. She'd seen the fanzines I'd started to buy – surely one of those might want to print it..? The meeting was arranged and Louise, one of life's good people, couldn't have been more charming and patient as I worked through my list of painstakingly prepared questions. I transcribed the result, wrote it out long hand and my mother typed this up. The result looked, well, professional. I thought, "Bugger the fanzines, let's see if I can sell it to *Doctor Who Monthly*."

I sent it in to the publisher, Marvel Comics, with what I thought was a grown-up sounding covering letter. In retrospect, it was hilariously pompous. But it seemed to work. I got a note back from the *DWM* editor, Alan McKenzie, saying he'd buy it and would I give him a call? My hands shaking, I dialled the number and tried to assume a confidence I didn't feel. Alan didn't seem to notice anything amiss and explained that he was looking for more of the same. Could I deliver? Saying yes was easy – but how was I going to pull it off? The chance to interview Louise had been pure fluke. Then I thought about our local theatre. They often hosted touring productions of the *Not Now, There Go My Knickers* variety and these were almost exclusively cast with popular but somewhat faded

TV actors of yesteryear. I walked up to the place and inspected the schedule of forthcoming attractions pinned up in the foyer. In two weeks' time, Deborah Watling (1960s companion Victoria) would be in town. I persuaded the theatre staff to put the idea of an interview to her and she agreed. For a time, this became a regular source of interview subjects and it wasn't long before I felt emboldened to look up an actors' agent in the local library's *Spotlight* and make a call that began with the truth-stretching introduction, "I'm from the BBC's *Doctor Who Monthly...*" It worked almost every time and when, after a few months, I finally met my editor, Alan spent most of that first meeting exclaiming over and over again at my extreme youth. I was 17 years old.

As my input into *Doctor Who Monthly* steadily increased, I began to get the chance to attend studio recordings at BBC Television Centre and arrange official interviews via the production office. In the end, I was also compiling the news (which in those days had a laughable lead time of three months). And, so, inevitably, I began to deal with John Nathan-Turner himself. I'd actually first met him in April 1983 in a tent, away from the queues and chaos of the BBC's all-too-successful 20th anniversary convention at Longleat. He was standing, unsmiling, behind a trestle table, wearing a red bomber jacket covered in badges and a pair of slightly ludicrous dark glasses. I wanted to tell him that I had started to write for the magazine but before I could say anything, he had snatched my programme from my hands and signed it deftly, with the signature I had seen before. I loved the way he used the top stroke of the J in John to pull the whole name together – so showbiz. I've never much seen the point of autographs but I was impressed with the way he had just assumed that's what I'd wanted. "Have a great day," he drawled and the moment had passed because it was time for him to introduce the next interview panel.

Perhaps my favourite memory of him came much later, when I was at university. I was having a high old time there, working a little, directing a lot, and cramming in the *Doctor Who* writing, which paid for my plays to have the best costumes, lighting and sets around. There was also a not inconsiderable social life. It was work hard, play hard and somehow, inevitably, when it was *Doctor Who* news day, I would wake to the banging on my door from a disgruntled fellow student saying, "Marson, there's some woman from the BBC on the phone." Long before mobiles, our only link to the outside world was a payphone in a chilly kitchenette at the end of the corridor. I'd stumble out of bed, shivering and yawning, and make my way to pick up the dangling receiver, hoping that the frog in my throat wasn't too obvious. "Hello?"

Sarah Lee, the secretary, would snap efficiently, "I've got John on the phone. He's been waiting five minutes."

A click and a buzz and then the familiar soft drawl of the man himself. "Hi – how are you?"

"Fine, thanks. How are you?"

He rarely answered my return courtesy. Instead, the next line was invariably, "Would you like a scoop?", the word "scoop" drawn out to bursting point. I loved that and it always made me want to laugh. With lamentable frequency, I'd then discover that I hadn't got a pen with me or if I had, nothing to write on except my hand – or the wall – which would end up defaced with odd lines like "*Reign Terror* 6 found" or whatever the "scoooop" was that month.

Over the next four years, I met John many times, regularly spoke to him on the phone and some of these encounters will feature in this book. As I went about my *Doctor Who* business, frequently I heard people praise him to the skies and bitch him to oblivion. *Plus ça change.*

I saw him last towards the end of the 1990s, walking despondently down Wood Lane. He looked different without his beard. He didn't clock me. It had been years since I'd had anything to do with *Doctor Who* and I was now fully absorbed with my own career in production. He was yesterday's man. I wish now that I'd stopped him to say hello ("Hi, how are you?") and tell him what I was up to because I sensed he would have approved – but perhaps it would have been unkind and insensitive.

The early 80s, the heyday of John's era, was a wonderful time in my life, full of change and opportunity, and unsurprisingly, it holds a powerful nostalgia for me. It's another of the reasons I was driven to write this book – because so much of it is rooted in the *Doctor Who* with which I became most familiar. Even when the going was good, John was a controversial figure. But, as the fortunes of the show waxed and waned, friends and foes swapped sides or became increasingly polarised. Equally, I wanted to explore the personality and impact of an individual who, more than a decade after his death, still has the power to divide opinion with such staggering ferocity.

It's said that history is written by the survivors. Certainly, plenty of what has been written and said about him would probably have been rephrased or suppressed altogether had its subject not died so prematurely. In his lifetime, John often promised to set the record straight and tell the story as he saw it. But when the camera was rolling or the tape set in motion, he always seemed to think better of it. Perhaps surprisingly for a man with such a talent for publicity, John was never keen to shine a spotlight on his own psyche and thinking. Although in private he adored gossip, in public, loyalty and discretion were important to him, both offered and expected in return. Not long before his death, John did write his own memoirs, appropriately in serial form, but these are, perhaps inevitably, frustrating and elusive, offering only momentary glimpses of emotion amid the parade of *Doctor Who* anecdotes. There is no anger or passion, surprisingly little humour or strong opinion – no real sense of the man who dazzled the world with his wardrobe of multi-coloured shirts.

What would John have made of this biography? "I think he would have loved it," says Colin Baker. "He would have asked, 'I don't want copy approval but let me have it and I can correct any mistakes!'" Nicola Bryant (who played Peri) believes that "he'd love the idea that he is still that important and then he'd pick holes in everything you did." Close friend Grahame Flynn points out that "he was a showman. You wouldn't do your own memoirs if you didn't expect people to talk about you." Script editor Andrew Cartmel says, "He'd have been delighted – if he's anywhere, he'd be smiling. He would have wanted lots of pictures in it." "I think he'd bloody love it," laughs another friend, Mark Jones. "I can see him sitting there with a fag in his hand, laughing."

It's my hope that this book reveals John as he really was, why he inspired love as well as loathing, deciphering his life with all its many triumphs and tragedies.

Richard Marson
December 2012

ONE

IT'S NOT WHERE YOU START

"In triumph ever modest,
In danger, ever cool,
They win, throughout the world, boys,
Fresh laurels for the school."
King Edward VI Aston school song

During his golden years, with the eyes and ears of thousands of fans on both sides of the Atlantic trained upon him, those who ventured to ask John Nathan-Turner when he was born were likely to be answered with a characteristically raised eyebrow and the old-school theatrical, mind-your-own business reply, "In nineteen hundred and frozen to death..."

In fact, he was born on 12th August 1947 and came into the world as plain John Turner. He was never Jonathan as has sometimes been claimed – this is a confusion from his early days in the theatre, when he was briefly credited as Jonathan Turner. The double-barrel came soon after, the earliest professional use I could find dating from January 1968. John Nathan-Turner sounded more stylish, was certainly more eye-catching and later ensured that he would, as they say in television, "give good credit" – but the pragmatic truth is that there was already a successful actor called John Turner registered by Equity, the theatrical union, and so an alternative had to be found.

His parents, Samuel (always known as Sam) and Kathleen (Kath) had met during the war, in which Sam served with the Royal Artillery. They married in 1944, when Sam was 23 and Kath 21, and settled in 245 Perry Common Road, a semi-detached council house in Erdington, a humble but pleasant suburb of Birmingham. The house had a decent-sized garden at the back, with a smaller one at the front. It was to remain their home until, decades later, illness and old age deprived them of it.

John was their only child, and as is so often the case with only children, he became the absolute focus of his parents' hopes and ambitions. "They were very proud of him," says Fiona Cumming, a director and close friend, "and in turn, it was very important to him to show them that he was doing well."

Whenever he made his not infrequent appearances in the pages of newspapers and magazines, he would dutifully send the cuttings up to Birmingham. The only other close member of the family was John's Auntie Joan, who lived nearby, and to whom John referred to as "mad Auntie Joan."

"She'd come out with silly things," recalls close friend Anita Graham, "and they were always running round looking after her. They all looked after each other."

After his demob from the army, Sam Turner had worked for a time as a fruiterer's assistant but eventually he became a bookmaker and this remained his hit-and-miss profession. John later commented, "I never got into the habit of betting myself because I was too close to it."

"I think his father, who was a very nice man, could be quite difficult," says close friend Barry Hannam. "One week he would have all the money in the world and Kath would have diamonds and minks and the next week it would all be gone again."

"For his 21st birthday," recalls Cumming, "he'd give John the keys to a car and then suddenly a few weeks later things wouldn't be going well for him so the car would have to go back. But he was very aware of his own position. For instance, Kath had a beautiful fur coat, which I don't think that she particularly liked, but it was important to Sam that he was seen to be able to have his wife in mink."

"Sam was a real man's man and could tell a few risqué stories," says Hannam.

"He was outrageous and outgoing, like John," says Cumming. "And he could always make things work."

"Dad was really a flat-cap type of chap," says Grahame Flynn, who knew John in later life, "whereas she was always particular. It was hats and long coats."

John adored both his parents but was especially close to his mother, who worked for some years as a catering assistant. "He was very thoughtful about her," says Cumming, "always looking for a dress he thought she might like, with the shoes to match. He was very particular about finding just the right thing for her. I always remember him sending her irises on her birthday, because Iris was her middle name."

Another close friend and colleague, Jane Wellesley, remembers, "I was an only child too and we were constantly commiserating about the fact that you had to deal with every crisis because there wasn't anybody else. As they got older, there were a lot."

Kath Turner never found life easy. Her great sadness was the tragic death of her brother, who had committed suicide at a time when this was seen as a stigma and rarely discussed. Over the years, she developed serious mental health issues and John often had to race up to Birmingham at short notice to deal with some aspect of her care. Cumming adds, "There were various other members of her family who'd also had the same problems. She was very unsure of herself and just had fragile health, which is one of the reasons John never finished up in America. He would never give up on the responsibility of looking after her."

Years later, he confided in Wellesley, "The trouble with my mother is my father," but despite the inevitable stress and uncertainty that blighted their marriage, his parents remained together until the end of their lives. He spoke to them most days and took them on holidays abroad. Carol Snook, another friend from the BBC drama department, remembers, "He said they'd done a lot for him so it was his turn now. I admired that tremendously."

Sam Turner, cheerful and ebullient, was passionate about music hall and old-time entertainment. From the age of three, John was taken to a pantomime every Boxing Day. He never lost his love of the genre and showed early signs of being able to hold an audience himself. Aged eight, he was given his first part in a church play, playing the part of a squirrel. The Turners were a standard Church of England family – religion played little part in their daily lives. They put their faith into their hopes for their only son's future.

In 1950s Britain, there was only one escape route for bright children from a working-class background and that was to pass the 11-plus exam to gain entry into a grammar school, with all the promise that a good education could provide. John was put up for King Edward VI Aston. Founded in 1883, this taught about 630 boys and was one of the top schools in the city with a solid academic and sporting reputation. Entry was highly competitive but John didn't let his parents down, passing his 11-plus and arriving as a new boy in September 1958. Hannam again: "He always said that his mother was very intelligent. She went to grammar school and he thought he'd got his brains from his mother and his practicality from his father."

The school was divided into four "houses" – John was a member of

Temperley House, named after the school's first headmaster, John Temperley. "The ethos of the school was wonderful, really," says Harold Jessop, who was then the head of physical education. "It was a very nice atmosphere."

Like most schools at the time, sport was regarded as hugely important and, although John played his share of rugby and cricket, and took part in athletics and swimming, as Jessop puts it, "He wasn't going to be an Olympian! But even if he couldn't do forward rolls, he could do something else, couldn't he? He wanted to participate in everything and did so to the best of his ability. He'd got a very nice attitude to life, I thought. He was very popular."

Jeffrey Richards, two years his senior, remembers: "Anybody who made other people laugh was popular. I would describe him as one of those characters who stand out at school. He was a performer – a personality. He was a kind of bustling, busy, flamboyant figure. He was very funny. He had a well-developed sense of the absurd. There was a lot of laughter around when he was there. He used to do imitations of the schoolmasters and that went down very well."

At the end of his first year, his report commented, "Tends to be rather fussy about things," and contained the rather grudging words "satisfactory progress", qualifying this with the warning note "but the effort must be sustained from now on – it is only the beginning."

Over the years that followed, his reports record consistent effort rather than any noticeable academic success. His interests in these early years were listed as stamp collecting, bus and train spotting, cycling and reading.

In 1961, John (sometimes known as "Turner the Bunsen Burner") became fast friends with another boy in his year called Roy Hawkesford. Although he wasn't an only child himself, Roy's elder sister had married when he was 11 and so there was a comparable absence of a sibling to play with. For the next four years, Roy and John became inseparable: "My parents liked him. We didn't live that far away from each other," remembers Hawkesford, "a mile or so but quite a way outside town. We spent hours walking slowly home from school – being able to talk about anything and laughing, the way boys are. He loved gossip – any kind of gossip – about other boys or teachers. Boys tittle-tattle just as much as girls, especially if you're not talking about rugby or football.

"His father wasn't there much because you tended to 'knock around' during the day when he would have been out. But his mother was very amusing and quite rotund and she'd give us tea and cakes. John liked his cakes. I remember her storming in once when we were sitting in the front room and having a rant at him – 'It was yo what ate that cake!' It sticks in my mind because the look on her face was so classic, telling him off but only in a mock kind of way.

"His father had an unusual collection of records, which pre-dated 78s, the content of which probably came from the 1920s, often bawdy, like his favourite one, *Bollocky Bill the Sailor*, sanitised as *Barnacle Bill the Sailor* in a *Popeye* episode. We laughed at that record and played it over and over again, revelling in the risqué nature of the lyrics and the 'broad' way the song was sung."

Aston was not an affluent area and one of King Edward's more forbidding masters, Harry Tyson, arranged after-school visits for boys to the local children's hospital where they might play with the patients cooped up there or sent them to call on old people, to talk, clean and shop for them. "John and I used to visit an old man called Mr Dodd," says Hawkesford. "He lived in a small terrace house with a side entry. He was practically deaf and blind and we'd sit, coal heaped in one corner of his room, listening to him talk about the old days, as it got darker and darker. We always found it difficult to make excuses to leave, but John would usually be the one to break the sad monologue and tell him we had to go home. At some point, he would inevitably turn to a condemnation of his children who never went to see him. On one occasion, in late November, it was actually dark in the room, when Mr Dodd offered us a biscuit. We thanked him and declined but he insisted that we take the biscuit tin in the sideboard. He offered us the tin on subsequent visits, too, and we always made our excuses – we were going home for our tea and so on. The last time we visited, we discovered from a neighbour that he had died. At the funeral, Mr Tyson asked us if we knew anything about any money. Of course, we said we didn't – feeling as if we were being accused of something. It turned out that there had been £2000 in the biscuit tin. We could see then why Mr Dodd wanted us to take it, when we assumed we were just being offered a biscuit by a poor old man. I'm sure we would not have taken the money, if we had found it; but no one would have suspected that there would have been any money in that house."

When boys reached the fourth form and their 15th birthday, the school required them to spend at least one term boarding at its Longdon Hall house near Lichfield. The idea, explains Jessop was that "you're away from home, looking after yourself and it gives you a greater independence. I haven't heard of anybody who didn't enjoy it. They still have reunions." Longdon was run by the headmaster, Leonard Brandon, and his wife, with the support of a resident teacher. John's turn came from September to Christmas 1961.

"In the mornings we used to do lessons," recalls Hawkesford. "We'd have masters come over from the school. You'd have a whole morning of English, science or languages and in the afternoon it was farm work because the hall was associated with a small farm. We all helped out – we had a kind of rota so that everyone did the different jobs like tending the sheep or mucking out the horses, digging the very large allotment. It was self-sufficient in vegetables. None of us were exactly adept at farm work but it gave us some kind of insight as to what it was like to work on a farm and it got us out of the city environment. Then we had games on a Wednesday afternoon – rugby or cross country.

"One evening a group of us were socialising in the classroom and were talking about whether any of us had ever fainted. John jumped up and said, 'You can make yourself faint!' Of course, we asked 'How? Show us.' John obliged by jumping onto a desk, crouching down, breathing heavy for about a minute then blowing as hard as he could on his thumb. Sure enough, he passed out immediately, falling forward off the desk and landing on his head where he seemed to perch before tumbling sideways onto the hard floor. We were horrified. He came round after a minute or so, looking very sorry for himself, but happy that he had entertained us. That was John Turner. He loved to be at the centre of things, entertaining us in some way, occasionally despite himself."

Apart from the usual academic reservations ("He does not always find it easy to settle down and learn facts") John's Longdon report was glowing: "He has done good work on the farm... and taken the trouble to see something of the countryside. On the rugby field, he has learnt to run well with the ball and put some effort into games. His general conduct has been agreeable and his manners pleasing. Early on, he had a little difficulty settling down to the routine of life here and was rather forgetful about keeping to time but he soon overcame this and has proved himself most reliable and trustworthy."

John belonged to the first generation who grew up with television as an integral part of the family routine. One of his favourites was the perennial school comedy, *Billy Bunter*. The Turners were also avid viewers of popular series like *Coronation Street*, a lifelong addiction for John and, later, *Doctor Who*. "We were both *Doctor Who* fans," says Hawkesford. "We used to find William Hartnell amusing as he was fairly poor as an actor."

Favourite television and radio programmes, and the stars who appeared in them, fuelled hours of conversation. "I remember him mimicking people from *Round the Horne* and *The Goon Show*. He was fascinated by Kenneth Williams and the whole camp thing. Two of John's favourite comedians were Tommy Cooper and, especially, Frankie Howerd. We all used to take off Frankie but John bore a certain facial resemblance to him, though many years younger, of course – and he got the voice perfectly."

"John also liked to talk about Noele Gordon, first in *Lunchbox* and then, from 1964, in *Crossroads* [the ITV soap]. We had a good old laugh at *Crossroads*, which was hilarious because it came from Birmingham and it was so bad. We both loved Beryl Reid, the Brummie Marlene in [BBC radio comedy] *Educating Archie*, and we saw her in pantos at the Birmingham Hippodrome. She wore amazing earrings that lit up. We loved whatever was outrageous or just plain hammy, camp or silly."

As they got older, the two friends were trusted to go out on their own, to the theatre and cinema, clubs and concerts. In August 1963, aged 16, they were even allowed to go on holiday to Bournemouth together: "We stayed at a guest house where my parents had taken me when I was younger – the funny thing was we turned up at the place having been given the address, and the lady said, 'We don't do bed and breakfast any more.' But she took pity on us because it was pouring with rain and we were obviously two young lads. She said, 'But I'll put you up anyway.' We went to the beach and wandered about but it was raining so hard that we went into a department store and bought pakamacs – those thin, grey waterproof ones that kept the rain out. They did keep the rain out if it wasn't also blowing a gale. Within five minutes of setting off proudly in our new macs, they were torn to shreds by the ferocious weather and we ran along the Square doing impressions of Gene Kelly (minus umbrella) in *Singin' in the Rain*. People looked at us as if we were mad. We probably were; who would be so mad as to wear shorts and a T-shirt in August in Bournemouth? We found everything a laugh then, except for the spending money we'd wasted on the pakamacs!"

The highlight of the holiday was a trip to the Gaumont Cinema to see the band who defined the decade – the Beatles: "We couldn't believe our luck to get tickets; we didn't know they were playing there until we arrived." They knew what to expect, having already seen the Fab Four live at Birmingham Town Hall, with Roy Orbison in support, on 4th June 1963: "We were knocked out by the Big O's voice and stage presence; you could hear a pin drop. Unfortunately we didn't hear a single word of the Beatles because of the girls' screaming – but they looked good!"

Sixties pop culture enticed them both. Hawkesford, who later became a professional jazz musician, still has the tickets for most of the shows and concerts they went to: "We saw the Rolling Stones at Birmingham Hippodrome on 27th September 1963, having box seats to the right of the stage – which meant not only could we see them very well, we could also hear them as well. Then we were in the audience for the *Thank Your Lucky Stars* that went out on 20th October 1963, in which the Beatles sang *All My Loving, Money* and *She Loves You*. We found [presenter] Janice Nicholls hilarious, with her broad local accent and 'Oi'll give it foiv!' catchphrase. We went to see the Beatles twice more, on 10th November 1963, at Birmingham Hippodrome and a year later, on 11th

November 1964, at the Odeon Cinema, Birmingham.

"Everyone would buy the Beatles albums. LPs were quite expensive in those days and we used to save up – you could only buy one a month. When John bought their second album, he took it home and then told me, 'I've taken it back to the shop'. This was a shop that we often used to stop at on our way back home from school. 'What's wrong with it?' 'Oh, it's got a terrible hiss on it.' The lady who owned the shop knew us quite well and she said, 'You have a listen to it, Roy, see what you think.' I listened to it and said, 'There's no hiss on that' – 'Yes there is, there it is,' replied John. I said, 'That's the cymbals, you chump!'"

It was one of the Beatles' support acts who really captivated John, though, another of the era's defining talents – panda-eyed, peroxide-haired torch singer Dusty Springfield: "He seemed to find her some kind of icon and he was always fascinated by her."

Roy could play guitar and often he would accompany John, who had a pleasant if unspectacular singing voice. Eventually, they decided to audition for the talent show of the day, *Opportunity Knocks*, presenting themselves for the initial heat at the Alpha TV studios on their doorstep in Aston: "We did *Move over Darling* – which was probably a strange choice but we used to like doing camp versions of middle of the road songs rather than pop songs. We also sang *Walk on By* but two boys singing *Move over Darling* was probably what did for us! We'd also rehearsed quite a nice harmony rendition of *A World without Love*, but we were out on our backsides by then, so never got to perform it or to meet [host] Hughie Green! My mother loved that song when we rehearsed in our back garden. I think we sounded quite sweet – when we weren't giggling."

When they were 17, John and Roy passed their driving tests: "His father let him borrow his car which was a Ford Consul – quite a big car – which we drove down to Bournemouth for the day. His dad, always amiable and friendly, was quite relaxed about that sort of thing."

Out of school, the boys were blagging their way into clubs too: "Our favourites were the Carlton Club, in Erdington, above a furniture shop on the High Street, which later gained fame as Mothers and the Elbow Room opposite the Barton's Arms in Aston. We also went to the Metro on Livery Street. As we were under 18, we used to dress smartly – John liked pointed shoes – and tried to look grown up in order to get in – which is amazing really as I looked about 12. John looked older, maybe 14!"

The general air of liberation swirling through British society reached schools like King Edward's too. As a great concession, boys in the sixth form were allowed to abandon the wearing of caps. Blind eyes were turned to lengthening hairstyles and record players were permitted in common rooms. Much of this had to do with the benevolence of the headmaster, Leonard Brandon. Jeffrey Richards again: "There was an extraordinarily rich after-school life, with a school magazine, school play, school choir, school orchestra, jazz club, chess club, photographic society, historical society, regular trips to Stratford to the RSC, and regular trips abroad. John came on the historical society trip to Provence in 1963.

"A group of us were sitting in a pavement cafe in Avignon when he came up, burst into tears and sobbed uncontrollably. His beloved camera had been stolen. Teenage boys simply didn't burst into tears in those days. We all sat there absolutely tongue-tied and shocked. It revealed to me that he was a considerably more emotional and complex person under the surface than he ever revealed."

Two years later, Hawkesford remembers another school trip, to Paris: "We were there for a week, that was good fun. We were in a large dormitory. The idea was to go and see a couple of plays but most of the time we were able to go out, teaming up with people from Stourbridge Grammar School.

"When we were on our way back to England, we arrived in Calais and were warned that it was going to be a very rough crossing – which didn't impress John at all. When on board, and still in the relative calm of the harbour, he recalled that the best way to avoid seasickness was to have big meal before setting off, to settle your stomach. When we were at sea, the rest of us were clinging to the railings on the deck above the restaurant. I turned to see John emerge from below with a big smile on his face. Just as he got to the top, he shouted out, 'That was grea....!' But he never finished the word as a huge dinner emerged from his mouth and spread across the deck in our direction. As you can imagine, we found it hilarious, but poor John, white as sheet and looking very sorry for himself, slumped against the railings for the duration of the crossing."

Perhaps inevitably, both boys shared a slight inferiority complex, rooted in their relatively humble backgrounds, marked out by their broader accents and the fact neither of them had the necessary talent on the rugby pitch, which was, at the time, the pre-requisite of school stardom. But this was about to change. Drama, once confined to the obligation of an annual school play, was steadily transformed. It started under the influence of Gordon Doble, who had arrived at the school to teach languages but whose real passion was the theatre. "We were pioneers," he says. "We used to do plays in the old assembly hall but in 1964 an extension opened which contained a rather marvellous assembly hall with a well-equipped stage." Doble can still remember John Turner as a "bright-eyed boy, very willing – indeed, falling over himself to help".

1963 was the year of the great satire boom, led, on television, by the BBC's *That Was the Week That Was*. The ripples from this explosion of cynicism and humour reached Birmingham and that year, somewhat tentatively, King Edward's began to mount their own school revues. "It was fantastically amateurish by present day standards," laughs Jeffrey Richards, the boy in charge. "There were about seven or eight of us. We used to sing Noël Coward songs and parody television programmes. One of our big hits was doing Freddie and the Dreamers. All the audience were screaming and it was very funny."

"Jeff was a cousin of mine," says Hawkesford, "and he directed. John and I were roped in, despite being a year too young, as we were clearly regarded as potential comic material. I was mostly involved in the music, while John played some parts in the show."

"John was a full participant," Richards remembers, "acting and mimicking and so on. He was terribly good. Terribly creative and contributory. We all thought he'd become an actor."

"More than any of us," says Hawkesford, "he had a real love for 'light entertainment', variety and the like. He was captivated by the whole world of it. He loved stars and stardom. We watched Ethel Merman perform on *Sunday Night at the London Palladium* [this was on 15th March 1964]. She was well past her prime and had a very wide vibrato and those big vowels used by vaudeville and stage singers. Of course she sang *There's No-o-o-o Business Like Sho-o-o-w Business*, which we found hilarious, but the fact is that John wanted that song as the opener to our first revue, done in the vaudeville style. I remember he also got us to do '*A' – You're Adorable*, the 1948 song later recorded by Perry Como, which I can still sing from beginning to end! Further evidence of his love of 'light' music with a comical or cheesy character."

A sort of cultural coterie developed within the sixth form. This small group used to spend its free periods in the art room under the aegis of Gordon Doble where, says Richards, "We drank coffee, played records and discussed culture. John Turner came into the fringes of that group because of his involvement in the revue. We set up the Wagner society in order to justify being in the room. It was a fantastically productive and wonderful time. I think he flourished in that environment, where you could be in a group of fellow creative people."

"It was a 'secret' little club," says Hawkesford. "John took me along too, once. This met in the art teacher's small office and seemed to consist of Mr Barlow, the art teacher, Gordon Doble, Jeff Richards, and John. They were rather surprised when I turned up, and faintly amused. Anyway, I remember they were all discussing a new play by Joe Orton, called *Loot* – further evidence of John's fascination with the outrageous and camp. I felt uncomfortable in that circle, which clearly evinced certain leanings "

Despite his suspicions and the closeness of their friendship, Hawkesford was still unaware that John was gay: "I suppose the signs were there – his adoration of Kenneth Williams and fascination with Dusty Springfield – but then there was a general campness about the popular culture. When we were on holiday together in Bournemouth, we had to share a double bed and I never had to fend him off."

"We weren't aware that anyone was gay," says Richards. "It didn't crop up at all. And anybody who was gay wouldn't have mentioned it."

No wonder – homosexuality was still a crime and looked on by most people as a shameful perversion. John conformed in as much as he had a steady girlfriend for some time, Angela Collins, who went to nearby Hodge Hill School. But, as Hawkesford points out, "Relationships with girlfriends in those days were not highly sexualised – they were more friendships with a bit of snogging. It never went further than that."

When Gordon Doble announced that he was leaving to pursue a career in the theatre, John was among a group of boys who got together to produce *Le Médecin Malgré Lui* (*The Doctor in Spite of Himself*), a one-act play by 17th-century French dramatist Molière, which they performed as a valedictory surprise for their departing teacher – impressively, in the original French. "Although it was in French vernacular," recalls Hawkesford, "it still had the audiences laughing. John wasn't a serious actor at all, but he knew how to entertain."

The school magazine, having referred to a year "spectacularly jam-packed with drama", commented: "John Turner, in the role of the rich gull Géronte, bursting both literally and figuratively from his costume, gave the richly amusing professional performance we have come to expect from him, and during the course of it, he succeeded in demolishing part of the set."

Doble was succeeded by David Collins, who wrote that "Mr Doble has left... a legacy of exacting standards. They must be maintained." Young, enthusiastic and ambitious, Collins ensured that these were not just hollow words and drama continued to flourish under his leadership – with John installed as the industrious secretary of the drama society. As well as the major school productions, Collins encouraged regular play readings, small studio-type productions and extensive theatre visits, including a backstage visit to the Birmingham City Rep. Eileen Barry, an actress then appearing in the local soap *Crossroads*, was persuaded to deliver a talk on technique, voice control and her experiences of television and theatre. Tellingly, given his later predilections, when writing about this visit in the school magazine, John noted: "There was a pleasing response to publicity."

John himself took the lead role of the Mayor in a production of the classic farce, *The Government Inspector*. He received his now customary rave review: "...Turner's mixture of pomposity and thinly disguised panic was a tour de force."

By John's last year, his Aston star reached its zenith. He was made school vice-captain and had carefully eradicated his Brummie accent, replacing it with something close to received pronunciation. Years later, recalls *Doctor Who* fan Ian Levine, "He used to go on at me, 'Your Lancashire accent's coming through – never say Bath, say Barrrth.'"

John was now the undisputed leading light of all the school's dramatic endeavours and was beginning to explore the professional world beyond it too, moonlighting at the local television studios, appearing as an extra in *Crossroads* (made at ATV's New Street studios) and in *United!* and *The Flying Swan* (produced at the BBC's Broad Street). These appearances came to an abrupt end when Mrs Brandon, the headmaster's wife, spotted him on her television two nights in succession.

Meanwhile, he persuaded the school to allow him to produce their first pantomime, carefully presented for an all-male school and so titled *Cinders' Fella*. "John devised the whole thing," says Hawkesford, who played Buttons in the production. "It was only when we got to put shows on that John definitely began to show leadership qualities. I was quite happy to support him. It was songs and a series of sketches but brought up to date. It involved some sixth formers who had never thought of acting before. It was quite amusing having a big galumphing chap as a fairy. It was slapstick but very funny and went down extremely well."

The school review proclaimed: "One cannot but admire the skill of John Turner in writing and producing an entire pantomime, which captured so completely the spirit of the traditional Christmas panto. With the aid of surprisingly good sets, an enthusiastic cast, chaotic lighting, inventive ad-libbing and an unbelievably tatty selection of costumes, he put on a riotously funny slapstick extravaganza, which contrived, wittingly or unwittingly, to satirise the pantomime genre, while keeping within the accepted bounds of that particular kind of theatre."

It was the first public expression of his lifelong fascination with the world of traditional pantomime – which was to have a lasting impact on his work and reputation.

During his final year at the school, John set up an elaborate scam for his old friend and deputy, Roy Hawkesford: "Senior prefects used to have a duty rota, sitting in pairs in the headmaster's ante room; we took messages out to staff, ran errands and so on. I was on duty on one occasion when a story broke about me having ordered some soft porn photos that had been delivered to the secretary's office for me. She had opened them by mistake. Mysteriously, everyone knew about it except me. John had set the whole thing up and even enlisted the secretary in the performance. He carried his role consummately, being both 'understanding' but also 'disappointed' by what I'd 'done'. I, of course, protested my innocence and denied any knowledge of the photographs, but the more I protested, the more I seemed to be digging myself into a hole. They kept this going for several days, until John's accomplices (who were friends of mine) eventually lost interest and stopped playing along. I was pretty traumatised by the whole thing, while it was obviously a huge source of fun for the others. John never admitted it. I should have laughed it off but I was hurt by it. I don't suppose I would have told him how I felt, out of pride. After a week it was all forgotten by everyone except me. I don't think John intended to hurt me at all; he obviously saw me as someone who could take a joke. It shows how, away from the stage, he could stage-manage an 'event'. It was very convincing, like being in a play, in a situation where there's no escape. I was ashamed of myself for acting as if I were guilty! Though painful, it still makes me shake my head in admiration. That was John. He could get people to do anything."

The Aston Revue of 1966 was all John's, the school magazine praising his "two splendid virtuoso solo spots, his all-too-short Frankie Howerd monologue and an off-key rendering of *Climb Ev'ry Mountain*, as well as impersonating Fanny Cradock, Ginger Rogers and Hylda Baker with characteristic aplomb. Sad to say, it was the last of those productions with the inimitable Turner touch. For producer-author-star John Turner, Aston's own Val Parnell, has left, with two revues, a pantomime and many plays behind him."

Invited to deliver a speech at the final summer term assembly of the year, John used his wry sense of humour to elevate the usual dull list of goodbyes and thank yous. It was a typically confident performance, beginning with a slightly camp joke: "If the nine leaving members of staff were placed end to end, they would stretch from the corner of Victoria Road to Ansell's Brewery... and undoubtedly people would start talking..."

A year later, John was invited back to receive a special prize for outstanding contribution to the school. By then, he had already embarked on his dream career. Having applied to Hull University, to read drama and German, he found his A-level grades weren't quite good enough with a C grade for German and a D for French. He failed General Studies altogether and, even after resitting this, only scraped a D. It was a disappointing result and he decided to reject Hull's revised offer – to read drama and theology – fixing his sights on a life in the theatre instead. "He couldn't wait to get on the inside of showbiz," says Hawkesford. "He was drawn to it like a moth to a flame, one might almost say."

The two boys, who had been such firm friends for the past few years, now drifted and went their separate ways. "I regret that I lost touch with him," says Hawkesford, "but I think it was necessary for both of us to discover who we were, and what we were capable of, outside our teenage friendship. Our lives really started in about 1964, and we never looked back. John wanted to move into theatrical circles, whereas I went into music in a big way and decided to go to university. When we saw each other at parties, after we'd left school, he wanted to be the centre of attention. It was obvious now that he was gay, playing it up for his audience. I suppose I found him somewhat sad – which says as much about me as it does about him. I think he found *him*self quicker than I found *my*self."

Teachers and schoolmates may not have been surprised that John had decided to go on the stage but his parents were less than pleased. "I was constantly being told I would 'starve in a garret'," John recalled in his memoirs.

"I don't think his father was at all happy when he went into the theatre," says friend and colleague Ian Fraser. "His mother was secretly OK about it but his father wasn't. But the great thing about John was once he started working on something you always had the feeling that he was going to succeed. I think his father picked that up quite quickly."

His first job was as a stage manager in the Castaways nightclub in Birmingham town centre. "I got my first real taste of showbusiness there," John reminisced in a 1990 *Doctor Who Magazine* interview. "It was a vast place with a floor covered by a carpet with footprints all over it. In the Galleon Bar they had cabaret six nights a week with such artists as Lonnie Donegan, Little and Large and Shirley Bassey. But my father insisted that I should learn a trade. The job I was doing was an evening one, so during the day I became a settler in a betting office working out how much was owed to the punters."

At Christmas 1966, he made his break into the theatre proper as property master on that year's pantomime at the Alexandra Theatre (known as "the Alex"). Said John: "It had a very starry cast – Rikki Fulton and Des O'Connor – and this experience finally decided me on where I wanted to go in life. I started to do a bit of dressing on touring productions, including a Brian Rix farce in which Wendy Padbury [*Doctor Who* companion Zoe] played a little Indian prince."

During this period John met a trio of men who were to play a significant part in his later life – the first was future producer Graham Williams. Williams's future wife, Jackie, worked as a clerk to the head of costumes at the BBC's Gosta Green studios. "There was a sudden crisis," John recalled, "which meant that they urgently needed a male costume assistant. Well, I can't sew and I can't knit but it was more a case of checking the gear and brushing the artist down before they went on camera." John was given a month's contract and worked on soap operas *The Newcomers* and *United!* where he met their respective producers, Bill Sellars (later to produce *All Creatures Great and Small*) and Tony Cornish. In his memoirs, John says, "I'm sure it was this first foray into television that made me determined to work in the industry."

When his contract came to an end, it was back to the "Alex" as acting assistant stage manager for owner and impresario Derek Salberg's 1967 repertory season. "Rep" involved the same company of actors and technicians (occasionally augmented with guest artists) putting on a new production on a regular basis throughout the season. He was paid ten guineas a week when ASM only, with a two guinea per week supplement if he was also appearing in a production. The company's leading lady was Janet Hargreaves, later to star as crazed, gun-toting ex-wife-on-the-rampage Rosemary Hunter in *Crossroads*. "We did a try out of a new thriller by Henry Cecil called *According to the Evidence*. The guest stars were Douglas Wilmer and Michael Gwynne and Naunton Wayne. John played a small part in it [as Detective Constable Parsons]. He was not very good but it was love at first sight. He had this cherubic face, I can see him now. He always had a slightly surprised look on his face, slightly poppy eyes, eyebrows up, very pink face with black curls that bobbled about. He was not exactly chubby but well rounded. We opened and I remember vividly I was in a purple swimsuit and purple tights and masses of hair pieces and false eyelashes, lying on my back doing bicycling exercises and he was minning about – I can only use that verb – as the secretary to my husband [played by Douglas Wilmer]. We only had to look at each other and we would corpse. We were very naughty and wasted a lot of time at rehearsals. He just had this expression that was hugely funny. We all liked him very much – he was a lovely, easy chap."

Having "tried out" in Birmingham and Leeds, *According to the Evidence* should have opened in London but wasn't ready. A film within the play featured John and although he had left the company by the time the play eventually opened in London, the film wasn't reshot with the new cast. He always delighted in the strange achievement of having enjoyed a nine-month run in a West End theatre without ever setting foot on the stage.

It was during his time at the "Alex" that John formed a friendship that would last for the rest of his life. "I was 18 and at drama school in Birmingham," recalls actress Anita Graham (who is still known to friends as Gladys Gumboot

– the nickname John gave her). "I was working as a barmaid in the evenings in a pub called the Vic next to the Alex. I remember he'd come into the pub and after a while we got chatting. He had this angelic face with lovely curly hair. Wonderful eyes and lovely little expressive chubby hands. He said, 'Do you get any tips?' and I said, 'Well, I get a few.' Everybody wore short skirts then and he said, 'If you put a bottle of everything on the bottom shelf, you'd probably get more.' So I did and it worked!

"We both had a silly sense of humour, similar backgrounds, loved the theatre. He absolutely adored the Alex – it wasn't worthy theatre. He'd come in with all sorts of people like [actor] Ray Bowers. The pub stayed open late, we'd sit around drinking and then go out to a club. He was always up for going out and getting into some sort of mischief."

John introduced Graham to his family and, she says, "I was wheeled out a few times. Maybe I was a smokescreen for a bit. I remember going to see a Danny La Rue pantomime. My real bloke came along to have a drink with us and Auntie Joan said to John, 'You want to be careful there, because I think he's got his eye on Gladys.'

"But although John was gay, he did love women. Loved squiring them around and he was very old-fashioned and gentlemanly in that way. I think because of the way he also loved his mum, he was always very well mannered and behaved properly."

For a while, John persevered with his own acting aspirations, while stage-managing the 1967 *Puss in Boots* pantomime at the Grand, Wolverhampton, with Dick Emery and Ted Rogers – the first trace of him being credited as John Nathan-Turner. But it was slowly dawning on him that "gradually the parts were getting smaller and my responsibilities on the stage-managing side were growing greater and so I thought someone was probably trying to tell me something." Later, he claimed that he made the final decision to abandon acting when a review poured scorn on his performance in a production of *Treasure Island*.

In August 1968, John came of age. His father threw him a big party, hiring the Ambassadors club in Birmingham and booking a comedian he liked, Bob Hatch, to entertain the guests and a musical double-act, the Morgan James Duo, to provide the dance music. One half of this duo was the late John Lee, who married actress Lynda Baron. Years later, their daughter, Sarah, would become John's secretary.

His next professional engagement was a season at the Cheltenham Everyman Theatre, where he again encountered Tony Cornish, producer of the BBC's *United!* Cornish was in Cheltenham to meet artistic director Michael

Ashton and discuss a couple of forthcoming radio plays. Ashton, who'd obviously taken a shine to John, invited him to join them and spoke so flatteringly about the young man's talents that Cornish suggested he might apply to the BBC for a "general exploratory interview", mentioning his name in the process. A reply came by return of post, with an invitation to apply for a vacancy as a floor assistant (with a starting salary of £870 per annum) in the television service.

A reference was required and John put forward his old headmaster, the benign, enabling Leonard Brandon. In a letter dated 27th November 1968, an MEM Harvey from the appointments department wrote: "Your views are requested on the candidate's: 1) Integrity, standard of values and general suitability; 2) Initiative, organising ability and capacity for sustained effort; 3) Originality, judgement and imagination; 4) Capacity to work both individually and as a member of a team; 5) Family background; 6) Ability to appreciate the differences of outlook of various sections of the community; 7) Outstanding characteristics and weak points."

On 6th December, Brandon wrote back: "I found him completely dependable in character, an excellent senior prefect and a fine influence in the upper sixth. He is tactful and pleasant in manner, he has a very good sense of humour, and he has abundant energy and enthusiasm. His activities outside the classroom were well balanced... He gave us great pleasure as an actor and the revue sketches which he wrote were particularly entertaining. Besides working in serious drama he organised the Sixth Form Revue and Pantomime, showing that he could work well as the director of a team and that he could achieve remarkable results in inadequate time. His originality, initiative and drive all left their mark upon our social life, and he was greatly missed when he left the school. I recommend him with no reservations whatsoever."

John was quickly summoned to BBC Television Centre in London, for what the corporation still refers to as a "board" – an interview process in which the candidate is usually grilled by two or more members of staff (the "board"). Years later, chatting to a nervous colleague about a forthcoming board, John advised, "Don't let them intimidate you. When you look at them, just imagine them sitting on the toilet – it's always worked for me!"

Basil Adams, the head of studio management and his assistant Colin Leslie were the men he had to impress and he obviously did a good job. He was given an initial four-month contract and the option of working either in Glasgow or London. He chose London and, just before Christmas 1968, John took up his appointment. Birmingham's "boy most likely to" had a foot in the television door. He was on his way.

TWO

STAY TUNED

'Cause you've started something, oh, can't you see?
That ever since we met, you've had a hold on me,
It happens to be true, I only want to be with you
Dusty Springfield, *I Only Want to Be with You*, 1963

BBC studio management, the department that John was joining, was the thriving home to the Corporation's scores of vision mixers (the people who actually cut the shots in a studio gallery following the camera script and the director's instructions), floor managers, assistant floor managers and, at the bottom of the pile, floor assistants. Almost exactly 20 years later, I would join the same department in the same job and nothing much had changed. In a corner of the duty room tucked away in one of Television Centre's circular corridors, amid the functional armchairs and stack of pigeonholes for the staff, there was a strange bespoke piece of furniture, a kind of long teak cabinet with a sloping glass top. Beneath this were pinned a series of paper sheets meticulously laid out in pencil – a hand-written schedule covering the next few weeks' assignments for all the department's staff. It must have been a hell of a job to service this schedule – hence the use of pencil, as amendments and alterations were constant.

Though productions could and did make requests for key personnel, there was no guarantee their demands would be met and even the most celebrated and in-demand vision mixer or floor manager had to resign themselves to the occasional day on a dull schools' programme or interminable sports show. Worse were the "duty standby" days, when staff were expected to report for work and hang around until every show was up and running at TV Centre, Lime Grove or the TV Theatre on Shepherd's Bush Green. The idea was that if someone phoned in sick, there was immediate cover to hand. Any new floor assistant joining on a temporary contract was lowest in the pecking order and it was in this capacity that John, staff number 141138X, started his BBC career. He was in good company – among his peer group were Paul Smith, Geoff Posner, Steve Goldie, Ed Pugh and Graeme Harper – all later to forge their own highly successful production careers.

The principal requirement of the job was to get an actor or presenter in and out of make-up and wardrobe on time and onto the studio floor. Easy enough on a simple show but much more complicated with bigger productions boasting larger casts and more elaborate changes. A floor assistant's week invariably took in the whole range and John worked on everything from *The Six Wives of Henry VIII* to *Play School, The Sky at Night* and *Ask Aspel* to *Blue Peter* and *Morecambe and Wise*. Looking back, he said: "I think the job was of great use to me because working on every different type of show at least gave me a flavour of all the different careers I might have pursued."

What he loved best were the dramas. This was the heyday of the lavish studio-based dramas and one of the very first productions to which he was assigned was the BBC2 colour serial *The Tenant of Wildfell Hall*. This and an early brush with *Doctor Who* (on *The Space Pirates*, in 1969) were, he later claimed, the reason for his determination to pursue a career in this field.

With his gregarious nature and affinity with actors, John was a popular floor assistant. Marcia Wheeler, then an AFM but later to rise to become the manager of drama series and serials, remembers him well: "He was a lively, bubbly go-getting type right from the beginning. He was a pro and a very hard worker. He seemed to me to be a born showman. That's the thing that struck me about John from the beginning."

Wheeler first met John not on the studio floor but at a party thrown by a mutual friend, the actress Vivienne Moore, who recalls: "Together with our good friend Anita Graham, we had this ridiculous little company we called Oompah Productions. We used to do Old Tyme Music Hall and pantomimes in old people's homes, hospitals and prisons. We'd rope in some mates and cram ourselves into a couple of cars with costumes we'd found and made up ourselves. I don't think we ever made any money – it was 30 bob and a bunch of grapes, if you see what I mean. We just had a laugh. I always remember John singing *Put on Your Ta-ta, Little Girlie*. He'd got white flannels on and a striped pink and white blazer and a boater. He was terrific, good-looking, very polished

– he sang well, he moved well. Years later, I used to ring him up at the BBC when he was producing *Doctor Who* and I just used to sing down the phone *Put on Your Ta-ta, Little Girlie!*"

"He loved performing and he was good," says Anita Graham. "He did a wonderful rendition of *I'll Make a Man of You* from *Oh! What a Lovely War*. He had a lovely voice. We were having a laugh and we all got to do things we wouldn't do normally. At Christmas one year we did *Puss in Boots* and the next year *Cinderella*. We did the music hall at a psychiatric hospital and I remember them telling us, 'If you want the audience to stay, you have to hand out cigarettes.'"

Doing these shows alongside the day job wasn't just a chance to have fun with mates. The writing, directing and performing, John later explained, "helped to get it out of my system. I could only write rubbish – pantomime, revue and sketches, parodies of song. I think that's the extent of my writing talent."

Home was a series of bedsits and flats. "At one time," says Anita Graham, "John shared a flat with a dancer and a musical director from Birmingham. [Actor] Ray Bowers was there for a while, too. They used to cook something they called Liver du Ponce, which was the main meal when anybody came round. We'd all throw something in because it was cheap.

"Once a year, we used to do trips down to Brighton. We'd all make picnic things and, whether it was raining or not, sit relentlessly on the beach. There'd be Viv Moore, Marcia and anybody's boyfriend that happened to be around. There was a lady called Georgina Symons (John called her Tits a Gogo) and another he called Desperate Dan because of the size of her jaw."

After two years on contract, John was offered the chance to join the staff and on 1st December 1970 he was accepted as a member of the BBC pension scheme. Having set his sights firmly on the drama department, he applied for any suitable vacancy and it was while he was floor assisting on another *Doctor Who* story, *Colony in Space*, that he learnt he had been accepted for an initial four-month "attachment" as an AFM to drama serials. He would never return to studio management.

In the early 1970s, the BBC's drama group was divided into three separate departments, under the overall leadership of Shaun Sutton. These were Plays (headed by Gerald Savory), Serials (Ronnie Marsh) and Series (Andrew Osborn). Plays were based on the fifth floor at Television Centre but series and serials shared a maze of poky offices in a rundown building overlooking Shepherd's Bush Green which the BBC had bought from the Post Office. This was Union and Threshold House and John would be based here for the rest of his staff career. "In the 1970s, it was a really happy ship," remembers director's assistant Carol Snook. "Everybody got their work done, controlled their budgets and did what they had to do but there was an element of fun too."

Fellow assistant Janet Radenkovic agrees: "The whole atmosphere at the BBC in those days was totally different – much nicer. It was not quite like a family but there wasn't that sort of cut-throat ambition which came in later – I mean, yes people were ambitious but not in a cut-throat way."

"We were turning out the best drama in the world, for Heaven's sake," says department manager, Brian Spiby. "The men in suits didn't really bother us – we were just a bunch of luvvies. They didn't understand what we did and they couldn't understand why we all went around kissing each other! We did have quite a young crowd. It had a sort of vibrancy about it. We all loved what we were doing and we were successful and that added to the zing of the atmosphere. I suppose it was the golden age."

"Serials was a relatively small department in Threshold House," says colleague and friend George Gallaccio. "One knew most of the people reasonably well. John quickly made his presence known. You couldn't not be aware of him."

"He was so outgoing and so gregarious," agrees Fiona Cumming. "There was a tea trolley which used to come round every morning and afternoon and this was a marvellous way to get together and find out what was going on. It was group therapy – you'd talk as you queued up for your sticky bun and your coffee. John was always good with the gossip."

"Gossip – yes!" laughs Gallaccio. "If you wanted to find out anything about someone, you went to John. He was very shrewd about people."

Karilyn Collier started as an AFM in serials on the very same day as John. "He bonded with everybody straight away," she remembers. "He really was a great friend – so charming and funny, a unique personality. And he was fabulous at the job. All the artists and directors regarded him as a friend as well as a colleague. We used to mark up the rehearsal room floor together. Because we were new, if somebody was away filming, they'd say, 'Would you do it?' so John and I constantly found ourselves out at North Acton [rehearsal rooms] on our knees. One day we asked, 'Why is it always us?' and they said, 'Because you always say yes!' So we said, 'From now on it's no!'"

His first few months were spent working on a new twice-weekly serial called *Owen MD*, starring Nigel Stock (who would join the ranks of John's many actor friends). This was a spin-off from an earlier effort called *The Doctors* and the first drama to be made using the BBC's new Pebble Mill studios, back in John's home city. "He was very reliable," comments producer Bill Sellars, "and very good with artists. A great sense of humour and always there to help. 100 per cent professional."

"He was the only AFM I knew who made the rehearsals fun," says Collier. "He used to pin up the schedule on the wall along with 'recipe of the week' and he'd do a fun recipe. He'd make people laugh, kind of making fun of himself, never other people. He never really said a bad word about people. He took up a lot of lame dogs – people who needed help. And he was a damned hard worker."

As 1971 gave way to 1972, John added the perennial *Z Cars* and a Sunday classic serial, *The Hole in the Wall*, to his list of credits. It was a happy time. He was where he wanted to be, making friends and contacts, working hard and, just as importantly to him, partying hard. "He was having a bloody good time!" says his friend Barry Hannam. "At this point, he was renting a room somewhere but he never had a proper base. He lived out of the boot of his car – everything was in there, all the clothes."

"He was one of my best-est friends," smiles fellow AFM Sue Hedden. "He and I were called the 'two twisted twins' because we both had the same attitude – we knew we were very good at the job and we didn't suffer fools gladly. We were mavericks but directors kept asking for us. He was brilliant, so efficient and full of fun."

"I really liked him," says production assistant Jane Wellesley, who first worked with John on *Owen MD*. "He was very chatty and very witty – he had a wonderful wicked turn of phrase, which rather appealed to me. He had nicknames for everybody – I was the Dowager – because my name was Wellesley." (At that time Lady Jane Wellesley was in the public eye as one of Prince Charles's girlfriends.)

John's penchant for bestowing a nickname on friends and foes (as well as on programmes) was a lifelong habit. Throughout the rest of this book, I'll note them as they crop up. My own favourite is "Attila the Mum" – coined for Bonnie Langford's formidable mother. They give some clue to his sense of humour, one of the hardest aspects of a personality to capture in print. While he frequently re-christened his friends, they tended to call him "Nathan" – the now more familiar soubriquet JN-T didn't come until later, originating from his habit of initialling production paperwork.

The only vacuum in John's life was someone to share it with. "John was always looking for his other half," says Anita Graham. "He had lots of boyfriends, including a couple of mine – well, I felt they were leaning that way anyway! A couple were actors. Generally, they were attached to the theatre in some way. He was very romantic and very tactile. He had a little place in Victoria and sometimes we used to share a bed and he'd love to have a cuddle."

Gary Downie was a tall, lugubrious-looking man, with the look of an animated Mr Punch (in years to come, his unkind nickname among famously catty BBC dressers was "Jugjaw"). He wore his light brown hair long and his bright eyes were often beady and suspicious. When he spoke, his vowels betrayed his South African roots while his quick gestures and fluid movements gave away the fact that he danced for a living.

He was born Roderick Gary Pinkus in Johannesburg on 17th July 1940. His mother was a dance teacher who had been ballroom champion and his father, known as Poonie, was a boxer. Gary was their middle child – he had an elder brother called Barry and a younger called Derrick. They all grew up on the big family farm. From an early age, Gary took after his toe-tapping mother, showing a precocious aptitude and ability for dance. It can't have been easy for a young boy growing up gay and dreaming of tripping the light fantastic in the overtly macho climate of rural 1950s South Africa. It probably accounts for some of his characteristic "strike the first blow" attitude, which so often antagonised people in later years.

His talent got him noticed, as Barry Hannam recalls: "They were sitting on the veranda when they saw all these African Zulus coming up the main drive. His father said, 'Right, go inside,' to them, and to the eldest brother he added, 'Bring my gun.' The Zulus were standing there and the father asked them, 'What do you want?' – 'We want him' – 'What do you mean, you want him?' 'He wants to dance with us!' they replied. At the time, the Zulus used to do their national dance before the rugby. Everyone threw money at them on the pitch so they earned good money. And Gary ended up dancing with them – he used to say he was the only white man ever to dance with the Zulus in South Africa!"

When his family decided to leave South Africa and return to their native Australia, Gary didn't go with them. Instead, aged 21, he came to London to make a career for himself. According to Hannam, he'd often recount, "I've been through the school of hard knocks – you have to learn to take rejection when you're a dancer."

"If you've ever been through that," points out actress Lynda Baron, "it affects you. If you're a dancer everybody tells you exactly what a spade is – one is used to people coming up and saying, 'What the hell do you think you are doing? Get off and come on again.' Nobody mixes it up and ties it with a ribbon. You just get on with it and nobody takes it the wrong way. I'm quite sure that's why people misunderstood him."

Assistant floor manager Lynn Richards, who worked with him in a 1974 theatre production of *Hans Andersen*, recalls: "He mainly played character parts because he was slightly strange looking."

Despite his unconventional looks, he made a go of it and worked solidly throughout the 1960s and into the decade beyond. Some of his many theatre credits included *Stop the World – I Want to Get Off* (1962), *Enrico* (1963 with Roger Delgado), the UK tour of *A Funny Thing Happened on the Way to the Forum* (1965), the legendary Lionel Bart musical disaster *Twang!* (1965–66), the West End run of *Sweet Charity* (1967) and a long run as principal dancer for drag queen Danny La Rue at the Victoria Palace Theatre, which culminated in a 1972 ITV special *Danny La Rue at the Palace*. Years later, John would sometimes tease Gary by calling him "Downie La Rue", claiming there was a resemblance between the dancer and the drag queen. On film, Gary appeared in *Tom Jones* (1963) and *The Devils* (1971) and was one of the knights dancing on the tables in *Monty Python and the Holy Grail* (1975). He also shot a commercial for Typhoo tea, directed by a fledgling Ridley Scott.

Towards the end of 1968, rising choreographer Flick Colby hired him to work alongside her all-girl dance group Pan's People. They'd been booked to back diminutive Scots singer Lulu in her eponymous BBC1 show. It was to run for 13 weeks and each programme was broadcast live from Television Centre. For many years, the entire series was thought lost, wiped in the same cultural massacre that obliterated so much *Doctor Who*. But then, in 2010, three episodes surfaced from Lulu's own collection, recorded on a pioneering home video, set up by her techno-friendly husband of the time, Maurice Gibb. These recordings, though poor, give some sense of Gary in his dancing heyday, hair flying and limbs akimbo as he go-gos himself silly in the ridiculous *Austin Powers* style of the time.

Colby booked him for other jobs too, including spots on the BBC's Bobbie Gentry shows – but he never appeared with them on *Top of the Pops* as BBC bosses wanted a "chicks only" group on their flagship chart show. Nevertheless, dancing with Pan's People remained a kitsch boast for the rest of his life. Pan's girl Dee Dee Wilde remembers him well: "Gary's long face was tailor-made for comedy. He wasn't the best of dancers but was certainly great company, always great fun and he had a wicked sense of humour. I seem to recall he was always looking for love!"

He was about to find it. By the summer of 1972, he had been living and working in London for over ten years, and was now employed as assistant choreographer on a new musical, *Tom Brown's Schooldays*, at the Cambridge Theatre. Heading the cast as the villainous Flashman was the young actor Christopher Guard: "It was rather a good show, actually, and my fellow boys included hopefuls like Keith Chegwin, Richard Willis, Russell Grant and one Simon Le Bon. Gary was wiry and disciplined and did not like mess; he was also warm and funny and good in company. He had a fine line in withering, waspish put-downs and didn't suffer fools. When he narrowed his eyes... you wouldn't want to be on the wrong side of that."

It was during this summer that John and Gary met, at a party, and, according to Gary in his 2003 interview with *Doctor Who Magazine*, it was a classic *coup de foudre*: "It was a friend's party, at the flat where Dennis Nilsen murdered all those boys and cut their bodies into pieces – he moved in after my friend moved out. I was pissed out of my brains because I'd just been dumped. In my alcoholic haze, I saw this very good-looking guy with beautiful black curls. The rest is history."

"The morning after," says Hannam, "they went to the King William pub in Hampstead, which was popular with gay men. Gary went to the bar to get some drinks and it was packed so he was a long time. John nearly left because he thought Gary had dumped him and wasn't interested."

Actress friend Jessica Martin recalls how "they used to tell this lovely story about their first date when they had spaghetti vongole – that was their dish."

"John was so good-looking then," says Jane Wellesley. "When he later put the weight on, I always remember Gary producing this photo of John and saying, 'Look, this is what I fell in love with!'"

They stayed together for the rest of John's life. Apart from sex, showbusiness and a thriving social life, they shared a deep emotional connection. They were both passionate, demanding, sometimes jealous, frequently protective – a pair of mutually obsessed, interconnected drama queens. Like many gay couples of the time, theirs was an open relationship. Sometimes they shared partners, sometimes they went solo, but always they returned to each other. Anita Graham believes that "when he met Gary, Gary was a gypsy, struggling a bit and John sorted him out and really looked after him. I think they became a family."

"It's interesting that we always spoke about 'John and Gary' – no-one ever referred to 'Gary and John'," says Fiona Cumming. "John was the star and had such a wide circle and was so confident within it that Gary would feel perhaps a little on the edge, a bit insecure. He could be spiky."

"Much spikier than John," says Anita Graham. "I can remember thinking, 'Oh God, I'm not going to say that to Gary because I'll get a mouthful.'"

"Without Gary," Hannam believes, "I don't think John would have made it. Gary was the strength there. He was very practical and did all the driving, whereas John was more creative."

"Gary absolutely adored John," says friend Mark Jones. "He worshipped him, thought he was the most wonderful, talented, creative person ever. From the outside, Gary always put John up front."

"Gary was a rock," agrees actor and old friend Christopher Biggins. "It couldn't have been easy living with John. I think he had a lot of agendas – he was a workaholic, and very much needed to be in the limelight. Gary was always there for him."

Sophie Aldred (*Doctor Who* companion Ace) thinks that "John was the one who relied on Gary more than the other way round – Gary was so strong. They weren't completely faithful to each other but they absolutely loved each other. They would have done anything for each other."

"They loved a bicker, though," laughs their hairdresser and friend, Barry Hannam. "And stand-up blazing rows and fights. Then they'd laugh. I remember John going hammer and tongs once and banging down this beautiful cut glass onto a glass table. The bowl of the glass just fell off. He went to Gary, smacked his face and said, 'That's your fault!' Then they just burst out laughing."

"I think they were a perfect match for each other," says another friend Stephen Cranford (Miss Cranford). "There was an occasion when they were living in Brighton when John and Gary had a fight – Gary stormed out and drove all the way to London. John phoned him and said, 'Your dinner's on the table.' Gary had cooled down by then so he just said, 'Right, OK,' and drove all the way home again. Preposterous!"

The relationship posed a challenge to many of John and Gary's families, friends and colleagues because, like any couple in love, they came as an absolute package – you couldn't have one without the other. For most people I've spoken to, the compromise meant putting up with Gary for the sake of John. Carol Snook (Snooky) says, "You could sit in the pub, on your own with John, and just howl with laughter. Then Gary would come in and it would be different."

"I never really warmed to him," admits Janet Radenkovic. "It was always Nathan who was my friend. I never did anything with Gary alone – it was either both of them or John alone. There was one time when they'd had a major row and I went over and had a heart to heart with John. He was really upset because it looked as if it was all falling to pieces. It's chemistry, isn't it, when people like each other?"

The bleak truth is that Gary was often tolerated rather than liked and some of John's friends couldn't even bring themselves to that. "John was alienated from a lot of people because of Gary," says Sue Hedden. "Gary's attitude to people was 'Who are you?' whereas John was always warm and lovely. Gary was just the sort of gay man that John wasn't. I never understood what he saw in that arsehole. I think Gary hated women. He could be vicious and downright evil."

"Without any doubt at all," says Colin Baker, "Gary held John back because there were so many people who couldn't abide Gary. I adored John but I was very wary and occasionally rather disliked Gary. Gary was not nice."

"He used to make appalling comments about women," admits Fiona Cumming. "Then it was almost as though he'd notice me and say, 'Present company excepted.' I sometimes felt like an honorary gay!"

"Gary would often refer to women as 'fish', which I always found quite unpleasant," recalls Grahame Flynn (Flynette). "John loved being around women but I only saw Gary totally relax with a few women like Fiona Cumming, June Brown and Sophie Aldred."

"Gary and I got on really well from day one," says Aldred. "I got his subtext. We'd just take the piss out of each other. Yes, he was a complete bitch and he could be nasty to people but I think it was a bit of a camp act. You'd say, 'Oh, *Gary...*' I feel quite emotional thinking about him. I really know that he loved me. I was less sure about John. It's interesting because people often say it's the other way round."

"I never felt that Gary was misogynist," says actress and friend Clare Clifford. "He was a very sensible person, down to earth with a lot of common sense. You knew that if you were friends with him, you were friends."

Ian Fraser acknowledges that "Gary could be very cutting and unless you knew him, you might take offence at some of the things he said. If he was going to be nasty, he would be nasty – but most of it was humorous. He was a very caring man. But he wouldn't let people get inside him. He held them away."

"I wouldn't say I had no time for Gary but I was cautious," says Snook. "Gary could be very, very sharp when he wanted to be but fortunately I got on with him and he was fantastic to my son – they both were."

"They were sweet as a couple," says actress Sarah Sutton (Nyssa in *Doctor Who*). "Whenever someone opens a bottle of champagne, I think of Gary!"

"I always thought Gary was very funny," says fan, writer and friend David Roden (The Rodent). "But not the brightest bunny. John was a lot more sensitive and thoughtful. I don't mean he was ever guiltless in any of their endeavours. He could be pompous and aggressive and a bully but by the same token he could also be incredibly sweet and quite emotionally delicate, very funny, very witty, very quick."

"Away from Gary, he was a wonderful person," agrees fan and former friend Ian Levine, "who would do anything for you – larger than life, the life and soul of the party. But Gary was like a black widow spider, spouting venom into his ear. It's the yin and the yang."

"Good queen and evil queen!" laughs Jessica Martin.

"Like any couple, you have to take the rough with the smooth," shrugs another fan turned friend Stuart Money (Moneypenny). "John had more generosity of spirit. Gary could be difficult with people he didn't know. John was always trying to smooth over things. Often, when they were together, I found the whole was greater than the sum of the parts – there was this sparkiness. But Gary was protective of John."

"He was more suspicious of people," says Anita Graham. "John was always popular but he also went through this time when he was terribly powerful. Gary was always suspicious of why people wanted to know them."

This was something that Downie himself acknowledged in his *DWM* interview: "I'd be the suspicious one, always suspicious of people, whereas he was more generous and trusting. He called me mean-spirited! I suppose I wanted to protect him, I don't know. I'm not as subtle as John was. I'm not as discreet as John was. Gary Downie as a person? The chorus boy comes out."

"We're all screwed up but Gary was screwed up probably more than most," says actor Mark Strickson (*Doctor Who* companion Turlough). "He had a vicious tongue on him. John was positively normal – he was the wife, the settling influence on everything. To a certain extent that's another reason we got on so well together because in my heterosexual relationship with my (first) wife I did all cooking and was more emotional, she was slightly more waspish – so John saw me as the John in my relationship."

For John's parents, the arrival of Gary on the scene – and the fact that their son no longer made any attempt to hide his sexuality – inevitably caused tension. "I don't think anyone's parents are ever 100 per cent happy when a child is gay, especially from that generation," says Barry Hannam.

"His mother was a spitfire who did not hold back on her opinions about gay people," says American fan turned friend John Frank Rosenblum. "She was disappointed, she wanted grandchildren."

"His mother was totally upset by it," agrees Ian Fraser, "and used to give him a very hard time about not giving her grandchildren. She could be quite vicious to Gary too."

Even years later, "His father used to say, 'You want to watch that South African. I think he might be after your money,'" chuckles Hannam. "John used to laugh and say, 'I don't think he is going to run off with my money!'"

"They would always meet up at Christmas," says Stephen Cranford. "The four of them – and they would always have turkey. Then one year, I think his dad plucked up the courage to say, 'You know what, John? I really don't like turkey.' And there was this awkward silence and then Gary went, 'Well, actually

I don't either,' and his mother went, 'Oh, I'm so relieved because neither do I' – and it turned out they'd been going through this routine every year and none of them liked it!"

At first, John and Gary shared a place in Clapham and then they bought a flat in Brockley, south London. Paying the mortgage was a strain and so for six months Gary, who was appearing in the West End, got an extra job dancing two late shows a night at the Stork Room nightclub, just off Regent Street. As John later emailed a friend: "We needed the money desperately for important things like food!"

Hannam again: "It was a house that had been converted into a maisonette and a one-bedroom ground-floor flat, lived in by an old couple. They bought them out and turned the house back into one."

"They obviously spent a lot of money on it," says George Gallaccio (La Contessa Gallaccio). "It was flashy but discreet, a mixture of rococo – John was the rococo one – and stainless steel and glass. That was Gary."

"The most garishly decorated house I've ever seen," is how Ian Levine puts it, "like something out of *Alice in Wonderland*. On the walls of the living room was this huge pair of red lips – like a Chaka Khan caricature – with a mirror in the middle of it. Big red lips. It made my skin crawl."

"I remember some wonderful parties there," Gallaccio continues. "They were terrific hosts and John, particularly, was very generous that way. You could do anything you like, somehow you were able to release your inhibitions at John's parties. You could really enjoy yourself."

"Their place was over the top, very theatrical, like they dressed," laughs another friend and colleague, Ralph Wilton. "They had a very flamboyant lifestyle, nothing boring. They drank quite a bit but, having said that, didn't we all?

"They had these wonderful Elsa Maxwell-style dinner parties," says Jessica Martin, "with really interesting characters. There was one lady in particular, who they called the Countess. She was from some part of Eastern Europe and had this beautiful silver grey hair all done up nicely. She was called Elizabeth Templeton and she'd been an actress, married to the man who'd written all kinds of 1950s and 60s American TV series. They'd lived in Hollywood and she'd met Bette Davis and she was full of these stories. She was barking!"

"If you went round for a meal, you could guarantee that you wouldn't be out of the door until one o'clock in the morning," says Mark Jones. "'Come round for half past seven, Markie and we'll have a good old catch-up.' It was sit down, chat, chat, chat, drink after drink...."

"I remember going to dinner," says Snook. "It was shambolic and fun and they were hilarious. They made this sort of moussaka which had baked beans in it – it was slap happy but there was a wonderful atmosphere."

"John did all the cooking," says Fiona Cumming, "and was a very good cook. He would say, 'Eat, eat, eat' – like the classic Jewish momma. Ironic that it was Gary who put together the *Doctor Who* cookbook!"

"In all the years I knew them, Gary only cooked once," laughs Grahame Flynn. "He had made the mistake of making a negative comment about dinner one evening so John said, 'Right, you can cook tomorrow!' Gary got up and made a superb full English breakfast. John reluctantly acknowledged that the food was excellent. Gary had made his point. The fact is that John liked cooking and Gary didn't."

"John would potter around in the kitchen," recalls Stephen Cranford. "Even if you just popped round, he'd say, 'Hold on,' and he'd disappear off and ten minutes later he'd come back with a plate of food. When he came to my house, he would open my cupboards and say, 'Let's see what we've got,' and superintend my cooking as I was a shit cook! 'Do this and try that and add this.' He would have been fantastic on *Ready, Steady, Cook.*"

"He loved having people to stay," says Anita Graham, "and changing the duvets and bringing the cups of tea in the morning. He was very good at fried bread. He loved to feed people."

Stuart Money remembers inviting John and Gary round on several occasions and "a couple of times we'd got no food in because my partner Robbie and I were working. The freezer door would open and I'd think, 'Well, you can't do anything with that,' and within 20 minutes this magnificent meal would appear for all four of us. You couldn't believe what he could get out of it."

Not everyone shares this view. "His food was bloody atrocious," laughs Mark Jones. "You worry when someone gives you a meal and they're not eating it themselves. 'I've been picking at it in the kitchen, darling.' There'd be a starter – some sort of prawn thing – I was grateful when it was a piece of melon because all you've got to do is cut that up. I dreaded it when he did a soup – 'What the hell's this?' – it was just gross. Then the main course – some charred piece of meat and vegetables turned into mush. There were occasions when it was far simpler and it was OK. 'It's only going to be tinned peaches and cream tonight for pudding,' and I'd say, 'Don't give me any cream or any of the syrup from the tin – just put the peaches in the bowl, that'll do me fine,' and every bloody time without fail there would be my two tinned peaches sunk under a litre of syrup and disgusting cream! 'John, I didn't want this' – 'Oh shut up, darling, it's good for you!' Maybe the ones who say it was OK had had too much to drink."

"If *you* were having a dinner party," says Jane Wellesley, "he'd be number one on your list. He was such fun and he could talk to anybody."

"You had to have him," agrees Lynda Baron, "because he could talk to anybody about anything. I once gave a garden party that was a mix of ex-RAF chaps and their wives, actors, of course, and a few odd bods from America, one of whom owned a brothel and was very grand – quite the grandest person there, you never saw the like. It was the weirdest collection of people and I thought, 'All we're short of now is John Nathan-Turner,' so we phoned him up and invited him. He chatted to everybody and by the end of it he knew all about flying and running a brothel in Miami – they all adored him. It was a love of life, I think."

According to Hannam, "John's party piece was doing a fake fortune-telling act. People he'd never met would all come away saying, 'He's so clever – that's exactly right!' – and it was all rubbish! Even at my mother's funeral, he had this woman convinced that he was a fantastic palm reader. He would say the most stupid, silly things and she'd say, 'That's exactly right.' It was just hilarious."

"We had a soap opera party at my house in London," remembers fan and friend Paul Mark Tams. "This was the 80s and the time of *Dynasty*. I borrowed a dress off Sarah Lee [John's secretary] and a great big diamante waterfall necklace off Lynda Baron [Lee's mother], and I said, 'Right, I'm going to be Krystal Carrington.' John had got wind of this and decided to come as Alexis. He turned up in full drag with a big fur wrap and the lipstick and eye shadow on and his cigarette on a stick. This outrageous outfit – and his beard – made him look more like Rita Webb than Joan Collins. He had this great big hat on his head and I said, 'Why are you wearing a lampshade on your head?' and he looked at me and said, 'You're a fucking cow.' That was John. He was fun to be with."

"When he was at a party," smiles Stephen Cranford, "if he had a glass that was in need of topping up, rather than be as unsubtle as asking for more to drink, he would hold his empty glass aloft and say, 'Don't these glasses sparkle when they're empty!'"

Although they later spent most of their time in Brighton, John and Gary never sold 118 Upper Brockley Road. They bought a chow puppy to share it with them, named Pepsi after a dancer with whom Gary had worked. "She was beautiful, a lovely, good-natured dog," says Ian Levine. "Poor dog, they'd leave her in the car at ten in the morning in Threshold car park with the window slightly open. Gary would go down at one o'clock and take her for a quick walk and a wee and put her back in the car until six o'clock. She spent five days a week sitting in their car."

Sometimes John would let Pepsi sit under his desk, although this was strictly against BBC regulations. John, ever the star-maker, was delighted when Pepsi's temperament made her ideal casting as one of Siegfried's dogs in *All*

Creatures Great and Small, based on the stories by James Herriot. "Robert Hardy wanted to echo the books and have Siegfried with dogs constantly yapping at his heels," John told *Doctor Who Magazine*. "Being a mean PUM [production unit manager, John's job on the series], there was no way that I was going to spend money on hiring all those dogs every week, so we used two of Bill's [Sellars, the producer], one that belonged to script editor Ted Rhodes and Pepsi." Later, this canine television veteran made a couple of appearances in *Doctor Who*, too.

With a blossoming career, a boyfriend, a base and a four-legged friend, life was sweet, busy and fun. At Christmas 1972, John made a brief return to the stage at Thames Ditton village hall. The Ember Players, an Esher-based amateur dramatics group beloved of producer Bill Sellars, who lived nearby, wanted to present some kind of Christmas entertainment. "He came up with the idea of doing a panto," Sellars recalls. "He was a delightful man and his humour came out in the writing." Sellars compiled the music and lyrics to go with John's "book" or script, customised as *Emberella*. They took the star parts for themselves – Bill as Tilly and John as Lilly, the ugly sisters. Gillian Beaney played Emberella: "John was terribly good and very funny. And he mucked in and never once made any of the amateurs feel like amateurs. My three-year old daughter was in the audience and when he tore up Emberella's invitation to the ball, she cried out 'Mummy!' and was very upset so John came to see her afterwards to show her it was just pretend."

On the other side of town, Gary was opening in a new show on a somewhat larger scale, *The Good Old Bad Old Days* at the Prince of Wales Theatre. The following year, he was cast by the hottest choreographer of the moment, Bob Fosse, in a musical called *Pippin*. But at 33 he was only too well aware that he was on the senior side for a dancer. "He wanted to get doing something else before he came to the end of the road," says Jane Wellesley. Like many experienced dancers, for Gary the obvious next step was to try to become a choreographer. He'd already had some experience as an assistant – but it was a difficult and crowded market to break into. John helped where he could. As AFM on the BBC2 classic serial *The Song of Songs*, when he learnt that a choreographer was required, he put Gary forward. This little gig led to a few others, on *Poldark*, *I, Claudius* and *The Duchess of Duke Street* but it was a patchwork of showy credits rather than a lucrative or durable career.

After he had risen further up the ladder and consequently held more sway, John eventually smoothed the way for his partner to join the BBC too, as an AFM, the junior role in which he had himself excelled. "I knew them both socially," says Brian Spiby, then the manager of drama serials. "John asked me if I'd consider Gary for one of the contract jobs. I had my pick of the best stage managers out there and he had very little experience but it was my decision to give him a chance. John didn't have to twist my arm because Gary had a personality which I knew would go down well with artists. Working as a choreographer with dancers was just a good a background for that and, other than being competent at the technicalities, personality is the key to it all."

"I think there was a little bit of antipathy towards Gary coming in to the department because it was only because of John that he came in," says production assistant Margot Hayhoe. "He wasn't the best AFM – he didn't have the experience, hadn't come up through the ranks at all. And also he knew he could get away with a bit because of the backing of John – that didn't really help. In any department there's always an element of bitching. I think that people felt that maybe Gary wasn't the best of influences on John and that maybe he had changed a bit when Gary came in and I think that there's quite a lot of truth in that. He was a bit of a stirrer, certainly."

Although the BBC Rule Book firmly proclaimed that marriage between people working in the same department was "subject to special approval", same-sex couples enjoyed an obvious loophole. Notoriously intimidating serials director Joan Craft usually worked with her partner, Jane Shirley, as her number two. "This caused no problems at all as Joan was so hard to work for that everyone else was grateful," observes Marcia Wheeler. "When I became manager, and John was producing, I would certainly have tried to keep Gary off *Doctor Who* but he wasn't the easiest to allocate. It would also have been OK if I knew the director was happy with the arrangement."

Although John habitually sprang to his lover's defence, there were exceptions, as Wheeler recalls: "Thea Murray, a production manager in the department, didn't like Gary. He was her AFM on an episode of *Shoestring* and behaved very badly, refusing to get artists to early make-up calls, or to set props in mud – he didn't want to spoil his new green trousers. He evidently went home and told John about this, who was furious and made him apologise to Thea. It is another example of John as a professional, even when his partner was involved."

In one of those coincidences which litter the relatively small world of "the business", this episode, *Knock for Knock*, featured Chris Guard, who remembers: "Both Gary and Trevor Eve (who played Shoestring) tended to be quite uncompromising in their opinions and it may well have been that they had their differences. Certainly, that fight by the Severn Bridge should never have happened. The light was fading and the only way we could get a sequence was to abandon most of the choreography, shoot it hand-held and just go for it. That would not have been Gary's way."

"I worked with him several times," says Sue Hedden. "He was basically lazy, and did the bare minimum. There were never any props there!"

"Ah, Gary – what a tart!" laughs fellow AFM Val McCrimmon. "He was good fun but not really competent. I think John kept him in the job, really. He always had someone to help get him through it."

"John got Gary into the BBC and then kept him there," says director Andrew Morgan. "They had a very loving and caring relationship and that was all great, but actually Gary wasn't good at his job and John was. Gary was difficult to place. I always dreaded working with him because he was unreliable and he didn't have his finger on the pulse. 'Oh, if you want to do it that way, I suppose you'd better...' That was the sort of attitude. That was difficult. It was a shame that Gary worked in the same line of business. I don't think it helped John's career, actually – so many people thought, 'He's with this awful guy who is not good.' He was a bad influence, really, a bit of a vicious queen."

"I have to be honest," says Janet Fielding (Tegan in *Doctor Who*), "and say that as much as I loved John, Gary's was a very pedestrian mind. John was a lot smarter than Gary. Gary wasn't very good and wasn't very popular, whereas John was liked. He wasn't perfect but he was very much liked. He was a smart man. I don't mean that he was an intellectual. But Gary played to the lowest common denominator in John. If John had wanted to make it, he needed a different partner. He chose the wrong partner. I never understood it. I never doubted that the two of them loved each other – but Gary would have been happiest in a gay ghetto – but John wasn't a gay ghetto man."

Gary may not have been winning friends and influencing people but John's own star remained in the ascendant. By the time his partner joined him in serials, he had leapt two places up the production ladder helped not only by his talent but by fate and good timing. Martin Lisemore, the producer of *The Song of Songs*, had rated and liked John and now wanted him to join his team for his epic 26-episode serialisation of Anthony Trollope's Palliser novels (known within the BBC as "26 Trollops"). It was to be the drama highlight of 1974, a worthy successor to the fabled *Forsyte Saga*. "In those days," explains Wheeler, "producers had an enormous amount of power. Martin used to plan what he wanted to do and just send the list up to the head of department to pass on to the channel controller."

Lisemore was the drama serials wunderkind, joining the BBC in 1963 as an AFM and becoming the producer of BBC2's colour classic serials in 1969 when he was just 30 years old. This might be a good moment to address the frequently repeated myth that John was the BBC's youngest ever drama producer. Lisemore may have beaten him to the job by a couple of years but the first producer of *Doctor Who*, Verity Lambert, was just 28 at the time of her appointment.

The Pallisers was split into two blocks of 13 episodes, the first directed by Hugh David, the next by Ronnie Wilson. John joined Wilson's team along with director's assistant Janet Radenkovic (The Tesco Queen, because she shopped there so frequently!). She says: "Raymond Hughes was the costume designer and the three of us used to go out for meals together while we were on location. We were just always laughing. We went filming in Scotland and it poured with rain. We spent a whole day sitting in the coach, waiting for it to stop. There was absolutely nothing one could do with period silk costumes in the rain. We told jokes and played silly games. It was great fun."

A greater crisis erupted when the production assistant, John Harris, had to be rushed to hospital to have a kidney removed. Lisemore refused to have the replacement he was offered and insisted on John stepping up and taking over instead. "I was promoted overnight," John later recalled. "So there I was, suddenly doing a job I hadn't been trained for.

"It must have been *Monty Python* time," says Radenkovic, "because he wore a sort of toy parrot on his shoulder in the studio and the head of department, Ronnie Marsh, came down and looked on in disapproval. John said, 'Well, you know it's quite difficult having been an AFM and suddenly to be a PM on the same show. I don't want to try the authority bit, I want to try the jokey way.'"

Director Ronnie Wilson recalls: "It was a huge production. He was so successful and so popular with the cast and everybody we were working with that I did ask for him after that. People enjoyed working with him and he was efficient."

It was no accident that many of the cast of the second block of *The Pallisers* later appeared as guest stars in John's *Doctor Who*, among them Philip Latham, Martin Jarvis, Barbara Murray, Moray Watson, Donald Pickering, Clifford Rose, John Hallam, and most notably, Anthony Ainley (who became the Master). John wanted Sarah Badel to join their ranks, writing to her on 11th July 1984: "You may not remember me... I am delighted to hear from your agent that you would be interested in reading a script. The part I would like you to consider is the Rani, who first appears in the script as a crone. I do hope you enjoy it..."

Two weeks later, Badel politely declined, but started her letter with a reproach: "What do you MEAN I may not remember you!!!! Who could forget those sandwiches on the train on the way to Bonnie Scotland with Ray [Thompson] playing his bagpipes. Of course I remember and I'm delighted to hear from you again. I read [the scripts] with much interest and find the tremendous care to detail with which they are written most impressive. I think the Rani is going to turn into a whizz kid and attract a cult following of her own! However, I have got to be honest and say that I can't see myself doing justice to her. I truly don't think that I'd be much good in it. I read it and instantly thought of Eleanor Bron!"

John loved actors and they tended to reciprocate. While immersed in *The Pallisers*, he was contacted by Nigel Stock, with whom he'd worked on *Owen MD*. Radenkovic remembers: "Nigel wanted to raise some money for his child's school swimming pool so John put on this pantomime – *Cinderella* – at the Theatre Royal, Drury Lane with some money also going into Save London Theatres. We were working on the panto and setting up our half of *The Pallisers* at the same time – and we had the cast list for both on the back of the office door. Ronnie Wilson got quite upset that the pantomime was starrier than his cast! It got to the point where agents were ringing up and saying, 'So-and-so would love to be in your panto.'"

Interviewed in the glossy souvenir programme, "author and director" John commented: "Pantomime has always fascinated me. It's totally illogical. The numbers often have no special reason and it's a marvellous spectacle."

The one-off performance took place on a Sunday (the theatre's only "dark" day), 16th December 1973. The cast was indeed spectacular – Judi Dench as Mirazel ("a fairy of the right kind"), Simon Oates as Baron Hardup, Sheila Hancock as the Prince, Julian Holloway as Buttons, Richard Briers and Donald Sinden as the footmen ("your fetish in their hands"), Peter Gilmore as the Major Domo, Elaine Stritch as Lady Carmen, James Bree and John Normington as the Broker's men and Bryan Pringle and Victor Maddern as Dolores and Fabrina, the ugly sisters ("just a pair of drags"). Cameo roles were played by a host of other star names, among them Penelope Wilton, Patrick Cargill, Jessie Matthews, Joss Ackland, Bernard Lee, Peter O'Toole, Frank Windsor, Alan Stratford Johns, Norman Bowler, Peter Byrne and John's leading lady from his first days in rep, Janet Hargreaves. Gary was the choreographer.

'Two of the "friends of Buttons" were played by actors and brothers Dominic and Christopher Guard. Chris says, "I remember thinking, 'What is this jumped up AFM doing hiring the Drury Lane and putting on this charity show?' Then he said, 'Would you be in it?' He was going round the North Acton canteen getting Richard Briers and Peter O'Toole and anyone else he could persuade into this preposterous show. My brother and I and a couple of others were dressed in velvet waistcoats with stockings and buckled shiny shoes. We did a song turning over big alphabet blocks as the letters rolled round, '*A*' – *You're Adorable*, but it had been rewritten – 'A, you're an artichoke, B, you're a broken boot, C, you're a clock with no alarm.' – I remember that much. I think the show was pretty dire but hugely entertaining, in the tradition of quality amateurism."

Tickets sold well, more than enough money was raised and the whole occasion did no harm to John's growing reputation as a young man of promise and pizzazz. When "26 Trollops" was finally completed (a strike delayed the last two episodes), the "jumped up AFM" was not required to return to fretting over props lists and marking up rehearsal room floors. Instead, he remained a production assistant and during the rest of 1974 was scheduled onto routine fillers like *Barlow* and *The Venturers*. This last project had been on the shelf for a long time. Its producers, Brian Degas and Michael Glynn, had been planning a glamorous international series about art forgery, a project part-owned by its intended star, film icon Stewart Grainger. When this fell apart, *The Venturers* was hurriedly dusted down and put into production instead. The lead director was Darrol Blake: "It was about merchant banking, which is quite fascinating. The script, however, was rather old-fashioned with powerful men talking to each other across desks. I remember Brian and Michael bombarding me from either side – 'How are we going to make this series look like no other series? How are we going to make it so special that they can't turn off?' So I said – 'Get another writer?' We did what we could with it."

Blake found John "efficient, affable, with a nice sense of humour. He had authority over the studio without shouting. He was quite excited to hear that I was married to Anne Cunningham because she'd been Elsie Tanner's daughter in *Coronation Street*. He was very impressed and chatted a lot to her. His greatest, greatest desire was to helm a soap."

Before production had got very far, *The Venturers* was hit by another round of the strike action so endemic at the time. This dispute involved production assistants, so John was temporarily forced into idleness. When the strike was over, and production completed on a curtailed run of the dreary banking saga, he began work on a rather classier proposition, a BBC2 serialisation of Frederic Mullally's *Looking for Clancy*.

Later in 1975 John was reunited with Lisemore and Wilson at their request on a prestige production of *How Green Was My Valley*. The script editor was Betty Willingale: "I got to be very friendly with him. Even though those were the good old days, the floor people – the production team – didn't really like script editors. If anything went wrong, it was always the script editor or the producer's fault; we were the lazy ones who never really did anything and all that. John wasn't like that. He knew that I was having a lot of trouble with Prue Handley, the costume designer who was a real misery and kept complaining that the scripts were late. They weren't. Poor Elaine Morgan was writing a script a fortnight, beautifully. And John said, 'Would you like me to talk to her? I could help?' I told him not to because it was my battle.

"The other thing I liked about him was when he found one or two things in the scripts which he thought didn't work, he came and talked to me. He didn't, as a lot of them did, say to his director, 'Oh, look! She's made a mistake here – she's let this through.' I admired that."

How Green Was My Valley starred Sian Phillips with a difficult co-star in the form of one-time film actor Stanley Baker. "I was terribly scared of him," says make-up designer Liz Rowell. "He wore a toupe and wouldn't be seen in the main make-up room so I had to make him up in his dressing room. He'd sit there in silence, an awkward, critical man. He was so frightening that I took Valium when I had to make him up. Everybody laughed about it but John was terribly sympathetic. He commiserated, made me laugh and took me to the bar."

John's old friend, Sue Hedden, recalls, "Sian was still married to Peter O'Toole at that time and he came down to location and said he wanted to be an extra. He was to be a hot chestnut man and the costume people dressed him up in sacks and tied string round his middle. John told me Peter wanted to stoop, so John said, 'What? More than you already are?' He got the prop lads to make him a hot chestnut tray with heavy stones in the bottom and then the chestnuts on top. They came to do it and put this thing round O'Toole's neck and he said. 'Thank you, John, you've now damaged my spine for life!'"

"The extra we'd originally hired objected violently to the Union," says Wilson. "But Peter did it and I didn't use it in the end because people would have recognised him and it would have been so distracting."

John was also responsible for saving the day when the script called for a dazzling field of daffodils. Unfortunately, the shoot was taking place in October. Hedden again: "John got loads of plastic flowers and the prop men spent hours arranging them in the field but the cameraman said, 'Well, they're obviously plastic,' so then John had boxes and boxes of the real thing flown over from South Africa. They planted them in the ground in these bitter conditions and John said, 'You're going to have to be quick!'"

After every studio, John organised a party. "John always loved to party," laughs Willingale. "There was lots of singing and stuff, totally organised by John. He always made a nice party atmosphere. He'd really get people going." Wilson agrees, adding, "He was a bit critical of me because I wouldn't go out to drink with the actors at lunchtime. He said, 'I think you ought to.' But I didn't drink at lunchtime because I had work to do!"

"It was very sociable," says Rowell, "We all gave parties, John gave a party in his flat in Brockley. I gave a party in my little flat in Ealing. Stanley gave a party in his place on the South Bank. The costume designer gave one."

When John came to write his memoirs, one passing reference to a "girlfriend" intrigued me. It stuck out in so careful and cautious a text, it was like a cryptic clue to a part of John's life he never publicly discussed – and so it proved to be. The mysterious girlfriend was 33-year-old Liz Rowell, the make-up designer on *How Green Was My Valley*. "He just fell head over heels with her," says Ian Fraser. "I think from time to time because of the situation with his mother he would get a little sad about not being able to have kids."

"Lizzie had the most outgoing personality," says Fiona Cumming. "They would share the most incredible jokes."

"John said to me that it actually had been quite serious," recalls Jane Wellesley, "and it had been a toss up as to whether he would leave Gary or not. He said she has just such a wonderful personality and that was what appealed to him."

The relationship started during the pre-filming. "I did love him very much at the time," says Rowell. "We just got on so well – he had a great sense of humour, he was so social – he was an absolutely lovely guy. It was a wonderful time of my life. We had a lovely time and a good relationship. He was very romantic in our early days. We used to have dinner – he'd come round to my flat after rehearsals. Gary was working in the theatre every night. I'd been a dancer in my early days and been to ballet school. I'd grown up with gay men – I have an affinity with them and love the sense of humour."

When Gary decided to visit his family in Australia in the New Year of 1976, Liz suggested to John that it would be a perfect opportunity for them to get away too. "I had a great friend in Barbados so we decided we would go there. It was very expensive so we had to book 12 weeks in advance. But by then John had obviously re-thought it and didn't feel the same. We sat on the plane and he said, 'Oh Lizzie, I don't think I love you any more,' which was a dreadful thing to hear. I thought it would be all right once we got there. We were there for three weeks and we were sharing a bed. John said to me that what was exciting about our relationship had been that he was doing it behind Gary's back.

"Our host, my great friend Chris, was also gay and he had a cousin who John met and started a relationship with. He would be getting himself ready to go out with this guy. I really wished that I was at home because it was so hurtful. I felt very unhappy and miserable and kept crying. Poor Chris used to say, 'Oh, it's not of fair of John to do this to you,' but it wasn't really John's fault. I knew what I was getting into. But, of course, the more you get into situations, you can't help it. I didn't think I would ever change him but I tried to think it would end well. I should have known better.

"I ended up really unhappy for a long time – it took about a year to get over it. Gary didn't know until after we came back from Barbados and I felt terrible because John told him that I seduced him. It wasn't like that at all – it was very mutual, I can assure you."

When I told Liz about John's reference to her in his memoirs, she told me, "I'm quite flattered and really pleased that he had some feelings about me. I think it was a great surprise to people. Even though it ended in tears, I am very proud of it."

THREE

SURPRISED & DELIGHTED

"The qualities of a good producer are difficult to define. To the layman, his work is not easily identified. Only those who work with him can properly assess his value..."
Jack Pulman, programme notes for *Martin Lisemore – A Celebration*, 1977

From February 1974, there was a new man in charge of the serials department. His name was William "Bill" Slater and he had a solid background as a director of popular shows like *Z Cars*, *The Regiment* and *The Onedin Line*. "A lot of people thought Bill wasn't a very good head of department," says George Gallaccio. "He was a bit shambolic – but I loved him. There was a sense of equality. Most of the office doors were kept open, people popped in and out and there wasn't really a great sense of hierarchy."

John, never backward in coming forward, took advantage of this to lobby Slater about his aspirations to produce. "One day, during an annual interview," he recalled in his memoirs, "I restated my ambition yet again. 'Well, if you're serious, you'd better learn the PUM's job by doing it, then the script editor's job, then we'll talk again.'

'When do I start?'

'Tomorrow as far as I'm concerned.'"

John was told to go and trail Lovett Bickford, a disgruntled PUM – or production unit manager – working on the hospital series *Angels* but dreaming of becoming a director. The series was being produced by Ron Craddock, of whom John wrote, "He taught me a great deal about how to spend money that shows on screen, and I shall be eternally grateful to him. He challenged the BBC system and usually won."

"Ron was nice but pretty mediocre," says Bickford. "There were an awful lot of those kind of people. There were very few people who had flair. John had flair. He was a talented man."

"Oh yes," agrees Craddock himself. "The job was done well. He was jolly good company – I liked him a lot as a person. He was warm and had a sense of fun and was conscientious alongside that, which was a nice mix. He had the priorities right. PUMs were a new invention. They were there to control budgets."

"He was tough," says director's assistant Carol Snook. "You didn't get away with anything. He kept a very tight control but in a nice way. He was so funny – the master of the quick quip. When he was working, the shutters came down. John commanded respect because he was fair and there aren't a lot of people you could say that about."

"To get there that quickly..." ponders another director's assistant, Jane Wellesley, "...well, he was very, very good with figures, very efficient, wonderful to work with. When you arrived, everything was really well organised. When we were working in Birmingham and went up for the two days to do the studio, he would go round to all the departments and get all the costs from them and give you a piece of paper with them all on. He made your life a lot easier than it would otherwise have been."

Marcia Wheeler, a fellow PUM, explains, "We had a variety of titles over the years (PUMs became production associates and then production executives, among others), the main problem being that basically we were line producers but the producers didn't want anybody else to have the word 'producer' in their title. The reason we were there is that most producers were editorial types, some of whom found production incomprehensible and others who found it extremely boring."

Gallaccio, another PUM, recalls, "The job got created to take the pressure off producers in the planning and financial terms. It was what you made of it, basically. There were four of us to begin with. John arrived a bit later. We were working with producers – two or three each. Each year we had a meeting with the department organiser when the programmes and producers were handed out – and as it went on it became 'I'm not going to work with him – no way!' It became a sort of bidding war – 'OK, I'll do that programme if you give me so and so.' There was a lot of trade off."

"When John joined, there were only five of us covering the whole department," says Wheeler. "The skill was to know where to be and when. One juggled the conflicting schedules and kept up with the office work in the gaps. I'm sure John did what I did, looking through the filming schedule (backed up by having been on the recce) and picking out the times to be there – days with many extras, stunts, night shoots that looked over optimistic, also, the start of anything especially with a new or inexperienced director or production manager, or a particularly tricky actor (if the producer wasn't going to help). You might be asked to attend rushes if the producer was on location, or to cover a dub or music recording. Some producers never attended any of the post-production; some hovered over it anxiously.

"Occasionally, the head of department would deal directly with a PUM," continues Wheeler, "if for example they wanted an opinion, cost and schedule for a project before they had appointed a producer.

"Some producers were hands-on, others hated the whole production process (or were too busy struggling with writers or another production) and left the PUM with a pretty free hand. Once a production got under way, about 90 per cent of the money and resources were committed; the task was to make the remaining money fit changing ideas, assuming the budget was OK to begin with; often it wasn't. Having organised the basic framework for the production, the PUM handed over the detailed running to the production manager(s).

"The role varied not only with the producer, but also the director and the team or teams. Some wanted to be left alone as much as possible, some wanted (or needed) help. Requests for additional recording time, or extra days on location would be channelled through the PUM, who also booked the (sometimes very complex) post-production schedule, and checked that it was achieved. PUMs knew the shift patterns of, for instance, scene crews, VT editors and OB units and would help planning by working to fit them. PUMs devised their own systems for tracking costs, and more importantly forecasting where the costs would end up. The longer the serial/series, the more room for manoeuvre, balancing the expensive episode with the cheaper one.

"Different PUMs had varying techniques; Frank Pendlebury *looked* as if he never did anything, had no idea what was happening and no hope of being on budget. He used to wander around locations like a figure of tragedy (despair in wellington boots), more or less crying, 'Woe is me.' He regularly brought his productions in under budget, probably by frightening his producers into sensible ways. Whereas I think John just had a very good business head, a very competent, capable person."

Actor-friendly as ever, John got on like a house on fire with the fresh-faced cast of *Angels*, especially Julie Dawn Cole, Angela Bruce and Clare Clifford, who played Shirley Brent (or Shirley Shagpile he as called her). "It was my first television job and we just took to each other. He was camp, smiling, outgoing, loved the fact that I had been in *The Rocky Horror Show*. I was deeply, deeply fond of him. He and Gary were really dear friends. We'd hang out and be outrageous."

Clifford's flat was just around the corner from Union and Threshold House. She began to join John and Gary for the weekly after-hours drinks parties that affable Bill Slater hosted in his office, popular as they gave serials staff the chance to socialise, gossip and plot. "The BBC was so different then," sighs Clifford. "It was creatively accessible. I was never happy just being an actor; I was far more fascinated with behind the scenes. On the Wednesday night in Threshold House there would be a get together and you would see all the well-known producers and directors and they would be talking about what they were going to do next. It was a wonderful creative environment, which, sadly, has long gone."

Carol Snook, who also worked on *Angels*, will never forget John's thoughtfulness to her at this time: "I'm a single mum and when I went in hospital with high blood pressure, John used to come and visit me at Queen Charlotte's. As soon as the baby was born, he was one of the first people to come and see me. I came home when Tom was ten days old and had a phone call from John saying, 'Right, you're doing nothing tomorrow – Clare Clifford's collecting you and you're coming over here and we're doing everything' – and they did, nappies, feeds. And I can't tell you, for a new mum on her own with a new baby, it was the most wonderful thing in the world. They just gave me that confidence I needed for that first day alone with my baby. I couldn't have asked for better friends. When I was back at work, John would organise the troops to check I was all right. Although he was tough work-wise, he was one of the kindest men I've ever known."

"He always looked out for me," says close friend Anita Graham. "I was living with some bloke that I was having a really terrible time with and didn't have the courage to say, 'Well, actually, I'm off.' This man was going away and John said, 'Right, I'll be there with a van,' and he got everything out and moved me onto his sofa for a couple of days. He was wonderful like that.

"He did a lovely thing when my second child Gabriel was born. He'd had a long day filming and he turned up with teddy bears and books for my elder son – I was living in the middle of nowhere in East Finchley but he made the effort to come over."

When another friend, Jane Wellesley, extricated herself from a long-term relationship which had ended badly, it was John who provided the practical support to get her life back on track. "I didn't have a job," she explains, "and I had tcrrible debts because my ex-partner had basically reneged on what he owed me. I had absolutely no money and John was instrumental in getting me back into the BBC as a freelance. He told me who to go and see and very quickly I was back working. He really was a great mate. I'd come back just before Christmas to find the house was flooded. Gary had gone off gaily back to see his family in Australia. John was on his own and I was on my own. Neither of us had a bean. Eventually, between us, we scraped together enough money to meet up in Shepherd's Bush. I will never forget that all we could afford was half of lager each. We sat in this really dreary, dreadful pub where we knew that we wouldn't bump into anybody that we knew and commiserated as long as we decently could and then went our separate ways."

Another friend who remembers the caring side to John's nature was actor Christopher Biggins: "He was very similar to me in a way, very infectious, great style – loved life to the full. We shared the same sense of humour and the same dress size – we were both big girls!"

When Biggins's relationship with the man he loved came to grief, he fled to John and Gary's for vodka and sympathy. "I was very low at the time. When you're younger, it hits you a lot harder and he was a great shoulder to cry on. He was very good to his friends and what also was marvellous about him was he had a really acid sense of humour so he could be bitingly funny and if you were on the other end of that, it wasn't too clever because he didn't hold back – he actually said what he thought. But we used to laugh all the time – I think the secret of our relationship was laughter."

As well as *Angels*, recorded in the Pebble Mill studios at Birmingham (and to which he managed to get Gary attached as AFM), John's reputation for industry and efficiency was rewarded when he was handed a new series called *All Creatures Great and Small* (which John quickly re-christened *All Creatures Grunt and Smell*). Just as he would become a hands-on producer, John was a hands-on PUM. Wheeler remembers that "when he was on *All Creatures* he became concerned at the escalating numbers and consequently rising cost of location catering so he went on location, stood by the van and asked everyone he didn't recognise who they were and what their connection to the shoot was. One man replied confidently that he was the goat handler's brother. John instituted a ticket system, giving cast and crew tickets, telling the caterers no-one was to have lunch without one, and only giving out tickets to those with a good reason. After that, whenever I saw the caterer's bills, I always thought of the Case Of The Goat Handler's Brother."

Another old chum, Janet Radenkovic, worked with him on the new series too and remembers, "There was a drive over the Yorkshire Dales he christened the yellow brick road and as we went across it, he used to sing *Follow the Yellow Brick Road.*"

Alongside the day job, John continued to make plain his ambition to produce. He submitted the idea for a new seafaring serial and on 26th July 1976, Bill Slater responded to this: "For the past two years I have been discussing the possibility of doing a serial set on board an ocean liner. Brian Finch wrote an episode of *Owen MD* set on a Frank Olsen ship and Bill Sellars and I discussed a spin-off. I eventually involved Brian Finch again and two days before your idea arrived on my desk I received that back from Brian. I would like you to look at it and come and have a chat when you can. Might I say I always welcome ideas from within the department. Thank you very much for sending it to me."

John needed no second bidding and was given the task of liaising with the writer. On 9th November, he reported back to Slater: "I have met and talked with Brian Finch twice now... I enclose copies of two storylines." Work continued and on 6th December, John was able to send Finch's treatment for *The Captain's Table*, a serial set on a cruise line, "concerned with the staff and guests who dine or are concerned with the Captain's table."

Slater was unable to interest controller of BBC1, Bryan Cowgill, in *The Captain's Table* (not surprisingly, it sounds woeful) but his successor did eventually sell an idea on the same lines. *Triangle* is still regarded as one of the worst drama serials ever made by the BBC, though it did well enough to run for three seasons. "John certainly wanted to produce it," remembers Marcia Wheeler. "It was his idea but Bill Sellars was put in charge, though John negotiated the ship, for an amazingly low figure, including accommodation, which was something Bill could never have done. In some ways it was ahead of its time – almost a reality show. Done now, it would probably use the real crew and passengers instead of actors. It might or might not have been better if John had been in charge. Discuss."

Script editor Christopher Bidmead laughs at the memory of *Triangle*. "It was so wonderful to have something to despise below you!"

In February 1977 there was a definite whiff of scandal hovering around the department. Bill Slater, married to *Onedin Line* actress Mary Webster, suddenly resigned, ostensibly to return to directing, but in reality because he had become embroiled in what the BBC of the time regarded as an inappropriate liaison. Ronnie Marsh, his predecessor and now head of the sister department, series, recalls that Slater "had to depart under something of a small cloud. It was of a slightly sexual nature with a scene boy," adding with startling old world lack of political correctness, "He must have been a bit mentally disturbed."

Whatever the justice of the situation around his own peccadillo, Slater was history (he died in 2006) and all eyes were on the new man, Graeme McDonald, who arrived with a reputation for producing a string of triumphs in the *Play for Today* slot. McDonald was gay, though discreetly so, and his appointment was well regarded. Producer Michael Cox worked with him at Granada, the ITV company sometimes known as "the BBC of the North" and he says that "Graeme was an astute backer of talent and that was one of the qualities which made him so good at his job. To a large extent his work was his life but he was a loyal and generous friend."

"He was very kind and caring," says director Andrew Morgan. Another who liked him was Ron Craddock. "He was terrific. Very intelligent and handled things very well."

"He was a very private person," says George Gallaccio. "You had to get to know him. Absolutely the opposite of John. I liked him."

"We used to call him Miss Piggy," laughs Carol Snook. "That was John again. Graeme believed in helping people along – a very different sort of head of department to many of them, very approachable."

"I had enormous respect for him," says director Ronnie Wilson. "He used to want to see a rough cut of your programme and he always made extremely good suggestions."

In the 1970s homophobia was widespread and even though the BBC was more liberal than most companies at the time, it was a factor here too. Writer Christopher Priest remembers script editor Douglas Adams explaining who John was and using a distinctly dubious pun – "Oh he's one of our PUM boys..."

"There was a distaste for being publicly gay," says actor Mark Strickson, "and celebrating being a homosexual in that culture. Even though the BBC was riddled with it."

"The BBC was so strong and so important," points out Christopher Biggins. "You see now also how they were dealing with sexual activities and they dealt with it in such a bad way. You were frightened. In *Rentaghost* [1970s and 80s children's comedy in which Biggins appeared] there were lots of people who were gay and you had to be really, really closeted because not only were you gay and it wasn't approved of but you were thought to be paedophiles. And it was very, very wrong. Everybody was schtum. Now of course if you're not gay you can't get a career!"

Some do talk of a "gay mafia", in drama especially, of huge benefit if you were "one of the boys". "There could be accusations of a gay mafia," script editor Betty Willingale allows. "It was a little bit jobs for mates."

Peter Davison believes that "John was very much part of and initially took successful advantage of this thing affectionately known as the gay mafia – which was headed by Graeme McDonald – where for a while, if you were gay, you could do no wrong. I had no objection to this because it was to my advantage!"

"The strange thing was," says AFM Val McCrimmon, "when I left the BBC in the 60s and came back in the early 80s, I couldn't believe how everybody seemed to be gay. People I had worked with before I had left – I thought, 'I don't know what's going on here.' The BBC had got ever so camp. There were men who, when I'd left, were married. When I came back, they were gay. I was just amazed. You think, 'What's going on here?'"

The most fabled example of the emergence of a more overt gay sensibility was John's good friend and colleague, producer Bill Sellars. Peter Davison, whom Sellars set on the road to *Doctor Who* by casting him in *All Creatures*, recalls, "He was a corduroy jacket-wearing, bald-headed married man who left one Friday night, saying to his secretary, 'Good night, see you on Monday' – and when he came in on Monday morning, he had a toupée and a new wardrobe and was gay. No-one knew who he was when he walked in!"

Despite the sniggering this inevitably caused round the tea trolley, Sellars should be admired for having the guts finally to embrace his true sexuality, empowered by the more liberal sensibility of the times. Just a few years before, gay men, terrified of prosecution and prison, often convinced themselves they could make a go of it in a straight marriage or, like director Peter Moffatt, they entered into a marriage of convenience, useful camouflage for both parties. But I'm not convinced that there was any kind of organised gay mafia at work within drama in the 1970s, any more than there was a Jewish mafia or an old boys network of former public school boys. These cliques certainly existed, as they do in most areas of money and influence, but no one set can really be said to have dominated drama. There were certainly plenty of straight men in key positions, for instance the group responsible for most of the police series.

According to Jane Wellesley, "John always said that the BBC were quite happy about you being gay as long as you were out – what they didn't want was people who could put themselves in a position to be blackmailed. There was a lot of that going on."

"Nathan was very flamboyant," says Carol Snook, "and never hid what he was or who he was as a person."

"He was never apologetic about it," says Bob Richardson, who worked in Enterprises, "and Gary was always introduced as his other half."

"He was holding up the flag," says Biggins, simply.

Russell T Davies, the man who brought *Doctor Who* back from the dead, celebrates this: "I admire no one more than an out gay man – I admire them now, never mind back then. It wasn't easy for him. Partly they had to be loud because that's how they had to exist. I love him for that. You go into those studios – they are full of hairy riggers and cameramen. It's a very straight environment. He was broadcasting it – literally with those shirts – loud and proud. That's hard work."

McDonald continued with the weekly drinks meetings for staff. "Once," remembers Fiona Cumming, "we all turned up with hats with M on them, from the McDonald's on Shepherd's Bush Green. The deal was that you brought your own bottle of wine. John was very good at getting everybody together for these."

This was an era when heavy drinking was the norm – at lunchtime and after work. "You'd do the work, helped with alcohol," says Cumming. "Life was so different then," says production manager Ralph Wilton. "The number of people who got nicked for being over the limit on that roundabout coming out of Television Centre. People didn't care that you came back from the club pissed at three o'clock in the afternoon. Secretaries would write a schedule and come back in the morning and find it was rubbish! But we got it done and we got it done well – it was part of the creativity – so much more relaxed. It was tough – hard, hard work – but a very different ethic. Less to a formula. It was much more diverse. There was room for everybody, before later it narrowed down."

John favoured red wine or Pils, a beer that was fashionable in the 70s, and vodka or "Vera Vod" as he usually called it. "When you'd finished work," smiles Colin Baker, "he'd say, 'Come on, love, one for the gutter.'" John drank heavily but at this point he was still some way from being an alcoholic and it never interfered with his work. He also chain-smoked extra-long Dunhills, carrying two packs at a time, and the ashtray on his desk was usually brimming. "He smoked very flamboyantly," recalls Sophie Aldred, "taking great long drags. Very theatrical – even lighting up was a performance. It was really all a performance."

McDonald, like so many others, was entertained by John but more importantly, he was impressed – taken by the young man's obvious energy and enthusiasm. "John had a good sense of humour," says Cumming, "but he was also very astute. He knew what he wanted."

What he wanted was to produce, but, in an era of staff jobs, these opportunities were infrequent. A vacancy had just occurred on *Doctor Who*. Interviewed in 1990 by fan magazine *DWB*, McDonald claimed that *Doctor Who* was "a bedrock part [of the output], a very important element... with Tom it was very much on a winning streak." But in utter contradiction of the facts, he also peddled the falsehood, "You can't just hurl a novice [producer] in to do *Doctor Who*... I never regarded [it] as the nursery slopes."

Be that as it may, novice producer Graham Williams (known as Grum) had been appointed in the final months of Bill Slater's reign. Williams had always been one of Slater's protégés and now he was Slater's replacement for Philip Hinchcliffe. Despite superb viewing figures, Hinchcliffe had pissed off management by pushing his luck with the levels of violence and horror in *Doctor Who*. His approach caused the kind of embarrassment and concern that higher levels of the BBC detest and Hinchcliffe was removed to produce a new film series called *Target*. Williams was told that the violence had to go. He had been working as a script editor in the department (John had already encountered him on *Barlow*) and was intelligent, diffident and boyishly handsome. In a 1998 *Doctor Who Magazine* interview, writer Chris Boucher recalled, "He was completely different from Philip Hinchcliffe, though they were both elegant young men. Philip was more pushy, a man on the way up, whereas I always sensed that Graham in some strange way was a man on the way down. I don't think he was sure of himself. Graham was related to Emlyn Williams, a very famous writer. Emlyn Williams was major and I got the feeling that Graham knew that he would never match that in any way, shape or form. It's easy to look back and see that he was a depressed man."

In 1985, Williams himself told *DWB* that "*Doctor Who* drove me crackers – it nearly killed me – the hardest work I've ever done in my life."

Hinchcliffe's PUM, old hand Chris D'Oyly John, was leaving with him, and so John, already hard at work on *All Creatures*, was asked to take over. Whatever McDonald (a seasoned diplomat) later said, within his department it was a programme that was regarded as a low-budgeted, serially troublesome children's show, weighed down by the baggage of behind-the-scenes horror stories to chill the blood of any newcomer. *Doctor Who* was the show that nobody wanted, the pre-requisite of those cutting their teeth and on the up or those biding their time, unwanted elsewhere in the department.

"It had a very small budget," remarks George Gallaccio, who'd been the PUM before D'Oyly John. "It was one of those very cheap and cheerful programmes. You had to improvise like mad on it in terms of getting it to work. I think the feeling was 'It's just *Doctor Who*' – like the bi-weekly serials, it was all done very quickly and not a great deal of attention was paid to them. It was bread and butter stuff – people thought there's nothing particularly interesting about that."

"Oh yes," says Val McCrimmon. "It was – 'Oh God you've got *Doctor Who*, poor thing.'"

"I wanted to do something creative so I asked to do it," recalls costume designer June Hudson. "My allocators said, 'But it's a kids' programme!' In other words, why would you want to do that? Good designers would often avoid it."

"The programme was a bit maverick," says Carol Snook. "People liked it or they hated it. The budgets were ridiculous. They worked miracles on peanuts."

"*Doctor Who* was regarded as a sort of loss loser," says producer Joe Waters. "It didn't have the budget, it was very studio-bound or stuck in a quarry."

"It was technically always on the edge of what was possible," points out Marcia Wheeler. "I remember doing it as a new production manager and thinking, 'I suppose the rationale is that if you can cope with this, you can cope with anything.' They were tough shows – very little time. It was not my cup of tea. I always thought it was a kids' show."

"There was a sense within the BBC that *Doctor Who* was just a training ground," says Bidmead, "a passing through kind of thing, just rolled in and out. The general feeling you had was, 'Oh, it's another *Doctor Who* – let's bung a light on it and get on with it...'"

"I think undoubtedly there was a snobbery," says Ralph Wilton. "People pretended it didn't exist but it certainly did."

Even the naturally confident John was daunted by the horror stories he'd heard in the BBC Club and around the corridors of Threshold House. On the other hand, he was bright enough to realise that, if he could make a go of the job, tame the overruns and overspends, it might help him on his self-proclaimed mission to the top.

The first two years threw plenty of white knuckle challenges in the path of both Williams and his chain-smoking PUM. Graeme McDonald forced them to abandon a vampire story at the last minute, fearing it might clash with his own plans for a lavish Christmas production of Bram Stoker's *Dracula* (which, ironically, John costed for him). Another story had to be recorded in the Pebble Mill studios, where staff were keen but unused to the tricky technical demands of a *Doctor Who*. A new companion arrived in the form of K9 but this gadget, though obviously box office, constantly malfunctioned, causing the kind of delays that the tight-as-a-tick recording schedule simply couldn't accommodate. Strike action was an ever-present threat, script editors came and went and the stories for which they were responsible frequently needed heavy rewriting, sometimes by the producer himself. These were just a few of the headaches. Meanwhile, the rampant ego of the star, Tom Baker, was growing unchecked.

Whereas Williams seemed to many a man with the cares of the world on his shoulders, John thrived on the heady combination of stress and showbiz, offering his producer sterling support but keeping his own counsel on his opinion about some of the whys and wherefores of this singular programme. When friends were occasionally scheduled onto the show, he looked out for them, too. *Image of the Fendahl* (1977) had a director new to the series, the flamboyant George Spenton-Foster. He was assigned Prue Saenger, a production assistant also new to the show and terrified by the prospect of working with Tom Baker. The AFM was Karilyn Collier, John's mate from his first day in the department and happily, she got on with Baker like a house on fire. Alas, this didn't endear her to either director or PA. "They were absolutely awful," she recalls, "knocking me all the way through the studio. John came down during the break one studio day and said, 'They are tearing you to pieces.' I said, 'Why? What have I done?' They got a lecture from the producer and that was thanks to John. When I hit problems, he was always there." Unsurprisingly, Spenton-Foster joined the ranks of those for whom John had no time whatsoever.

In 1978, he came close to being moved from the job, as fellow PUM Marcia Wheeler recalls: "There was a hilarious meeting with the manager Brian Spiby, who, I suspect, had been told by a producer that he didn't want a particular PUM. Instead of being open about this, to try to hide it, Brian decided to shuffle everything round. He allocated me onto *Doctor Who* and Chris D'Oyly John onto *Tinker, Tailor, Soldier, Spy*. I was speechless with horror because I didn't want to do *Doctor Who*. Luckily, I didn't have to say anything because the others were all so furious – John certainly didn't want to have *Doctor Who* wrenched from his grip – and Chris didn't want to do *Tinker, Tailor* because he wasn't really a literary type either."

By his third year as PUM on *All Creatures* and *Doctor Who*, John was handed responsibility for yet another drama, a family saga called *Flesh and Blood*. This was to be produced by Bill Sellars, script-edited by Teddy Rhodes and directed by another old hand, Terence Dudley (who had also directed several episodes of *All Creatures*). The cast included Bill Fraser, Nigel Stock, Michael Jayston and Richard Willis, all later to feature in *Doctor Who*, and the serial was created and written by John Finch, who recalls, "I realised very early on that Sellars wasn't enthusiastic about producing *Flesh and Blood*. His first words at the read through were to say to the actors that the script had 37 'bloodies'. This was virtually his sole comment. I think the casting was faulty in three or four instances too. I felt he was very unfriendly, but I don't know why. Terry Dudley, on the other hand, was a delight to work with. Bill complained about the size of the audience, but Terry told me it was very high in the audience appreciation index. We had a first-class review by the eminent critic John Peter, where he compared it very favourably with *Dallas*. On the whole though, mainly because of Bill's unfriendliness, *Flesh and Blood* was an unhappy experience."

John had come a long way since early 1977 when his PUM portfolio had started to expand. But of all the dramas and developments in John's life during that career-defining year, perhaps he was least aware of the one that was to have the most significance. Producer Martin Lisemore, whose belief in John had elevated him from AFM to production assistant, was overseeing his latest adaptation, a serialisation of Colin Watson's *Flaxborough Chronicles*. It had been retitled *Murder Most English* and, like *Angels* and *All Creatures*, was being taped in the Pebble Mill studios. On 3rd February 1977, after a long day's studio recording, most of the cast and crew were staying overnight but, as script editor Betty Willingale recalls, "Martin lived in Buckinghamshire and decided to drive home."

"He always went back to his wife and family," says director Ronnie Wilson. "I went with him as he got into his car and I was the last person to see him alive. He was driving on a country road and there was a blind hill. He went up over the hill and this other car, without its lights on, came and smashed into him."

"Thank God I declined a lift," shudders Willingale. "He was taken to the John Radcliffe Hospital in Oxford but died almost immediately. He was only 37. Oh, I can't tell you how awful it was, horrible, horrible."

The aftershock of Lisemore's tragic death reverberated through the department. The decision was taken to present a one-night-only charity gala evening, *Martin Lisemore – A Celebration*, with proceeds going to the National Association for Gifted Children and to help establish a trust fund for Martin's two young children. John was roped in to direct and produce and he persuaded close friend Ted Rhodes, the theatrical and ultra-waspish script editor of *All Creatures*, to join him. In the introduction to the brochure produced to accompany the performance, they wrote: "Mounting a show of this kind filled us with dread. The associated problems of finding a place to rehearse, assembling the cast, musical arrangements, obtaining scripts from many sources... Is it any wonder our ulcers grew?"

"John was very good at begging and borrowing things from lots of people," says Margot Hayhoe. "From costumes and lighting to props and it looked very good. It was comedy sketches and singing and dances at the Victoria Palace."

The performance took place on Sunday 26th June with sketches by writers like Elaine Morgan, Peter Ling, Michael Palin and Terry Jones and music from, among others, Richard Stilgoe. Among the stars persuaded to take part were Christopher Biggins, Brenda Bruce, Chris and Dominic Guard, Nerys Hughes, Jeremy Irons, Anna Massey, John Normington, Michael Robbins, Gareth Thomas, Christopher Timothy, Fiona Walker, Derek Waring and Moray Watson. Gary Downie choreographed the number *Tap Your Troubles Away* and the grand finale was John's favourite, *It's Not Where You Start* from the 1973 Broadway musical *Seesaw*.

Among the audience were John's parents, who rarely travelled to London or saw their son in his professional life. "He brought them backstage and introduced them to me," says Karilyn Collier, who, like everyone else, was working on the show as a favour to John. "I was struck by their quietness and ordinariness. They were very sweet people who had produced this amazing personality in the son. I thought, 'I didn't think his parents would be like that' – they were very meek and humble."

Unfortunately, the show wasn't as successful as John had hoped. "Unlike the pantomime at Drury Lane, we didn't have the publicity machine," explains Janet Radenkovic, "and it wasn't anything like full, which was quite disappointing because there were some wonderful actors in it."

Nevertheless enough money was raised to fulfil its compassionate intention of establishing a trust fund for Lisemore's children.

McDonald, meanwhile, was left with the problem of who might follow in his footsteps as the producer of the prestigious BBC2 classics. Despite the status of the slot, it was, typically of the serials department, a treadmill of production often with one adaptation filming or in studio while others jostled either side in various degrees of readiness. At the point of Lisemore's untimely death, *Murder Most English* was only two episodes in. "We had to go on," sighs Betty Willingale. "Graeme was marvellous and really stepped forward to help. He came and did things that a producer would do and kept us all going." Having done some firefighting of his own, he handed the production over to Bill Sellars ("utterly useless", in Betty Willingale's view). Sellars was never a contender as a long-term replacement – whatever his professional shortcomings, he was in any case scheduled to produce *All Creatures Great and Small* where actor Christopher Timothy (who'd been one of the *Murder Most English* ensemble) would, after John Alderton and Richard Beckinsale had turned it down, be his third choice to play James Herriot.

Uninspired by the choice from within, McDonald looked further afield and his eye was caught by a young man he remembered from Granada. Jonathan Powell had started attracting attention as a writer and script editor (notably on the acclaimed *Country Matters*) and progressed to producing popular dramas like *Crown Court* and *The Nearly Man*. Someone who worked with him there and remembers him well is the writer John Finch: "He obviously came from an upper-class set-up of some suit. I think Jonathan fancied himself as a writer. He was my assistant on *A Family at War*, and he did write an episode, which I edited. He also ghosted one of the *Sam* novels, using my scripts. I remember picking up a copy on Cologne Station and finding that my name was not anywhere mentioned! He was ambitious. In fact, I never met anyone who was more ambitious than Jonathan. At the time I was having considerable success and I think Jonathan decided to hitch his wagon to my star. Denis Forman [chairman of Granada] once asked me if Jonathan had the potential to be a writer. I replied in the negative, but said that I thought he would make a good producer. I always had the impression that Jonathan could be pretty ruthless. He could be very charming, but very irritating too. I once took him to task for clicking his fingers at waiters."

"His nickname up there was 'Bopper' Powell," chuckles George Gallaccio. "He was quite a wild young man. When he first came to the BBC, part of him was trying to be the respectable producer but we used to have parties and things and he would let his hair down. There were two sides to him – the daytime Jonathan and then, when he'd had a few drinks, the other Jonathan came out."

Powell, born on April 25th 1947, was just a few months older than John. His youth seemed to count in his favour. "Serials were a bit like that," says Marcia Wheeler. "They seemed to make a conscious decision to appoint a fairly young generation."

"Graeme was very, very good – he appointed me!" smiles Powell himself.

It should be said that being young and ambitious wasn't all. It helped if you were a man too. A kind of "glass ceiling" held back female members of staff from getting to the top. Women's lib, like gay lib, was making inroads into attitudes as well as the law, but it was a slow process. Marcia Wheeler still remembers her annoyance "when John and George Gallaccio got trainee attachment producer posts and I'd applied and hadn't even got an interview. I was more experienced and at least as well qualified."

As successor to Martin Lisemore's kingdom, and, paired with the brilliant Betty Willingale, Jonathan Powell began to produce a string of distinguished dramas, introducing regular adaptations of contemporary novelists alongside Austen, Dickens and the usual suspects. The best were recognised as productions of extraordinary quality and worth – from John le Carré's *Tinker, Tailor, Soldier, Spy* (1979) and Angus Wilson's *The Old Men at the Zoo* (1983), to Vera Brittain's *Testament of Youth* (1979) and Iris Murdoch's *The Bell* (1982). "Jonathan liked nothing but the best," says Willingale. "He was the embodiment of the pursuit of excellence – and a bit snobbish!"

Wheeler, who worked closely with him for many years, believes that "he was a classic example of the kind of producer who found the production process deeply boring and wanted it to go away. He had an extremely low boredom threshold and an extremely short attention span. He tended to make sudden decisions and that was that. He had a huge flair for putting a project together and an equal flair for publicising it but very little interest in anything between."

Aged 30, in charge of one of the BBC's most important shop-window slots, bringing with it direct access to the crème de la crème of British writing, acting and production talent… it must have been apparent to all but the most obtuse that new arrival Powell reeked of ambition. "He was obviously going to become head of department," says Ronnie Wilson with a sigh.

Lovett Bickford "didn't like him terribly. I don't think he was interested in anybody but himself and getting up the greasy pole which he of course did."

"Daytime" Jonathan, his manner quiet, cool and softly spoken, was the very antithesis of John Nathan-Turner with his jazz hands style, love of the trivial and personification of camp. They represented two aspects of the BBC – Powell was one of the university-trained thinkers, analytical, inscrutable, high brow, John one of the grass roots programme makers – instinctive, effusive, populist. For the time being, this was of no consequence because the department valued both, and their interests and paths were seen not as conflicting but complementary. But it is an unmistakable irony that by acting as "kingmaker" to both men, Graeme McDonald inadvertently put in motion a clash of cultures and ideologies, which, a few years later, would erupt into a bitter, personal, political struggle, consuming the career of one of them and ending the life of *Doctor Who*.

FOUR

THE GREATEST SHOW
IN THE GALAXY

"It felt to me as though the show needed to progress in order to survive..."
John Nathan-Turner, *Myth Makers* interview, 1990

In 1979, Britain was in crisis. The year began with the infamous winter of discontent, in which widespread strikes combined with freezing conditions created an atmosphere of misery and depression. Inflation, running at 11.3 per cent, seemed to be out of control. The government seemed to be out of touch and the Prime Minister, James Callaghan, out of reach, beleaguered and on the back foot. "Labour isn't working," sneered the brilliant Saatchi and Saatchi-coined Conservative catchphrase in the spring election campaign. On 3rd May, the country handed victory to the Tories and their twin-set dominatrix, Margaret Thatcher. She recognised the appetite for drastic change and, over the decade that followed, provided it with ruthless gusto.

Against this backdrop, 1979 started with business as usual in the microclimate of the BBC's Union and Threshold House, but here too, drastic change was on the way. In April, the serials department merged with the series department, creating one larger group under the leadership of Graeme McDonald. At the same time, production was under way on the 17th season of *Doctor Who* and all was not well. Tom Baker had resigned at the end of the previous season, a bluff in the battle for control of the show between him and his producer, Graham Williams. An uneasy truce was brokered between the two men but Williams was physically and emotionally exhausted by the ceaseless demands of the job. He was drinking heavily, some say in an attempt to keep up with his wayward star. "But it was insane," says costume designer June Hudson. "No-one can keep up with Tom in that way."

"I must say I kept a back seat in all this," John commented in his memoirs. "I really couldn't fathom it out – they'd often be very close and spend hours together, talking and drinking, and other times, they'd be at loggerheads."

The problems posed by Baker's proprietorial approach to the job did not lessen. His behaviour in rehearsal and on set was often outrageous, rude, bullying and unprofessional. Whispers of this enlivened the gossip doing the rounds of Television Centre. "Tom would end up goodness knows where," says AFM Val McCrimmon, "without his script, which he'd leave wherever he'd ended up and then he'd come into rehearsal and say, 'We'll rip that up and do this instead' – and he'd been allowed to get away with it by Graham. Tom often wasn't there. If he got bored during rehearsals, he used to go to some club in Soho. He was impossible. I think he thought he *was* Doctor Who. He had taken control and it was all getting very silly."

"Tom wasn't easy to work with at all," says director's assistant Jane Wellesley. "He was going a bit mad then, leading it, instead of being led by the producer, who was a bit weak, though very nice."

Wellesley was part of the team working on one of the planned highlights of that season, a story in which *Doctor Who* would film on location abroad for the very first time. The destination chosen was Paris, the story was *City of Death*, and it was John who made the shoot possible, costing it to within an inch of its life and persuading Williams to go ahead. But the four-day lightning filming trip was a sorry saga of dismal weather and narrowly averted disasters. Says Wellesley: "The PA had spent quite a lot of time in Paris with her young son, supposedly sorting out these locations and had basically totally failed. We arrived the first day and went for lunch. That went on a bit, so about 3.30 it was decided that we really ought to go and shoot something. It had been arranged that we were going to shoot in this art gallery on the Champs-Elysées and we all trooped off only to discover that it was a French bank holiday and everything was closed. The next morning we were scheduled to film in some café and it had become a building site. We were supposed to film outside the Louvre and it suddenly transpired that permission hadn't been granted and at one point it was a case of 'Right – everybody run!'"

Baker became embroiled in an on-off relationship with his co-star, Lalla Ward. Sometimes they'd be flirting, but more often they were feuding. "I had Lalla crying on my shoulder because he was horrid to her," remembers McCrimmon. "He just ignored her and made her very miserable." For their colleagues, the vagaries of this behaviour were tiresomely unpredictable and had to be sensitively navigated. "I think Graham had quite a few personal problems at the time, too," says Wellealoy. "John used to have open bar in his hotel room. When we got back from a day's filming, he'd say, 'The bar's in my room,' and we'd all troop along and sit around and drink. One night it went on and on and on and people didn't go. John wanted to go to bed, so in the end he just went into the bathroom, got undressed, got into bed and said, 'Last person turn the light out!'"

It was during this tricky, uncomfortable shoot that Williams confided in John that he had decided to quit. John's loyalty and support had moved Williams to suggesting that for this third season in their collaboration, he might be credited as associate producer. This was apparently not acceptable to the craft unions (it was this kind of rigid demarcation which Thatcher would eventually sweep away, along with so much else) so, left with the option of sharing his producer's credit, Williams understandably declined to change the status quo. "Nevertheless," commented John, "I have always felt, with extreme gratitude, that Graham's impassioned request resulted in my being asked to take over."

During the summer, as production staggered on, McDonald was considering the succession. Some people have hinted that, in some way, he "owed" John a favour or that John, as one of his obvious protégés, and someone who had been signposting his ambition for years, was the inevitable choice. But, even if this were true, there is evidence that others were considered. During 1978, John's fellow PUM, George Gallaccio, had been "on attachment" (the inspired BBC scheme whereby a member of staff can "try out" in another job or department) to BBC Scotland, producing a hokey series called *The Omega Factor*. "When I finished that," says Gallaccio, "I had a meeting with Graeme and he said, 'What would you like to do next? Would you like to do *Mackenzie*, by Andrea Newman?' And he did actually say, 'I wonder about *Doctor Who*?' I said, 'No, I don't want to do *Doctor Who* but I'd love to do the Andrea Newman.' So whether it was actually *offered* to me or whether Graeme was just exploring the possibility, I'm not sure, but I made my preference clear and was given *Mackenzie*."

During the production of *Shada*, the final story of the season, John was summoned to McDonald's office. He noticed that Tom Baker had been in just before him. "I can remember exactly what he said," he told *Doctor Who Magazine*. "'Your time has come, John,' said Graeme. 'I'd like you to produce *Doctor Who*. And I've told *that* man.'"

"I remember," says director Andrew Morgan, "Graeme saying to me, 'You know JN-T's going to produce *Doctor Who* – I think it's very good casting, he'll do it marvellously,' and I said, 'Yes, he will.' He was on the road and everyone thought he was going places."

"I was pleased," says eminent script editor Betty Willingale, "and thought, 'Oh that's good.' Whereas so often I used to think, 'What the..?!' So many idiots were made producers."

Ronnie Marsh, McDonald's predecessor and now elevated to special adviser to the head of drama group, believes: "It was the sort of programme best done by someone who loved the theatre and make-believe. If a producer hasn't got enthusiasm, he isn't going to communicate that enthusiasm. It's very wrong to throw a project at somebody and say, 'How do you feel about this?' It's death and disaster unless the producer shows enthusiasm for the project he's doing."

Grahame Flynn, a close friend in John's later life, says, "The first thing he did when he was made producer was to go to Carnaby Street and buy that black leather patchwork coat he used to wear for filming. He was a very, very young producer. He told me that he grew the beard to make himself look a little bit older, so that when he was talking to people, they would take him more seriously."

There was a caveat. McDonald explained that former producer Barry Letts, now in charge of another departmental warhorse, the Sunday classic serial, would take on the new role of executive producer – insurance against John's lack of creative experience. John swallowed his disappointment with apparent good grace, though it rankled with him. Letts, a sensitive and tolerant man, was himself uncomfortable with the position this placed him in and tried to reserve his interventions for advice about scripts and key appointments. Letts's long-time collaborator, writer and script editor Terrance Dicks, later recalled in an interview for DVD producer Ed Stradling: "Barry felt immensely embarrassed being executive producer because he felt that John was the producer and he mustn't undermine his authority. Nothing was done about bad habits which started then. When the show later declined, I used to say to him, 'This is all your fault, Barry.' And he'd say, 'What do you mean?' I said, 'You were the executive producer. You saw JN-T at work. You should have put in a report saying this man couldn't run a whelk stall or organise a piss-up in a brewery, but you didn't because you were too kind-hearted.' And he didn't, bless him."

"Barry took his role seriously," says director John Black, "in the sense when he had a complete novice producer in John. It was Barry who had the ultimate say on script changes but he was an extraordinarily nice and intelligent man who was very keen to develop John and make him feel he was in control. He was very aware of John's strengths and weaknesses. But his whole idea was that support should be withdrawn over time."

Just like Mrs Thatcher, John felt he had been given the remit for sweeping changes. The three years he had spent on the show as PUM meant that now he showed little hesitation in making them. There would be a glossy new title sequence, with a rearranged version of the theme tune. The incidental music was to be revamped, too. On 25th September 1979, even before his appointment was confirmed, John sent a memo to McDonald: "Enclosed are the two records I mentioned to you by Jean Michel Jarre. I would be grateful if you could listen to them when you have the time. Although many of the tracks on these LPs are highly commercial, I think this kind of 'synthesizer music' would be very useful in next season's *Dr Who*."

John never forgot his mistake in inviting long-term composer Dudley Simpson to lunch to tell him that his services were to be dispensed with. "My intention was to break the news over the main course," he wrote in his memoirs. "Dudley said that I was the very first *Who* producer to take him to lunch and how delightful it was. There was only one thing for it – I had to tell him there and then. Dudley was very unhappy and it felt like the longest lunch I'd ever had. I learnt a lesson – if you're giving someone bad news, do it over a drink or a cup of tea. Only give good news over a meal!"

The new broom had a new office as *Doctor Who* moved from 401 Threshold House to 204 Union House. He retained the services of the efficient and friendly Jane Judge, the production secretary who had worked for Williams since October 1978. The series ahead was to be an extended one – 28 episodes rather than the usual 26 – because John had suggested that seven four-part stories would be a better mix than five four-parters with a concluding six-parter. With production due to begin in February 1980, there wasn't much time to get the show on the road. Williams's script editor, Douglas Adams, was leaving with him and so, as a priority, John needed to find a replacement. Johnny Byrne, one of the regular writers on *All Creatures*, wasn't interested, too busy with his freelance career, though he did offer to contribute some story ideas. It was Robert Banks Stewart, then producing the very successful detective show *Shoestring*, who suggested a 38-year-old actor turned writer called Chris Bidmead. He was interviewed by John and Barry Letts and believes that "it was Barry who got me in really – I said how silly I thought the programme was. John was still finding his feet."

Having got the job, Bidmead was horrified by the paucity of the material on offer, a ragbag of rejects and leftovers. One of these was revived, the Terrance Dicks vampire story abandoned a couple of years earlier on the instructions of Graeme McDonald. John had a few ideas of his own, based around a "futuristic Butlin's holiday camp" and he had commissioned a jobbing writer with previous

Who form, David Fisher, to work these up into a four-part story. John was toying with *Errinella* too, an offering from a director he liked, Pennant Roberts, but this never got off the blocks.

With the cupboard so bare, it may seem odd that John turned his back on one obvious contender. The final story of the troubled 17th season was the six-part *Shada*, cobbled together by Adams and partially shot when one of the habitual strikes of the time forced production to a halt. Attempts at a remount were planned and costed and could certainly have filled either of the first two recording slots of the new series with no major problems. But to John, salvaging *Shada* was only ever practicable on the basis of its being scheduled as an extra, on top of his already increased episode count for the next run. It's hard to see how this would ever have been given the green light but it clearly indicates John's determination that different was better. *Shada* was effectively thrown away. "John was not keen, I was not keen," says Bidmead. "I think we shared the view that we wanted a new broom that swept clean – we didn't really want to have all that baggage, a bit of leftover stuff from last time. I would have been quite happy not to have *The Leisure Hive*, quite frankly, and indeed Terrance's. John was insisting on them and the only compromise was a huge amount of rewrites.

"He was very charming and affable. Afternoons he almost completely left me to my own devices. After you came back from lunch, you closed your door and you didn't see anybody. He was wonderful at getting star casts and getting the budgets fiddled so that we got the best things for the directors – that's not nothing, that's really important stuff – but missing at the heart of this was that a producer's job is to understand what you're putting on the screen and why. I felt that John had absolutely no sense at all about storytelling and script. I don't want to sound too whiny about this but the way this showed up was you'd get a bunch of stories on one page of A4 – a stack of ideas from writers and you'd read through them and pick out some really cracking, good ones and you'd put them in front of John and he'd go, 'Not that one, not that one,' and you'd say, 'I want to understand you, John – why?' 'It just doesn't work for me' – I hated that phrase, it was not at all specific. There was no educational process between us – I could not learn his mind on this.

"Very early on," continues Bidmead, "I realised that I was on my own when it came to getting the stuff on the screen. John was going to be terrific as the guy for getting all the material together but as far as understanding stories, he didn't even know how television worked."

"Too pleased with himself by half," observes Lovett Bickford, the first director of the season, of Bidmead. "He thought he was the bees' knees."

Inevitably, John's casting of directors has provoked much comment and some criticism over the years but, in the main, he was only working in the way that he had been trained and which was familiar within the BBC of that time. Producers of long-running, multi-episodic series tended to employ a mix of directors. Some would be favourites, who might be relied upon to come in on time and budget, get on with the cast and do a good creative job – note the order of these assets. But there was also an expectation that room would be found for both the up-and-coming aspiring directors (often on attachment from the grade below, production manager, having passed the internal directors' course) and the staffers who nobody really wanted any more who, for a variety of reasons (age, laziness, drunkenness, unpleasantness, profligacy) were difficult to place and yet needed to be employed. For his first season, John managed to avoid the "time servers" and put together a mix of young thrusters and old reliables. Into the former category were Bickford, Peter Grimwade, Paul Joyce and John Black. In the latter fell father figure-types Terence Dudley and Peter Moffatt, both of whom he had worked with on *All Creatures* (and, in Dudley's case, *Flesh and Blood*, too). He'd tried some long shots, too, approaching Ronnie Wilson, who'd directed *The Pallisers* and *How Green Was My Valley*. Wilson had other fish to fry and declined. Similarly, Herbie Wise, who'd masterminded *I, Claudius*, was uninterested. Another *All Creatures* alumnus and veteran *Who* director Christopher Barry offered his services but he wasn't John's type, but then nor was he top of anyone's list. "Chris was a pain in the fucking arse," says Sue Hedden. "He used to have tantrums and stamp his foot. I used to say to him, 'Stop taking yourself so bloody seriously!'"

"He was a kind of wheedling figure," says Peter Davison. "When things went wrong, he'd say, 'Why does this always happen to me?'"

"He was very capable and competent and organised," allows Marcia Wheeler, "but not hugely inspired. A journeyman director."

Barry could evidently be tactless, too, later annoying John by suggesting to Peter Davison that the actor was wrong for the job and subsequently by implying to journalists that *The Tripods*, a much-hyped (but pretty awful) science-fiction show which he was directing might ultimately be a replacement for *Who*. John was irritated by some of the directors and writers who had preceded him and would refer to them disparagingly as "old toots".

He wanted to start his reign in style and when Bickford waxed lyrical about "balls and pizzazz", he liked the cut of his jib and booked him with Letts's blessing. "It was my first job as a freelance," says Bickford. "I'd just done *The History of Mr Polly* for Barry – which had a distinctive style – John liked that and frankly wanted a new style for *Doctor Who* – and he asked me whether I would do it and of course I would because it was interesting to do. It was a bloody awful script but it's been recognised as quite groundbreaking visually. I am much more visual and filmic than most of the directors used to be. They were just dull –

there was no excitement – I don't think they had much idea of script either. I was pretty difficult and demanding. He probably lacked confidence when he first started and he had Barry sitting on his shoulder a bit. Barry was a nice man but very straight down the middle, pretty dull, really, and a very modest director."

Modesty was not Bickford's strong suit. Cumming remembers that "even as an AFM, he would the answer the phone as 'Bickford of the BBC here' rather than 'Hugh David's office' or whichever director he was working with!" He needed every ounce of confidence because *The Leisure Hive* was a baptism of fire. His filmic approach required an overrun of a whole extra studio day – a major blot on John's copy book so early on in his producing career (although, conversely, he was almost certainly cut a degree of slack for precisely the same reason). "I did him a huge favour," asserts Bickford. "I don't think he would admit it but it was interesting, he made a stir and it was a new beginning."

"I was 18 when *The Leisure Hive* was on," says future showrunner Russell T Davies, "and I remember the way it looked. The camera was just in there and tight. You'd still hire a director like that now. I love the feel of it. It was absolutely gorgeous."

"He should have taken it further," says Bickford, "but he went back on it. He never used me again. We overspent, doing an impossible script, and he was quite careful I think. He wasn't adventurous with the directors – he wanted people that he could control."

Tom Baker loathed the story, especially its requirement that the Doctor stay looking aged for a good chunk of screen time. John had lost no time in establishing his authority over his new fiefdom. He insisted that, from now on, Baker should wear make-up. "It was one of the major issues," says Flynn. "Tom didn't want to wear it but sometimes he was coming in after too much lager and Benedictine or whatever and when they edited the show together, he would look different in every scene. He also had this health scare, which meant he had sudden weight loss and lost the curls in his hair. So John made him wear make-up."

He also commissioned costume designer June Hudson to transform Baker's increasingly scruffy clothes into something altogether smarter and more streamlined. He knew that Baker was inordinately fond of Hudson and it saved him yet another battle. June smiles when asked to remember John. "He was so boyish – I can see his face now, the brown eyes looking at you. You didn't have to watch your back with John – he didn't play games – there was none of this guarded and cagey behaviour you get with so many producers. He had great faith in me – never for one minute did John ever question my judgement. He trusted me so much and for that reason I would have moved heaven and earth for him. He was actually a frustrated costume designer. In later years he did panto and that's a clue as to why his influence could be bigger than was needed for television – it was more theatrical.

"John wanted a completely different look – I persuaded him to keep the scarf. To get rid of it wouldn't have been practical because Tom used it as a prop. There was a danger that he could have used the old scarf with the new costume so I thought I had to incorporate it with the new costume – I made it of chenille, which is very light and the colours are good. John wanted the question marks on the shirt for marketing and though I understood that, I didn't like them. What I said to him is that Doctor Who is above all a gentleman and gentlemen don't wear logos."

John was adamant and the question marks remained a part of the Doctor's "look" for the rest of his time on the show. The cosmetic changes he was instigating were, however, mere window dressing. Encouraged by Letts and Bidmead, John was determined to eradicate the somewhat smug, all too knowing, clever clever, undergraduate comedy that had become the signature style of the show under Williams and, especially, Douglas Adams. John didn't like the almost invincible line-up of two Time Lords and a robot dog either. K9 could be written out easily enough, the departure milked for all the publicity it was worth. Early on, John lunched with Lalla Ward. He was relieved to find that she was of the same mind – it was time for Romana to go. Interviewed on an American radio show after John's death, Ward commented, "I think it was quite difficult for him with Tom and me in that he inherited us and we'd already known him. It's quite difficult when you come in as the new person having been on it in a different guise – and have to change your role with people who have been playing the same role for quite a long time – that's quite a lot to take on board."

On 3rd April 1980, *Blue Peter* transmitted a film all about the *Doctor Who* exhibition at Longleat House in Wiltshire. This had opened in 1972 and was the responsibility of BBC Enterprises' tiny exhibitions team run by Lorne Martin with the help of Julie Jones (Punkette) and Bob Richardson. "*Doctor Who* was our biggest money-spinning exhibition," says Richardson. "It was our bread and butter, really. We were looking at ways of getting free publicity. Getting *Blue Peter* involved was my idea – I suggested it to Lorne and he made the call to Biddy [Baxter, the programme's editor]."

The film was a fairly run-of-the-mill entry in which the presenter, Tina Heath, helps to spring-clean the exhibition. What made it significant was the star interview – not with Baker or Ward, but their new producer. The director of that short film was Alex Leger: "With his unkempt hair, rotund and dressed in jeans and a blue serge sweater, John had very particular ideas about how his programme should be portrayed. In direct conflict with *Blue Peter*'s boss of films, John Adcock, he believed that the mystery of the *Doctor Who* monsters should remain just that – a mystery – and he told me so in no uncertain terms. Imagine my disquiet when Adcock told me that the purpose of the film was to get 'behind the scenes' and show *Blue Peter* viewers what the monsters were really like as the exhibition was put in place. Tina showed various monsters being man-handled into their displays and the monsters were shamefully revealed in all their homespun glory. It left me wondering what would result from this fairly tedious piece of filming.

"The first cut was shown to both Johns although John Adcock had a few minutes tinkering before Nathan-Turner arrived. I watched with some interest. Which of the two personalities, I wondered, would prevail? The film was shown and I retreated. There was a brisk argument and I heard John Adcock say that it was his film and he would do what he liked with it. Nathan-Turner made several comments but recognised that in the greater scheme of things he didn't have much choice. Adcock was a believer of 'possession is nine tenths of the law' and now the filming was over he (and *Blue Peter*) were the rightful owners."

It was John's first appearance in front of the cameras but many more would follow. He became known within the BBC as one its few producers perfectly willing to sit on a sofa and emote about his output. His credits mounted up, from children's programmes like *Saturday Superstore* and *Take Two* to magazine shows like *Breakfast Time* and *Behind the Screen*. Most names on end credits remain faceless – not John's. His characteristic drawl and bright, Hawaiian shirts became familiar to an audience far beyond the hardcore fans. The shirts were a clever touch. They were flattering to the fuller figure ("You bitch", I can hear him retort) but they also served to make him stand out. They were his costume as producer and ambassador-in-chief for *Doctor Who*.

As if to prove the old Western cliché "This town's not big enough for the both of us", the struggle for supremacy between actor and producer played out on location, in rehearsal and in studio and, for a time, neither was backing down. "Tom hated him," says McCrimmon. "He was out of control and John stopped that. He came in to try and make it a bit more sensible and that pissed Tom off because he wouldn't let him do all his silly things – whereas Graham had allowed him to. It was about time for Tom to go, really."

"He'd worn himself out," says Bidmead, "and was into the booze in a big way, causing serious problems on the set. One of the things I hated about Tom was the way he ingratiated himself with the extras but with his peer cast he just wouldn't bother at all. He wouldn't even look them in the eye when playing with them."

"Later on," says Colin Baker, "John used to say to me that he'd been burnt a bit by Tom – because Tom was so powerful and insistent. He'd battled with Tom and never again wanted an actor to have the kind of power in a programme that Tom had had."

"Spoiled, undisciplined and impossible to work with" was director Terence Dudley's damning verdict in an interview reproduced in *Talkback: The Eighties*.

"Tom would arrive 40 minutes late," recalls fellow director Paul Joyce, "demand a box of BBC pencils and proceed to go through his script and take all his lines out. Terry Dudley brought in a tape recorder and Tom said, 'What's that? Are you spying on me?' 'No, no, no – I don't want to lose one of your bons mots – I'm trying to keep on top of these script changes.' That stopped him in his tracks. Terry wasn't a great director but that was a good tip."

"I was very worried going into *Doctor Who*," says AFM Lynn Richards, "because Tom had this terrible reputation. For some reason, I don't know why, Tom took to me straightaway. John nicknamed me Snow White. My hair was very dark then so I said to John's secretary, Jane, 'That doesn't make sense,' and she replied, 'It's because you look after everybody.' Tom and John didn't get on at all. Tom said, 'I don't suffer fools and I don't spend my time with people I don't like' – and he had no time whatsoever for John. Tom thought he was it and John wasn't. I was sort of the go-between. Tom would say something and I would have to tell John and vice versa because they literally didn't talk at that time."

Baker was further destabilised by John's decision to replace Romana with a teenage boy called Adric, played by Matthew Waterhouse. Waterhouse was an 18-year-old *Doctor Who* fan and getting the part, only his second professional engagement, should have meant that he was living the dream. The reality was a shock, with Baker, the actor he admired so much, treating him with undisguised contempt. As he recounts in his sparkling memoir, *Blue Box Boy*, one day at rehearsal, Baker turned to him and snarled, "Why don't you piss off?"

"He went into that show and no-one looked after him," says Russell T Davies. "The lack of care from the production team – was it all like that in those days? Now you get led in, you get helped."

Waterhouse himself is more forgiving. "I do think that was a problem, not particularly with John, but with the way the programme was run and probably the way the BBC worked at the time. John couldn't be there all the time. Peter Moffatt [the director] was very sweet actually but when you're working with an actor as difficult as Tom, I don't think people were taking care to prepare me for what this was going to be like. Bidmead said, 'Watch out for Tom,' which was very well meant but it's not enough – I was thrown into it and when I rethought it to write [my book] it all came back very vividly. That first day was very, very difficult."

Around the BBC, and within fandom ever since, hovers the persistent rumour that Waterhouse owed his big break to a close encounter with the casting couch. "I was in the BBC at the time and it was being said," recalls Davies. "He was a pretty thing in his day. We had a PA who said, 'Oh, those two are at it like mad!' – hardly proof but..."

"I think it's funny," says Waterhouse himself. "It's ridiculous. I don't think John was that corrupt actually. We once sat in the BBC bar discussing our fantasies and he said he wanted to be the controller of BBC1 by the time he was 40. I remember that absolute phrase very clearly. I think he thought that he would do *Doctor Who* for a year or two and then something on the lines of *Dallas*, which he absolutely loved, a British version of *Dallas*. He was very, very ambitious for the programme and himself. Particularly when you were as ambitious as John was, I don't think it would have been a logical step to say, 'If you have sex with me, I'll put you in this programme.' I'm absolutely certain that he never cast anyone in that way."

I wondered if Waterhouse's sexuality had ever been discussed, even light-heartedly, but, he says, "We never mentioned being gay. I do think that John was someone who didn't see very deeply into people. Apart from in a light, social kind of sense, he didn't deal with people on a more complex level very well. In a light, camp, jokey way in the bar – fine. He was only just beginning as a producer but he hadn't figured out the best way to deal with people. I'm not sure that he was ever a touchy-feely person anyway. If I'd started to go on about being gay, I think his reaction would have been to make a pass at me. It wouldn't have been to sit down and say, 'Tell me about your struggle.' I think he'd have thought, 'Oh maybe I can get in his pants.' But if he *had* tried it on with me, I'd have run a mile. There would have been no casting couch because I wouldn't have been anywhere near the couch, I'd have been out the door!"

Waterhouse's debut was in the story *Full Circle*, written by another teenage *Doctor Who* fan, Andrew Smith. Smith remains grateful, not only for the opportunity, but also for the personal kindness John showed him. "Because John knew I was interested in the technical side he arranged for me to go and see some of the edit on *Meglos*. On location he also said, 'You might want to stand there, this will be good, see how they drag Draith [one of the characters] under the water.'

"An insurance rep used to come to my house every Friday and my parents mentioned that I was doing a *Doctor Who* and he said that he had a nephew who was about 12 or 13 with Down's syndrome and a mad *Doctor Who* fan. Afterwards, I looked up Down's and I think at the time the average life expectancy was 16 years. When I was in the studio, I was talking to John about the show and its effect and I mentioned this to him and he said, 'Right,' went away and came back with an annual which hadn't come out at that point, got some signed pictures and a Polaroid camera and we took some photos of the cast. I took a photo of Matthew outside the TARDIS. The sales rep came round and brought his nephew with him and we gave them to him and he was absolutely delighted."

The director of *Full Circle* was Peter Grimwade. "John called him 'Granny Grumble',", says Carol Snook, who was close to them both. "It was just a name which fitted." Grimwade was clever, catty and neurotic and didn't hide that he felt *Doctor Who* beneath him. "He was pretty vocal about what rubbish he thought it was," says Waterhouse, "though he was prepared to direct and write for it."

"I got on very well with him," says McCrimmon. "He was very horrible about Matthew because he probably fancied him. He could be ever so bitchy but also lovely."

Grimwade (whose other nickname was Grimbleweed) proved a gifted technical director but he was rarely popular with actors. "I found it quite a frustrating experience working with him," says Peter Davison. "He did have that sort of turn of nastiness about him sometimes – to me, he was ineffectual as a director."

"It was very rare," says Richards, "to find a director who was good with casts and good technically. Grimwade wasn't a people person at all, he was more technical."

Several years later, after Grimwade had fallen out with John, I interviewed him in his crowded flat. It was a disturbing, melancholic encounter. He had written a bizarre entry in the CITV series *Dramarama. The Come-Uppance of Captain Katt* was a satire about an ageing TV science-fiction show whose leading man was an egotistical monster. Grimwade told me that this character was a morph of Tom Baker and John Nathan-Turner, based on his experience of working with them both. The satire might have been lost on the play's juvenile audience but it seemed to please Grimwade, who still seethed with bitterness. But in 1980, he was John's coming man, commissioned to direct two stories in that inaugural run, and write a third, *Zanadin* (although pressure of time pushed this on to the following year).

Grimwade was one of a clutch of inexperienced writers coming to the show through Bidmead's combination of aspiration and desperation. Most established writers simply weren't interested in attempting a *Doctor Who*. Bidmead had nurtured Andrew Smith through the process and he was gambling with two authors who were new to the medium but curious and motivated. Steve Gallagher's story eventually made it to air in the fifth slot of the season, as *Warriors' Gate*. Christopher Priest, on the other hand, was to fall foul of the producer and the row was such that, decades later, he still felt the scars.

Priest was originally approached to write for the programme by Douglas Adams but it was Bidmead who commissioned him to write a serial called *Sealed Orders*: "The story was intended to write Romana out of the series," explained Priest to fan writer Richard Bignell in a letter dated 29th May 1990 and a further email dated 4th November 2009. "The plot involved the hopping back and forth in time producing multiple variants of the TARDIS and a spare Doctor, one of whom got killed. It was written with the usual mix of studio and filmed exteriors. I worked according to Writers' Guild protocols; submitting one episode for approval and payment before starting on the next. The thing was finally delivered. A long silence ensued. Then I was summoned to Shepherd's Bush. Turner and Bidmead told me that *Sealed Orders* could not be used as it did not fit the brief. It turned out that Bidmead had come up with some unoriginal bollocks about something he called E-Space and my story 'no longer worked in E-Space'.

"To cut a long story short, Turner and Bidmead offered me the opportunity to come up with a new story, to make up for having lost the earlier one. Everything was couched in terms of exaggerated praise for me and my work, so although these two struck me as being as plausible as a clockwork fish, insincerity ringing in every vowel they uttered, I agreed to send in another outline. Once again (E-Space aside) they wanted the programme to strike out into new and adventurous areas, and that a recognised science-fiction writer like me was exactly the person they needed. I came up with the idea for *The Enemy Within*. This raised the question of how the TARDIS was powered. Where did it get its energy? I suggested that the motive force was fear – somewhere hidden inside the TARDIS was the one being in the universe that the Doctor feared above all others. The psychic tension between the two of them produced the energy to move through space and time. The story dealt with him having to confront and ultimately defeat this fear. The story was again written round the removal of one of the characters, this time Adric. Turner and Bidmead said they loved it and I was commissioned."

Says Bidmead: "I hadn't read enough of Chris's previous work to have had any views on it, and would have simply been responding to the quality of what he turned in. The Hollywood-style flatter-and-batter procedure he claims to have been put through bears no resemblance at all to the method of working I recall at Union House. It's quite possible – as any TV writer would understand – that his first drafts were perfectly adequate and deserved encouragement to continue, but the work, once completed, failed to meet our expectations and/or needs. This is what writing for TV is like, although I can see how someone with a novelist mentality might not understand this. It's sad that Chris has these sour memories."

"In the end," recalls Priest, "I delivered all four episodes and was paid for them. It was during this period that I came to dislike Turner. He was difficult to work with. He often sulked, was abusive, or shouted. He was often unobtainable without explanation, and then would re-emerge petulantly complaining that things had taken place in his absence. I kept out of his way as much as possible."

Within a year, the tension between Priest and his producer would erupt into a messy row, which was only resolved when it was taken out of John's hands.

Meanwhile, *Warriors' Gate*, the replacement for *Sealed Orders*, had both a new writer and a director fresh to the show, too. Paul Joyce had been recommended by David Rose, head of drama at BBC Birmingham, for whom Joyce had recently made a *Play for Today*. "I liked John immediately," says Joyce, "because he didn't seem to give a shit about anything and he smoked and he drank. But he had no interest in me one way or another. I was trying to bring a film consciousness into a studio situation, to achieve a kind of poetry with that story and the way it was told. The problems started from day one. Steve Gallagher submitted what was basically a 16-page treatment. Bidmead and I had to produce 130 pages. Chris and I sat down and wrote it – they paid me but refused to credit me. I lost the first two weeks of rehearsal scripting. John never understood what the scripts were about. He didn't understand the original story. He had no idea about the final product – he just said, 'It looks good, Paul.'"

One of Joyce's team was Val McCrimmon. "He was an absolute con man," she says of the director. "He couldn't actually do it so it ended up with Graeme Harper [the production manager] and I more or less having to do the show for him. He didn't know what he was doing. It was a nightmare. I used to take rehearsals and this Joyce chap used to say, 'What do I do here?' He really had no idea. I mean, he could tell actors what to do but he wasn't actually writing his camera script as we were going along. I said to John, 'I think there's something a bit wrong about this chap.' Graeme had to take over."

"I felt that probably he'd like to see me go," says Joyce dismissively, of Harper. "He doesn't deserve the credit. He was no more than a production manager."

"I was trying to be as close an ally to him as I could," says Harper. "I knew my role and how to get it moving for him but things went wrong and at one stage John Nathan-Turner asked this director to leave and said to me, 'Look, would you like me to come on the floor and you direct, as you've planned it all for the director? You've done all the homework. How would you like to play it because we've got to get this done?' It was a fantastic opportunity but I decided not to and I think I was right. John made a fantastic job of that moment."

"John fired me three times," says Joyce. "He rehired me within 20 minutes because he realised he was fucked. It was on the basis that I was using too much of the studio rehearsal time. I compromised and moved much faster."

"It wasn't done out of hatred," points out Harper. "It was done out of desperation to get the thing done. Paul managed to persuade John that he would get himself together and to be honest, he did. He wasn't experienced and hadn't planned it well enough to be able to get himself out of trouble. But he was still there at the end and we did get it done."

"We were all deeply traumatised by the whole thing," sighs Joyce. "I'd given up smoking and I didn't want any smoking in the gallery. John agreed to that but then, when it got very tense, he had to light up."

"John was very supportive and very apologetic to us," says McCrimmon. "I must say this about John – a lot of people look down on you if you're older and doing a relatively junior job but John always respected me and valued my opinion and would say 'What do you think about this, Val?' He was lovely, very caring."

"As a producer, he was brilliant," says Sue Hedden. "I'd known him as an AFM so we had a slightly different relationship. He was very hands-on but he wasn't always over your shoulder. He would give everybody their space. 'Are you really going to do that?' he might say to a director. 'OK, if you think it'll work.' But behind their backs, he'd check, for instance going to visual effects and saying, "Is this the director's 'over the rainbow" moment?'

"He always said at the first read-through, 'Right, if anybody...' and he'd look around the room '...if anybody has a problem, don't moan and whine and whinge, don't go causing atmosphere, just ring me. And I'll sort out the problem.'"

"We were talking about meetings," says PUM Marcia Wheeler, "and he told me that every meeting he held as a producer, he always analysed it after so that he could work out if there was anything he could have done to make it go better. I thought that's very unusual. It showed me a different side to him."

"Very early on," recalls Bidmead, "there was a production meeting which I turned up to. Afterwards, he blasted me – 'What the fuck were you doing at that meeting? You are not invited to these meetings – this is a production thing.' I couldn't understand what he was on about. There's an element of Hollywood about that – you know, how writers are allegedly despised in Hollywood. They've got the practical problem of making what's in your head come true within the budget and there's some arsehole of a writer saying, 'Oh no, this scene is a huge panorama...' I was actually fairly silent at this meeting as I recall. It was just that my presence was thought to be obstructive."

Story six was Johnny Byrne's offering, *The Keeper of Traken*. This would introduce two new regulars, Sarah Sutton as Nyssa and Anthony Ainley as the Master. As Baker's time with the show was drawing to a close, John was concerned that he needed some element of continuity to smooth over the departure. He'd lunched both Elisabeth Sladen and Louise Jameson, launching a charm offensive to try to persuade first one, then the other to return, even if only temporarily, as a fillip for the audience. Neither agreed, so he decided that Adric would be joined by two fellow companions, to help the battle against the returning Master. Ainley was among *The Pallisers'* sprawling cast and John recalled his part as the oleaginous Reverend Emilius when thinking of who to succeed the late Roger Delgado. In later years, when Ainley could barely bring himself to speak of John (like others who first knew him in the early 70s, he tended to call him Nathan), he would tell interviewers that it was Barry Letts who cast him, following his turn as the evil Sir Mulberry Hawk in the 1977 version of *Nicholas Nickleby*. It was a half-truth (as it no doubt helped that Letts knew that he was capable of playing such a part) but also a petty gesture because if Ainley owed anyone a debt for the job, it was John. In a 1981 letter, he acknowledged this himself: "What I want you to know is that I will be grateful to you till I'm in my wooden box for giving me the most enjoyable work I've ever done – truly."

But these were to prove to be hollow words indeed.

The director of *The Keeper of Traken* was John Black, who'd worked on shows like *Softly, Softly: Task Force* and *Coronation Street*. He wrote to John directly in search of work. "John had a very practical approach to things. He was friendly and open and was also decisive – he made an instant decision that I could do one, having met me. He was quite keen to have young, relatively inexperienced directors, I think. People who hadn't done them before and I suspect that he may have quite liked the fact that he knew more than the director, certainly about *Doctor Who*. You have to accept the fact that the producer is a big part of an ongoing serial – the ongoing element has to be in his hands.

"There was an awkward moment in rehearsal quite late on when he looked at a run. Robin Soans [playing Luvic] had suggested it might be quite interesting if he had a stammer and he worked carefully on that to make that credible. I'd gone along with that because it did beef up and explain maybe why he talked less than some of the others – and John, when he saw it, came to me afterwards and said, 'I absolutely hate stammerers, I can't bear them – I just want you to change that.' No discussion. A good thing about John was that he was decisive – often you disagreed with his decisions, often you thought they were taken without sufficient consideration but at least he took decisions and made them, which is quite an important function of producers.

"John told me well after the event that he never thought that much of *The Keeper of Traken* as a script and was surprised I managed to do so much with it – and it was on that basis that he gave me other things to do."

It was Black who cast 18-year-old Sarah Sutton, who, unlike Waterhouse, joined the regular cast with several years of acting experience already behind her. "You were working in this *Doctor Who* world," she says. "It was a little bubble in some respects – I had a confidence that there was someone like John who was overseeing everything. I found him always very approachable, but a very strong presence. He was so passionate about the programme – it was definitely moving into a new era then."

Baker's departure, painful, protracted but inevitable, was announced to the press on 24th October 1980. The final decision had been effectively taken out of his hands when he tried the old blackmail of threatening to leave. This time John called his bluff. "I was there," says Bidmead. "Tom was saying, 'I've done this far too long,' and we said, 'You know, Tom, we think you're probably right.'" Two and a half years later, when he made an unexpected appearance at the BBC's *Doctor Who Celebration* at Longleat, Baker was asked by the audience why he had left. "I was pushed," he said, looking directly at a nearby John, "by a rat... (pause) ...the Master!"

John always flatly denied that there had ever been any hostility between them. There were reasons for this. It was partly to do with John's strong sense of professional etiquette and loyalty. But it had more to do with the fact that, some years later, a real friendship did develop between the two men – partly brokered by Nicholas Courtney, who was close to them both and therefore a bridge between them. They were both raconteurs who enjoyed carousing and drinking. Crucially, too, John never stopped asking Tom to be involved in the professional side of *Doctor Who*, offering him employment years after they had worked together on the series. It was a slow burn but when the friendship ignited, it was bright and lasting.

"At John's memorial," Lynn Richards recalls, "Tom got up to speak. I hadn't heard that Tom had worked with John subsequently and I thought, 'My gosh, this is hypocritical because they hated each other – I can't believe you're getting up to talk.' He gave a wonderful speech saying what a fool he'd been – and said that he got to know the real John."

Baker's final story, *Logopolis*, was written by Bidmead, who had himself decided to depart. "The job needed more respect. I was working totally crazy hours – getting locked in at night. I wasn't stressed – I loved working. Arguably, I even made the stress for myself. I asked for a 30 per cent increase in salary. Graeme McDonald was sympathetic but said, 'We just can't – there's a pay level here and we can't do it.' John wasn't delighted I was going."

Logopolis introduced the final new face of the season, Australian airhostess, Tegan Jovanka. "My take at the time," says Bidmead, "was that he had orders from on high to have an Australian." Interestingly, there is paperwork to bear this out. As far back as 2nd November 1979, McDonald had sent a memo to John (and Letts) asking: "Is there any mileage in trying to film a *Doctor Who* story or pair of stories in Australia? Would Australian TV, a major customer for the series, welcome such an involvement? The scenery within easy reach of Sydney could give a refreshing new look to a planetary surface."

Years later, McDonald told *DWB*, "I certainly don't think that the Australian girl that he put in was a successful idea. I never really knew why he did it, except to overtly woo the Australian interest."

Whatever McDonald's view, Tegan was destined to be one of the most popular companions. The actress who played her was Janet Fielding and her initial interview took place at 11.30am on 6th October 1980. "My first impression of John was his sense of humour. I was bullshitting him about being tall enough to play an air stewardess and he knew it and I knew it – but he liked the chutzpah.

"I think that he did very well with what he had and what was at his disposal. He had bugger-all budget. John was openly gay but other than that I don't think that he was in any way a social radical. I think that in some ways you need to be to understand sci-fi – you've got to be questioning the institutions – you've got to be looking at alternative versions of how we are and what we are. He didn't have a minority sensibility. We didn't always agree and I never made a secret of that. There was never any shouting. He might argue about costume, or the role of the companions or whatever but I never won. He had all the cards. 'That's the way it's going to be.'"

Logopolis went into production in December 1980. "We had such foul weather," says production manager Margot Hayhoe, "filming on a bypass – and waiting and waiting for the rain to clear. I can remember John keeping everyone's spirits up in the coach, making us play silly games. He wanted to keep things happy – he hated atmosphere, although sometimes people could irritate him and he might have a little short temper but it was so rare that was quite effective."

Saturday, 24th January1981 marked the final day of recording in Tom Baker's seven years as the Doctor. "He just went and he didn't say goodbye to anyone," John told fan Bill Baggs in a 1994 interview. John's first year as producer had been a whirlwind of constant change as he led the revolution from the old regime and began, ever more confidently, to imprint his own style and personality on the programme he loved. "That first year was exciting," says Paul Joyce, "because although he didn't always understand what was happening, there were challenges and he was up for that."

"I think he did a fantastic job on the show," says Lalla Ward. "He took it on at a time when science fiction was suddenly becoming incredibly popular and he had to keep a programme that had been going for a long time already and bring it up to date, not lose what we already had and not have the budget that they all had. It was a lot to do."

It had been an intense learning curve and he was keenly aware that he was still "on attachment", therefore "on trial" – but with his new leading man, Peter Davison, lined up and a second season on the horizon, the prospects were exciting and life was good.

(above left) John at school, 1958 *(courtesy: King Edward Aston)*

(right) Last term, 1965 *(courtesy: King Edward Aston)*

(above left) Roy Hawkesford and John Turner, rehearsing for *Opportunity Knocks* (Summer 1963) *(courtesy: Roy Hawkesford)*

(above right) School trip to Paris, Easter 1965 – John wouldn't wear his beret in case it flattened his quiff! *(courtesy: Roy Hawkesford)*

Christmas in Erdington – John with his parents
(JN-T collection)

(above left) John *(left)* and Bill Sellars *(right)* in *Emberella,*
December 1972 *(courtesy: Bill Sellars)*

(above right) Going Dutch in Amsterdam for
Arc of Infinity, May 1982 *(JN-T collection)*

Making hay while the sun shines -
John and Gary, circa 1979

(above left) Life's a drag – *(courtesy: Paul Mark Tams)*

(above right) Eric Saward and Jane Judge at Lynn Richards's
wedding reception, July 1982 *(courtesy: Lynn Richards)*

John in his element – supervising Sylvester McCoy's photo call, 1987
(courtesy: Grahame Flynn)

L to R – production associates June Collins and Angela Smith at Collins's
leaving party, 1994 *(courtesy: June Collins)*

The author on the set of *Dragonfire*, 13th August 1987

(Richard Marson)

Party animals at the Salisbury pub in St Martin's Lane, circa 2000 –
L to R – Nick Courtney, John, Rob Liston, Tom Baker, Stuart Money
(courtesy: Stuart Money)

(above left) John with Barry Hannam, the hairdresser who married Gary after
John's death *(JN-T collection)*

(above right) Happy birthday JN-T, 1989 *(JN-T collection)*

John and Gary with Stephen Cranford
(courtesy: Stephen Cranford)

(above left) Grahame Flynn and John in the front garden at Marine Drive
(courtesy: Grahame Flynn)

(above right) Biting back – John showing his feelings
about *DWB*, 1990 *(courtesy: Gary Leigh)*

Tits and teeth – John and Nicola Bryant relax in the hot tub. They fell out in 1996 and were never reconciled *(JN-T collection)*

FIVE

EVIL ANNIE & THE BARKERS

**"It was like feasting with panthers,
The danger was half the excitement..."**

Oscar Wilde, *De Profundis*, 1897

On the second floor of BBC Television Centre, behind a soundproof layer of thick plate glass, a series of observation rooms looks down into each of the main studios. They were designed so that visitors could catch a glimpse of the work taking place on the studio floor without getting in the way or causing a disturbance. For the privileged *Doctor Who* fan of the 1970s and 80s (I was among them), these dark little rooms were nirvana – the gateway to watching the programme being rehearsed and recorded. Under the relatively relaxed security system of the time, staff were able to sign in as many guests as they wanted. Sometimes the observation galleries would be crammed with devotees drinking in every detail of the recording taking place below them.

In 1979, Jan Vincent-Rudzki was top dog among this crowd. He was president of the Doctor Who Appreciation Society (DWAS), which he had formed in 1976 with his friend and partner Stephen Payne. He was also a clerk in VT cataloguing at Television Centre. "I was in a very privileged position and I wasn't going to abuse it," he says. "Graham Williams tried to use me to spread leaks. I remember he left a picture of Davros on his briefcase during *The Armageddon Factor,* hoping that I would go off and tell everybody, 'Oh, there's going to be another Davros story' – but of course I didn't. I used to go up to the production office and say this is what I want to put in *TARDIS* [the Society magazine] about what's coming up. For *Destiny of the Daleks*, Graham said, 'No, I don't want Skaro put in. That's meant to be a secret.' 'OK fine' – I took that out."

But still there were leaks and even before John Nathan-Turner took over from Williams, concern was being voiced about fans "on the inside" and the risks of gossip and souvenir hunting, or theft, from the studio floor. Accordingly, Graeme McDonald, head of series and serials, asked Graham Williams to deal with the problem and on 2nd October 1979, Williams sent him the following memo: "As spoken with you on Friday, I enclose a copy of my open letter to the president of the Doctor Who Appreciation Society, which is the largest of the many *Doctor Who* fan clubs throughout the world. It is, as I warned you, constructed in my finest patronising schoolteacher prose! I have spoken with the members of staff involved and with the principal organisers of the fan club and I hope these measures will be sufficient in preventing any more serious breaches of confidence. Should the situation worsen... I shall of course ask that a more official approach be made to members of staff and fans alike."

The letter Williams composed in his "finest patronising schoolteacher prose" was dated 23rd August and addressed to Vincent-Rudzki: "I'm faced with the odious task of pointing out that goodwill and co-operation are open to abuse and, I'm sorry to say, are being abused. Members of BBC staff, recognising the enthusiasm of the fans, invite guests to the studios or workshops, etc. Staff are, understandably, too busy to supervise their guests every minute of the day and night. So far I have left these 'semi-official' visitors very much to the discretion of the staff but in various ways have been aware that off-the-record conversations have been quoted verbatim, 'candid camera' shots have been taken, artists and staff have been pressured in recording breaks and there have even been accusations of 'souvenirs' being taken away from the studio (and with or without <u>anyone's</u> approval, that's not on!)

"The answer is simple – I can just ban <u>all</u> visitors to the studio and ask for staff to be read the riot act on BBC staff regulations re the subject of confidentiality, which, I might say, are severe. I do not want to do this – I would far sooner the matter was left to the judgement of the individuals concerned, but if the abuse continues I shall have to take whatever action seems necessary to ensure that the programme's prime responsibility to the public in general is not undermined by a few mavericks. At the risk of sounding pompous, privilege carries responsibility and those few fans who can take advantage of the co-operation we try to extend can very easily spoil it for everyone else. The Golden Rule for fans and staff alike must be – 'If in doubt, <u>don't!</u>' I have to work under the same rules as everyone else in the BBC – I don't make them up for my own benefit. Common sense and goodwill should be enough without me or someone else laying down a lot of boring 'rules and regulations governing...' There's quite enough of that about already, so if the situation doesn't improve, I'll bring the shutters down."

But the problem of "spies" (as John sometimes referred to them with a characteristic dash of melodrama) never really went away. According to Vincent-Rudzki, John made this a rod for his own back: "Graham Williams knew you worked in the BBC and would find things out, whereas with JN-T if you said you knew anything, he wanted to know how. It all went wrong from the start. I'd seen on the VT booking sheets that a booking had been made to watch *The Three Doctors*. I met him and it was all very nice and then I mentioned that I'd seen this – and that was it. Evidently he was absolutely furious because I knew what he was doing. He went away thinking I was cocking a snook at him and that wasn't at all what I was doing. The fact was that – me being me – I wouldn't have told anybody.

"He was a really insecure person. Stuff got leaked and I think he was convinced that I was coming up to his office, looking at things and going round nicking stuff. But he never ever said anything directly to me – he always told other people or he insinuated. Very weird. I used to go up and have a chat with Jane Judge [the production secretary]. She was really friendly and nice. JN-T took over and she went cold, totally cold. At a convention, JN-T said I really shouldn't go up to the office unless I rang them beforehand. There was another convention where he said in front of all these people – 'Oh Jan, I've put extra locks on the office door – I've made it very secure.' It was dig, dig, dig. Another time, when there was a circle of us around JN-T, he saw me in profile and made a comment about my big nose – for no reason other than he could and to demean me and put me in my place."

Vincent-Rudzki admits that he roamed the studios during lunch breaks to look at the sets and that, after recordings, he would return and casually remove items he felt were obviously destined for the skip. "I'd see what was left – find souvenirs. Once I had this lovely set model and was walking down in a basement corridor when I turned a corner and there was JN-T. He said, 'Oh, I see you've got that. I know where it is now.' I carried on – it wasn't his anyway, in my view. I also got a whole load of *Doctor Who* design plans. He rang me up and said, 'Jan, you've got some of my plans,' and that really annoyed me because it wasn't *his* programme – I always thought he was the caretaker. I was very wary of him. I stopped running DWAS for two reasons – one was the fact that the paperwork was incredible – but the other was JN-T."

In October 1980, David Saunders, a 32-year-old librarian who lived at home with his widowed father, took over and became DWAS co-ordinator. "I considered John a friend," says Saunders. "One of the things that he liked about me was that I was actually that bit older than the rest of the people he dealt with in fandom." Though he claims he "didn't yet know he was gay", with his mincing gait and fussy manner, Saunders was an easy target for mockery and send-up. But he won respect, too, by dedicating himself to the society and the many dreary chores that entailed. John eventually nicknamed him "the Garm", a dog-like monster from the story *Terminus* whose silhouette was curiously reminiscent of Saunders. Both characters shared an element of pathos too.

John held regular meetings with Saunders and was "exceedingly helpful" in marshalling guests for the society's conventions. He also allowed them the occasional "scoop" for the society newsletter, *Celestial Toyroom* and the magazine *TARDIS*. Saunders wrote letters to him in return, on the society's garishly headed paper, carefully sycophantic in tone: "The nineteenth was undoubtedly one of the best seasons of *Doctor Who* for many a year. Each story seemed to be better than the last..."

A notable feature of John's office was a large whiteboard carefully filled out with the details of forthcoming stories, titles, writers, crews and production dates. Other producers used the same system but John's whiteboard became the source of one of his fabled attempts to trace the information that seemed to haemorrhage from his office and end up, if not printed, then whispered widely among the fans. "I used to go to the production office," says Saunders, "and we talked and then went to the pub. Then it became that we just went to the pub. Until one day (in 1983) when it was, 'Oh, don't go yet, come back to the office,' and that's when I was ushered in and there on the board was a story titled *The Doctor's Wife*. But I'm not stupid. I thought, 'I haven't been here for over a year,' and I only mentioned it to Dominic May [then an admin assistant for DWAS]. I did hear that other fans had been to the office around that time and had been taken in. It was clearly set up as a trap."

The Doctor's Wife became part of the folklore of fandom to such an extent that, years later, after the programme had triumphantly returned to BBC1, Steven Moffat couldn't resist the in-joke of actually using it for one of the episodes.

The constant quest to trace the source of the various leaks did John no favours, making him seem as petty and obsessive as some of the fans. A waste of valuable time and energy, it was an itch he could not resist scratching and it triggered his worst control freak traits. In the summer of 1983, David Saunders attended a convention in Columbus, Ohio. "A lot of the American fans were talking in the bar," he remembers, "and came and asked about the casting of Colin Baker. I had heard this rumoured but I didn't know it was true.

"About a fortnight after I got back, I got a call asking if I'd like to come in for a drink with John in the bar at TV Centre – it wasn't the regular business meeting. I went along all innocently. When I arrived I was sat down in a corner with [press officer] Kevin O'Shea and I was grilled for a good ten minutes. 'Why were you telling everybody in America about Colin Baker?' They were trying to get me to confess but, in the end, they could see my reaction was genuine and I was innocent. I knew how it had got out there. Jeremy Bentham [a former DWAS historian] had passed it on to [US-based fan] John Peel. I didn't tell them that – I just said I would try to find where the leak had come from. Keith Barnfather [another fan] had just left the BBC and said, 'He can't do anything to me any more – go back and tell them it was me.' So that's what I did. And because the news had started leaking out, the public announcement of Colin's casting was brought forward by weeks."

John was fighting a losing battle. The longer he was there, the more fans found employment with the BBC, joining the ranks of the dreaded "spies". Today the programme seems largely to be made by fans and some of these spies, huddled regulars in the dark space of the observation galleries, later had their own high-profile involvement with the series – among them, Gary Russell in the press office, Mark Wyman and David Richardson in costume, John Ainsworth in design, Patrick Mulkern on the staff of *Radio Times* (he's back there as I write) while Marc Platt was toiling away in radio programme index.

Another fan "on the inside" was Bob Richardson, who joined the BBC in 1977, in the facilities department called premises operations (known as "bogs and boilers"). He had obligingly "signed in" Vincent-Rudzki as a guest before Jan started to work at Television Centre himself. "You used to get the daily duty sheets," recalls Richardson, "which showed everything in the studio for the next week or two. There was no restriction on the number of visitors you could have – sometimes in the observation gallery of TC3 or 4 there would be a dozen or 15 people – and I used to be in reception waiting for these people to arrive. It became a burden because I didn't always want to watch – I was a keen *Doctor Who* fan but I didn't always want to spend three or four hours sitting on the floor of an observation gallery. But I didn't feel comfortable about having people in the building when I wasn't there.

"I was sitting at my desk one day and the phone rang and it was a guy called Ian Levine. He said, 'I understand you're a friend of Jan's – can you get me into Television Centre to see *Doctor Who* being recorded? I want to take you out to supper.' So I went out to supper with him to a Hungarian restaurant in Queensway. It was dreadful food, really awful, and Ian said, in the way that he does, 'I *need* you to get me in.' So I signed him in and it became a regular arrangement."

No-one better defines the public perception of a *Doctor Who* fan than Ian Levine. Large, loud and earnest, his voice vibrates with passion for the programme. He machine-guns his opinions at the unwary and doesn't do shades of grey. With Ian, it's black and white; you're either with him or against him. "He was a fan in the true fanatic sense," says Vincent-Rudzki.

"The infamous Ian Levine!" laughs Ralph Wilton, good-naturedly, a friend of Levine's for many years. "Ian is, was, always will be a great *Doctor Who* groupie. He's like a dog with a ferret."

"I love the fact that he loves modern *Doctor Who* too," says Russell T Davies. "Technically he shouldn't. He's got all these saving graces and yet his view of the world is barking."

Levine grew up in the seaside town of Blackpool. He was the eldest of three children, part of a wealthy family, and privately educated. As a child, his great passions were music and television and most especially, *Doctor Who*. He would painstakingly write up his recall of each episode post-transmission. When domestic video systems began to emerge, he made it his mission to collect every episode he could find, a bewilderingly complex and challenging task in those days. "I joke that I have Asperger's," he says, "but I don't think I have. I'm too sociable and out-going. But I must be on the scale somewhere as I do like to collect and when I collect, I must collect *everything*."

By 1979, aged 26, he was a wealthy young man with a thriving career as a record producer and DJ, shuttling between Blackpool, where he worked for Mecca and the bright lights of London's gay club scene. Ian himself had only "come out" the year before and now he was right in the centre of the capital's pre-AIDS heyday when, it seemed, the only price to pay for rampant promiscuity was the occasional dose of the clap. He was seeing what he calls a "sex friend", a handsome Canadian doctor called Rob Piaggio. "One night, after Copa [a gay nightclub in Earl's Court], I went back to stay in the flat Rob shared in Maida Vale. It was a proper nice place and we got up the next morning and had breakfast and I was introduced to his flatmate – Ralph Wilton. Ralph was a camp queen who worked at the BBC and he said, 'I'm a production manager – I'm working on *Doctor Who*.' So I got to go and watch *Shada* from the floor as Ralph's guest.

"I saw Rob for about a year and one day Ralph said, 'I've got some exciting news for you – my friend John Nathan-Turner has been appointed producer of *Doctor Who*.' I said, 'I want to meet him – I'd love to be well in with the producer.' He said, 'He's got a very nice boyfriend called Gary and they live in New Cross.' So we had a late dinner. They came round the week Graeme McDonald appointed him producer, before he'd got a script editor or anything.

He was incredibly friendly. I'd edited together a best of *Doctor Who* clips for him on U-matic. I showed him them all and he was fascinated."

"A couple of days later," says Bob Richardson, "I got a call from Ian saying, 'I won't need you to sign me in any more.' It was a relief in some ways because I didn't have to tailor my evenings to fit in with what Ian wanted to do. I didn't really have any contact with him after that – he didn't have a lot of time for the other fans who he used to go and watch the show with either. He cold-shouldered a lot of people. Once he ingratiated himself, he was rather proud of the fact and would like to drop hints about what was coming up – 'I can't say any more, I'm sworn to secrecy.'"

From *The Leisure Hive* onwards, Ian was John's guest in the production gallery. It was the beginning of one of the defining relationships of John's career, twisted in that it was very much rooted in what each could do for the other. "He needed me as much as I needed him," believes Levine. "I'd hated *The Horns of Nimon* and I welcomed John as the messiah. Have you ever seen *I, Claudius*? They were so sick of Tiberius that they welcomed Caligula with open arms. It was like that."

John swiftly nicknamed him "Evil Annie" (an anagram of Ian Levine), knowing that he had found someone he could make good use of. In modern parlance, he lost no time in making Levine his "bitch", literally as well as figuratively. "I remember going to Brockley early in 1980," frowns Levine, "and that's the one time I had to get fucked by him – he wouldn't take no for an answer. I had no choice. It was, 'You want a favour, I want a favour back.'"

John's beloved *Coronation Street* had its own historian. Now he would have a pet expert of his own, albeit unofficially, an ever-willing, hard-working, virtually infallible and magnificently free resource for continuity and research. "Oh, yes," says Chris Bidmead. "Superfan. He was a go-to guy because he knew more than John about the show."

Levine was happy to act as "informer" too. When John sometimes had the doors to the observation gallery locked to deprive the "fan glitterati" (as he sometimes called them), it was Levine, knowing how the likes of Vincent-Rudzki and Richardson got round such obstacles, who tipped him off that some of the spies might be watching via a feed to the internal ring main system. John promptly had that switched off too, although Vincent-Rudzki comments, "His attempt to exclude fans simply made them more determined to find out."

At a time when tapes and the transfer of them cost a small fortune (which had to be funded from the meagre programme budget), "Evil Annie" was more than willing to provide this service free, gratis and whenever John felt the need. The perks of allowing Levine access to his court weren't only confined to the day job either. From 6th December 1979, the hottest gay club in London was Heaven and, as its resident DJ, Ian made sure that his new showbiz best friends John and Gary were a permanent feature of the VIP list.

"They got in free and they got free drinks," says Levine. "Every half an hour a barman brought up a pint glass of vodka and orange. They would come in at ten. John plonked himself in the VIP booth while Gary went cottaging in the toilets, looking for someone to join them in a threesome. Some days Gary found someone before half ten and they were off home. No messing. Other days they couldn't get anybody and were there till the bitter end at four o'clock. What they went home with was often the worst dross in the place – I can't believe the people they took back. Meanwhile, the more drunk John got, the more secrets he told me..."

"Ian used to ring me up and tell me all the latest gossip," says Vincent-Rudzki, "from when he went out drinking with John and Gary. Ian would tell me things and they'd be going round fandom – and the biggest supplier of the information was JN-T. On 23rd March 1980 I sent him an internal memo listing 20 things I knew about the new season. I said, 'Look, I've heard all this outside the BBC – I thought you ought to be aware that this stuff is leaking.' I was trying to establish some sort of trust. But he didn't like that because he thought I was showing off. Jane Judge rang me up and said, 'I have JN-T for you on the phone,' and JN-T said, 'I want to know who told you this.' I said, 'It was nobody in the BBC.' 'I want to know who told you this.' I didn't want to drop Ian in it, so I said, 'Somebody outside the BBC – I'm not prepared to tell you who it was.' How could I tell this bloke, 'You're getting pissed, telling everything to somebody and – it's your fault'? It would have been a really stupid move."

For the six years that Levine was in favour, the payback was legion. An eyewitness view of the entire production, an entrée to cast and crew, all manner of props and "souvenirs", scripts and tapes. "I got a lot of fantastic perks out of it," he says. "I was the only fan invited to the 20th anniversary party. I got the book from *Shada*, every rehearsal script, a cupboard full of time-coded 'Philips' tapes – and some influence on the programme."

After allowing Levine U-matic tapes of *The Leisure Hive* and *Full Circle* studio recordings, John had a change of heart about letting his lapdog have any more such treats. Looking back, Levine thinks it was another manifestation of paranoia, although it's possible that John realised that the BBC might take a dim view of him offloading scores of tapes onto a member of the public who happened to be a fan. Whatever the reason, Levine got round it with the help of John's secretaries, script editor Eric Saward and some of the directors. "They would say, 'Quick, come round – John's gone – there's a copy of *Mawdryn*

Undead on his desk, come and get it but it's got to be back before Monday.' I was his worst nightmare. Everything he was paranoid about, I was doing – squirrelling away tapes."

Thanks to this furtive piracy, several of the 21st-century DVDs include a range of deleted scenes and behind-the-scenes moments. Levine himself has an unusually gossipy take on many of the era's stories. A typical example concerns *Castrovalva*. "There was a scene when Adric was tied up in the Master's web," explains Levine. "Just before they recorded it, John had a word with Matthew and said, 'Make your dick hard and let's see if anyone notices!' It was a giggle. They were like two schoolgirls."

David Saunders offers partial corroboration of this tale. He says, "Matthew told me, 'If you look at that scene, can't you see I've got an erection?' But I think it was totally spontaneous."

Watching the sequence in question, it certainly seems feasible but when I asked Waterhouse about it, he simply laughed hugely and insisted that it was "a fabulous myth... completely untrue but I like it! If it had been true, I might have been tempted to stuff something a bit larger down there!"

Whoever you believe, Levine uses the anecdote as an example of his scorn for what he sees as John's inherent lack of professionalism. The tsunami of bitterness and bile that eventually erupted between the two men makes it hard to get him to focus on any healthy or happy aspect of the relationship. "He was fantastic company," Levine does allow, "very funny, witty and camp. The most wonderful friend. There were good times, happy memories. I had a family gathering and John and Gary had one of the early video cameras so Gary came and filmed about an hour of this for me. I've still got it. They went to Miami and stayed with my mother. I remember a lovely Sunday in Brighton with Peter Davison, Mark Strickson and his wife at the time, with Nicola Bryant and her very handsome American husband, Scott. Peter Davison's agent was there too and he had the worst wig, it was slipping all over the place. It was hysterical. John did have his good points but he liked crawling yes-men, which I had to be myself. It makes me sound terrible. It hurts."

Some feel that Levine, by nature (and the necessity of his business) a self-publicist, has increasingly overstated his influence and involvement. Another fan, Paul Tams, is now the producer of the *K9* series but in the early 80s he was an aspiring graphic designer, as well as a friend of John, Gary and, especially, John's secretary Sarah Lee. Tams believes that "Ian has his own agenda. He has created this mythos that they were close. The fact is that he was this sycophantic fan who wormed his way into John's affections by providing him with large bottles of vodka and forking out for things like meals out. He manipulates people and buys their friendship and that's what he did with John and Gary. They treated him as this fan that was basically there to be used. He got to see some recordings and read a few scripts but he offered to do it. He wasn't asked. He's a very pushy person – obsessive. I don't think there was any *true* friendship."

"I know that he and John got on very well at the beginning," says Wilton, "but then it just got heavier and heavier and heavier. John got a bit fed up with Ian pestering him all the time. I think it got a bit too intrusive – John was busy and there were other things to do. Ian was very much a *Doctor Who* freak."

Whatever the mutual benefits to their relationship, based on such an imbalance of power, it was toxic and dysfunctional from the start.

"They made fun of Ian when he wasn't around," remembers Richardson, "and said an awful lot of negative things about him, primarily led by Gary. Ian was very fat and because of his appetite and size, it was Gary who said, 'Do you think he's got a special reinforced industrial toilet?'"

Away from *Who*, Levine was a rich and, in his field, powerful man, used to having his opinion heard and respected. Within *Who*, his desperation to stay in favour made him perjure and humiliate himself. It brought out the worst in John, too, as, egged on by Gary, he bent "Evil Annie" to his will, the treats and rewards interspersed with rebukes and punishments to keep him firmly in line. "I got very abused," says Levine. "I was really put upon. I was his scapegoat. I had to put up with all sorts of crap. He would say, 'You're a piece of shit. Get out of my office.' I put up with it because it was a fan's dream come true.

"I was like an unpaid chauffeur. Because he had that much sex, John went to the clap clinic every single week. Muggins here had to pick him up from Threshold House, take him there and wait."

"That's rubbish," snorts Tams, whose partner at the time was John and Gary's private GU consultant. "I can tell you that the clinic in question was in walking distance of Threshold House, on Hammersmith Broadway."

Production manager and close friend Ian Fraser points out, "This was the time when AIDS was rife and John was actually being responsible in going to get tested. I know this as we discussed it. The only other discussion was to try persuade Gary to do the same. As for visiting the clinic *weekly*, there is no evidence for that, as far as I am aware."

Close friend Grahame Flynn recalls, "John once told me, 'You would have loved it in the 70s, Gray. You could have so much fun.' They were gay guys having fun and this was pre-HIV. But, in the time that I knew John [the early 90s onwards], he took his sexual health very seriously."

Having marked his territory early on in their relationship, John's sexual demands shifted so that Levine assumed the role of glorified producer's pimp, holding private sex parties at his own house in North Acton (where he says he would watch but only participate half-heartedly) and arranging a string of escorts according to John's whim of the moment. Ian was effectively handing him the keys to a licentious gay man's sweetshop. "There was a barman at Heaven that they fancied and I had to pay him to have sex with them. One birthday, he wanted a policeman to strip-search him. The next birthday he wanted a runner, all sweaty. There was one day in the studio when I'd lined something up for him – a birthday surprise – and he kept popping up and saying, 'Ooh, three hours to go, I can't wait.' He wasn't concentrating on what was going on, he was thinking about the sex. Then it was, 'I want you to set up an orgy for me' – a command like a Roman emperor. I had to have eight people in my house. In the end, I went upstairs and watched TV. It was just horrible. It made me feel sleazy and unclean."

"People in glass houses shouldn't throw stones," believes Tams. "He wasn't whiter than white himself. He would provide people for them from Heaven like pieces of meat. John was no saint but... well, they both needed to have their heads knocked together."

But Tams's testimony is disputed both by Levine and their mutual friend, and fellow fan, Mark Sinclair. "At the time," he says, "Ian, John and Gary and that sisterhood really did get on very well. Miss Tams says all this now because he hates Ian. They fell out over money and I can understand that from his point of view too. But I tend to lean towards Ian's version of events."

Unwilling to risk losing the keys to his own sweetshop of props and scripts and insider knowledge, Levine concedes that he shamelessly abased himself, sublimating his own views and feelings, never openly disagreeing with John or challenging him. On 31st July 1982, he insisted that DWAS present the producer with a special "fans' award" on stage at the PanoptiCon V convention. The award took the form of a gaudy portrait of John surrounded by a range of characters from his first two seasons – paid for by Levine. "I was mortified by it," says Vincent-Rudzki. "I thought that Verity Lambert should have got it, not this new bloke. I blame Ian a hell of a lot for some of what happened. He went completely over the top and fed John's ego."

But Levine, carefully kept in the background, was a time bomb – a vociferous gay man whose love for a television programme could suppress his common sense and dominate his instincts. As he puts it, "You can tread on a worm till it turns" and when he finally did, it would have devastating consequences for John.

By allowing a superfan to sit at the heart of the show, John had, almost from the start, a heightened awareness for what might please the die-hards. He was a crowd-pleaser by nature, a populist and a showman and as fan letters poured in praising the return of this monster and that character and his heartbeat quickened to the rapturous applause of convention crowds, he began to explore more and more ways of pleasing his audience. "The funny thing is that in many ways he courted the fans," says his secretary Kate Easteal, "because he wanted the show to have a fan base and he enjoyed the conventions."

"Hugely important to him, that adulation," says Janet Fielding. "Absolutely key. He could walk into one of those conventions and he was a big man. No other show was going to give him that. That's why John never gave them up."

He gave interviews to fanzines, in his office, over the phone or by answering questionnaires, often incorporating into his answers some of the stock catchphrases he adopted, chief among them "Stay tuned!" and "No comment". It took up a lot of time and was the cause of caustic behind-the-back remarks from some of his colleagues who felt his attention would have been better spent elsewhere. "I learnt the lesson from him – not to do it," says former showrunner Russell T Davies. "I never made contact with the DWAS – I never even said hello to them. I just thought, 'I am making the programme.' I protected *Doctor Who Magazine* because I loved that as much as the programme. But I wanted to keep it professional. Every interview you ever do is dying to get you to say which one you hated and it's all that fandom really wants. I won't feed that engine. By being so biddable he was probably the architect of his own downfall."

"He was always very generous to the fans," says Fiona Cumming. "I remember one boy who rang faithfully every Thursday at the same time. I think perhaps he had Asperger's or something of the kind – and Sarah, John's secretary, just knew that when he came on the phone, he was to be encouraged and listened to. He came to the studio on a visit and so on. John cared for the fans but some of them were too clever by half and they criticised everything. You do want to say, 'Grow up.'"

"There's so many different types of fans," points out Sophie Aldred. "Yes, there are the barkers but then there are lovely fans and children too. With any show you have to have a very thick skin – I meet people now who say, 'Matt Smith is a crap Doctor.' I think he recognised that some were bonkers – driven by something other than rationality. And to be honest it's meant to be a show for kids and there are these obsessed thirtysomethings. And there's nothing wrong with that – what would they do if it wasn't for *Doctor Who*?"

"There was a guy called Peter John Holloway," recalls Easteal, "who was in a mental hospital and he used to phone up all the time. He'd write letters or phone from a phone box and we'd just tell him what was happening that day. Then the pips would go and he'd be gone. I was very non-judgmental about people like that and I think John was too. On a show like *Doctor Who*, with such a tight time schedule, it would have been very easy to not allow people to visit. But he was never like that – he was happy for them to come. I remember once reading in a Sunday supplement about a family with these three boys who had inherited some terrible medical condition. They were all really ill and it was just a really sad article. I rang the journalist and said, 'Do you think it would be a nice thing if we invited these three brothers to come and have a picture in the *Doctor Who* studio? It doesn't say that they like *Doctor Who* but they are of an age where they probably do and it might be a nice treat for them.' The journalist agreed and we got hold of the mother and invited these three boys. John was like, 'Yeah, yeah.' They came and had a brilliant afternoon. It was us saying we have got this very special show, which means a lot to a lot of people and, rather than being precious, we are opening our doors and saying come and enjoy it and feel part of it. John found that kind of thing very rewarding."

"I think John got too close to the fans, really," says Lorne Martin, who worked for BBC Enterprises. "He was the only producer who got involved with them. There were all these little cliques of backbiting, bitchy fans and it was the tail trying to wag the dog in a way. You have to divorce yourself from that."

"In many ways, he was very good to the fans," believes production associate June Collins. "He let them have access. I often was quite surprised that he didn't mind talking to them and going off to conventions. I think it's questionable whether he should ever have got involved in all that though. A lot of them have probably got issues themselves – so can you really judge what they say? It's a spider's web. If you start to be that friendly and that involved, it can come back and bite you. I think that might have been because he liked to be loved. It was flattering to him. In some ways, it's nice because obviously the fans make the show... perhaps there could have been a middle way?"

"How extraordinary for a producer of a BBC programme to develop a relationship with fans," says actor Mark Strickson. "I mean, any relationship's better than no relationship. If you do nothing, you'll get nothing wrong – and if you form lots of relationships, some of those are going to be with people who bite you back."

"You don't want to get too close to those people," asserts script editor Andrew Cartmel. "John would get too close to them and would really worry if they didn't like what he was doing – he was the ultimate example of getting too close."

"I think it was inevitable that it would get very, very unpleasant, given the psychology of some of these boys," says Matthew Waterhouse.

"It may well be," believes Colin Baker, "that he had the same attitude to the programme as people like Ian Levine and Gary Leigh [of whom more shortly]. That they kind of own it and that they have such an emotional stake in it that they want it to go their way."

"He let the lion out of the cage," shrugs Vincent-Rudzki, "and then it mauled him."

It's true that, although always happy to accept their praise, John usually turned his face from fans' criticisms, dismissing them as the impertinence of "barkers", the term he coined and always used to define the *Doctor Who* fan stereotype of the era – pale, male and spotty, somewhere on the scale perhaps, certainly lacking in most social graces, all factors which made them easier to despise and dismiss. "Yes, barkers – and quite rightly so," says John's long-time secretary Sarah Lee, with asperity. "Some of the letters were *ridiculous*. But he did try to get everybody involved."

The biggest British fan event of the 1980s was the two-day Longleat convention, over the Easter weekend, on Sunday 3rd and Monday 4th April 1983. John announced the news that it would be happening on stage at that July 1982 PanoptiCon V, as an impulsive reaction to his "Fan's Producer" award. Longleat was *Doctor Who*'s Woodstock and you were either there or you weren't. I was there and vividly recall the endless queues, beleaguered celebrities, the tents with (slightly tatty) displays of sets and visual effects, the merchandise, the auction and the state-the-bleeding obvious announcements made over the tannoy system at annoyingly frequent intervals by John Leeson, in character as K9.

The programme notes, written by Levine, lavished hyperbolic praise on the producer (the original hand-written copy still survives in John's archive). As he concluded a potted history of the series, Levine gushed: "John Nathan-Turner, taking over as the new producer, was about to drastically change the style of the show. Suddenly, overnight, the show was back to a golden age period with visually stunning drama and colourful locations."

John was visible throughout, introducing panels, dealing with press, chatting to fans and generally giving it his best "eyes and teeth". For all the irritations and the uncertain weather, it was still a thrilling experience for any "barker", most of all, perhaps, in the visible acknowledgement, beyond dispute or mockery, that this programme was so clearly loved by so many people and the circle of that affection spread far wider than the narrow sphere of organised fandom. "I was at Longleat," says Russell T Davies. "I loved it. I didn't have tickets – my sister drove me there. Two people came out, complete strangers, and said, 'We've just been in, they didn't take our tickets – do you want them?' and they gave them to us. We jumped the mile-long queue, went in and had the most brilliant day. What a showman he was for doing that – absolutely brilliant."

The idea for some kind of "super convention" to be open to the general public, rather than just the die-hard 'barkers', had first been mooted before John became producer, as Vincent-Rudzki recalls: "Terry Sampson [the head of BBC Enterprises] had said to me and Graham Williams in the BBC bar, 'We ought to have a *Doctor Who* convention in Wembley.' I said, 'No way – you can do that but DWAS is not going to do that.' To me a convention is a big event but where there's some intimacy to it. What I loved was having the stars in the bar with all the fans – anybody could talk to anybody – none of this nonsense with hospitality rooms and signing autographs."

"John felt that we should celebrate 20 years of *Doctor Who*," remembers Lorne Martin of BBC Enterprises' exhibitions department. "He was very much the organiser of what would happen – we designed it and found the tents and did a lot of on-air promotion. We weren't really aware of the potential. We were flooded with people, the victims of our own success and the cause of logistical problems on the day. A load of 'experts' came out of the woodwork after the event, people with perfect hindsight, talking out of their arse, but it was the first time it had ever been done so it was a learning curve.

"John set the benchmark – I can see now that the BBC have learnt with that – they've taken back exhibitions."

John used all his considerable powers of persuasion to ensure the best roll call of talent he could muster for the event. "'Think of the fans' might have been his catchphrase," said Elisabeth Sladen in her memoirs. He pulled off the considerable coup of persuading the notoriously publicity-shy Patrick Troughton to appear, writing to him on 30th November 1982: "I am writing to ask you to reconsider your decision not to attend the *Doctor Who Celebration* on Sunday, 3rd April. I am very heavily involved in this instance with BBC Enterprises who want to make this one-off occasion as productive as possible and I am very keen indeed that as many artists as possible from *Doctor Who's* past and present attend. I can assure you that if you were to reconsider I would ensure that your attendance would be as brief as you would wish it. In other words, if you only wanted to attend the Convention for a couple of hours I would totally understand. I am prepared to organise a car to and from Longleat so that you will be able to leave exactly when you wish... I shall endeavour to make your appearance as painless as possible. Twenty years of a programme is no mean feat... and without you it won't be the same."

Troughton relented, enjoyed himself and began to agree to further appearances at fan events until his untimely death at an American convention in 1987.

As one of the (then) current cast, Mark Strickson accepted John's three-line whip and a car was sent to collect him from the council flat where he then lived opposite the Old Vic. "They thought, presumably, that a few thousand people would turn up. None of the actors could get to it because you couldn't get through in the cars. It was truly shocking – the impact of so many people being interested in *Doctor Who*. We were shuffling around with soldiers carting us through the crowds, doing as much signing as we could. It was mayhem."

"The whole thing was appallingly organised," says Vincent-Rudzki. "It was dreadful. Thousands had to be turned away. I'd never been to an event before where you had to queue for the men's toilets. There were all the sets for *The Five Doctors* and I was a bit taken aback by that. I thought, 'Here's JN-T going on about secrecy and yet the sets are up – what?'"

Given the head start about the event, Saunders had found a nearby hotel, the Mendip Lodge, and booked a number of rooms. "At least a dozen DWAS executive or assistants booked in there – Jeremy Bentham booked and it was he who organised the impromptu party on the Saturday evening and invited JN-T."

"He turned up," says Vincent-Rudzki, "looked at me and said, 'I see Worzel Gummidge has been doing your hair.' Another dig. I told this to Steve [Payne, Jan's partner at the time] and he flew into a temper – he was going to deck JN-T. I think it was a culmination of all the things that had been going on. I thought, 'I can't have this.' JN-T had gone into the bar where all the fans collected, to lord it with Gary. I went in and JN-T came up and put his hand out to shake mine and I said, 'No, I'm not going to shake your hand – you've insulted me again and I'm fed up with it.' He looked a bit taken aback and I said, 'This event is a complete mess and it's your fault.' He replied, 'It's not my fault, it's Enterprises',' to which I said, 'You keep going on about how it's *your* programme – well, it's *your* fault.'

"I was getting rid of all my angst. Then I brought up the sets. 'All this fuss you make about keeping things quiet and you've shown everyone the sets. That's a really stupid idea.' Bang. He just exploded and started calling me a thief – shouting out, 'Thief, thief, thief!' at the top of his voice in this pub. Everyone looked. I thought, 'What's everyone thinking?' Then he said, 'All you British fans – you're bullshit!' He kept repeating it, with absolute venom – in front of nothing but British fans."

"I remember thinking this is getting worse and worse," says Payne, "and I actually tried to step in and modify it all and calm things down – but that didn't work at all, it was already out of hand."

David Saunders adds, "I vividly remember, as John stalked off in high dudgeon with Gary in tow, Keith Barnfather [another fan and later producer of the *Myth Makers* DVDs, a series of interviews with *Doctor Who* cast and crew from over the years] shouted after him, 'Just remember – we'll still be here long after you've gone!'"

"He dragged me off with him," says Levine, "and said, 'How can these people exist?'"

According to Vincent-Rudzki, "John threatened to sue Keith if he entered the BBC and Gary was going on at David Saunders like a yapping terrier, saying, 'Expel Jan and Steve from DWAS – how dare they treat John like this?' David, bless him, said, 'No – they formed the society. Even if I could, I wouldn't – we're here because of them.'"

"From their point of view, they'd been insulted," says Saunders. "It was damage limitation. Jan and the others weren't there as representatives of the society and it wasn't a society event. It wasn't logical to expel them. I said, 'I'm sorry John, I feel we can't go along with this.'"

"To me that was very much the turning point," says Vincent-Rudzki. "After that, the really positive attitude from British fans changed. He fell from favour and they started to question him."

John did attempt some damage limitation of his own. On the first Thursday of every month, there was a regular gathering of fans (many of them the "glitterati" who had been present for the Mendip Lodge Hotel incident) in a London pub, the One Tun in Farringdon. On 2nd June 1983, John turned up (with Gary) and, says Vincent-Rudzki, "He made a specific point of coming over to me and Steve, shaking our hands and saying, 'Let's start afresh.' I knew that he didn't mean a word of it – he was doing it for show. However, I thought, 'That's quite a brave thing to do – all kudos to you.' But by then the damage had been done."

As Longleat began to fade into fan folklore, spring gave way to summer and London sweltered. One July night, a gay 18-year-old *Doctor Who* fan called Gary Levy missed his last Tube home to Harrow. "I had nowhere to go until the first train started in the morning," says Gary (who has since changed his surname to Leigh). "I'd heard of Heaven and thought I'd pop along. It was a big step for me at the time. I just remember walking in there and this big guy came straight over and introduced himself as Ian Levine. But I'd already recognised him because I'd been to Longleat."

Levine remembers it slightly differently: "He came toadying up to me, 'Oh you're Ian Levine.'"

"I was a heavy *Doctor Who* fan," says Leigh, "and I knew that Ian was supposed to have all these missing episodes so I decided to play dumb and see if I could use it to my advantage. At the time I had at the back of my mind to start a fanzine.

"He said, 'If you wait till the very end – my set finishes about four o'clock – why don't you come back with me and stay at my place? Then tomorrow I'm driving down to Brighton for a get together with John Nathan-Turner, the producer of *Doctor Who*.' I was like 'Who, who?' – 'He's doing a barbecue – there's going to be Peter Davison, his wife, Mark Strickson, Fiona Cumming...' In my head I was like, 'Wow!' but I just said, 'Oh, OK, I'll come.'"

It was already daylight by the time the odd couple reached Levine's house. "It was a very sweaty, hot, humid night," Leigh recalls. "For some reason the heating had been on full blast. It was just as AIDS was hitting and Ian was paranoid about touching people. He made me get into white gym shorts and pose for him."

"I didn't really fancy him," maintains Levine.

The following day Levine drove his new acquaintance down to Brighton. "That was my opportunity," says Leigh. "I had Ian to myself and there was nowhere to escape. So I was cryptically mining around for titbits – he gave me loads – I got a couple of episode titles, the exclusive that Target books were going to be releasing three historical novels, which at the time was huge because they'd only been releasing recent stuff. My first issue of *DWB* was all things I got from Ian."

Ian introduced him as "a friend of mine" and his uninvited guest was given a warm reception. "They looked after me – plied me with food and they were keen to give me some wine – but I've never drunk in my life. They were utterly charming. I was quite awestruck. I spent a lot of time with Pepsi."

As well as petting the dog, Leigh was letting his ears flap. "They were talking about forthcoming scripts and production. They would mention little bits and I was thinking, 'Oh for a recorder' – I had to remember all this stuff in my head. It was the basis of my first issues. OK, ethically it was wrong but I was 18 at the time. I always had a mischievous streak, not a nasty streak – people seem to confuse that."

The very first *DWB* (short for *Doctor Who Bulletin* or "*Doctor Who Bullshit*" as John nicknamed it) appeared in late July 1983, 12 pages photocopied on a friend's machine and assembled with a staple gun. "The first issue cost me less than £10 to produce. The profit I made kept being ploughed back in. As a typical fan, I would wander into Forbidden Planet [a genre bookshop then close to Tottenham Court Road] every Saturday afternoon and flick through all the fanzines. Alan Jones, who was working there, took a liking to me so when I took in five issues of the first edition, he was quite happy to put them out for me. He called me on Monday morning to say, 'Any chance of a reprint? We've sold all of them in an afternoon.'"

It was the beginning of a fan phenomenon and a constant thorn in the side of John Nathan-Turner. As soon as the first issue emerged, Lovine, furious and embarrassed that he had been conned, "hit the roof. He made it clear in no uncertain terms that, 'I confided in you and you've gone and backstabbed me.' There was a big rift between me and Ian for a while because I'd betrayed his trust. If he spotted me on the dance floor at Heaven, I would just twinkle."

Leigh was undeterred. The success of that first crude effort only spurred him on. "I didn't go after a particular market. I was writing for myself – these were my opinions – and this was what I wanted to read. I obviously tuned into how fans were feeling. It was the zeitgeist."

Leigh was the child of a Polish Jewish mother and a Greek Orthodox father. He was adopted and, ironically, years later, discovered that his birth mother had married Ian Levine's cousin, Lloyd Casper. "I had quite a lonely childhood," says Leigh. "I had a sister but she was quite detached. Lis Sladen [Sarah Jane Smith] was like a big sister to me. It was her portrayal that brought me into *Doctor Who*. I never missed an episode. Then, from the moment of the star-spangled flashy opening to *The Leisure Hive* and that dreadful electronic music, I sensed that something's not right here, something's changed. It was change for change's sake – Nathan-Turner wanted to make his mark. I was 15 at the time and it didn't feel like *Doctor Who* any more."

DWB's style – opinionated and gossipy – might, in other circumstances, have been just the type of material that John would have enjoyed reading. But he sensed a gauntlet was being thrown down and he was determined to respond. By issue three, Forbidden Planet had received a formal letter from Christopher Crouch in BBC Enterprises asking them to "cease and desist" selling the upstart new title. "That was my main outlet so it really looked like the nail was in the coffin," says Leigh. "The only thing that kept me going was that by then I'd built up a few subscribers and there was another comic shop nearby which agreed to stock. That helped to salvage the situation. I was banned from Forbidden Planet till issue 53 – they felt that they had to comply with Enterprises."

But, in a characteristic reaction to all subsequent attempts to subdue him, Leigh also published Crouch's pompous edict. "I think this made people realise I was a maverick not for turning. When they realised I wasn't going to lie down and die, about a year after the ban, I wrote to the production office requesting an interview – thinking that maybe this could be a way of pacifying the situation – and John was up for that because it gave him the chance to put his point of view. The interview went really well and I know John was very happy with it. It was very pleasant though I felt he'd already prepared his soundbites.

Then John and Gary asked me for a drink. They were very, very charming at first and we had a lot of laughs and then it was basically cryptic hints that if I played ball then the door would open for me. 'Of course, we could make trouble for you, but if you keep us happy, we'll make sure you stay in the circle.' But I've always been a person of principle.

"About a month after the interview, they invited me to dinner. It was August 1984. I was invited to their place in Saltdean, Brighton. I contacted Ian Levine. He was very up for me going along and seeing what would happen but he warned me that, 'You know they're going to try and get you drunk and pounce on you, so you've got to be prepared for that...' I said I'd be very careful. I booked a hotel – they had offered to put me up but I'd thought it would be safer not to.

"It was just the three of us and Pepsi. During dinner, a piece of cutlery fell under the table and Gary went rummaging under there – and unbeknownst to me he was actually tying my shoelaces to the table leg. When I got up obviously I fell down in a heap and Gary made his move towards me. He was trying to hold me down and I was laughing my head off because I'm very ticklish – if anyone touches me, I just burst out laughing. John Nathan-Turner loomed large over me, and started unbuckling his belt and I just thought, 'I've got to get out of here.' I yanked my shoelace, grabbed my bag and said, 'I'm sorry, guys, I'm out of here,' and made a dash for the exit. I think that was more or less the last contact I had with them."

But it was far from being the end of the story.

SIX

LET'S MAKE MAGIC

"John wanted it to be the late 70s or early 80s for the rest of his life…"
Mark Jones, friend, interview with author, 2012

The seaside city of Brighton, about an hour from London on the Sussex coast, has been a popular resort since the days of the sybaritic Prince Regent. "Prinny", the son and heir to King George III, built an opulent fantasy palace there, the Brighton Pavilion, a retreat that remains lasting testimony to the "prince of pleasure" and all his folly and flamboyance. It's a fittingly theatrical landmark for a place that's long been the gay capital of Britain and when John and Gary started to think about finding a weekend base, it is not, perhaps, hugely surprising that they chose Brighton. They bought their first flat there in 1982, on the top floor of a three-storey block called Teynham House. Soon after, their good friends Fiona Cumming and Ian Fraser moved into a flat on the middle floor. "They liked to socialise a lot," says Cumming. "We used to go out with them and make a four in Brighton, which is full of pubs and clubs. We all used Brighton as a switch-off place."

Brighton was popular with actors and entertainers of all kinds and many of these formed part of John and Gary's wide social circle, among them Chris Ellison (who later starred in *The Bill*), Michael Jayston, Hugh Lloyd and his journalist wife, Shan, June Brown, Carol Kaye and Michelle Collins. Soon, Brighton became more than a bolt-hole and they spent less and less time in the large Brockley house. "I don't know why on earth they didn't rent it," says close friend Stephen Cranford. "It was a three-storey town house with a massive garden. They used to go up there once every few weeks to open the post and then drive back – it was preposterous really. They had all this property and did bugger all with it."

Deciding that the Teynham flat was too small, they moved out but didn't sell or let that either. Their new address was 183 Marine Drive, in Saltdean, five miles east of Brighton. A 1930s art deco seafront cliff house, "it was ravaged by the appalling sea spray," says Cranford, "and blighted by leaks. There were two balconies and both let water in. There was a large lounge and a not quite so big dining room that John used as his office – both had damp-patched and repaired ceilings. It was always, 'That's going to be done on the insurance.' But their house was never finished. Because I work in construction, it was, 'Oh, Steve, come round to dinner – and bring your toolbox.' I'd put a telephone point in or sand their floors or repair their loo. When they moved into it, way before I knew them, it had these really manky old carpets and they said, 'Oh, we'll keep them for now until we get the place sorted' – but they never did. In their downstairs loo they had a pinboard with photos of blokes they liked and if they had a guest coming who was a little more mainstream, they would take this pinboard down!

"Upstairs there were four bedrooms – the master bedroom at the front where they slept with the view out to the sea on the east side of the property and then behind that at the back was their little *Doctor Who* room, which was racked out floor to ceiling with stuff. The stairwell was in the middle and halfway up the stairs there was a little landing where they had a couple of chairs and a table with a *Doctor Who* chess set on it. At the back there was a little bathroom and on the west side of the property there were two other bedrooms, which were guest rooms."

Another close friend, Grahame Flynn, used to stay in the main guest room, which was furnished with "a lovely original 1930s art deco bedroom set in washed-out green, which had been left in the Teynham flat when John bought it. There was a matching headboard, wardrobe, bedside tables and dressing table. This had original make-up and 1930s artefacts on it. The back bedroom was really a dumping ground and the drawers of the divan were filled with VHS tapes of *Doctor Who* stories from the production office."

"John loved the garden," says American fan-turned-friend John Frank Rosenblum. "The front one looked out over the sea and the back one was walled with a shed in which John stored stuff like bits of sets and costumes. He stored stuff everywhere. His office was off to the side of the kitchen – it looked out to the beach so that he could type and see the sea. It had a *Doctor Who* pinball machine in it – he loved that thing – and all sorts of props on the desk and giant brown folders filled with scripts and headshots [photographs of actors]. Both

London and the house in Brighton were like museums if you were a *Doctor Who* fan – there were shelves of it. I can see Adric's star on the shelf next to the bathroom. He had the chess pieces from *The Five Doctors* on the mantelpiece. The Key to Time was in his study."

Between their three properties, as well as original costumes and props, such as the Six Faces of Delusion helmet from *Snakedance*, John ferreted away prototypes of much of the merchandise sent to him for approval. Gary used to say, "That's the pension – when the cheques dry up, we're selling the *Who* stuff."

It wasn't just *Doctor Who* memorabilia that John and Gary hoarded. "They had all this junk all over the place," laughs friend Mark Jones. "'Mark, this'll be worth a fortune' 'Are you sure, John? It looks like a lot of broken tat to me!' Once I went round there as usual and on Brighton market he'd bought this big sovereign ring. He said, 'Mark, what do you think?' And I said, 'I can't stand sovereign rings, it's so Del Boy' and he opened it up and there was a watch inside it. He said, 'How camp is that, darling?' and roared with laughter!"

There was much entertaining. "My then wife Julie and I lived in Hastings and we'd go over to them and they'd come over to us," remembers Mark Strickson. "John would phone up and say, 'Look, we've got a little cold collation – it'll be on the table about two o'clock if you two would like to come over?' So we'd drive over to Brighton for the cold collation, have too much to drink and drive back again the country roads way. People would come down from London. We might go down to the beach. They liked playing party games like charades. It was very gay – there were always lots of flamboyant gay people there."

"I lived in Exeter when I first got to know them," says Grahame Flynn. "At home, I was a serving police officer, publicly living life as a straight man. In the 1990s, the police were not particularly tolerant of gay officers in their ranks. Even though I was very discreet, my sexuality was a problem. My gay life was in Brighton with John and Gary. Here I could relax, discover the real me and immerse myself in gay culture. John was very supportive to me and I used to drive four, five, six hours to see them. We would often go for a day trip in Gary's vintage 1950s Humber Hawk or John would say, 'Let's go and see an act,' meaning a drag show with great artists like David Raven, Maisie Trollette, Dave Lynn and Dockyard Doris.

"One of their great mates was [actor] Jimmy Bree. Wherever he went in the world, he would send John a naughty postcard – a soldier showing his arse or something – and it would go up on the pinboard! I remember Jimmy coming to dinner once with his partner, Al. During the meal Al suddenly exclaimed, 'John, why is there a plaster cock with teeth in your dining room?' This remark was aimed at the prototype design for the Haemovores from *The Curse of Fenric*, which was in the bay window!

"Because I had such a long drive home, I would always leave first thing the following morning. You'd have what he called 'brekker' and then he would present you with a little lunch box – toasted sandwiches he had prepared for you to eat in the car. He was always a very good host."

"I think," says Cranford, "John would far rather have a party at home and everyone come to him rather than going to a bar or restaurant. He liked it to be behind closed doors. John was the host, the social instigator."

"They used to invite me down at weekends," recalls actress Jessica Martin. "At that time I was young, free and fairly single. They'd say, 'Oh, Jessica would you like to come down Saturday and stay over – we're having a few friends over?' We used to make a regular trip to the Queen's Arms in Kemp Town – and I'd be introduced to the local drag queen set. Then, after dinner, he used to put on a record of *Mack and Mabel* and make me sing the songs. Then after a few glasses he'd get very serious and say, 'No, I don't want you to sing it like that – I want you to feel that song and really sell it and deliver it.' Those words really ring in my ears to this day. For all this campery, he was very insightful and he had taste as a director – he knew what he was talking about. It was such an important time in my life – it still feels very vivid, like yesterday."

"Those guys liked to party," says John Frank Rosenblum. "It would start with drinks and then we would go out to some place with a show, usually a drag show or a theatrical show where John would know everybody. There might be a party afterwards. We'd end up back at the house late at night, usually a smaller group of people, who were seriously going to town – more drinks and some drug use – nothing too heavy compared to what I see here in LA – poppers and coke and cannabis – it wasn't like an opium den – and then you'd end up heading off to the bedrooms and sometimes when you woke up, there'd be one or two attractive young men downstairs on the couch.

"The moment the off licence opened on the Sunday we would be walking over there almost in bathrobes to buy giant bottles of liquor and the morning papers. The kitchen was white and open plan – it had a seating aisle. John would always be serving food and made breakfast, 'Bloody Marys, anyone?' Then he would read the papers and cackle about people he knew."

Like many who work in the television industry, John wasn't much of a viewer himself – his insider knowledge generally made him too jaundiced to be able to switch off and suspend his disbelief. He remained devoted to *Coronation Street* (and was much less keen on its BBC rival, *EastEnders*, which he called *DeadEnders*) and enjoyed the high camp of the glossy American soaps, *Dallas* and *Dynasty*. Gary was a gifted pianist and would sometimes provide the accompaniment for a general sing-song. They both enjoyed a trip to the cinema.

One of John's favourite films was *The Producers*, while movie musicals were among his passions, among them *Singin' in the Rain, Hello, Dolly!* and *How to Marry a Millionaire*. "The first ten minutes of that are just an overture," says Mark Jones, "and he adored it. He'd say, 'This needs a line of chorus girls going through the middle'. He loved watching musicals and it always took four times longer than the film because we kept pausing it and deconstructing the scene. It was just great having that professional input."

"In a sense he was a great Vaudevillian," believes another fan who became a friend, Stuart Money. "He used to give me cassettes of music from the 20s, 30s and 40s – he had a fabulous collection of stuff. He kept cassettes of the annual Royal Variety Shows and Command Performances. He was an absolute wizard at the history of pantomime, classic pantomime, he had tomes of information and was fascinating about the Commedia dell'Arte."

Back in London, John's "home from home" was his office in Union House. Although he was moved a couple of times, the style remained the same. Not for him the usual BBC decor of pale beige. He had his office painted a deep, rich red and, leading the way inside, he would sometimes drawl, "Come into my *womb...*"

Inside, the walls were covered with a headache-inducing patchwork of publicity photos, with a BBC calendar for the year lurking somewhere among them. There were piles of scripts, props crammed everywhere space could be found and shelves of video cassettes. "There was this glass cabinet with a display of merchandise," remembers Sophie Aldred, "and right in the centre were a pair of kids' Y-fronts from the 1970s with the brown piping and Tom Baker's face right on the Y. There was John Nathan-Turner written in spangly letters. It was all very light entertainment and 'Here I am!'"

The number of people working on a major television series has proliferated over the years but, in the 1980s, producing 26 episodes a year and handling the entire brand was the full time responsibility of just four people – John, as producer, his script editor, production associate (as PUMs had been renamed) and the production secretary. John used collectively to refer to this team as "the front office", although in fact it was a series of offices (producer, script editor and associate all had their own while the secretary guarded the outer space). Over the decade, he maintained an extraordinary continuity within this core team and, despite the one monumental falling out that followed, this cannot be discounted. There were (and remain) plenty of television creatives whose personality and approach make it hard for them to retain staff for a few months, never mind year after year. Despite his quirks, occasional outbursts and subsequent sulks, John was good at keeping a team together. June Collins came from Science Features in 1983 to take over from Angela Smith as John's associate, winning the appointment over fellow contender, a certain Gary Downie. John nicknamed her "She who must be obeyed…"

"That's me!" she laughs when reminded of it. "I thought really highly of him," she says. "He was a perfectionist and he expected that from his team. The show was totally the first priority. There were so many producers who were just never around, getting drunk somewhere. He was a bit like a rock on the show – so strong and supportive. He had the most fantastic sense of humour – not bitchy, really witty. I think he liked to be liked, and was sensitive, even though he sometimes upset people.

"He was a very good manager of time. There's a saying of his that I still use today. We got hit by an editing strike and I had to rearrange the whole schedule. I wasn't getting a lot of help from the editing department. I got off the phone, stressed, burst into tears and said, 'I can't sort this out.' He said, 'Look, darling, it's only somewhere to come during the day.' He helped to keep things in perspective. They were some of the best years of my life. Nothing has ever matched my career there. It was like family.

"The pressure was incredible – we would be running three teams at the same time. I've read that the new series is often behind schedule, despite oozing with money. But I mean going over budget and being behind schedule was just not in John's vocabulary. He was a professional – the best person I've ever worked with."

Chris Bidmead had been briefly followed as editor by a trainee, Antony Root (later to rise to wealth and prominence in the industry both in Britain and the States), who filled the role on a temporary basis. The eventual long-term successor was 36-year-old writer Eric Saward, who had been recommended to Bidmead by a senior script editor in the BBC radio drama department. Saward's first effort, *The Visitation*, was judged a success and he took up his role in the spring of 1981. In the months that followed, a relationship developed between Saward and the secretary, Jane Judge (they are still together). Both declined to be interviewed for this book, which perhaps tells its own story. But, over the years, Saward has hardly fought shy of sharing his opinions about John and the years they worked together on the programme.

"This concept that we were always arguing, every day for five years, is a myth," he confided to *Doctor Who Magazine* in 2004. "John had many qualities. He could be very supportive. It's just… well, you never quite knew where you were with John. You never really knew what he was thinking. You were never included. When you listen to Barry Letts and Terrance Dicks [1970s producer and script editor], you get a sense of two people who worked very closely together. I'm sure they didn't agree all the time but there was a rapport there, which there never was with John and me."

"I liked Eric," says Matthew Waterhouse. "I thought he was a very talented writer who understood *Doctor Who* very well. I remember him saying something about *Time-Flight* – that it had been a complete bloody mess and he'd had to rewrite the whole thing. He said, 'Basically that's my script,' and idiotically I casually said to John that the script wasn't very good and had had to be rewritten. John snapped, 'Who said that?' and I had to admit that Eric had mentioned it. I got a feeling from that they weren't pals."

"I was aware of a tension," says Fiona Cumming, "but as a Libran, I hate discord and I put blinkers on and look at what I want to see. I never really had much to do with him. I always liked to talk to the author though – even if it was just a chat on the phone and I don't think he liked that. You had to go via Eric and, in many cases, it left you with three days' work when a ten-minute phone call would have cleared everything up. It wasn't that you were trying to undermine him in any way but Eric's a very, very insecure person. He should never have been scared of John, though, because John always relied very heavily on his script editor."

"They were very different people," says Strickson, "the opposite ends of the scale. If I was Eric, I would have got a bit frustrated with the fact that John was, rightly, so obsessed with building the brand that he was probably wasn't giving Eric enough support in terms of stories. Eric would have felt fairly insecure – out there on his own, having to do it, thinking, 'I need some more help here. I need some more feedback from my producer – and what's he doing? – he's flying away to America all the time.' As script editor, it wouldn't have been your job to understand the commercial imperative."

"I always got on with Eric," says June Collins. "They both could be moody. But with John it wouldn't last very long. Eric was a good script editor, there's no doubt about that. He worked hard and cared about the stories. And I think that John respected Eric."

But John was uneasy about Saward and Judge's initially on/off romance. His tendency towards paranoia was an Achilles' heel of which he could never rid himself, especially as it tended to be stoked by Gary. John wanted always to be the first to know anything and he worried that his secretary and his editor might conspire or share secrets with each other rather than him. Finally, there was only one way this could be resolved. In May 1983, Judge moved on. Her replacement was 18-year-old Sarah Lee, who had already "tried out" on a temporary basis, helping to open the fan mail.

"It was a lot of work," she remembers, "very, very full on. We were producing more drama in terms of screen time than anyone else in the department at the time. John threw himself into work 150 per cent, really, and was gregarious and a lot of fun. He was a very generous spirit. I don't think my strong point was spelling and I wasn't the greatest typist in the world but I got things done. Maybe one of the things that swung it was that I came from a background of theatre and television [Lee's mother is the actress Lynda Baron]. He needed to have someone who had some idea of how to speak to actors, how to ring them up. We might have a major photo call in the middle of town with all the press there and sometimes I had to go and do it on my own because he was in the studio. He'd say, 'Make sure you get this shot and that shot.' I was in charge and when I think back and look at my 20-year-old stepdaughter who'd have no idea what to do, well, I wasn't treated like the office junior. He never made you feel as if you were afraid of your boss. We were very much a team. It was a good atmosphere. I absolutely loved getting up and going to work each day. That's why I stayed there so long. I was happy, confident and it was fascinating."

In July 1981, there was another reshuffle in the continuing power game upstairs. Graeme McDonald was promoted to succeed Shaun Sutton as Head of Drama Group and in his place as Head of Series and Serials came David Reid, who had a long track record as a director and producer at companies like LWT and ATV, where he had been head of drama. John had nothing to fear from the new arrival. "John was immediately someone you liked," says Reid. "Just one of those characters, lovely, flamboyant, sparkling eyes – with enormous enthusiasm. He lived and breathed *Doctor Who* and that meant it was a little bit of the department that was running itself. To some extent, it wasn't something I had to worry about. I could get on with other concerns because I knew I could trust John with that completely. He was just someone with that project you felt complete safe with and you just let him get him on with it."

It was a summer of good news, as he was granted his wish of being made a permanent producer and told that Barry Letts would no longer act as his exec. As John had grown in confidence, this supervision, no matter how tactful, had increasingly rankled. Now John was flying solo and *Who* was his oyster. But he remained thirsty for what might lie beyond it. It has been one of the biggest fallacies of John's career that he was content to remain on *Doctor Who*. Whatever his undoubted affection for the programme, the perks and compensations of staying in post, the evidence is overwhelming that, almost from the start, he was actively trying to move on.

"John wanted to get out of *Who* very fast," says director Paul Joyce. "He was always looking beyond it and he certainly was ambitious. He wanted Bill

Cotton's job [Cotton was, at that time, controller of BBC1]. He told me that he was in Bill Cotton's office one day and somebody came in and said, 'You've got to make this decision today about the Gracie Fields drama' – and Bill said, 'No, I'm not interested in Gracie Fields.' Afterwards, Nathan-Turner said to me, 'It was madness – I would have said yes. I want Bill's job.' I would have loved him to have that chance – to get to the top. Then he would have found himself. *Doctor Who* didn't really accord with his vision of himself as an executive."

John's paper archive is groaning with attempts to get other projects off the ground. In January 1980, just weeks after becoming producer on *Doctor Who*, he did his best to interest McDonald in a script of his colleague and friend, Peter Grimwade, as he explained it in his memo, the "basic idea of a modern-day trio whose names happen to be Holmes, Dr Watson and Mrs Hudson [which] appeals to me enormously.

"I like Peter Grimwade's style of writing as displayed here and his flippant Holmes, his fastidious Watson and his student Hudson have been well drawn." Noting that "for my money, the whole thing is over 'gay'," he nevertheless goes on "I should like to develop this idea with him as a series for television, possibly as an all-film project. Are you interested?"

McDonald wasn't. On 14th January, he replied: "It seemed overheated and overblown to me. You might be interested to know that Tom Baker once had the idea of a present day detective who happens to be called Holmes and so got all the cases that are still sent to Baker Street. A nice idea I haven't been able to place yet."

John replied at once: "Although you're not over keen on the Peter Grimwade script, some more information about this project has been revealed... it was written as a full-length TV movie ending with the installation of the latterday Holmes in Baker Street, with the series Tom Baker mentioned to you to follow on. Indeed this script, it turns out, was written specifically for Tom Baker, with Trevor Baxter and Miriam Margolyes in mind as Watson and Hudson."

This intriguing idea was not pursued but it would be interesting to know what John would have made of Steven Moffat's dazzlingly successful 21st-century *Sherlock*.

At the same time, he was trying hard to interest light entertainment in a camp Australian performer called Jeanne Little, whom he had first seen on a visit to Gary's family there. He devised a 6 x 30-minute format, *The Little Jeanne Little Show*, which sang her praises as "one of the most talked about stars in Australian television. To Jeanne, everyone is 'daaarling' and everything is 'stunnning' or 'brilliiiant'. As well as being a very funny performer, singer, dancing ballet, ad-libbing or doing sketches, Jeanne has been a super-scorching model and dress designer."

He persuaded the Michael Parkinson team to book Little for a guest slot and used this to bolster his proposal, which he sent to Robin Nash, the head of variety. Nash's response, on 22nd January 1980, was dismissive: "Personally, my reaction to the *Parkinson* appearance was not very favourable. It seemed to me that she was an 'over the top' performer of whom the English viewer does not seem to be usually 'over fond'."

John didn't give up. Nash finally rejected the series on 13th May, saying "the idea... has been given every consideration." On 27th May, Nash's counterpart at LWT also rejected the proposal and on 26th August, Philip Jones, director of entertainment at Thames, followed suit, saying that he'd "keep her in mind for suitable guest slots". Little went a long way – John didn't finally give up until the following year when producer Paul Jackson wrote to him on 18th February: "I have had further discussions with both Robin Nash and Michael Hurll [an executive producer] – I have to say that it does seem to me that, lovely and loony though the lady is, she is definitely more of a guest slot than a series."

On 13th April 1981, John sent an enthusiastic memo to Reid putting forward the idea for *National Champion*, a serial telling the inspiring story of jockey Bob Champion, who won the 1981 Grand National after winning his battle against cancer. "I am confident we could achieve an exciting and moving two-part serial... Antony Root, my script editor, is as excited as I am... we are confident that this is an extraordinary and unusual story which we would both love to develop."

Reid says, "I thought, 'John's got a good idea here,' and I tried to interest Alan Hart [who succeeded Cotton as BBC1 controller] and Brian Wenham [BBC2 controller] and they could neither of them see it. But, you see, John was right because a year or so later Lew Grade went ahead and made the movie with John Hurt and Jan Francis [*Champions*]. I wished then and I still wish that I could have pushed on with John – my guess is, had I been there longer, he would have come up with other ideas, which one might have got off the ground."

There was no shortage of them. In 1982, he pitched a variety of literary adaptations and original concepts. Among the former was a 26-part version of John Christopher's *The Prince in Waiting* trilogy ("possibly using the basic characters for a further series if required") – suggesting that this could be made during the summer using OB cameras. Reid, who had already committed himself to another Christopher trilogy, *The Tripods*, suggested he offer this instead to Roderick Graham, head of drama at BBC Scotland but on 20th July, Graham turned it down: "I think this really takes a Stephen Speilberg [*sic*] or a radio production and I don't feel that television... is really competent to deal with it." Graham also turned down another of Reid's rejects ("There is no way we shall get resources for three films") *Villi the Clown*, to be based on the unusual autobiography of one William Campbell, who toured the Cold War Soviet Union under cover as a circus performer. Graham judged sniffily that "I really don't think this would be worth the expense involved, although it would have had wonderful title music!"

"Personally, I think the BBC is mad," John wrote consolingly to Tudor George, the man who had brought *Villi the Clown* to his attention. Neither could he find any takers for an adaptation of Catherine Cookson's *Hannah Massey* (brought to him by an old actor acquaintance from rep, Jeffrey Holland, then starring in *Hi-de-Hi!*). Within a few years, Tyne Tees would do very good business with an ongoing series of Cookson serials.

During the previous year, Gary had been a production manager on *Angels* and one director with whom he worked closely was Matthew Robinson. "I had a couple of parties during that period," says Robinson, "and Gary brought John – that was the first time I met him. He was somebody you couldn't forget – he had a huge presence. He was entertaining, very friendly, positive and fun."

Robinson had a pet project of his own, which he had devised and was trying to get off the ground. "John was trying to expand his empire," Robinson recalls. "He said he'd try to move it forward." *Rye Spy* ("which I like enormously", John emoted in his accompanying memo) was to be a 13-episode film series, subtitled "the adventures of an industrial investigator", following one Jim Rye, who works on the inside to uncover industrial fraud and wrong-doing. The outline suggested hopefully that "Rye could be a well-known American actor should this attract co-production money". This seemed unlikely. Even then, the format creaked, reminiscent of those ho-hum rent-a-plot ITC series of the 1960s. The supporting characters, Rye's landlady and her 23-year-old daughter "both have occasion to help Rye... answering phones, opening letters... even solving problems on occasions". Very emancipated. Sniffing a dud, Reid turned it down flat, though Robinson got the consolation prize of an offer to direct *Doctor Who*.

As producer, John's ultimate prize remained a twice-weekly soap opera. "In a way he was ahead of his time," believes Peter Davison. "I remember him talking to me very early on that his ultimate aim was to do a soap opera. He wanted to bring back *Compact* [an early 60s serial set in a women's magazine]. This was baffling to me at the time. I was thinking, 'Why on earth would your ambition be to do a soap opera? Why would you want to do that?'"

"He was constantly working on proposals for soaps," recalls Janet

Fielding. "John adored soaps. That was where he would have loved to have gone."

In 1982, the grapevine was buzzing with the news that the BBC, having half-heartedly flirted with the twice-weekly format for years, were finally beginning to think about a fully-fledged rival to ITV's seemingly invincible *Coronation Street*. "I was the person who pointed out to the BBC that they needed a soap opera," says Reid. "You have to commit to three years minimum. It is not a drama you can put on for six months; it is habit-forming, you can't interrupt it."

John tried to seize the day. On 19th February 1982, he submitted a format for his own bi-weekly, *Lives*. This would "follow the loves, experiences and fortunes of eight London school leavers – four female and four male – who will end up sharing a large London house divided into apartments. A topical and youthful programme which will appeal to all ages. I envisage both parental and career involvement with the above characters. This is a sketchy format at present as requested – more details and development are obviously needed." Interestingly, he added a postscript suggesting that "after an initial period of recording episodes, I would envisage returning to the *Compact* style of making programmes... a weekly turnaround with one of these (two episodes) transmitting LIVE."

Despite the vagueness of the outline, *Lives* was drably reminiscent of the last serial to adopt this approach, Southern's pitiful *Together*. John had misread the scale of the BBC's ambition. A few weeks later, on 17th April, he tried again, this time presenting Reid with *Catwalk*, credited both to him and Gary Downie. This was a bi-weekly "concerning the business and intrigues of a West End fashion house. The accent will be... glamour fashion parades, beautiful models etc and rivalry within the company, even espionage involving rival fashion houses. Four of the five company directors take active roles in running the business – these are namely Adrienne, Katherine and Dinah, three mature ex-models, and Burgess, a successful designer and ex-husband of Dinah."

It was tripe and even the suggestion that "it is proposed that the technical advisers would be the internationally famous 'Emmanuels'" (the strange use of single quotes was all theirs and seemed to imply that the Emmanuels were themselves fictional!) wasn't enough to raise a ripple of interest.

Third off the blocks, and most drawn-out, was John's tenacious attempt to revive *Compact*, the serial he now held up as the model of what a new BBC1 soap might be. He involved the original writers Hazel Adair and Peter Ling and even retitled the enterprise *Impact* but Reid was never tempted and gently fobbed him off. If John had only done his research he would have known that, as an ex-ATV drama man, Reid would not have welcomed anything with the same DNA of the turgid, embarrassing *Crossroads* (another Adair and Ling creation) on his patch and neither would the BBC.

The winner in the race for the new soap was *East 8*, later renamed *EastEnders*, the clever invention of script editor Tony Holland and (to a lesser extent) his tough-talking, frequently hatchet-faced producer, Julia Smith. Its success was a career turnaround for Smith, who, just a few years before, was nearly dismissed from the staff as nobody wanted to work with her. John and Julia cordially detested each other and her victory in the soap contest can't have lessened the antagonism. Sadly for him, *EastEnders* possessed everything that his own ideas lacked – it was utterly contemporary, conceived on a grand scale and populated with characters drawn from life rather than cliché and fantasy.

Though he never stopped trying, John's only success in winning a commission outside *Doctor Who* was its 1981 spin-off, *K9 and Company*. Intended as a pilot for a series, to star Elisabeth Sladen as Sarah Jane Smith and John Leeson as the voice of the dog, here John was ahead of the game in pursuing this idea. It took the BBC over a quarter of a century to catch up. True to the inherently sexist spirit of the Corporation's approach to female artists, though ostensibly the star, Sladen's fee was noticeably lower than either Leeson's, or even guest actors Bill Fraser and Colin Jeavons. Despite an indifferent slot and a transmitter failure depriving a sizeable slice of audience from watching, the pilot rated well – over eight million viewers – more than seven times the number who would regularly watch *The Sarah Jane Adventures*, still seen as wildly successful because measures of success in a multi-channel world are so different. Back in 1981, the BBC could still afford to be lukewarm and picky with its successes and *K9 and Company* was not pursued. "It was probably me," admits Reid. "I never pitched a series to the controllers. I thought of it as a Christmas special, that's all."

"Very much in the back of John's mind was empire building and 'let's get another series on the go'," thinks John Black, who was taken off a *Doctor Who* story, *Black Orchid*, to direct the special. "He was keen it should go on. I think he had always had a slight sort of impresario edge to him and that could have taken him far if he'd had the right-hand man who could fix the scripts and do the casting. I did feel that some of his casting was a bit dubious – of running characters."

John had instructed contracts to engage his new leading man, Peter Davison, on 21st October 1980. "He rang me up and asked me if I wanted to do it," recalls Davison. "It was a great thrill to be asked but he did have to persuade me. My agent [John Mahoney] thought I should do it because it was a lot of money."

On 30th October, John wrote to Mahoney: "I am so glad negotiations are now settled for Peter Davison to play the part of the Doctor. I look forward to enormous success with the programme and to our further healthy co-operation. As previously mentioned, it will be necessary for Peter to have streaks put into his hair and within the bounds of safety to perform his own stunts. It will also be necessary during Peter's contract for him to drive."

The contract, for 28 episodes ("although we expect to record only 26") followed on 18th November, at a fee of £600 per programme. "I didn't really realise," says Davison, "that when I was being cast, I was sort of being turned into a gay icon – that's why he insisted on highlights in my hair. I knew John from *All Creatures* and when we were all away filming in Yorkshire, he would always be right in the thick of it. He was for the most part very, very affable. I liked him very much and I think we always got on very well.

"I look at it now and think I wish I could have done it better. I was very young and you never quite realise – you've been cast as this iconic figure that you've been brought up with – and I don't think I quite grasped it in the way that I could have."

Originally, John asked one of his favourites, "Baby" June Hudson, to design Davison's costume. "I said, 'I see Peter Davison in cricket whites – he's the quintessential young Englishman – blond, good-looking, the very essence of the First World War generation. I fitted him in these cricket whites – very simple – it didn't need more, with his looks and charisma. John seemed to like it but when it came out I thought, 'What the hell is that?'"

John later claimed that it was a photograph on his office wall of Davison playing in an *All Creatures* charity cricket match that inspired the look. Either way, and unbeknown to Hudson, another designer, Colin Lavers, was instructed to take this basic cricketing look much further than she had ever anticipated. On 6th February 1981, John wrote to Lavers: "I've been thinking some more about the Doctor's costume and I've come to the conclusion of basically a "cricket" image is the best! The morning suit idea would seem to me to be in danger of looking too immaculate or if ill fitting as we discussed, too clownish – baggy pants etc.

"A cricket pullover with white *Doctor Who* shirt and white shirt with the introduction of colour into the trousers would be very appealing – add to this some kind of top coat, when needed, and we have the practical, effective, casual look, which we so wanted. Possibly the topcoat could be a morning suit jacket and the collapsible topper might work with this, I'm not sure. I'm being pressurised by the merchandising department to settle the image so that franchises for products can be negotiated."

Hudson was not impressed with the result. "Colin, sorry, but oh my giddy aunt!" she exclaims. "Striped trousers and that edging. I thought 'Hell's bells.' The great problem with costume for men particularly is that you've got to be very careful – it should be tailored and serious and not look as if it's made by a dressmaker because immediately the character loses strength. You look at an actor and think, 'Why did they cast this actor?' and that is what you're emphasising."

Davison himself didn't mind the costume – such tensions that did emerge between producer and star focused principally on areas of artistic interpretation. From the start, John was keen on "stars", living to rue the day he referred to the "*Morecambe and Wise* effect". He meant that big names were so fond of the show (or their children and grandchildren were) that they flocked to appear. But the words were twisted and used against him to imply a deliberate light-entertainment focus in the casting. His guest-star policy (funded by what John referred to as "knicker elastic money", cash he'd spirited away to fund the fees) still divides opinion.

"He wanted to have a name," says Davison, "which I don't always think correlated to the best actor available. I remember when we had Leonard Sachs in *Arc of Infinity* and he couldn't remember his lines. I said to John, 'This is not a good choice.' Leonard had been doing *The Good Old Days*, that's why he had him in there – he was a lovely chap, don't get me wrong – but I think there was another name that came up and he rejected this other name and I said, 'Why? Because he's a really good actor!' It was frustrating, definitely.

"Beryl Reid was such a huge mistake in a way. I mean, maybe it worked because you know, it's Beryl Reid but she really had no idea what she was doing. We had to guide her through – 'What am I saying, darling? I've no idea.'"

"I loved that," hoots Russell T Davies. "I'd cast Beryl Reid. I'd cast Joan Sims. I love that kind of thing, getting people off the soaps, getting famous faces – I think that's really clever and it really works. Well, not every bit of it worked – I'm not convinced that Joan Sims worked – but here we are, talking about her 20 years later. That showman side of John was really broad and clever I think."

"He had a very strong grasp on what entertains people," says Strickson. "As soon as you bring in people like Lynda Baron, you bring in people who wouldn't normally watch it. People so underestimate what John was doing."

Grahame Flynn recalls how "he pointed out to me that there was a wealth of talent sitting at home, waiting for the phone to ring. Faded stars of the stage and screen. He would always say, 'If you don't ask, you don't get! If you want to cast a Broadway star like Dolores Gray, why not ask if Dolores Gray will do it?'"

"Casting was all to John," says Robinson, "the bigger the name, the better it was. When we came up with the idea of Koo Stark [booked for *Attack of the Cybermen* before a contract dispute ruled her out], he just went absolutely crazy for that. If you tapped into John on that basis and came up with big ideas and if John didn't have a block about somebody big – and he did have a blind spot with some people – then he was ideal."

"Some of the fans used to moan about his casting," says Sarah Lee, "but I think the interesting side of that was he believed actors who were very good comedians or perhaps a bit more music hall would also be good playing straight. When you look at what's going on now and who is in things, with stand-up comedians getting parts in movies or Lenny Henry playing *Othello* – that was all he was trying to do, but on a shoestring."

Much of popular series television is crisis management. Scripts were always a problem on *Doctor Who*. Saward had to navigate his way through piles of half-baked material commissioned by his predecessor or John himself. An early trial was wrestling with the problem of author Chris Priest and his second attempt to write for the series, *The Enemy Within*. "After I had delivered the last episode," recalls Priest, "I heard nothing more from Turner. I soon forgot all about *Doctor Who*, which even at that stage had become an unforgettably bad experience. Several weeks later, I took a call from Turner. He was in one of his moods. He demanded to know when I was going to go in and meet him and revise the scripts. What I had sent in, he said, was unusably bad, did not conform to the brief, and the whole thing had to be rewritten from beginning to end.

"I asked if that was a firm commission [the Writers' Guild has an agreement with the BBC about rewrite commissions] and Turner flew into a rage, insulted me and my scripts, said my story had been cancelled and threw the phone down. I thought that was the end of it but a year or so later someone sent me an interview Turner had given. He was asked why the programme never used 'proper science-fiction writers'. His answer was that they had tried this, named me, but said that I could not write well enough for the programme and had behaved unprofessionally."

Priest considered legal action and lodged a formal complaint via the Writers' Guild. Eventually, he received written apologies from the BBC and both John and Saward in person, the situation having escalated upwards so that head of department David Reid had to resolve it. But Reid stresses that an incident like this needs to be seen in context. "This wasn't a one-off – very much not so," says Reid, somewhat ruefully. "I used to feel that no one in the department ever walked through the door to tell me something nice or with good news! Producers were habitually having problems with writers/agents/directors and, always, with budgets. What kind of problems..?

"Betty Willingale, eminent script editor, arrives in my office one morning (obviously at the behest of eminent producer, Jonathan Powell) to tell me that after shooting for four days on *Bleak House* they realise they have hired the wrong director [Lawrence Gordon Clark]! What to do – stand over them brandishing a whip, screaming get on with it? No, it's cards on table with central planners – rushing script to new director (actually in Africa at time) and delaying production by three weeks. On another occasion I was very pleased with the first episode of a series starring Robert Lindsay and Paul McGann, *Give Us a Break*. 'Commission another series,' I cry. Later the same day an ashen-faced producer admits to me that the BBC have made no provision for Lindsay or McGann to do a second series. What should have been standard practice had simply fallen through the net!

"Anyway, how does all this relate to JN-T?" continues Reid. "I think the big difference was that – in virtually all cases – producers forewarned me of trouble brewing so that I was rarely ever caught out with a situation that had got as far as John's had with Chris Priest. As a matter of interest, I very often found myself defending producers or the BBC for decisions that personally I might not have agreed with. Therefore, where appropriate, I never thought it weak or wrong to apologise or offer a degree of compensation. The spat with Priest does, I think, show John in a bad light – an insistence to run his own small empire in the way he decided and then get into what can only be called a paddy when it doesn't come out the way he wanted. Though his independence and self-reliance were admirable in many ways, I have no doubt, had he talked and involved me sooner, we could have avoided a collision course without John losing face."

The loss of *The Enemy Within* left a gaping hole in the schedule and Saward stepped up to fill this with a hurried script of his own, first called *Sentinel*, later famous as *Earthshock*. This killed off Matthew Waterhouse's Adric. "I'm delighted you enjoyed *Sentinel*," wrote John in response to a memo from Reid, on 21st September 1981, commending a "good, exciting story".

"I intend to make the ending as moving as possible. At the start of the next story, the regulars will still be recovering from the loss of their companion. Incidentally, this is the first time a companion has 'died' since the late 60s."

Waterhouse was shocked to be told of his character's imminent demise but the news reached him, not from John, but via Davison, who, rather unkindly, sprang it on him at the Acton rehearsal rooms. "John was in many ways a nice man," says Waterhouse, "but he didn't really know how to deal with it, so he thought it was better not to say anything. Which is of course not the best way of dealing with it. That was his approach, to keep it secret. He had this idea that I would freak out and burst into tears."

"I adored the ending of that," says Davies. "I loved killing him, and I don't mean that cynically – it was shattering. The silent credits were perfect, that was the most emotional thing to do. My favourite was always *Earthshock* – the size of it, the sacrifice, the darkness of that story. I love the fact that Adric sacrifices himself for nothing. You can guarantee that now he'd fly that spaceship into the Earth to make sure the dinosaurs were killed to create the human race. They do the opposite of that and he dies for no reason at all. He's just trapped. History takes its course. I do love that story. It's very bleak. I think it's absolutely brilliant. In soap operas, the episode I always love best is the episode after a death – someone comes into a room and there's a hush and they'll reminisce over a pint of bitter – the after events of a death are more dramatic than the death. I was so looking forward to the first episode of *Time-Flight*. What do you imagine that episode's going to be like? The Doctor's going to be guilty, maybe the companions want to go home, will they build a shrine to him on some distant rock, where will the journey take them? Two flipping lines of dialogue and they go to Heathrow. I remember feeling so dislocated from the programme by that – it was the first time when I sat up and thought, 'This is wrong.'

"The story of television is the story of the increasing emotionalisation of stories – you look at the 60s and everything was *Man in a Suitcase* and *Randall and Hopkirk* – there was not an emotion to be spared. They were larks, adventures. By the 1980s, telly was wising up. *Time-Flight* had such good storytelling material. When I start to describe the Doctor, Nyssa and Tegan going to some rocky patch, building a cairn of rocks to remember Adric by, that's already twice as dramatic as anything we got. And cheap! Not unfilmable! It's utterly bizarre that they couldn't see the drama in that. That episode one is a bizarre decision and badly done – badly written."

Looked at as a whole, Davison's first season was a mish-mash of leftovers from the previous year (Grimwade's *Xeraphin* became *Time-Flight*) and rush jobs to shore up the space left by a sudden disaster. One of these was John Flanagan and Andrew McCulloch's *Project Zeta Minor*, intended to launch Davison's era. When this feeble effort was delivered and, in John's absence (he was attending a convention in America) deemed unusable by Barry Letts, Terence Dudley's *Four to Doomsday* was rushed forward to take its place in the schedule. "Terence was always trying to write for *Doctor Who* when I was doing it," Robert Holmes told me in August 1985. "The ideas weren't there. I saw one of his, *Black Orchid*, and realised why I hadn't used him."

"He'd written some stupid story about the brother in the attic," grimaces Davison, "and turned it into a *Doctor Who* whereas in fact it was just a bit of nonsense. I could not stand the man. The trouble is that he had such contempt for the programme. That it was beneath him and he should be doing something far more worthy. He was arrogant about his ability. He was a hack who would knock off these terrible stories."

John Black was the director charged with making *Four to Doomsday* work and helping the new lead to find his feet. "It was a difficult ball game," he says, "in that I didn't have a huge amount of confidence in the script. I sought from John on several occasions the rationale for the casting of Peter and above all for the cricketing theme because I couldn't get my head round that, really. I thought that Doctor Who was eccentric whereas this was more whimsical – almost a parody of eccentricity. It didn't seem to be fundamental in the script, even with the cricket ball. In my own heart of hearts, I had doubts about the casting but it was entirely down to John, how he saw it all continuing and fitting, but I never got any explanation that was rational enough for my comfort. Peter was extraordinarily nice to work with – I was very aware he was searching around for approaches. We were all slightly at sea."

Davison's actual screen debut was farmed out to Bidmead and pushed to fourth in the recording order. People have praised John for his canniness in letting Davison gently find his way by recording three stories before his debut but in fact this was mere pragmatism, a necessary reaction to yet another script emergency. Bidmead cooked up *Castrovalva*, inspired by a series of Escher prints on the walls of Graeme McDonald's office, which John disliked so much he always sat where he couldn't see them. While McDonald may have appreciated the in-joke, he didn't think much of *Castrovalva*, sending David Reid a damning memo on 5th January 1982: "*Dr Who* is too valuable a show to us to let its standard slip so dramatically and I think we need to be sure that John is aware of the shortcomings of that opening episode. Chris Bidmead's script was not only unimaginative but it forced the action into the visually uninteresting TARDIS for far too long. I think too you would agree that the performance of the two girls was bad, which, since they were regulars last year, one can only put down to poor direction. The spotlight the new Dr Who puts on the show makes this halting start the more embarrassing. I suggest we will have to monitor John's scripts and choice of directors more carefully in the future."

Despite McDonald's concerns, there is no evidence that they did so. Happily, the audience loved Davison from the start, embracing this dashing young Doctor and the programme's new twice-weekly slot, with enthusiasm and huge numbers. Davison may have felt he was partially there as some kind of gay subtext (and maybe he was) but the mainstream BBC1 crowd took to his deceptively gauche characterisation. There were a few bitchy remarks about "the wet vet", but Davison's arrival reinvigorated the series and temporarily lifted its sagging credibility within the BBC.

That Christmas, Davison, then wife Sandra Dickinson and Anthony Ainley headlined a production of John's old standard, *Cinderella*, at the Tunbridge Wells Assembly Halls. John took unpaid leave to direct the show. "That was kind of John's strength," says Reid, "that innate understanding of end of the pier – and I don't mean this in a derogatory sense in any way – he understood tat – what people enjoyed even if it wasn't mainstream, wonderful and up to date. He had an instinct for 'that will work'."

On 13th April 1982, John sent a memo to Biddy Baxter: "It occurred to me that you might be interested in following the mounting of a theatre production for *Blue Peter* considering the link with *Doctor Who*. Any interest?" This time, Baxter passed.

"It wasn't part of the deal to do a panto," points out Davison. "I think he just sold us very cleverly because he was good at that kind of thing. 'It's going to be fantastic.' But the location was terrible. It wasn't a proper theatre. Outrageously, we would quite often spend *Doctor Who* rehearsal time rehearsing for the pantomime. I wasn't mad about that. But it was quite fun."

Cinderella was the bright idea of sometime director Lovett Bickford, who was now attempting to make a living putting on plays and shows. "I had children," says Bickford, "and was very keen that the children should see good theatre. I spent far too much money on the production and I was very pleased with what John did, because he was very inventive, brilliant at pantomime."

Inevitably, John engaged Gary as choreographer. "I wasn't too keen on his friend," says Bickford. "He was a very nasty queer if you get my meaning – and John was just not. He could be bitchy but always funny. Gary was never funny. John could have anybody he wanted rather than that nasty piece of work."

"That wasn't good," agrees Davison. "That was one of my very few tantrums in my professional career – I hardly ever lose my temper – but Gary was so horrible to the dancers that I basically just stormed off and said that I'm not going to stay in the rehearsal room if you're going to be like this. I think it kind of had an effect but I should imagine he was just horrible to them when I wasn't there. But Gary I really didn't like. It was baffling as to why they were together."

John might have said the same about Davison's peroxide-blonde wife, the squeaky-voiced Dickinson, whom he could not abide. Despite Davison's considerable pulling power, *Cinderella* lost money and Bickford, bruised, happily sold the sets and costumes to John, who had decided he might try his own luck as a theatrical impresario. He roped in his close friends, *Doctor Who* director Fiona Cumming and her husband Ian Fraser in a new extra-curricular venture, Teynham Productions, formed on 19th September 1984. This was designed to allow them to present their own shows and pantomimes and named after the block of flats where they had all started their lives in Brighton, the backdrop to their happiest hours.

SEVEN

WHETHER YOU LIKE IT OR NOT

"Each producer has altered the emphasis of the programme, and the changes thus made, combined with the talents of the five actors who have played the Doctor, are, I feel sure, major reasons why the programme has been so successful for so long. Bringing about my own changes was very stimulating..."
John Nathan-Turner, introduction to the commemorative programme for *The Doctor Who Celebration*, 1983

For John, 1982 to 1984 were his golden years, his supremacy over *Doctor Who* questioned by few, the future apparently secure and a time when he could enjoy all the immediate rewards of his tenancy – the attention from fans, the extra-curricular income, the social and sexual perks and, perhaps more than anything, the fun and fellowship of sitting right at the heart of a diverse family tree of actors and technicians, all looking to John as their ersatz father figure. There were a few dissenters, some who bitched behind his back, but during this halcyon period, John had every reason to feel that he was unassailable, trusted to get on with running his empire.

"John wasn't a needy person," points out his personnel officer, Pat Dyer. "There were a lot of people in drama who were luvvie and precious but he wasn't one of them. He just got on with his life."

Most of the battles that came his way were internal and did nothing to dent the public image of a show refreshed by the arrival of its new star and twice-weekly schedule. Some were amusingly trivial, like the exchange of snippy memos between John and his old friend (and fellow ugly sister), Bill Sellars, over the saga of Davison's hair. This needed to be short for an *All Creatures Great and Small* special (which Sellars was producing) and long for the series of *Doctor Who*, which would start shooting immediately afterwards. John wrote: "I do hope an acceptable compromise can be reached with regard to Peter Davison's hair length as in the first story to be filmed of the next season of *Doctor Who*, Peter will be seen swimming underwater."

Sellars teased back: "I would have thought hair length underwater could be covered up by a bathing cap or general snorkel gear. Have we any guarantee that Peter Davison will have any hair left at all by the time he resumes filming for you? We are, of course, concerned that his hair is not caught in a threshing machine while filming for us."

The previous year, however, Davison's availability had presented significant headaches. Regarded as key BBC1 talent and not exclusively as Doctor Who, he was one of the stars of an ongoing (and now forgotten) sitcom about two brothers, called *Sink or Swim*. The uninspired controller of BBC1, Alan Hart, wanted to keep this going. *Doctor Who* was a bedrock of his winter season, so he decided that, to avoid overlap, *Sink or Swim* should transmit in the autumn. But this meant that it would have to be recorded during the summer of 1982, forcing a two-month shutdown in production for *Doctor Who*. On 6th October 1981, John Morell, head of programme planning, noted drily: "I can imagine there will be much gnashing of teeth," and indeed, John entered the ensuing row with gusto, even, briefly, suggesting it might require a recast.

"There were all these arrangements," remembers Matthew Waterhouse, "and John worked very hard to make it work. But I stood in the bar with Gary and he was saying, 'It's absolutely disgraceful – the man [Davison] should be grateful to have one job and we shouldn't be having to work around him."

Finally, John was forced to surrender and alter his schedule, sending all concerned a memo in which he warned prophetically, as it turned out, "I would point out that the *Doctor Who* schedule is now very tight and there is little manoeuvrability with regard to any technical and servicing problems. Indeed... the final episode will be Sypher-dubbed very close to transmission." His only pyrrhic victory was the controller giving his "undertaking that the production run of *Doctor Who* must not be interrupted in this way in 83/84".

This was of little consequence when, in the autumn of 1982, the BBC was plunged into yet another round of industrial action. Having to work so close to the wire meant that there was not enough leeway to rescue all the affected episodes. On 25th November 1982, the planned finale, Eric Saward's four-part Dalek story, *Warhead*, had to be abandoned, its story code bumped onto the next show in production. The director of the cancelled show was John's old friend Peter Grimwade. On the day the news was made final, Grimwade took his team – and Saward – to commiserate over lunch at Television Centre. But, whether by accident or design, he omitted to ask John. The resulting row has become part of the folklore of the programme, an oft-quoted example of producer as diva. "It was a lunatic situation," Saward told *Starburst* magazine in 1986. "We get back [to find] John Nathan-Turner had been shouting and screaming all over the building, 'How dare they all go off to lunch together and not invite me?' He was furious and it's so silly. 'How dare they? I am the one who does the hiring and firing round here – how dare he take my script editor to lunch and not me?' He took that absolutely as an out-and-out insult and that was a contributing factor to why Peter was never invited back. Pathetic, isn't it?"

John later gave his own version of events to *Doctor Who Magazine.* "I went to ask Saward and Grimwade for a lunchtime drink to drown our sorrows, only to discover that they had already left with the rest of the production team, excluding only myself and the associate. I had not been invited to the wake. I was deeply upset and annoyed. I blame Saward. If one insists on playing two roles on a production, ie being the script editor and the writer, then one makes sure you don't have two faces as well. It's not at all attractive. I tackled him about this later and he simply didn't appreciate that the producer, or indeed the associate, could be affected as much by the situation as he, the writer. It took a long while for us to recover from my outburst about loyalty and, in some ways, I don't think we ever properly did."

"It did unravel," says mutual friend Carol Snook. "Granny Grumble [Grimwade] was very upset about it. That was a terrible misunderstanding which was stirred up and which should never have happened. He liked John and hadn't deliberately left him out at all. He blamed Gary for stirring it up because they were the same sort of era but Granny was directing and Gary wasn't."

During the following season, when a rechristened *Warhead* finally went before the cameras as *Resurrection of the Daleks,* the director was not Grimwade but Matthew Robinson. During location filming in London's Shad Thames, he had his own experience of one of John's sudden explosions. "Even these days I am still pained to think of it," says Robinson. "We stayed friends – indeed he offered me another show, so it clearly didn't mean a lot to him but as a freelance director it was a very vicious public attack and completely unjustified.

"I was just saying I was quite excited about the sequence I'd dreamt up and telling Eric about it. John wasn't around at the time: it wasn't as though I did it in front of him and ignored him. Then he strolled up and just completely bawled me out. It was quite shocking in the manner in which it was delivered –

WHETHER YOU LIKE IT OR NOT

face contorted, shaking with rage over something so, in my mind, unimportant. Surely, he could merely have had a quiet word in my ear that that was not the way he wanted things to happen on his show? I'd have abided by it in future, the incident blowing over in a couple of minutes. I think it's unforgivable, frankly. I can see absolutely no reason why I shouldn't discuss with the writer what shots I am taking."

"I wonder how he'd feel," postulated John in his own memoir, "if the boot was on the other foot now that he's producing *Byker Grove*? A little differently, I suspect."

But Robinson disagrees. "I don't run my sets on the basis of hierarchy; I run them on the basis of everybody working together. I'd discuss shots with the actors. The row was like water off a duck's back to him; perhaps, rather, it was just part of his life's rich pattern. I myself harboured no long-term grudge."

Television has always been brimming with behind-the-scenes divas and drama queens. John's BBC contemporaries included producer/directors like Stewart Morris and Michael Hurll who screamed, shouted and bullied their way through work on a day-to-day basis. Powerful women execs like Esther Rantzen and Biddy Baxter were lethal in heels and no less unpredictable or frightening. For all his sudden, sometimes inexplicable, tantrums, John was not in the same league. Even Saward admitted that "incidents such as the lunchtime row were not a common occurrence".

Robinson proposes an interesting theory about John the producer. "It was like there were three separate John Nathan-Turners – one for the pre-production, one for the production and one for the post-production period. He was mostly first class during pre-production, an ideal producer, very supportive and enthusiastic, particularly if one came up with good casting ideas. He was relatively flexible with the scripts if you had a slightly better idea – which was unusual in a producer, particularly in those days. He was very enthusiastic and he loved big ideas – the bigger the idea you could go to him with, almost the better he liked it.

"During production, 50–60 per cent of the time he was fine but the moment the pressure began to build then he became a bit of a different animal and got quite irritable and very defensive of the traditions of shooting *Doctor Who* and indeed very aware of the hierarchy on the shoot. He became very much the big producer and you were very much under his control and he didn't like you putting a foot wrong at all.

"In post-production he was fine, mainly, but very pernickety about certain points. There were a couple of times when I tried to extend a shot by slowing it down but he spotted that and absolutely wouldn't have it at all – I don't quite understand why – he'd got a bee in his bonnet about tricked-up shots but, frankly, I would have thought the whole thing was tricked up. On music I had a pretty free rein with the composer and, generally, he was very supportive.

"He had absolute commitment to *Doctor Who* – you've got to really love the programme that you're making and John completely lived and breathed it."

Actor Mark Strickson, now an eminent producer himself, agrees. "What does a producer do? If a programme is a success, it's a team effort – if a programme is a failure, it's the producer's fault. I know that from bitter experience. John led from the front – he had more energy than anyone else. He would be there all hours of the day and if you put as much energy into *Doctor Who* as he did, he had enormous respect for you and would give you the time of day."

For all John's ambition and despite his great skill at making a little go a long way, the programme's budget was still a significant cross to bear. He had already attempted to get an increase directly from Hart's predecessor as controller, Bill Cotton, working hard on a carefully thought out presentation, "giving him carefully backed up facts and figures why we needed more money," as John told DWAS fanzine *TARDIS* in 1988. "And he let me rabbit on and he let June [Collins – the production associate] throw me the figures and at the end of it, he said, 'John – I loved last season. It was terrific. All I want is another 26 exactly the same.'"

The BBC maintains a strange financial caste system where a programme's potential budget is capped by the slot in which it is going to transmit. "*Doctor Who* was in an early evening slot which didn't get that much money," explains drama department manager Marcia Wheeler. "There was this peculiar idea that programmes made for small children could be made for small money, which I never understood. You still had to use full-sized actors!"

"One of the things that astonished me," says writer and script editor Chris Bidmead, "was that here was a show that went out worldwide and earned a lot of money and yet the time and budgets were so restricted. Once I understood how broad the appeal of the show was, I couldn't understand why they were being so mean. I came to the conclusion that the people upstairs didn't really care."

"There is no doubt about it," says David Reid, then the head of series and serials. "Floating around at that time – and I never discussed this with John at all because it would have been unfair – but there were many people, controllers included – who every year would go, 'Ummm, I *suppose* we go on with *Doctor Who*?' There was that feeling about it. It's what nowadays you would call a cost-effective programme. If you were looking for cuts in budgets, you could always take something off *Doctor Who* and you could still get the same number of programmes. My yearly brief was, 'Here's £26 million – we want 200 hours of drama.' It was almost like, 'Give it to me by the yard.' If you've got a banker like *Doctor Who* and you know what it's costing and that John will bring it in on budget – and more importantly, you haven't got another idea to replace it – you locked that off and studios knew what they were doing, how many episodes, how many personnel. It had considerable advantages.

"But it was John's enthusiasm for the show that really kept its momentum up. Things like, 'What about a Christmas special?' or getting all the Doctors together again, or what about the *Doctor Who* conventions? It kept a sort of impetus for that year and the year after but without those things, without John's input, it would otherwise have faded and gone much sooner."

John was forever beady for any gimmick that might give the series a boost or grab some press attention. From the first, he believed that filming abroad was one way of refreshing the show, with its necessary reliance on locations close to London. He tried to persuade Disney to let him film a story in their Florida theme park: "Our story, by an American writer, would be written specifically to incorporate the visit to Disney World by the Doctor." But he had underestimated the rigidity of their corporate mind-set. On 7th May 1981, Ami Halling from Walt Disney Productions broke the news that "it is against our policy to allow settings like Disneyland and Walt Disney World to be used as background for a programme in a non-Disney television series."

The following summer, however, he did rake together the cash for a lightning shoot to Amsterdam, for the story *Arc of Infinity*. Writer Johnny Byrne was invited to deliver the goods in a letter dated 1st October 1981. "We are allowing ourselves the luxury of filming in Amsterdam, which, of course, means that our story must be very strongly rooted there. Tegan, who was left on Earth at the end of story seven, is in Amsterdam on holiday. No longer a stewardess she becomes involved, accidentally, in some sort of criminal activity. Ideally, this activity should not include smuggling drugs, stealing diamonds, Dutch masters or the plans of the latest strain of tulip. Neither should her involvement be overtly political. Meanwhile, the Doctor is locked in some enormous tussle elsewhere, which eventually leads him to Amsterdam, a reunion with Tegan, a possible link between their respective difficulties, followed by a satisfactory conclusion. The above said, Amsterdam and what can be created in a television studio, is your oyster."

Arc of Infinity launched the 20th season of *Doctor Who*. This was generally felt to be something of a disappointment, curtailed of its spectacular Dalek conclusion and slightly weighed down by the continuity conceit, pointed out by Ian Levine and used by John in publicity, that each story would feature someone or something from the Doctor's past. Production became increasingly fraught as strikes disrupted the tightly planned schedule. One story in particular, *Terminus*, might fairly have been rechristened *Interminable*. It was directed by Mary Ridge, a one-time staff director, for whom John had worked as an AFM on *Owen MD*. Ridge, old school and approaching retirement, found herself out of her depth among the strenuous demands of *Doctor Who*'s frantic rehearse/record schedule. She was unlucky too. She battled with one hurdle after another, from problems with scenery to costumes and delays caused by strike action and when, during the final evening's recording, it became obvious that an entire day would be needed to complete the serial, John lost his temper and stormed out of the gallery. "He went ballistic about that," says production associate June Collins. "She was quite sweet and I felt a bit sorry for her, really."

"He did upset her greatly," says Davison, "because she didn't finish and that was a sort of crime."

It didn't look good and the party for departing cast member Sarah Sutton (who, in any case, would now need to return to complete her contribution) was a muted affair. But fellow producer, Joe Waters, has some sympathy with John's position. "I was pressured from above into using Mary on *Dixon of Dock Green*," he recalls. "The result was not a happy collaboration. She was extremely hard-working and I gave her some of the best scripts but she would burst into tears if I criticised anything or made suggestions to improve the episode."

Davison, well known to loathe tension in his working environment, found the making of this constantly interrupted second series a strain. "I really wasn't very happy with it," he says. "It was a bit flabby, story-wise and we ran out of money.

"The directors were part of the problem. A lot of them just didn't really understand the story, so you'd end up explaining the story to them. As a lot of producers do now, I felt that John leant towards directors who he could push around so that there would be a lot of bullying going on about certain things, quite often to get the thing done. And maybe that was necessary. But they weren't very spirited. We had nice people, like Ron Jones, who was a perfectly affable person but who never seemed to really grasp what was going on. Peter Moffatt also never knew what was going on but did it in such a charming way that actually you could forgive him anything. He'd had a long career and did in a way stand up to John and was actually a bit stronger than one suspected.

"When I left *Doctor Who* and moved on to a series called *Anna of the Five Towns*," continues Davison, "I was directed by Martyn Friend. He was the first really good director that I'd worked with. Before that it was all jobbing series directors. But Martyn on *Five Towns* and David Tucker on *A Very Peculiar Practice* never would have done *Doctor Who*. When I was doing *Doctor Who*, I remember thinking quite seriously – and I even talked to John about this – that I could direct – because I always seemed to know much more about it than the directors. You'd be going, 'Why don't we do a shot here?' They weren't interested. I did have the idea that things should be moving and not lots of shots of everyone standing there going, 'So what now Doctor?' But it wasn't until I left and worked with Martyn and David that I suddenly realised how little I knew about directing.

"John was ahead of his time in that he was the first of the producers who I worked with who imposed their will more than I think they should have done. Really, I think he interfered too much. When I worked with another staff producer, Ken Riddington, what he did so well was that he would hand it to his director and, apart from complaining about the number of extras, he would leave him to it. John's problem is a problem which I think affects quite a lot of series now – where the producer thinks they know better than the writers or the directors. It's an imposing of their control. He shouldn't have had that firm a vision in his head. Almost always producers like that make the show worse."

"John was the best producer I ever worked with," counters director Fiona Cumming. "His judgment for the programme was the best. The way he could judge people. He was the one who put together the team, you see. If somebody didn't work, he had no compunction about getting rid of them. It does seem that the various major fall-outs that John had were in the main with male colleagues. Perhaps the regard he had for his mother left him with a respect and a protective attitude towards women? We had a couple of spats when I felt I was being pushed and dug my heels in but these were not long lasting and didn't affect our regard for each other. Professionally I trusted him completely. He knew me well enough not to give me the ones with the Daleks and other Metal Mickeys – mine were the more fantasy based ones. He played to my strengths."

"He was very manipulative," recalls another director, Michael Morris, "but for the good of the show. He lived it and cared about it so much. I was the new boy, learning my craft and I always felt that he was on my side. He was beautifully flamboyant. When he offered me the job, he called me into his office and said, 'Sit down, I've got something to say. If you get rid of those terrible Hush Puppies you're wearing, you can direct a *Doctor Who*.'"

The one director for whom Davison reserves effusive praise is also the only director to have worked both on the "classic series" and the 21st-century version – Graeme Harper. "I would agree that John was impulsive and quick-tempered," says Harper. "If something went wrong, he'd shout. Heads would roll. People jumped. If he got upset, you knew it was serious – he wanted it now, get on with it, do this. The whole of making *Doctor Who* was about time – you had no time to make it properly, that was the problem. But I think a lot of it was really good – John really brought it into the modern world – so it didn't creak."

Neither did Harper feel unduly pressured or bullied by John: "He just gave me my head and said, 'Do it your way, there's no house style – just make sure the Doctor's the hero.' I could shoot it any way I wanted, which was brilliant. He was trying to keep it moving forward all the time."

One way in which he achieved this was in the constant turnover of regular characters. John was never scared by a change in the core cast. His robust attitude was that the comings and goings of Doctors and companions helped to keep the show fresh and talked about and, from a practical point of view, avoided the Tom Baker trap of any one actor developing delusions of grandeur. "I like him for doing that," says Russell T Davies, "although I was obviously safer with those sort of choices. When you make those changes, it's a burst of energy and newness. But I couldn't really work out how much of it was planned – I mean, Turlough's departure seemed really quite random. I love Tegan – she's one of my favourite companions ever and much underestimated but even then I was a writer and I sat there with that departure scene going, 'Oh come on, there's a lot better ways to write that.' Surely if you knew in scene one that she's leaving, then why haven't you built up to this?"

"We were much more disposable and interchangeable," shrugs Janet Fielding.

"It was this vision he had," believes Sarah Sutton, "of the programme being in the public eye and how you generate interest – getting rid of a companion and bringing in a new one was a trick to hook an audience. I would happily have stayed but I wasn't given the choice."

When John decided to dispense with Sutton's services, he gave his reasons in a letter dated 3rd March 1982: "I wanted to let you know that I am not proposing to ask for an option on your services beyond the current contract. Nyssa will leave the TARDIS sometime during the next season. This is no reflection on your portrayal, which I must say has been super, but merely that I feel the companions should change every couple of years."

Davison, who had become close to Sutton, wasn't happy with the decision. "It was another thing that we disagreed over. I felt that if he wanted to get rid of companions, I should have continued with Sarah because – and I may have been wrong about this – she was the most sympathetic character to the

Doctor. What happened is that he would end up with Janet – through no fault of her own – sort of gritty, feisty and never wanting to be there or wherever we went – and then he got Turlough, Mark, who was trying to kill me all the time. In a way, he was trying to get to the point that Russell T Davies achieved so brilliantly, which was to make an interesting companion, but he missed the real, simple truth that you simply have to make the companion an interesting character. You can't just make them feisty and bolshy or trying to kill you – you have to give them a proper character."

Mark Strickson started filming as alien public schoolboy Turlough during the summer of 1982. His arrival in the programme came about after some subterfuge worthy of the devious character he played: "I was in a series called *Angels*. When one of the lead actors, Al Ashton, became ill, they wrote me in as a regular. While that was very gratifying, I didn't really want to be in *Angels*. I asked my agent, Jan Evans, if I was up for anything else and she said, 'Yes, *Doctor Who* – but they're not going to see people for another three weeks or so.' So I took history in my own hands! Because I was a regular in a series, everybody knew me and I was able to walk into Union and Threshold House, find John's door and introduce myself. He knew who I was because Gary [Downie] worked as a production manager on *Angels*. I said, 'If you've got ten minutes, this is the situation – I don't particularly want the part in *Angels* – I would much rather do *Doctor Who* and if you'd audition me for it, I'd be very grateful.' I realised I was stepping out of line. John was terribly friendly and approachable. Here was a chance for him to poach somebody that Julia [Smith, producer of *Angels*] wanted and that was interesting to him. But I have to say, too, that I was right for the part. Eric came in. They said, 'We think you could do this part really well – don't tell anybody but we'll offer it to you.'

"John came from near Birmingham – so do I – he wore his heart on his sleeve and I wear my heart on my sleeve – we're both very open, honest people. We got on from day one – from the moment I walked in that office I thought, 'What a nice guy.' He was enormously kind. An example of that is on the first day's filming. You've got to remember there's no rehearsal for filming so I was establishing Turlough as a character on location. I did my first scene and he came across and put his arm round me and said, 'Let's have a little chat,' and said, 'Could you do Turlough with a posher accent?' – I said, 'John, I could but it wouldn't be natural – it wouldn't be me. And Turlough does come from another planet. He is pretending to be a public school so I'm hoping it will work and people will almost think there is something wrong with this public schoolboy – I'm not Rupert Everett.'

"He said, 'If that is better for you, I'm happy. You go that route. Because you're in this for the long run and I want you to have a performance you can repeat.' And this is how good John was – I want you to give a performance you can give every episode and doesn't change. There's no point in damaging an actor but a lot of producers would have told me to do what they wanted. I found John very protective of me. We had a very healthy, strong relationship."

As Strickson was settling in, Davison was struggling with the decision on whether he would continue beyond the agreed third season. "I think that if the third year had been the second year," he explains, "I probably would have stayed. I'm glad I did it but I'm glad I left when I did."

John was disappointed but, not being stupid, he wasn't surprised either. He began to plot the new shape of the programme, setting himself the challenge of writing out Davison, Fielding and Strickson, and finding two new leads to play the sixth Doctor and companion all within the space of the next season – the 21st. Hindsight, useless though it always is, tells us that he might, perhaps, have been wiser to attempt more of an evolution instead of revolution, keeping some continuity of companions perhaps, but his confidence was at its peak and the reckless bravura of the revamp reflected this.

Fielding was the first to go. She'd been a hit as the "mouth on legs" Tegan, and, despite her reservations about the show and the part, had already agreed to a contract for 22 of the 26-episode run. This was curtailed to just 14 (though she was paid for the unmade episodes), making her the first of the established faces out of the door. "He had to get everybody off and I had a pretty good run. Funnily enough, John and I became really friendly after I left the show. Looking back, I think if he'd left with me, Mark and Peter, everyone would have gone 'fantastic'. He would have left on a high."

Strickson was next to bow out, in another story with overseas locations, *Planet of Fire*. Here the volcanic Spanish island of Lanzarote played both itself (as a sop to the Tourist Board) and the alien world of Sarn, a location suggested to John by director Fiona Cumming, who had holidayed there. Even shooting in October, it was going to be hot and John broached the subject of what Strickson might wear. "He didn't insist and he actually put it in a very heterosexual way – 'Look, the girls are always showing off their legs, Jamie wore a kilt, you've been in a black suit all this time, come on, get your legs out.' I used to cycle from Waterloo, miles and miles a day, and I remember coming in wearing shorts one day and Janet saying, 'You've got bloody good legs, Mark.' When John asked me to get into shorts, I remembered that and I thought, 'Why not?' I flattered myself that I might become a gay icon and that some girls might like it too!"

Make-up designer on the shoot was John's old flame, Liz Rowell. At the fag end of the previous, curtailed, season, she had worked in very tense circumstances on the nonsensical two-parter, *The King's Demons*. This tension had been unwittingly caused by John. Aware that Rowell was in a long-term relationship with production manager Jeremy Silberston, John had thoughtfully requested the pair of them to work on the serial together. Just before production began, Silberston left Rowell for another woman. "I should never have done [*The King's Demons*]," she says, "because it was very difficult. Jeremy obviously wanted nothing to do with me. I had been given the choice by the make-up department who'd said, 'It's too soon.' It was awful but John was wonderfully supportive to me – he'd always come to pick me up and take me to the bar or the restaurant. Jeremy had put me and my assistants in a completely different hotel miles away from the him and the rest of the unit. He was probably embarrassed – maybe he didn't want to face me. John said, 'I've got a foreign trip coming up. Would you like to go to Lanzarote?' I said, 'Oh yes!'

"That was lovely except for ghastly Peter Wyngarde (who John had cast) – he was awful." The main guest star in *Planet of Fire*, he was "overweight and had dyed hair, all backcombed and lacquered. Because it was an all-male cast, I took the least items possible – nothing very special – but the minute we got to Lanzarote, Peter Wyngarde said, 'Have you got the eyelashes?' so the poor prop buyer Paul had to scout the island looking for some eyelashes. Peter obviously didn't like ladies and would do anything to put me down. He wanted eyeliner and something round his lips as well as the eyelashes so it all began to look like drag. I wouldn't go as far as he wanted and so he said, 'Oh, darling, you need glasses,' and John marched up and said, 'Don't you speak to her like that – she's very capable. She's been here many years. She's very good at her job.' He would back you to the hilt whereas a lot of producers would say 'Oh, darling, don't worry about that. Keep him sweet.'"

Rowell's other challenge was to create the "look" for John's latest discovery, Nicola Bryant, signed to play new companion, Peri Brown. "I thought long hair was important," says Bryant. "I said, 'I'm playing an American college girl,' and in those days, they were all about long hair. The bob was Liz's idea and John agreed with her. I did get my agent to argue it. It was one of those bizarre things where I actually felt it was very much Liz's decision and I just totally disagreed with it. It was very unpleasant. I thought she didn't like me or something. It was very personal and horrible but somehow John had been convinced that this would make me look even younger."

Rowell confesses to feeling "awful" that Bryant felt this way. "It is my favourite ladies' hairstyle and suited her face shape," she says. "Neither John nor I could remember that style being used on any previous episodes and we wanted her to look a bit different. I think she really suited that look."

"Before they cut my hair," says Bryant, "there was a Peri passport shot. John asked me to send an old one to the props guys. I didn't have one so he asked me to be imaginative. I put my hair into plaits and took a black-and-white shot in a photo booth. He didn't see the shot until *after* I'd had my haircut. He went all gooey over it saying how adorable I looked and asked how old I was when the shot was taken. I told him, 'About three weeks younger than I am now.' His face fell. He was genuinely shocked. He didn't speak for quite a while – as though he was computing something. He then said something like, 'So you could have looked like this now... for the show?' He explained to me that he'd wanted me to look even younger and then maybe mature on my journey with the Doctor. A nice idea. He'd been led to believe that the new haircut would make me look younger. I was never told he was thinking about that, otherwise I would have suggested it. Poor John!"

Bryant was presented to the world as the show's first American companion. The truth was that she had grown up in Guildford and was faking it or, as Bryant herself puts it, "I was doing what Dominic West and Damian Lewis are doing in reverse, in American TV today – but I was doing the whole thing under cover." Had the deception taken place and been uncovered 25 years later, it might well have provoked a media storm of criticism and rebuke. As it was, the British press accepted the fairy story and asked no awkward questions.

"She was basically telling us that she was American," says Davison. "She was speaking in a kind of weird voice. You could obviously tell that her accent wasn't very good and it was clear to me as, at the time, I was married to an American. I think she said, 'Oh I'm American, but I was brought up over here, you know.' I was very aware that the Americans would not buy into it. How could you do that and not think that you're going to be caught out?"

If he, too, suspected that there was something fishy about his new signing's story, John was giving nothing away. "It started," explains Bryant, "because my agent had seen me playing an American in *No, No, Nanette*. When he got a casting breakdown for Peri, the BBC said they were only looking at genuine Americans. He didn't have anybody on his books but he thought, 'I just saw that girl in the drama school,' so he contacted me, thinking I was genuinely American. When he found out the truth, he said, 'I want you to do the whole thing American and if you get the job then we'll tell them.'

"At one of the auditions they had a film crew from Denver making a documentary and they were asking about my school. The story was that I was half American – my father, who was dead, had to be American! I just acted my way through it. It got very complicated. My final audition turned out not to be a final audition – and this says something about him – John didn't want to phone the agent and say I'd got it; he wanted to say it to me face to face. That was wonderful. Then he had to impress upon me that I wasn't allowed to tell anyone. And I was like, 'Er... well, I'm going to have to tell my husband,' at which point he fell off his chair – 'You have a husband?' and I was like 'Yeah' – 'That's something we're going to have to talk about.'

"At this point, I'm still doing the American accent and I'm thinking I'm not sure what I do at this point – I'd better ask my agent. I said, 'Well, now we need to tell them...' and he went, 'Oh, yes, in due course we will – let me sort all the contracts out first.' After everything was finalised and signed he came back and said, 'I think it's best if you carry on being American.' Everyone goes, 'Oh, JN-T made you pretend to be American but it was my agent.'

"It did put me in a weird position," she admits. "I had to keep it up the whole time I was with Peter. The only time I was off was on the phone when I got to call home. My husband was very supportive – he was American so I had a base to check every sound and every word. Weirdly, I never really had the confession with John. It was one of those things – it was never said. It was a strange relationship. Part of it was absolutely beautiful and part of it was difficult."

John's primary concern remained that the press and public shouldn't know that Bryant was married. "He was like, 'You've got to be available – that's your job.' You are hired for various qualities, one of which is your appeal to the male audience. At the time it was just how it was. Now as a mature woman I have issues with it but in reality, it didn't bother me at all. I just thought it's part of the job, suck it up and deal with it. Everything was controlled – when I look back on it now, it seems ridiculous – it was like something from the 40s. I did say to John, 'I'm really bad at lying – please don't make me,' and he said, 'You can't be – you're an actress!'"

Bryant complied, wearing her wedding ring on her right hand and "if I went to a West End opening or something like that, I went with a lovely gay actor friend, Dursley McLinden [who later appeared in *Remembrance of the Daleks*]. Luckily, Scott, my husband, was a very nice man and he was great mates with Dursley so it was a joke amongst us all.

"In the end, it was Colin who blew the whistle about me being British. My husband and I had been invited to dinner at his house with his wife Marion. It seemed wrong to be 'acting' in that situation, so I told them the truth. Colin admitted he had no idea. He thought both Scott and I were American. He kept it under wraps until he left the show and although he mentioned it in a newspaper article, there was very little response, probably because there was so much more going on at the time of Colin's departure. I had, of course, already left the show by then myself."

39-year-old Colin Baker was the final addition to John's gallery of changing faces – and the most significant. Bright, handsome, a good, established character actor, he was an unexpected choice to play the sixth Doctor. The journey to his surprise casting had started the previous spring. "It all started with a phone call from my agent. I was doing a play in Brighton and my agent phoned up and said, 'You've been offered a part in *Doctor Who*' And the very first thing I said to him was 'Oh dear, that means I'll never play the Doctor!' My agent said, 'Well, there's fat chance of that!'"

The story was *Arc of Infinity* and Lynn Richards was the AFM. She remembers: "Ron Jones [the director] was casting and he wanted Colin as Maxil, a guard. I knew about the part Colin had played in *The Brothers* and I said, 'Oh, I don't like him, no, thank you very much,' but Ron said, 'No, I want him.'

"My job was to make sure the actors were there at the right time on the first day of rehearsals for the read-through. In those days, very few people had answerphones, never mind cell phones. I got through to everybody except Colin. I thought, 'I don't believe it – the guy I can't stand, I'm having such trouble with!' I was ringing him at midnight. I'd let the agent know but you never totally trust agents – you had to make sure you spoke to the person yourself. So I kept calling and calling and calling and in the end I got in early to set up the rehearsal room and the only person there was Colin. He came over and said. 'Lynn, I'm so sorry, I've been so terrible.' I fell in love with him straight away."

That same morning, Baker met John for the very first time. "He went after that and came back a few days later for the producer's run. That's the first time I really spoke to him. He came up to me afterwards and said, 'Are you under the impression that this programme is called *Maxil the Guard*?' and I said, 'No, it's called *Doctor Who*' – 'That's not what I'm getting from watching your performance!' I said, 'Well, nobody thinks of themselves as a bit part in anybody else's life. Maxil is in his universe in which the Doctor is playing a fleeting part.' He said, 'Yes, that's probably true but in any scene that the Doctor's in, my eye is drawn to what you are thinking and doing' – I said, 'Well, you don't have to look at me!' 'Can you tone it down a bit?' 'If you like, since you ask so nicely...' It was a nice opening relationship because I'd been in shows where producers just come up and say, 'That performance is over the top. It's just ridiculous.' But something about it had piqued his interest, because he was over the top himself. I did tone it down a bit."

John later nicknamed Baker "Archie" because of his arch wit and turn of phrase. "We both love the bon mot. I've always got on well with overtly camp men," smiles Baker. "John could be very queeny and I'm a kind of gay manqué, really. I can be camp with the best of them and I rather enjoy it – I find it fun."

The story was recorded and Baker thought that was the last he would hear about *Doctor Who*. "But because we'd been such bosom pals," says Richards, "we asked Colin to our wedding reception. He was the life and soul."

There was a strong *Who* contingent at the reception, held on 22nd August 1982, including Peter Davison, Sarah Sutton, Eric Saward and Jane Judge. "And John and Gary were there too," says Baker. "I'm not very gregarious, normally and I nearly didn't go but I liked the girl so much so I went, with my wife, Marion, and even she said afterwards, 'Gosh, you were on form today.' It was one-liners and having fun. By that time, John knew that Peter Davison was leaving and when he left, he said to Gary, 'I think I've found my new Doctor' – meaning me.

Baker heard nothing more for some months, until John rang him out of the blue and invited him to lunch on 10th June 1983. "I still had some vestigial fame from *The Brothers* and I remember saying to Marion, 'I know what this is about – he's got some charity gig in Brighton that he wants me to do.' We had lunch and then he dropped the bombshell that he was thinking – it wasn't an offer – he was thinking of offering me the part. It's not cool to say this but I went, 'Yes, please!' and tried not to show it because normally you're supposed to say, 'Oh, I don't know... It's typecasting.' I don't care about being typecast, cast is the main thing!"

At 4.30 p.m. on 22nd June, Baker returned to Union and Threshold House, this time to meet John's boss and head of department, David Reid. "John and I had talked about the kind of eccentricities that you're looking for in a Doctor Who-type person. It was very much his fiefdom. I did make a mistake in casting the lead for an ongoing series. We'd got the rights to do *Miss Marple* and Guy Slater [the producer] had come to me and said, 'I know who I want – Joan Hickson,' and I said, 'Are you sure? I don't see it but Guy, you're the producer, if you want her you have her.' But Guy was right and I was wrong. I always felt that John knew 100 times more about *Doctor Who* than I did so I was very much in his hands. He brought Colin in to see me and said, 'That's the person I want,' and I said, 'Well, John you're the guy – OK, fine.' I did have reservations about the casting but they were in my head. I never said to John that I did – perhaps in retrospect I should. No, I felt that John knew entirely what he was doing. He needed backing not undermining."

"As I was driving to Threshold House," recalls Baker, "I was listening to the cricket on the radio and I waited till the very last second because it was the Birmingham Test and, to all intents and purposes, we'd lost it. Then up steps Botham and starts pasting it all around the place – and I thought, 'Bugger, I've got to go and meet this David Reid' – for the best job in my life – and I go in there and he's got the cricket on. So I start talking about cricket. JN-T hardly knew what these two people were talking about. We talked about cricket for a while and my memory of the conversation after that was that he said, 'You are aware of what kind of world you're entering?' I said, 'Yes' and he said, 'Well, good luck then.' That's how I remember it. John took me back to the office and loaded me up with tapes and sent me away and asked me to come back and tell him how I'd like to play it."

He returned for another lunch on 28th June, when John formally offered Baker the job. In view of the BBC's disappointment that Davison had only stayed for three seasons, this time the option would be extended for a minimum of four. Baker happily agreed the condition. "Peter Davison saw us having lunch together and says that he guessed!"

John swore Davison to secrecy but the news quickly began to leak. A delighted Ron Jones told Lynn Richards, who explains, "It was Ron who'd said to John, 'What about Colin?' The minute I heard, I thought Colin will actually be better than Peter because he's larger than life and a little bit eccentric. Then Colin rang me and said he was out of work. Knowing what I knew, I said, 'Don't worry, I'm sure something will come about.' That must have panicked him a bit because next thing, Colin rang John. John called me in straight away and said, 'How did you know, how did you know? I have to know where it came from.' Of course, I didn't want to tell him that Ron had told me but in the end, he literally slammed his fist down – 'TELL ME!' – so I said, 'I got it from Ron,' and then ran into the other room to ring Ron and say, 'John wants to see you – I gave it away, I'm so sorry.'"

Before long, the press were onto the story and, on 19th August, John hurriedly arranged a photo call to unveil his two new stars – Baker and Bryant. They looked relaxed, natural and attractive, with Baker wearing the same clothes he'd sported at Lynn Richards' reception the year before. By the time they actually began working together, both had been given top-to-toe John-friendly makeovers which, even for the 1980s, were a sight for sore eyes. Indeed, of all his leading ladies, Bryant was possibly the least fortunate. No matter how much Janet Fielding complains about the infrequency of her wardrobe changes ("Anthony Ainley's had more costumes than me!") or the skimpy styles she was made to wear, no matter that Sarah Sutton refers to her long-running Traken gear as "smelly" or that Davison branded the replacement "like something worn by a McDonald's waitress", more often than not, Bryant was packaged like a piece of meat in a parade of dayglo shorts and leotards. "It was a gay man's idea of what heterosexual men want," says Baker. "Poor Nicola hated it. But if you came and said, 'Nicola looks awful in that,' you'd be his enemy for a day or two.

If he asked for advice, he'd listen. John didn't respond to unwanted advice very well."

"The reason they bothered me," explains Bryant, "is that, like most women, you know what your assets are. I've got a nice smile and an hourglass figure. The outfit that I wore for the press release for Colin was mine but those shorts and leotards couldn't have been a worse look for my shape. That was the issue I had. If he wanted sexy, I could do sexy – it just wouldn't have looked like his idea. He had a very strong opinion of what sexy was and our two opinions were not the same. The day before the first shoot he rang me up with instructions about what to wear – 'Do you have any really short skirts? What's the shortest thing you've got?' and I said, 'Well, shorts.' These were shorts that you'd wear if you were at the beach so he said, 'Right, well bring those.' Then he said, 'What's the clingiest top you've got?' I didn't have anything in my wardrobe that fitted that bill at all. Bearing in mind I'd had five auditions and he'd not seen me in anything like that – I was wearing mostly jeans and American college sweatshirts – I was trying to dress as the character."

Baker came off even worse than his companion. John went through the motions of consulting him about what he might wear and, as Baker puts it, "the costume I described to JN-T was the one Chris Eccleston [who played the ninth Doctor] got. Why can't Doctor Who just have clothes?"

Instead, John commissioned costume designer Pat Godfrey to come up with a "totally tasteless" design, rejecting several early efforts, until approving an end result that was part-clown, part-carnival, a multicoloured nightmare of clashing patterns and eye-watering colour. As director Chris Clough puts it succinctly, "It was a horrible costume – just crap."

"Absolutely hideous," in the judgement of Godfrey's fellow designer, June Hudson. "She should have had the strength and the confidence to say, 'No, I'm sorry, I disagree with you.' His idea *could* have worked but it needed to be less in your face – the idea that it was somewhat bizarre. A gentleman can be eccentric and can still have enormous dignity and class. You'd say, 'OK, John, I see what you're heading for – how about eccentric? There are plenty of eccentric earls and nobles around.' It was not high quality enough either – it needed to be made by Mr Davis at Morris Angels – in expensive material, beautifully tailored – eccentric rather than garish."

"I seriously think that the costume was the greatest mistake in the history of television," says Russell T Davies. "To this day when it comes on screen, I think why did no-one pick up the phone and say, 'Dress him in a black suit'? One of the big problems with the show would have been solved with one phone call. That's how little care was being shown above John Nathan-Turner. I can quite understand his position – you're busy, you're tired, there's not enough money – you get too close to things. You can't always see your own mistakes. There were people sitting above him with very colourful mistakes screaming out of the television and they didn't even pick up the phone. I think that's disgraceful."

Years later, John himself admitted that the costume had been a mistake, telling *TARDIS* "It was totally my fault, I take the entire rap. It's not Pat Godfrey's fault. She came up with a very tasteful costume but I kept pushing it, saying, 'It's not tasteless enough.' I don't think that worked very well."

There is a theory that the coat was just a take on John's love of his Hawaiian shirts and that in insisting on dressing Baker in this way, in curling his hair and encouraging him to give an extravagant, theatrical performance, John was, even if subconsciously, casting himself in the part. "Oh I think absolutely," chuckles Peter Davison, "*absolutely* he was casting himself!"

"That makes total sense," agrees Sutton. "I think that's a fair point. *Doctor Who* was everything for John; it was his passion, his life, it encompassed him – and I think that's where it could have all gone wrong, not to be able to stand back from it. I think it was slightly dangerous in that way."

"Colin Baker did seem to be him," says Jonathan Powell. "I think that *Doctor Who* was his fantasy and he was Doctor Who. He got sort of trapped into this thing, which became his ego and he became synonymous with it. I remember absolutely thinking 'He's just creating something in his own image.' I'm sure that's true."

"It's kind of irresistible," says Davies, "but it can't be true! It's so obvious I keep wanting to deny it. It's weird."

"I've never heard that theory," says Matthew Waterhouse. "That's very interesting. Now you've mentioned it, it sounds quite convincing. So basically John thought he had become Doctor Who..? Yes, that's fascinating and certainly rings very true. He certainly behaved like that at conventions. He saw himself as the main star."

"I don't think so at all," refutes John's secretary, Sarah Lee. "You have to remember when you're shooting something multi-episodic and you've got very little time to make a lot of decisions, you look around you sometimes and think 'Maybe something bright and clashing, like this shirt?' No, he definitely wasn't trying to recreate himself. I think that's bullshit. He would be laughing up there and saying, 'Don't you think I would cast someone far better-looking?' That is not the case. With Colin, he was kind of looking for someone a bit cerebral maybe. Somebody who was going to be quirky and funny but a bit deeper. He saw this guy who was amusing and had a big personality."

"John and I were very different in most ways," says Baker himself, "but we did get on extremely well and we liked to giggle. I liked the work to be fun. John was like that too. With him, it was just a simple organic thing. Whatever job he'd done, if I'd met him and he was running my local garage, we'd have got on well. Very quickly after I started work for him, we would phone each other up. Just to tell gossip – he was an inveterate gossiper. 'Have you heard about so and so?' He loved showbiz and he loved having the status – he loved being the producer of *Doctor Who*, it's certainly true, and he was very protective of his domain."

Michael Morris, who was asked back to direct for Baker's first season, says that there were whispers about the casting within the department. "Colin Baker wouldn't have been my first choice, and I think a lot of people thought, 'Oh shit, what's John done now?'"

In December 1983, there was a changing of the guard in drama series and serials too. David Reid had decided to move on and return to writing. "It was a 24-hour-a-day job," he says. "I'm not sure we used the word 'stress' in those days. It's very adrenalin-making, which is actually very empowering. But Graeme McDonald had always said that head of series and serials was a job you should probably do for no more than about three years and I think he was probably right."

Reid had supported John and allowed him a level of autonomy unheard of now but fairly typical at the time. In the main, he had confined himself to commenting on scripts and screenings of finished episodes. Admitting that "I never, ever understood *Doctor Who*", he sometimes worried about the direction it was taking. For instance, when he'd read the scripts for *Snakedance*, he sent John a memo, urging, "I think you are making a mistake pursuing this line of storytelling. I genuinely believe it is far too abstract and obscure. I really haven't got a clue what actually happens in the last episode." He offered what he hoped were constructive suggestions. Down in the *Doctor Who* office, Saward raged, "the more I read this memo and the more I read *Snakedance*, the more convinced I'm [*sic*] David just doesn't like this sort of script. *Snakedance* does work. It is clear and does hang together." At John's behest, Saward composed a lengthy defence and explanation of his position, which John sent up to Reid as a joint effort. "Throughout the story we do learn all that is necessary," this argued. "The style of the story may be a little eccentric but is original and we feel, works very well indeed. As you will see, the other stories in the 1983 season are much more conventional sci-fi adventures. That being so, we feel there should also be room for a more unusual tale, especially when it is as well written as *Snakedance*." Whether he was convinced or not, Reid let them get on with it.

The search for Reid's successor was conducted discreetly. "Remember," says Reid, "those were the days when jobs like that were not advertised or boarded for – they were very much 'old boy network' appointments. Head of series and serials was not a job that too many people were falling over themselves to do – mainly, I think, because mostly it meant virtually giving up what most of us were good (or better) at – directing or producing. I certainly sounded out a couple of people, [producers] Guy Slater and David Askey. Graeme McDonald, I am fairly sure, 'put out feelers' to Michael Cox at Granada but Jonathan Powell was, as I recall, very much [director of programmes] Brian Wenham's front runner."

Powell was duly appointed and, as Colin Baker's first stories went into production, it fell to him to read the scripts and raise any concerns. Ironically, given what was to follow, John can be forgiven for not being too concerned by comments like this one, sent by Powell in a memo dated 24th April 1984: "I've now read *Attack of the Cybermen*... It seems to me to be a well-told story with some decent characterisation. In short a script which is coming along nicely." On 15th June 1984, he followed this with: "I enjoyed *The Two Doctors* and found *Vengeance on Varos* absolutely excellent."

But whatever he said on paper, Powell was no fan of *Doctor Who* – or John Nathan-Turner. He says, "My memory is that whenever he came into the office, what I really wanted is for him to leave. We didn't fight but we didn't get on. I don't think he understood quality work. There was just something about him. I wanted him to go – *and* his bloody programme actually."

John's world was about to fall apart.

EIGHT

HANKY PANKY

They tell me I'm up to no good
I should just settle down
But I don't wanna stay with just one man
I wanna sample what's around

Miquel Brown, *So Many Men, So Little Time*, 1983

In September 1983, I made my first visit to the *Doctor Who* studio. It was a seminal moment, not just because I was a fan, but because I already knew that Television Centre was the place I one day wanted to work. I'd been invited by John to write a set report on *Resurrection of the Daleks*. I can still conjure up the excitement I felt as the Central Line Tube snaked out of its tunnel revealing a first glimpse of that famous building. John's secretary, Sarah Lee, met me in reception with a big smile and took me to TC6, where the air was acrid with smoke guns and production manager Corinne Hollingworth was keeping order with a wonderfully imperious tone. "Will the Daleks *please* keep quiet! We *are* recording!"

It was a magical afternoon and by the end of it, I was already feeling a little punch drunk when John suddenly appeared from one side and smiled, "Had a good time?" Naturally, I assured him that I had. The smile was replaced with a frown. "I will get to see *every word*?" with the emphasis on *every word*. I don't know why he asked this – it was the deal that Marvel (the publishers of *Doctor Who Magazine* in those days) had with him. His blue pencil scored through my purple prose on a regular basis and he can't have forgotten that. But I nodded and reassured him. The smile returned. "Do you want a drink?"

The BBC Club is on the fourth floor of Television Centre. It was given a hideous corporate makeover in the early 2000s but even in its heyday, it wasn't an aesthetically pleasing place. Back then, the decor was motorway service station chic, and it was thick with cigarette smoke and heaving with people. The main part of the club was split level, the lower area leading to a roof terrace. A balcony fenced off the higher level and the *Doctor Who* crowd congregated next to this, some of them leaning on the rail (handy for spying on whoever was sitting below), with the bar just a few feet away behind them. I was star-struck and (unusually) tongue-tied. Rula Lenska (a guest star in *Resurrection*) was very much in evidence, tossing her mane of hair this way and that, laughing throatily at some gossip I couldn't hear. Janet Fielding seemed tiny in real life. Mark Strickson was entertaining a small group, looking flushed and animated. Weaving in and out of them all, exchanging a word here and a word there, John bought and dispensed a couple of rounds, raising an eyebrow when I asked for an orange and lemonade.

After a while, he came back to me and chatted for a few minutes, asking me where I was from and what I liked about the show. He seemed incredibly friendly. I was flattered. Then he asked me if I'd ever been to Brighton. I had, but long ago, as a small child. He told me he had a place there and that I should come and visit. I said I'd love to. Looking back, this seems ludicrously naive but then, for all my assumed confidence, I *was* ludicrously naive. John beckoned to someone I didn't recognise, who came over and smiled at me as we were introduced. This was Gary. More chit-chat followed and then I was asked a question, whispered in my ear, which stopped me in my tracks.

"Have you ever had two up you?"

It was noisy and I thought I must have misheard. The question was repeated and this time, as its meaning sank in, I felt myself blushing and the combination of a pint of sickly soft drink and sudden panic made my stomach turn over.

"Er... no, I haven't and I don't think I'd like that."

I felt very stupid. They were amused. "Oh, you're so fucking provincial," John said. I thought, "I come from Bishop's Stortford, I *am* provincial." But I said nothing because I couldn't think what to say. John rolled his eyes and moved off, giving me up and Gary followed him. I put down the empty glass and fled. I was 17 years old.

In the years that followed, I quite often told this story to friends, because in retrospect I did find it funny. It was a joke against myself – because I hadn't read any of the signs. John had been right – I was "fucking provincial".

That was my only "close encounter" with John, although about a year later there was a sequel, this time with Gary. I'd been told I could collect some *Two Doctors* production photos from Union House and that I should turn up at six thirty. I arrived early, waiting in the depressing little entrance, where a bored commissionaire behind a desk phoned up to the office to say I was there and then went back to his *Evening Standard*. Presently, someone rang back and I was told to make my way through to the lifts, where I'd be met. I walked along a long, thin corridor, with production offices either side, all deserted. Everyone must have gone home. I reached the lifts and waited. They were the kind you get in rundown hotels, small, noisy, arthritic. I could hear it creak its way down to me. The doors opened and there was Gary, all smiles, super-friendly. I stepped inside and felt immediately uncomfortable. There was barely enough room for both of us.

The lift had scarcely started its lumbering elevation when Gary said, "Ooh, I like that jumper. What's the logo?" and, without waiting for a reply, leant over and squeezed it. It was a Cecil Gee jumper, in bright blocks of colour and the logo happened to be positioned just above my right nipple. At the same time he was squeezing this, which hurt, he lunged forward and tried to stick his tongue in my mouth. I can still remember the sickly sweet aroma of his aftershave. For a moment, I froze, pinned against the side with Gary trying to thrust his tongue further in. Meanwhile, his other hand had released my nipple and slid between my legs, where it was forcefully investigating access.

The lift shuddered to a halt and, as the doors opened, I slid down and wrenched myself out from under him, haring off round the corner, feet slipping beneath me on the polished floor, along another long, thin corridor. There was no-one around here, either. I was thoroughly freaked and full of panic. My instinct, ridiculous and child-like as it may seem, was to hide. I shot into an office, closed the door and folded myself up under the desk, trying to slow down my breathing so that I could be as still and silent as possible. I heard Gary walk past and further on and then terror gripped me again at the thought that he would come back, find me and I'd be trapped here. I peered out from under the desk to see if there was anything I might use in self-defence. All there seemed to be were piles of scripts. I seized one and rolled it up tight. It would have to do. I waited.

Minutes crawled past and there were no returning footsteps. I began to feel scared that I would get locked in or find myself accused of being an intruder, which technically I now was. Eventually, I don't know how much later, I clambered out from under the desk and, still holding the rolled-up script, dashed back out into the corridor, retraced my steps and, shunning the horrible lift, pelted down the stairwell instead. Back in the entrance area, the commissionaire didn't look up from his paper as I sped past and found myself back in the welcome noise of Shepherd's Bush Green. It was only when I was on the Tube travelling home that I finally unrolled the script. It was a copy of *Timelash*, episode two.

For days afterwards, I expected a call to say that my services were no longer required by *Doctor Who Magazine*. In my head, obscurely and, looking back, quite wrongly, I felt that somehow it must have been my fault and that I was to blame. But it was never referred to and after a while I stopped worrying and began to see the funny and farcical aspect of it.

The significance of these stories is that I need to declare my own experience of the most controversial aspect of John's life – the degree to which he, and Gary, crossed lines in their dealings with the young men around them, over whom they exerted sometimes considerable influence. When I started researching this book, there were plenty of whispers and unsubstantiated reports about the "the dark side of their relationship", as Sophie Aldred puts it. "I don't know everything that went on," she told me. "There was quite a lot of stuff that I wouldn't have been comfortable with and I believe some of the fans may have suffered... young men."

"Interestingly," ruminates Colin Baker, "he never, ever saw me as someone who he would share that with – he might say, 'Oh that's a pretty one over there.' I used to stay with John and Gary when I was working in Brighton and they never remotely tried to hit on me – they never crossed the line. We had a kind of emotional connection and it was certainly nothing to do with his usual predatory attitude to males. But they used to tell me all sorts of things that I probably shouldn't have known, Gary in particular."

"I was on a visit to Brighton," recalls former Doctor Who Appreciation Society coordinator David Saunders. "We were all very merry. It was after one of their pantos and there were always two lads who, I think, were between 17 and 22 and, when it came to cabaret at the ball, appeared naked to the waist. I remember making some comment about how these lads were a delight to the eye and Gary said something to the effect of, 'Hand-picked, David, *and* tried and tested.' So I said, 'Do you mean..?' and he said 'Yes... and only two of them ever said no!'"

"I went to Southampton to see this panto," says director Alan Wareing, "and spent the night in the hotel. One of the chorus boys ended up in John's bed that night and the following morning this young bloke was at breakfast with him."

"John would quite often regale us with his sexual adventures," laughs Peter Davison.

Others are less relaxed about it. "While he was on stage at conventions, he had Gary going round checking out young lads," asserts Ian Levine.

"Gary was the fixer, I think," says Aldred.

"There were rumours that I used to hear," recalls John's secretary, Kate Easteal. "It's amazing that nobody went to the papers."

"John was a promiscuous guy and I had the impression he slept with a lot of people," says script editor Andrew Cartmel. "With the fans there's a line you shouldn't cross and the ultimate thing is if you're banging them, that's potentially really dangerous because there's the question of exploitation. John called them barkers. So instead of feasting with panthers, it was feasting with poodles!"

"I think you'll find there were an awful lot of people who had scars," believes close friend Grahame Flynn. "People younger than me who were out of their depth. I think that happened to a number of people."

"Certainly with the young men thing," says another close friend David Roden, "I think John would send Gary out to find people and bring them back. He was definitely the foot soldier. His endless stock chat-up line was, 'I could get you in *EastEnders.*' In that respect, John was very passive and Gary very active."

"I know that Gary hit on a couple of guys at our conventions," says Ron Katz, who ran the Doctor Who Fan Club of America. "That happened here."

But Norman Rubenstein of the rival Spirit of Light organisation is adamant. "That never happened with us. I would guess that John might have kept a tighter leash on Gary because there was a lot of press there so it would have been noted and commented on."

"He didn't pursue people," maintains Gary Russell, a fan with a long and multi-faceted *Doctor Who* career. "He didn't need to – because if someone turned him down, there were another six people at a convention who might not."

"They were having sex with young men in their hotel room," Levine continues. "They only got these young men because he was the producer. I can't understand why they haven't spoken out…"

It's a valid question. Although I did meet some people who felt that their treatment at the hands of John and Gary was inappropriate, it would not be true to say that I've found anyone willing to testify to coercion or abuse. The gay age of consent in the 1980s was 21. Clearly, neither John nor Gary saw this a barrier, but then nor did thousands of other gay men at the time. Many felt it was unjust and unrealistic and when, in 2001, it was finally lowered to 16, in line with heterosexual law, there was little outrage. But I don't believe that John and Gary showed much curiosity about the precise age of their potential conquests. They were highly sexed men with broad tastes and it clearly became almost a reflex action to explore the possibility of an encounter with the young men they met who might seem available, interested or persuadable.

They belonged to the first generation of homosexuals liberated by law in 1967. The revolution in culture and attitude that brought these reforms about wasn't confined to a gay sensibility, as actress Jacqueline Pearce recalls. "It was liberating because women had got the Pill – so for the first time they had control over their own fertility. There was a lot to celebrate for gay men and straight women. But there always is a price to pay – women weren't showing much respect for themselves – perhaps the same was true of gay men. I felt it was too much. We had to go to one extreme before it could balance itself out."

One of the hardest acts of imagination and empathy is to think yourself back to how people really felt and why people did things that, years later, no longer seem right or acceptable. The 1960s and 70s ushered in a pre-AIDS sexual permissiveness that to many now seems crude, dangerous and counterproductive. But that era of "Let it all hang out", "Make love, not war" and "Love is all you need" cannot simply be dismissed as an unfortunate aberration. It was not. It was a necessary reaction to years of oppression and inhibition. John and Gary, already outsiders by the nature of their sexuality, were both immersed in a profession that accepted them for what they were and was much less likely to judge or condemn promiscuity or underage sex. The attitude was: so long as everyone is happy and enjoying themselves, what does it matter? Who is it hurting?

Part of the significance of my own experience is that, while John came on to me in the BBC Club, when I made it clear I wasn't interested, he didn't force the issue. This seems paralleled by others' experiences. In 1983, 18-year-old fan Patrick Mulkern (who would later write for *DWM* and *Radio Times*) was given the chance to go to Television Centre and watch stories being recorded from the studio observation gallery. "I remember my granddad warning me, 'You wanna watch those BBC types. They're all Ho Mo Sexual.' He really stressed the first two syllables! I first met John and Gary in the BBC Club bar. John had little to say to me and eyed me warily –Gary, however, was all over me. It was a 'charm offensive' – double meaning intended. A weird blend of lascivious and *faux* coquettish.

"He was always trying to chat me up: 'It's the boy from north of the Watford Gap!' became his greeting for me. (I used to Tube it in all the way from Chesham.) They also referred to me as That Doxy Boy, I imagine because of my naff clothes, bleach-blond hair and the fact I was hanging out with much older fans, as if I was some rent boy. I was mortified but it makes me laugh now.

Despite Gary's best efforts, they soon realised I wasn't 'interested'. In fact, I thought he and John were repulsive specimens, physically. But if you weren't interested, they didn't push it. I grew to quite like both of them eventually. A few years later I remember standing in a corridor at a DWAS convention with Gary, who had his own blond highlights by then, as he was casually talent-spotting 'doable barkers'. It's easy to be puritanical with hindsight but I always thought they were pretty harmless, really."

In the spring of 1986, Dominic May, then a member of the DWAS Executive, attended a dinner with them and the cast and core team from the *Doctor Who* production office. They went to a restaurant in Holland Park. "There was a fair amount of drinking," recalls May. "I offered to drive John back home – I thought it was an interesting opportunity to get to know the guy a bit better. He asked me if I'd like a drink and poured out the biggest glass of vodka and coke I have ever seen in my life. Suddenly, out of the blue, he asked, 'So how's your love life?' I said, 'Fair to middling,' but felt a bit uncomfortable and so beat a hasty retreat. It felt evident to me that he was slightly propositioning me. He didn't push it in any way but it was very clear that if I had responded in a different way, that was how it was going to go."

Five years earlier, Bob Richardson was working for BBC Enterprises and had got to know John well enough to share the occasional drink in the BBC Club. "I liked John," he says. "When he was talking to you, he would always take your viewpoint on board. Quite often he'd say, 'Do you think so? Do you really think so?'

"Enterprises had always had the pick of everything that was made for the show unless it was hired. John was great because he gave us carte blanche. Then, one day, I went over to the studio and John said, 'You can't have anything – I'm not letting you have any more stuff.' I went back to see Lorne [Martin – Richardson's boss] and John told him, 'Enterprises are making a fortune out of my show and I don't see a penny of the money and I'm fed up with it, so until you actually come up with some cash for my production, you don't get any more props or costumes or monsters. That's the end of it.'

"Lorne said to me, 'Look, you get on very well with him, take him out for dinner somewhere nice and butter him up and see if you can persuade him.' So I met him in the bar with Gary and, in fact, we didn't end up going for a meal. We just stayed in the bar all night and drank and drank and drank and then Gary propositioned me. 'John and I would like you to come home with us for a bit of fun.' They were driving down to Brighton that night and said they'd drop me at the station the following morning. I was really taken aback and quite shocked because, although I'm gay, I didn't really envisage getting myself involved in a threesome with John and Gary. I wasn't attracted to either of them and I could just see all kinds of complications. I very politely said, 'I'm seeing someone at the moment – if you don't mind I'd rather not.' John was actually very pleasant about it – Gary, on the other hand, was not. He was quite difficult. He said, 'So there's someone else is there? Well, be honest – which one of us don't you fancy?' John was about to buy a drink but Gary just said to John, 'Come on, drink up.' It was late, about 10.15. I was just left standing on my own with my half-finished drink, panic-stricken. I thought, 'This is a complete nightmare – I'm going to go into the office and it's going to be worse – he's going to be ringing up and asking for stuff to be returned.' In fact, when I went in the next morning Lorne said, 'I've spoken to John and everything's fine.'"

Within the BBC, it was always said that there were two clear rules which, if broken by a member of staff, would lead to instant dismissal. One was not having a television licence. The other was having sex on the premises.

In 1980, Mark Sinclair, who was then a 20-year-old member of the DWAS Executive, travelled from his home in Whitstable to meet John with Society coordinator David Saunders. "In those days," smiles Sinclair, "I could have been served with salt and pepper – I was a dish!

"John was very friendly. I told him how beautiful I thought *The Leisure Hive* was. I asked, 'Who's the guy who played Pangol?' and John said, 'Oh, he's not as good-looking in the flesh!' and I thought, 'So the rumours are true.' After about an hour he said, 'Let's go for a drink,' so we went to the pub on the corner. I got pissed out of my head. He was a delight to talk to – we chatted about *Round the Horne* and *Carry On* while David, who was as queer as a concrete parachute, sat in the corner in his safari suit, belching and farting. Afterwards, I remember getting on the Tube with a sense of euphoria that we'd got on so well. Blow me pink, about a week later he phones me. 'When are you coming up to London again? I thought you'd like to come to TV Centre and have a drink – what are you doing tomorrow?'"

Sinclair took the day off work and travelled up to London. "I thought, 'I'm on my own here.' He said, 'We'll have lunch at the BBC Club,' and for some reason, he gave me a calculator – a really nice one – 'That's for coming up.' He said, 'I want to show you a trick,' and he typed a number in and I said, 'Yeah, it's a number.' 'Turn it round,' he said and when I did, it read 'Bollocks'. I remember I had steak and chips for 42p and lots to drink because it was really cheap. We had a quick walk round the studios and ended up back in the pub on the corner. His dog was on the cover of that week's *Radio Times* because she was in *All Creatures* and he said, 'Perhaps you'd like to meet her?'

"We got to about the sixth pint – it was about half four and I said, 'Don't you ever do any work?' and he said, 'I work at other times to make up for it.' As we left the pub, he said, 'I'd like to see you again,' and gave me a kiss on the cheeks, right outside Currys! I thought, 'Poor old queen' – because at that age he seemed so much older than me. Next day, I had a hell of a hangover. A week later I got another phone call: 'When are you coming up?'"

This time, John told Sinclair to come to the production office. When he arrived he discovered that Jane Judge, the secretary, was off for the day.

"I went into his office and he locked the door – it had a Yale lock – and then he pulled his trousers down. I won't go into details but you get the idea. Halfway through this romantic encounter, the phone goes. It's Biddy Baxter. *Blue Peter* were doing a *Doctor Who* item and it was, 'Yes, Biddy?' He stood there talking away to her with his trousers round his ankles. You've got to laugh, haven't you? When he put the phone down, we wet ourselves. We ended up in the pub and it was 'When are you going to come up again? Do you fancy a threesome?'"

Sinclair, an aspiring actor at the time, admits, "It was a situation where I was thinking, 'What am I going to get out of this?' But I liked John too. I liked his very dry wit and he was very clever. I didn't really fancy him, though he had lovely teeth."

Sinclair confided what had happened to his best friend at the time, fellow fan Paul Mark Tams. When John arranged the next meeting, at the Champion, a gay pub in Notting Hill Gate, Tams offered to come with him. "He was worried about me. I had my car outside and John and Gary turned up. 'Come on we're going.' Miss Tams says goodbye. I was shitting myself and thought, 'Why am I doing this? Why am I with this other awful man who I didn't know from Adam? They're going to have all the pleasure.' John gets in my car and Gary drives the other car. I hit the kerb because I'm nervous.

"We end up in the flat in Brockley where it looked like a bomb had gone off. The three of us had sex. We all ended up in the bath and it was no Busby Berkeley movie, I can tell you. I was still there in the morning. When it was just John and me, he said how impressed he was with me and I felt like I'd had an A plus from a teacher! Then he asked me, 'When can we repeat that?' I told him, 'I don't mind repeating it but not with Gary there.'"

Although they did continue to meet, the sexual liaison petered away and eventually, after acting as organiser and MC of the 1981 DWAS Panopticon, Sinclair walked away from fandom. I asked him what he felt now about what he refers to as the "affair". "I liked John. I didn't like his methods. He was a spoilt child in a sweet shop. And I think it was a mistake, in a nice way."

Outside work, John and Gary had plenty of opportunity to meet potential partners. Like most gay men in their prime, they were regulars on the club circuit, often visiting the London nightclub Heaven, where resident DJ Ian Levine made sure they had VIP access. But they also spent a sizeable amount of their time attending *Doctor Who* conventions in the UK and America. It was at a convention that John came face to face with his future successor, Russell T Davies. "I went along to a convention in Manchester about 1991," says Davies. "I'd never really been to a convention because I'm not particularly interested in Jon Pertwee telling stories and things like that. I went to the dealers' room to buy some stuff and at the same time I thought I might get laid! I mean, come on! I was young and thin and wore a leather jacket.

"John literally made a beeline across the room towards me – I'm 6ft 6 and very thin in a leather jacket – zoom! I must have been about 28 and I was kind of embarrassed because I was a script editor at Granada at the time, which I think was the first thing I said to him. I went, 'Hello, I'm a script editor at Granada,' because I thought I don't want to look like a young fan boy on the prowl! I never tell this story because nothing happened. I can imagine hearing it and saying, 'Oh yeah, what happened then?' We sat down and had a nice chat – I wanted to know if [the series] was coming back. I went away feeling quite happy because I'd met John Nathan-Turner and he was the *producer*."

There had never before been a BBC producer with such a high profile. To *Doctor Who* fans of the time, John was as much of a celebrity as the actors who appeared on screen. Many held him in awe and were keen to meet him face to face, get his autograph, have their photograph taken with him, and, if they had the guts, ask him a question or two. His job had elevated him into a unique position of power and responsibility among a fan base that, especially in the UK, was largely composed of teenagers and young men.

When Antony Wainer, the press officer of DWAS since 2002, first met John and Gary in the bar at a convention, he was 17 – the same age I had been at my first meeting with them. Wainer recalls, "Gary was physically vetting people to meet John – 'Yes, you, not you' – almost like a conveyor belt of talent. I laugh to think I passed as crumpet then! I was naive and just thought this man was interested to talk to me because of my interest in *Doctor Who*. He would beguile me with stories – it was all quite enthralling.

"Gary asked for my telephone number and they would phone me at home. My mum would always answer and, particularly when John would ring, she would say, 'Antony – the producer of *Doctor Who* is on the phone, why does he want to talk to you?' They gave me more of a heads-up as to what they were about. When my dad picked up, it was, 'What do you want now?' so John asked me to use the pay phone at the bottom of the road. I would phone him from there – Gary would always answer and then they would phone me back. It was,

'Are you sure you don't want to come down to Brighton ai.d rifle through the goodie trunk?' The goodie trunk was a collection of props and costumes, which they implied I could choose from."

The phone calls went on for a period of two years until one day "they had these Swedish friends staying with them – I was invited to have sex with all four of them and they would video it. I was only 19. I just wasn't interested. I probably just laughed it off – I didn't think badly of it. Now I think it's awful – they were in a position of power. They wouldn't take no for an answer."

But in the end they had to. I asked Wainer what he feels about them now. "The other side of the story was that John was very, very funny and very kind. Gary was funny too. They made me laugh – I had good times with them. At conventions, John would always buy me a white wine spritzer. He used to say, 'Do you want a white wine spritzer or a spritzer that's dry, a spritzer that's oh so terribly dry?' I was really fond of him towards the end – after the nastiness was out of the way."

Shaun Dellenty first met John at Stoneleigh Town and Country Festival in 1985 when he too was 17. "I was shy but my teacher had said, 'You need to be an actor' – and I was interested in that." The star attraction at the event was Jon Pertwee. "He looked at my father and said, 'Dellenty, you old bastard!' and it turned out that they had been in the navy together. He was lovely to me and very taken by the fact I was called Shaun [Pertwee's son is also called Sean]. There was a sort of green room for the day and we went in there and the next thing John is there. He went, 'Who are you?' I said, 'I'm Shaun, I'm a really big *Doctor Who* fan.' He said, 'Tell me about yourself,' and I immediately went, 'I want to be an actor.' 'Doing what?' 'Anything. Television. I'd love to be in *Doctor Who*.' He said, 'When you get home, write to me.' So I did. I got a letter straight back saying, 'You must come and visit me in my office.'"

For various domestic reasons, Dellenty couldn't take up the invitation straight away. "Then I started to get more letters, 'You must come and visit my office – do ring my assistant Kate Easteal.' I've still got some of them. He must have sent about five or six. I just thought he was going to get me into acting. So in the end I saved up and rang the number and said, 'John's written to me and said I should come down,' and I got this message to meet at a pub on Shepherd's Bush Green. Coming down to London for the first time on my own was a big thing. I walked in the pub and saw John with Gary so I went over and stood there, awkward and shy, for about ten minutes. Then he just span round and I said, 'Hi, John, I'm Shaun, you arranged to meet me,' and he said, 'What? Did we?' and I was just crushed. Gary leant over and said, 'Who's that?' and they had a good old cackle.

"I'd got enough money to buy them one drink each – and I remember coming back, spilling the drinks on the way and then I stood there for a good half an hour like a lemon while they chatted to each other. Eventually, he turned round and said, 'So what do you want to talk about?' and I said, 'Well, if you remember, I want to be an actor.' 'Oh, right – what sort of actor?'

"He did give me some advice then. I must have stayed there for about an hour and right towards the end, John said, 'What are you doing now? Where are you staying tonight?' and I said, 'Well, I've got a ticket back,' and he went, 'OK, seeya,' – just like that. It was like I wasn't there any more and in the end I just filtered away."

Dellenty is now a deputy head in a primary school in London's Southwark. He's risen to prominence because of his championing of anti-gay bullying in schools. Looking back, he says, "I've seen enough gay men planning to know what was going on and there was a definite 'get him back' suggestion there. I recounted the story to a few people at the time and they said, 'You could have slept with him and got a part in *Doctor Who.*' But I felt stupid and humiliated and had learnt a lesson in life."

None of these anecdotes reflect creditably on either John or Gary. But they are not a complete picture by any means because they did manage to forge some meaningful, emotional and lasting relationships with a small circle of young fans. One of these was with a 20-year-old policeman called Stephen Cranford, who first met them in 1993. "I was their local beat officer for Saltdean," he says. "We were doing house to house enquiries. I said to the other officer, Dave, 'If you ever come across a guy called John Nathan-Turner – just ask if they mind me popping in. It was only going to be a case of, 'Hello, I'm Stephen, I'm your local policeman, pleased to meet you, here's my card if you need anything. I like what you did on the show, thanks very much.' We were knocking on doors to see if anyone knew who owned this car – and Dave came across John and said, 'I've got this friend who wants to meet you.'

"'Oh that's fine, send him round.' When I did come round and said I was the friend of Dave the policeman, they were a bit taken aback. They'd been expecting a 12-year-old boy not a police officer and they found this really quite amusing. They were massively hospitable straightaway. I now know that coppers were one of John's big fantasies. They found that highly delightful. I was on duty so after 20 minutes I said I'd better go and they said, 'Here's our number. Drop by another time when you've got more time.' I gave them my number too but I didn't really think anything would ever happen. About two or three weeks later I got a phone call, 'Oh hi, it's John Nathan-Turner. I didn't know whether you wanted to pop over for a dinner?'

"I did so and started to get to know them very much better. I think he had a fascination with police officers, never mind a fantasy thing. He asked what I did, what went on at the station and how I came to be a policeman. *Doctor Who* was a very tenuous part of our friendship and it was really very rarely discussed at all. It became almost irrelevant.

"I'm gay, always have been," Cranford continues, "but back then I never really knew or had faced it. I think he and Gary always did know. Police work is a little different now but back then it was very hostile environment if you were an out gay officer. My real dad is absolutely fantastic but slightly Victorian. All these issues were suppressed. From the emotional point of view, I didn't have anyone, apart from them. John and Gary were the ones who tried to reassure me that it's fine on the other side, if you like. They were so understanding because of the difficulties they would have had. They knew exactly what it was like having to lead a secret life. They would phone me every week and see how I was. At the time Gary was studying psychotherapy and he was saying, 'This is all perfectly natural'. They were almost like mentors. John, especially, was like my gay dad. I even bought them Father's Day cards for a few years."

I asked Cranford if they'd ever tried their luck with him themselves. "Only in a very friendly way. As a tease. 'Go on, unbutton your shirt' – Gary was a lot more pushy, John not at all so. They were always saying, 'You ought to meet this guy...' and 'Oh Stephen, what do you think of him?' John would do anything for you. When I was moving, he said, 'Right I'm coming over – tell me what I can do,' and even my really close mates didn't do that. There was massive generosity." Cranford remained in their close circle for the rest of their lives.

Another fan who became almost an adoptive son was David Roden, who first met John and Gary at a 1992 *Doctor Who* weekend at the University of Kent, where 21-year-old Roden was then a student. Roden's flatmate at the time had already met them and suggested he should join them for a drink. "My flatmate was tall, blond and terribly ambitious. He was doing this whole spiel about wanting to be a director of Teynham [the production company John and Gary ran with their friends Fiona Cumming and Ian Fraser] and pretending that he might be gay. I completely blew his cover and said, 'No, you're not gay – you've got a girlfriend,' and he stormed out, just like they write in scripts. John let out that massive guffaw he had and said, 'I like you,' and we just clicked."

Roden is now a drama development producer at the BBC. Then he was studying drama, had aspirations either to act or to write for television and, "John made a genuine offer – 'If ever you want to send me something to read, please do.' I stayed in touch and sent John some stuff. He came back to me and said, 'This is good but I've got some thoughts for you...'"

In the summer of 1993, Roden was invited to stay with them. "I was met outside the station by John and Gary in their Humber, their vintage car, and driven – it must have been a Saturday lunchtime – to Marine Parade. They immediately started to ply me with alcohol – within seconds of getting in the door it was, 'Do you want a vodka? I'm having one.' I knew what the game was. 'Come on, come on, drink up, we'll get you a top-up,' and, of course, they were giving themselves a decent measure and handing me harmful measures. I knew that if I let all that alcohol get into my system, I would pass out. I just felt really awful. I went and made myself ill in their downstairs loo. Gary did make an attempt. I made it very clear that I wanted to be their friend but not at the cost of greasing my arse up. They tried endlessly – it was always Gary – it was always the pint of vodka in a plastic tumbler and a smidgeon of Tango trick."

Later that year, John employed Roden to write the script for the 30th anniversary *Children in Need* special, *Dimensions in Time*. "John and I genuinely clicked. I was terribly fond of them both but... it became incredibly nasty at the end..." The falling out, bitter and final, is described in chapter 13, but it follows the same sad pattern as several of John and Gary's intense, all-or-nothing relationships.

Grahame Flynn became closely entwined with John and Gary in his late 20s. "John had many acquaintances but only a few very intense friendships. He formed long-term relationships with David Roden, Stephen Cranford, myself. We all became very, very important to him."

Flynn's own friendship started when he met Gary at a *Doctor Who* day at Longleat in the early 90s. "Gary said he'd kept continuity Polaroids and floor plans from the show. We got chatting, exchanged numbers and before I knew it, I'd been invited down to Brighton for a weekend. It was only when I got to the house that I even knew that John and Gary were an item."

Although Flynn "had an interest in production design" (which he has subsequently made his career), at the time he, like Cranford, was a policeman. "We hit it off straight away – John and I became very close friends. John could be fiery – he was a typical Leo – had a big roar but he was a great listener. He became like a mix of partner, older brother, and almost a surrogate father figure, I suppose. He would have been an excellent father. I had never experienced a friendship like it in my life. When it was fun, it was great; when it was hell, it was awful. We did have a major fall out in 1996."

"Grahame was a police officer," remembers Colin Baker, "and he was all hugger mugger with John and Gary – it was all very weird. They were at a convention and it all went wrong."

The conflict centred around Colin's co-star and friend, Nicola Bryant. "John phoned me and asked me to this convention. I hadn't been to one in ages.

I was having a terrible time with relationships – I was celibate and I was going to stay that way for quite some time because I'd had enough of dating dreadful people! We had a really in-depth personal conversation. He was like, 'Oh, I'm really sorry to hear that.'"

At the convention, John and Gary introduced Bryant to Flynn. "He seemed like a nice chap," she says. Bryant had brought with her a stack of glossy photographs to sign. "I'm always very true to copyright law and the photographer had given me a stamp with his details. Unfortunately, because the photos were glossy, you could wipe the stamp off. The only thing I could do was go and get a batch of sticky labels, stamp the labels and then stick them onto the photos."

Bryant set off to her hotel room and "happened to pass Grahame and this other chap in the corridor and he said, 'Where are you off to?' When I said, 'I'm going to stamp a few hundred photos,' he said, 'Do you need a hand?' So he and another guy came and helped. We came back into the green room an hour or so later, thinking, 'Oh my God, I can't believe we just did that,' laughing and in good spirits and Gary came over and said, 'Did you have a good fuck?'

"I thought, 'You're seriously suggesting I just slept with a gay guy?' He was obsessed with this guy and I didn't realise they all had a relationship. From my world this makes no sense. So the only thing to do was to joke in the most camp and flamboyant way – 'Well, darling, it was marvellous, thank you!' He flounced out of the room and I thought, 'Oh', and that made me a bit nervous."

"I never understood the attitude to Nicola," sighs Baker. It was jealousy of a supposed relationship between Grahame and Nicola. "That's where all that viciousness started."

"As we were getting ready backstage to do the auction," Bryant continues, "JN-T came up to me, spat in my face and said, 'How dare you?' I was shaking. I can't believe that he would think that I would do that. I was shocked and I'm still shattered at the thought of it now. I adored John and from that point on, I never spoke to him again."

"Gary was so jealous," says Flynn, "that he went and kicked in every panel of my car. I made the mistake of intimating to John that I thought Gary had done the damage. He was very angry and defended Gary. I found out many years later from David Roden that Gary had confessed and John didn't speak to him for three weeks. We didn't speak for about a year, until he found out the truth. I didn't know that he had spat at Nicola. That is just awful."

"I stopped going to any conventions that he attended," says Bryant, "and then I got something horrible from Gary basically saying, 'You bitch, you're ruining our conventions – how dare you take money from us?' And it was completely the other way round. I just stopped attending. Also because I was on my own, I didn't have anyone that I felt would stand next to me or protect me. It was just ludicrous. What was even more ludicrous was that about five or six years later I was going to a convention and Grahame came to pick me up in the car and was like, 'Oh everything's all right now – they know nothing happened.' I said, 'So why didn't anyone come and apologise? Why didn't anyone put it right?'

"I wrote a really long letter, which killed me to write, because I thought they need to know the truth – and I was just about to post it when a very dear friend of mine who's a top psychologist phoned me and said, 'Don't send it because I promise you anything in there that can be twisted will be. You know the truth – you know the situation. If they're decent, they will come back and apologise and if not, you cannot go back in there. You'll be punished for the fact that they were wrong. And I found that very hard because I thought 'No, no, no – when John reads this, he will understand.'"

"I am sorry that I never had the opportunity to speak to Nicola about it," says Flynn. "I did write to her via her agent but heard nothing back. This is something I deeply regret. She is simply a beautiful person who didn't deserve John's unspeakable behaviour."

"I think John adored Gary," says Bryant, "and was madly in love with him. On paper you could say John held all the aces. He looks like the powerful one but Gary was in charge."

"Gary would get something into his head," sighs Flynn, "and would become very cold, angry and bitter. Massively paranoid. He could not see the truth if he got something in his head. It's a sad fact that I forgave Gary on many occasions to maintain my friendship with John. And it would always be John who would pick up the phone or send a postcard and, before you knew it, you'd be back in the bear pit."

"I do not think Gary was a good influence on John," says Jackie Pearce. "I didn't like him. I don't know why John was with him. It's always been a complete mystery to me. Gary did not like women but he knew that John did and women responded to him. Maybe he saw them as a threat."

"John needed somebody like Gary," says Sinclair. "When he didn't feel comfortable being nasty, Gary would do it for him."

In Colin Baker's view, "Any big disagreements that John had, Gary either caused or wound up out of nothing, like with Nicola, like with Sandra [Dickinson, Davison's wife]. I'm sure after I'd left the programme, I'd have seen more of John had it not been for Gary. I think Gary was even a little bit jealous of my relationship with John."

The weight of evidence seems remorselessly to suggest that John's worst excesses were usually at the behest of his partner. "John and Gary had a fantasy about twins," says Levine. "Gary kept saying, 'John, why don't you have a *Doctor Who* with twins in it?'"

The almost-unwatchable result was *The Twin Dilemma* and the two lisping teenager leads, Paul and Gavin Conrad, were only part of the problem. "Gary was like, 'Oh look at them, aren't they gorgeous?' Never mind that they couldn't act!" snorts Levine in fury. I well remember that camp old slyboots Peter Moffatt (whose hands had a tendency to stray, too), director of *The Twin Dilemma*, dropping less than subtle hints to me about this. "I can't think why John insisted on having boys... I found quite a good, talented pair of twin girls... but for some reason, he *insisted* on boys."

Was John Nathan-Turner a paedophile? It's a question that must be asked. There are plenty of whispers. "I'm very well aware of the rumours," says a fan who became a friend, Stuart Money. "John enjoyed the company of all sorts of people and certainly liked to encourage young actors and actresses but I would certainly never attribute the words predatory or pederast to him. I can't speak for his partner."

"Those stories were around," confirms former DWAS co-ordinator and convention organiser Andrew Beech. "They were dreadful flirts. On the one hand, I wouldn't expect the same stories to keep on and on and on unless there was something to it. Although I know from my own experience it's very easy for someone to take a little incident, blow it out of all proportion and get the wrong end of the stick. Equally, some of the stories are so hair-raising that I find it very hard to believe that anybody would get away with that kind of thing. Surely somebody would have said or done something about it by now? They have had every opportunity to speak out and other than these Chinese whispers, nobody ever has."

"I could put my hand on my heart and say that they weren't like that," says another friend Mark Jones. "They were fantastic with my son. The evidence that I saw was that they only copped off with chaps who were gay and were looking for a party after a convention. I don't really know how young it went."

"I think he liked younger fellers," says Sinclair, "but I don't think he was a paedophile. He was breaking the law – the gay age of consent – but it was a ridiculous law."

"I think people have in their heads that things were happening," says Flynn, "but I honestly don't think that would be the case. The agenda was fun. They helped a lot of young gay guys come to terms with their sexuality... which is why I am annoyed about the idea of a sex scandal coming out."

"There's a difference between a bit of fucking on the side and paedophilia," says Pearce, emphatically.

"They loved kids," says Stephen Cranford, "but not in a perverse way. They would spoil them and then hand them back. When they lived in the London house, they used to have rails of costumes and the local kids, if they were there, used to come round and dress up – much to the horror probably of the parents! It was all totally innocent. The problem is nowadays that would be seen as seedy grooming behaviour but it couldn't have been further from the truth. They were wonderful with kids."

Another long-term friend, Jane Wellesley, agrees. "The first time I actually met my then partner's two young children, we decided that the best thing to do would be to take them down to my mother's with John and Gary – so that they weren't just alone with us. We had the most wonderful weekend – they were brilliant with the kids. They had friends that actually put in their will that if anything happened to them, they wanted John and Gary to be the guardians. That was quite unusual then. A lot of people would think twice about wanting a couple of gay guys to foster their children in the event of their death."

As I put the text together, the BBC was immersed in the shit-storm of the Jimmy Savile allegations, which shocked the nation and prompted a scale of concern and a series of high-profile investigations. One of these was into the culture and practices of the BBC during the years when Savile, who appears to have been a monstrous serial paedophile, was most active – the 1970s and 80s. Context is certainly crucial. However dim a view today's BBC management might take of John's activities, there is no evidence whatsoever that he was a Savile-esque character. John was clearly attracted to young adults – but not children.

However reprehensible some of his behaviour, he was far from alone and far from being the most extreme contender. Senior producers and executives often had a reputation that made younger staff wary. As television presenter and sometime executive Janet Street-Porter said on the BBC's *Question Time* in October 2012, "There was a culture that made me feel uncomfortable, of inappropriate sexual behaviour. Not just a BBC thing. I think you'll find across it commercial TV as well. There was a culture and it was a generational thing – behaviour was tolerated."

It didn't matter whether you were straight or gay. When I joined the BBC in 1988, plenty of my female colleagues were resigned to the casual gropes and leering comments of men higher up the ladder, production or talent – some of these being very famous names. During the interviews for this book, I compared notes with Russell T Davies about the (internally at any rate) notorious light entertainment executive Robin Nash, who, at different times, made a pass at us both. We were nothing special – that was just his routine for the young men within his orbit. Similarly, I, like others, turned a blind eye to the wandering hands of Peter Estall, another executive I otherwise held in high regard, because it was easier to move away and pretend it hadn't happened than to make a scene and perhaps risk my job. Lest I should sound as if life at Television Centre was one long round of ducking from dirty old men or giving into occasional temptation, I do go back to the point that life was different then. The positive aspects of political correctness – enshrining one's right to work unmolested either verbally or physically – had yet to be established in either law or people's thinking.

Even in the subculture of *Doctor Who*, John cannot be said to be the only "celebrity" who has fucked fans. Whether gay or straight, some of the best-known and most revered names in fandom did or do cross the same line as John and Gary. Arguably, some go even further and are lucky to have avoided the potential fallout. Conventions invest these actors with the same spurious aura that makes teenage girls throw themselves at boy bands with adoring abandonment. Some of these stars have the taste and judgement to stay behind an invisible barrier or have developed genuinely meaningful and lasting relationships with partners who happen also to be fans. But plenty are happy to play away from home and indulge in a chance to punch above their weight, their pulling power fuelled by a part they often played decades before. Perhaps the most complex aspect of all this, especially in the wake of the loathsome revelations about Savile and others, is that apparently some victims go willingly to the slaughter – groupies, star-fuckers, wannabes – even the names are damning and derogatory. Disturbingly, very often the last thing on either party's mind at the moment the line is crossed is whether one of them is of a legal age of consent.

Sex remains an inseparable part of the alchemy of showbusiness. In television, "sexy" is one of the most over-used adjectives there is – shots, scripts, shows, ideas, all can be "sexy". The whole process of casting is driven, to some degree, by who fancies whom and why. Although John was fond of saying, "There's no hanky panky in the TARDIS," *Doctor Who* was as riddled with this as the rest of television drama – whether it's the young girl bursting out of her top or the boy in a kilt, you pays your money and takes your choice.

The world has moved on a long way since John was in charge of all things *Doctor Who*. He would not recognise or feel at home in the BBC as it is today. Had he lived and worked in the world of the internet and social media, he might have behaved differently, taken fewer risks, tempered some of his more dubious and questionable behaviour. Today, we live in a culture of exposé, apology and resignation, when the merest hint of scandal can destroy people's lives and careers, and not always fairly. Media hysteria and hypocrisy often appear to cloud the central issue, with any real victims frequently seeming lost in the furore. The lines that John undoubtedly crossed and the poor judgement he sometimes exercised in pursuit of high jinks and good times now make uncomfortable reading. It's not enough to blame his love and loyalty for Gary, the "foot soldier". They are part of his legacy too.

NINE

DOCTOR IN DISTRESS

"The people who make Doctor Who have got rather complacent. The show got rather violent and lost a lot of its imagination, a lot of its wit, and had failed really to capture a new audience..."
Michael Grade, interviewed on *The Jimmy Young Show*, September 1985

Doctor Who was back on a Saturday. Much was made of its return to this traditional slot for the 1985 season and of the fact that each episode now ran 45 minutes. The original request had been for 50-minute episodes, the standard drama length of the time, but John had tried to use the decision as a new angle in his perennial argument for more resources, arguing that he was being asked to produce more screen time for less money. He based this on the simple maths of adding together two 24-and-a-half-minute episodes and subtracting the titles and recaps. Predictably, no extra money was forthcoming and the unsatisfactory compromise was a running time of 45 minutes. As the season progressed, John discovered that he could have filled the 50-minute slot after all, and lots of material had to be jettisoned.

Otherwise, things had gone his way for the making of his fifth season in charge. For the first time, it was a year without the headaches and complications caused by industrial action. He was delighted with his new leading man, with whom he was already on much closer terms than either of the predecessors, and he was fond of Nicola Bryant, too, whose school nickname he appropriated, calling her "Knickers". (Gary preferred the fuller version, "Knickers with the Knockers".) He had an established court of reliable, if sometimes humdrum, directors around him, adding just one newcomer (Sarah Hellings) to the mix. Although his long-held ambition to shoot a story in America derailed at a late stage, he managed to salvage this by shifting the locations to Seville in Spain. This showcase story was *The Two Doctors*, commissioned to bring back Patrick Troughton and Frazer Hines (who had played Jamie in the 1960s) after the previous reunion of *The Five Doctors*.

"It was the only time I ever fell out with John," remembers Colin Baker. "We were filming in the heat in Seville. John cracked open the champagne at lunchtime and, well, he wasn't very abstemious, let's say. Nicola and I had been getting a little irritated in the morning because Gary, who was the production manager, would say, 'Could you stand by please?' So you'd come out of the shade and stand at the top of a hill and ten, 15 minutes would pass and so, in the afternoon, I said, 'Gary, can you not call us out until you're going to use us, please? It's counterproductive' – which I thought was a perfectly logical argument. John came steaming over, 'Well, it's counterproductive drinking champagne at lunchtime.' And I thought, 'But you were the one who got it and offered it to us.' I was quite upset actually because he'd never done anything like that before but he was defending Gary, of course. Though I wasn't attacking Gary, just the procedure that left us pouring with sweat before starting a scene. It wasn't about my comfort; it was about my ability to do the work. By the evening, he was fine but it was the first time I had that rage. He was all hot and bothered because of that heat too."

The man who dreamt up *The Two Doctors* was Robert Holmes. Eric Saward had been championing the writer since watching much of the show's back catalogue and realising that Holmes had written, or edited, many of the all-time greats. Initially, John was resistant, using his defensive old line about not wanting some "old toot" on his show. Saward persevered, with Holmes his first choice writer for the 20th anniversary special. Holmes, himself wary of the Saward/Nathan-Turner set-up, had a go anyway, tentatively suggesting a story called *The Six Doctors*. As John outlined this in a letter to William Hartnell's widow, Heather: "I intend to get an actor to play the part who looks very like Bill, although it will be made obvious at the beginning that this Doctor is an impostor and one of the problems the other Doctors have to face is to unmask the impostor... the whole thing will be done in the best possible taste."

But, as Holmes told me when I interviewed him on 29th August 1985: "I found it too difficult to do. It was meant to involve every character who'd ever been in *Doctor Who*, as far as I was concerned! [But] that's when the talks began and they realised that I wasn't really the arrogant monster they thought I was. They were afraid, I think, that I would come in and be very autocratic and say, 'This isn't the way we used to do it,' and stuff like that."

Saward persisted and Holmes's triumphant fifth Doctor swansong *The Caves of Androzani* was reward for his tenacity. It helped that it had been brilliantly realised by Graeme Harper. But the director for *The Two Doctors* was John's old friend, sweet-natured Peter Moffatt, self-confessedly at a loss in the world of *Doctor Who*. "He'd say, 'I haven't got a clue, dear,'" smiles Baker. "'You tell me what you want to do' – which is very enabling!"

Holmes was not impressed. "I think the cast was very good," he told me. "I just don't think Peter got them into a proper *Doctor Who* mood. The story was basically a plea for animal rights. I was trying to point out how filthy it is to eat all this meat, although I'm not a vegetarian. There's no good killing off somebody who isn't important. If you get to like a character and then you kill him, the impact is much more important. I don't think they did [the death of Oscar, one of the supporting characters] very well. It should have been very moving. That, again, is down to the way they directed it. In the book I've handled the death scene, I think, a lot better than it was handled on television.

"[John] is not involved in the stories. As long as Eric can get a story, and gives it to John, he just says, 'Yes, OK.' I don't think he's got a story mind."

Holmes was right. The subtleties of characterisation and plot were not of huge interest to John. The look of the show was, on the other hand, always at the front of his mind, and he could rely on Moffatt to charm the turns and finish ahead of schedule. This was, however, the last time he would employ him. After John broke the news, Moffatt wrote to him on 20th February 1985: "It is I who should thank you, for so many things. For having me back yet again to work with you when you know my usual failing! Most of all for all your wonderful help, support, encouragement, creative criticism and the wealth of <u>love</u> which goes with it all. I shall miss you sorely. Thank you, dear John, for six exciting engagements."

As well as the routine of filming and studio recording, John had another distraction on the horizon. This was the debut venture for John, Gary, Fiona Cumming and Ian Fraser's Teynham Productions. There was a lot at stake. Hiring the theatre alone cost them £6000 per week. "We used to have Teynham meetings on a Saturday morning," recalls Cumming. "I was working in Scotland so would come down on a Friday night and we'd have a meeting that started at 11 o'clock with coffee – but the coffee was always laced with brandy! I couldn't keep up – I simply couldn't cope with that amount of alcohol. I would be drinking gin and tonic – by the time the fifth one was poured, the gin would be up to the rim. So I moved on to the wine but the glass was always being refilled. So my next ploy was to take up tapestry so I would have the glass next to me. I would be listening to everything that was going on and plying my needle –

which of course kept your hands occupied. That was the only way I could cope with the quantity of alcohol in the meetings."

As work started on the final story of the season, another Saward Dalek epic, rehearsals began for another version of John's *Cinderella*, this time billed as boasting "the stars of *Doctor Who*", at the Gaumont Theatre, Southampton. Baker was Buttons, Bryant Cinderella, with Anthony Ainley again Baron Hardup, Mary Tamm as Prince Charming and Jacqueline Pearce as the Fairy Mirazel. Ian Fraser recalls, "John directed, Gary did the choreography, I lit the thing and Fiona did all the admin and management. It was stressful during the rehearsal period – we worked all day and then went at night to the theatre."

"Initially," recalls Baker, "I remember saying, 'Well, I'd rather have Christmas off – but John was very insistent. It did seem to be getting a little bit too cosy to be doing everything together. It was fun to do but it was a very dangerous idea because the majority of the public who go to pantos aren't hugely interested in *Doctor Who* – they want a variety of people. He got the filming [for *Revelation of the Daleks*] scheduled outside Southampton so we weren't too far away. I was uneasy at the time about being told by the producer that I could have time off in order to work for him in something else! I thought, 'Well, you must have cleared it with the BBC.'"

As Baker was working on the series at the same time as rehearsing the panto, Teynham didn't actually pay him until the performances started. He also received 2 per cent of the gross box office. Alas for Baker and Teynham, the pantomime didn't make money but there was talk of mounting the same production in Singapore the following year, with profits to be split 60/40 between Teynham and the Singapore Tourist Board. The connection was not as random as it apparently seemed. John was already lining up a story for Colin Baker's second season, to be shot on location in Singapore during the summer of 1985.

Meanwhile, Baker's first full season as Doctor Who launched as part of BBC1's winter schedule on Saturday 5th January 1985. The ratings were not the disaster that some have subsequently claimed. There was a fall from the dramatically high opening figure but this was distorted by inevitable curiosity about a new series and new Doctor. Later episodes were averaging a more than respectable seven million plus, pretty much level with the previous two years. The stories were more fairly criticised for the levels of violence and cruelty involved. Saward's bleak worldview predominated – characters suffered and were tortured. There was little in the way of catharsis either, most ending up mere cannon fodder, their struggles in vain.

I put this to Saward when I interviewed him in the summer of 1985. John insisted he was part of this too, perhaps to ensure that Saward, who, the previous year, had given me a surprisingly frank interview for the time, stuck to the party line. It was an uncomfortable meeting and there are some awkward moments on the tape as John and Eric are scrupulously polite to each other and uniformly defensive in their responses to my questions. In particular, I took Saward to task about his disposal of the supporting characters in *Attack of the Cybermen*, most of which he wrote (though it was credited to a former girlfriend, Paula Moore). "It was quite a positive element," he told me. "Being pretentious about it, it's the energy and effort people put in to avoid death. They don't just sit there. They were being very determined about trying to escape and although they died in the attempt, I think the way they went about it lifted the show dramatically." I didn't buy this then, nor does it convince me now, perhaps because it was hard to care about most of the characters. Saward, who looked up to Holmes, had yet to replicate his skill.

"There was this tendency to do things that were too dark and too nasty and too hard-hitting," says Andrew Cartmel, who eventually followed Saward as script editor. "The interesting thing about Eric was his stuff was so full of good ideas – especially the stuff he wrote himself. He modelled himself on Robert Holmes – who is in my mind the great *Doctor Who* writer. I think he really liked and revered him. Eric's period was full of these Holmes-esque ideas which didn't come off, perhaps because of unsympathetic direction or it was miscast or badly shot.

"What is certainly right is that period saw the show at its nadir," continues Cartmel. "I really like and respect Colin and Eric but what they ended up doing under John's aegis was going well in the wrong direction. In my mind, *Vengeance on Varos* was the turning point. There's this scene with these baddie guards who are precipitated into an acid vat and the Doctor says something like, 'Enjoy your bath, I won't be joining you.' It was way too callous for the Doctor. That really hit me when I watched it. I thought, 'Fucking hell, that's not a good thing to do.' And all that stuff about changing people into animals – it was too much, like torture or something. As *Doctor Who*, the emphasis was all wrong."

"It's a very difficult show to write," Holmes told me, "because you're on a knife edge between *Grand Guignol* nonsense and *Monty Python* on the other side. You've got to be very careful what line you tread…"

Predictably, comments reached the pages of *Radio Times* and Mary Whitehouse, guardian of the National Viewers' and Listeners' Association pressure group, a long-term critic of *Doctor Who*, wrote to John, copying in BBC director-general Alasdair Milne and chairman of the BBC governors, Stuart Young, on 27th February 1985: "It is not only correspondents to the *Radio Times* who find the present series unacceptable. So do we. MA Murrell's letter surely hits the nail on the head – To see such cruelty (murder, sadism) now made part of 'entertainment' I find most repugnant and irresponsible. May I suggest that your responsibility to the children who watch at that time should be your first priority. There must surely be other ways of developing a new storyline."

Whitehouse was on surer ground than usual. Some of the imagery – from crushed hands and acid baths to cannibal cooks and syringes in necks – was distinctly questionable for the time of day, just after 5pm on a Saturday.

The series had been scheduled by Alan Hart, a controller of BBC1 whose time at the top had been undistinguished and whose departure was precipitated by the steady decline of what was supposed to be the mainstream channel. "Alan Hart was a nice man who'd come from sport," explains Jonathan Powell. "The story was that he had got the job of controller by mistake. The person they'd wanted was a man called John Gau but in those days the appointment of a controller of BBC1 was in the gift of the governors. The managing director of television had to come up with a shortlist that was sent to the governors. Alan had done a fantastically good presentation and they voted for him. A few years went past and BBC1 got into problems – not all Alan's fault – its share [of the available audience] had dropped to something like 32 per cent – and ratings were very low."

Panicked by such a poor performance, the BBC went looking for a dynamic new broom and when Michael Grade was announced as Hart's successor, the newspapers, who knew a natural showman when they saw one, pushed him centre stage whenever the BBC was in the headlines. With his chunky glasses and Gordon Gekko braces, Grade was a chip off the old block – his uncle was the legendary Lew Grade – and Michael even borrowed Lew's trademark cigar in his quest to stand out as a mogul in his own right.

"When Michael arrived," recalls Powell, "a lot of what series and serials was doing was already quite tied up. *Doctor Who* was looked at as part of the furniture, one of those things you could tick off for 12 hours or whatever, that's that little chunk of money. I realised that obviously Michael's job was to get the ratings up and, for the department to flourish, we had to have a relationship with him and give him what he wanted.

"It seemed to me that there were three kinds of drama – you needed the long-running series, 12 episodes or preferably more that would fill up the critical slots on Saturday and Sunday night at eight o'clock. It was the most difficult thing to find those programmes and you never got any thanks for it but it was an act of faith that the serials department supplied those slots. Then the entertainment department [drama's main rivals for these top slots] could go and fuck themselves. That was the first job – you had to supply Michael with those hit shows. Then you had to do a few slightly shorter-running things that supplied audiences. Then you could start to trade and have the high-end stuff – *The Singing Detective* or whatever it happened to be. Equally important. One never existed without the other. You could put as many *Singing Detectives* as you liked on BBC1 but if the channel was falling apart, nobody noticed. If the channel's a success, when you have your *Singing Detective*, then the thing takes off.

"In those days," continues Powell, "once you got past April, you were locked in the plan for the following year. Offers [the system where each department presented the channel controllers with their wish list for production in the year ahead] came in August and then your programmes were ticked off. Michael arrived quite late in the process and all the stuff we were doing was fixed. I remember sitting in my office and thinking, 'We've got to get on with this bloke,' and I wanted to ensure that when he arrived the series and serials department is the one that he knew was his friend and would deliver. So I prepared a memo for Michael to be on his desk when he walked in – it said, 'The BBC planning system says that you can't change anything – here are the programmes we are making for you next year. I'd really like to see you as soon as possible because, despite the planning system, I'd like you to know that we will change whatever you want because we have other ideas and if you don't like stuff we are doing, I'm very happy to cancel them and get stuff you like.' And I think that was one of the first memos he got. We got on like a house on fire – because obviously he walked in and thought, 'Here's somebody I can do business with.'"

Over the years, many theories, often convoluted, have been put forward to explain why, towards the end of 1984, these two men – with the knowledge and backing of the BBC's director of programmes, Brian Wenham, and the managing director, Bill Cotton – took the decision to cancel *Doctor Who*. Some have suggested that it was a knee-jerk response to the extra costs of the new soap, *EastEnders*. But this is a fallacy. As Powell's predecessor, David Reid, explains: "When they said yes to *EastEnders*, the deal was done on the basis that I also insisted, 'Listen, you can't take away from me the money that I already have – it has to be on top of it.' 'What? You mean you want 200 hours plus this twice a week?' 'Yes!' It was a long battle but we won it."

Nor was it a sacrifice made to help fund the launch of breakfast television (which had already been up and running since January 1983) or the new daytime service (launched in September 1986). The BBC had its usual financial woes – it was ever thus – but no, this was primarily an artistic decision rather than a financial one. The four men involved all believed that the show had had its day. "It was terrible. *Doctor Who* was a long way down the list of priorities, frankly," says Powell. "It didn't really figure. What it needed was triple the budget. It was made, as far as I remember, for nothing. But it wasn't worth investing in. It was a problem child, it really was. It was an embarrassment. It had become a laughing stock. Nobody wanted it to succeed – we wanted it to die."

The spurious reasons hinted at or given in subsequent interviews were all an early example of spin. Many of them centred on the idea that the BBC needed to make up a sudden shortfall of cash. As Reid puts it: "People will tell other people what they need to tell them. My guess is that the various reasons were probably a smokescreen. Michael Checkland [director of resources] was an excellent accountant and he just wouldn't have made that kind of mistake with the figures."

John, who always denied that the show had ever been cancelled, would often point to other programmes axed at the same time – among them *Crackerjack* and *Pop Quiz* – omitting to note that such decisions are part and parcel of each and every year's commissioning process. He got some of his facts wrong too, often citing that his old friend Geraint Morris had his *Juliet Bravo* series cut to eight episodes. This is untrue. At 16 episodes, *Juliet Bravo*'s final season in 1985 was, in fact, the longest yet.

Rumours about the imminent fate of *Doctor Who* began to seep from the notoriously leaky sixth floor of Television Centre. Robert Holmes knew a well-connected secretary who worked there and shared the gossip and, on Thursday 21st February, he phoned Eric Saward to tell him what he'd heard – that the show was about to be cancelled. "Eric phoned me up," says Ian Levine, "shitting himself – 'If I tell John, the only question will be, 'How dare you know this before me? I'm the producer!' I cannot tell him – it will be World War Three. You'll have to tell him. He knows you've got sources and hear things all over the place. Just tell him.' So I phoned up John and said, 'They've cancelled the show.' He said, 'Don't be ridiculous, you're talking out of your arse. Why do you listen to such rubbish?'"

Half an hour later, Saward plucked up the courage to face John and tell him that he had heard the same rumour, admitting it was Holmes who had told him. "I dismissed the whole thing out of court," John later admitted in his memoirs. "Arrogance, maybe, but I couldn't believe that such a major decision had been made without any form of discussion with the front office. It was inconceivable."

On Friday 22nd, John flew off as planned to attend a *Doctor Who* convention in America. While he was away, whispers of the imminent cancellation spread around fandom and it was then that I first heard them, over a crackly line on a pay phone in my college at a snowbound Durham University. Nobody could quite believe it would really happen. But, shortly after arriving back in his office on the Monday morning, John was summoned up to Powell's office and given confirmation that the rumours were true. It was, as Saward told *Doctor Who Magazine*, "a bizarre situation. John came down quite shortly after. He walked into my office, saying, 'We've been cancelled and they won't say why.' He was in a state of shock. That day we were due to have a playback for the second episode of *Revelation of the Daleks*. He said, 'I don't think I can do this.' I said, 'Do you want me to do it?' There used to be a pecking order for playbacks. John would sit behind his desk; I would sit in one of the armchairs; the director would sit opposite. 'Would you?' John said, so I sat behind the desk. Graeme Harper came in and did a double take. 'No,' I said, 'I'm not the producer yet.' I made a joke of it. We went through the playback and John just sat there. He had never been so quiet or un-opinionated. It took him quite a while to recover."

"I know he was very hurt by it," says Harper. "Very down and very depressed – they didn't know if [the series] was going to happen again."

"Oh yeah – there was a certain amount of shock and upset," says John's secretary, Sarah Lee. "To be honest, we thought, 'What a bunch of monkeys – they don't realise what they're throwing away.' We just thought how very silly of them. John tried to fight it, as any producer would."

"If he hadn't done that," says Levine, bluntly, "they would have cancelled the show. The BBC said they were going to rest it for a while and then bring it back. They had no intention of doing that. It was a lie."

"It wasn't a postponement; it was a cancellation," agrees Colin Baker. "Initially, John just told me that the programme had been cancelled. Then it mutated into being a postponement."

"John was very much putting a brave face on it," recalls Nicola Bryant, "and saying, 'Look, it's got nothing to do with you, it's a ridiculous thing – we're going to fight this. I've got plans.' It was all terribly personal."

In the days before the story broke, Gary Russell, fan, writer and script editor, was working in the press office. "Kevin [O'Shea – the drama press officer] told me, 'We need you to keep this quiet but is there any rumour in fandom? Because the show's been cancelled.' I don't think I believed it – I thought this was another JN-T publicity stunt, to get a reaction from *The Sun*. The BBC had no idea what they'd let themselves in for."

The news reached the public with a report in the London *Evening Standard* on the afternoon of 26th February. This, too, indicated a cancellation. With the story now in the public domain, the fight back could begin. Whatever his own feelings, John rallied himself and his friends, acting carefully and discreetly so that he could avoid any suspicion of involvement. The two prime movers were, on the inside, his close friend, Kevin O'Shea and, outside the BBC, Ian Levine. "Kevin got on with John because they shared a love of vaudeville, theatre and film," explains Gary Russell. "Kevin was a master at manipulating the tabloid press – John was too – but none of the big stories would been pulled off without Kevin. Kevin knew the journalists and which ones to target."

"John came to my house," says Levine, "and sat there, planning a strategy. He was livid. There was a code word called 'Snowball' – I had to phone Charles Catchpole at *The Sun* and quote 'Snowball' – the code word for a known BBC insider who leaked things. All the time I was talking to him, John was scribbling things on a pad for me to say. Next day, front page of *The Sun* – 'Dr Who* Axed In BBC Plot' – every word that I passed on was out of his mouth."

It was just the kind of story Fleet Street loved – showbiz, slightly ridiculous, which lent itself to a specious campaign (the *Daily Star* issued "Save *Doctor Who*" stickers) and gave the journalists another stick with which to beat the BBC, a popular activity even then. Day after day, they ran stories and hounded the press office and cast for quotes. There were items on television and radio shows. In the *Doctor Who* office, the phones rang non-stop – Patrick Troughton even popped in to show solidarity and answer some of the calls. The nadir of this media circus was the making of an ill-advised charity record called *Doctor in Distress*, inspired by the staggering success of Band Aid's *Do They Know It's Christmas?* the previous Christmas.

"I didn't want to do that," says Baker, with feeling. "That was an appalling lapse in taste, judgement and everything. All I know is that John rang me up and said, 'There's a big record producer called Ian Levine who's doing this record to save *Doctor Who* and he's got loads of big recording stars who care about the programme and they want you to come and do it. I said, 'I'm the last person who should come and do it. It's going to devalue it if I'm doing it because of course I want my job! I felt *desperately* squirmy about it. But one thing that John always did was to make it perfectly clear that he'd be very unhappy if you didn't do it for him, as a favour. It was just tacky."

According to fan Paul Mark Tams, who was closely involved in the project, the idea for the record started during a get-together in one of John's regular haunts, the Albertine wine bar on Wood Lane. "I'd go there after work," says Tams, "and meet Sarah [Lee], and Eric and Gary would turn up and we'd drink a couple of bottles of wine. At the time of the cancellation, John sat down and said, 'We've got to think of some ideas to keep this going in the press,' and we had this brainstorming session. I'd done a track for Gerry Anderson's

Terrahawks album so I said, 'Well, a tribute record using the *Doctor Who* theme would really be nice,' and he said, 'It's a really good idea – it would keep it fresh.'

"Bullshit – that's a complete lie," says Levine. "It was John and Gary's project. We were sitting in my house in North Acton, planning what to do to save the show and Gary Downie said, 'I've got a great idea. Let's do a Band Aid charity type of record.' John's eyes lit up and he said, 'Let's get Evil Annie to do it!' Tams's task was to pick all the singers, except for the ones under contract to Record Shack [the company Levine was working for at the time] and John who got Colin, Nicola, Anthony Ainley and Nick Courtney. Tams designed the cover, too, and he was in the studio every step of the way. John kept completely away – he couldn't be seen to be involved."

"I arranged for a lot of these people to take part," says Tams. "A lot of their PR people turned up for the recording session and then did a three-point turn when they heard it. The first time I heard it, I died inside. Ian is the only person responsible for turning that record into the travesty it became."

"I had no desire to do it either," says Bryant, "but once Colin was on board, there was no way I could wriggle out. John was a very persuasive man. The day itself was great fun but I hate listening to it for obvious reasons!"

The Hi-NRG sound was in vogue and Levine, who wrote the lyrics, worked with his then musical collaborator Fiachra Trench (with whom he'd composed the theme to *K9 and Company*) and employed future Oscar-winner Hans Zimmer to put all the music together. But, looking back, Levine shudders to think of it.

"It's the worst blemish on my 37-year history of making records," he says. "I've written and produced over 2500 records and that's the worst. I cringe because I hate it so much. There were too many cooks. *Doctor in Distress* is inexcusable. I've never lived it down."

Despite a *Daily Star* front-page story and TV-AM turning up to cover the circus, subsequent interest from programmes like *Breakfast Time* and *Blue Peter* soon withered away when they actually heard the thing. Tams swallowed his pride and took to the stage to harangue a largely apathetic audience of fanoraks at the DWASocial convention in April 1985. "How many of you have already bought the record?" he started brightly, like someone playing Buttons in an amateur panto. There were barely suppressed smirks and a squirming in seats as Tams went on – and on: "Just to run through a few people that are actually on the record, if you've never heard of them, I'll explain who they are. 'There's hardly any real stars on there' – that's what the BBC said. There's Faith Brown, I know you've all heard of her [Brown had guested in *Attack of the Cybermen*]. Miquel Brown, who is a very nice black lady singer from America who had a hit, *So Many Men, So Little Time*. From Bucks Fizz we have Bobby G, and you've all heard of him. Hazell Dean, a big chart topper... Hot Gossip... We had Julie Harris and Steve Grant from Tight Fit. We had Matt Bianco. We had Justin Hayward and John Lodge. The Moody Blues, and they are world megastars, who were as big as the Beatles. We had Phyllis Nelson who's at number 14 this week. We had the stars of *Starlight Express*... If that isn't starry enough for the BBC, then what is?"

"I knew who very few of them were," says Baker. "They didn't quite know why they were there either. I think they'd had their elbows up behind their back by Ian Levine and marched into the studio. So it was quite uncomfortable. It was just a bit, 'What's all this about?' It was cringe-worthy, it really was. I don't think it helped in any way at all. I don't think it hindered either. It just left a bad taste in the mouth."

Released under the unfortunately double-edged name, Who Cares, the finished track was, with dull predictability, excluded from radio playlists (the BBC rejected it on the grounds that it wasn't up to their artistic standards) and heard by only the die-hards and collectors – and most of them were startled by its plonky amateurism. "Eighteen months is too long to wait," ranted the group chant at the start of the track. Three and half minutes was too long to listen, one might counter. It seems unlikely that it raised much in the way of cash for the nominated charity, Cancer Relief, other than the £100 paid for the rights to release it on DVD in 2007.

But, despite this wretched misfire, in a strange way, the whole farcical hoopla that greeted the news that the BBC had derailed the Doctor was one of John's shining moments. If he had sat still, done nothing, said nothing, the fuss would eventually have died down and the show would almost certainly have ended there and then. Working incognito to stoke the fires of dissent, John was fighting for everything he believed in. The BBC, as so often, were caught on the back foot.

"There was such a hoo-ha from the public," says Harper, "and certainly from the fans that they embarrassed the BBC into giving it another go."

In a 1990 interview with *DWM*, John said: "As a staff producer, I felt it appropriate to say nothing. But as far as the fans were concerned, it was their finest hour. There was talk of jamming Wood Lane and marching to Downing Street with Daleks and Cybermen."

"I was summoned to a meeting," grimaces Powell, "after we'd cancelled it. The meeting was with Bill [Cotton], Michael [Grade] and Keith Samuels, who was head of press, and what had happened is that some fans had threatened to attack the House of Commons with the Daleks. We were all joking about this until Keith said, 'You have to do something about it,' and we went, 'What are you talking about?' He said, 'If they take the Daleks to the House of Commons, that photograph will be on the front page of every single newspaper in the entire world.' At that point we said, 'OK, maybe we haven't cancelled it – maybe it will come back in a year's time.' If that hadn't happened, it would have gone. But the judgement was that it simply wasn't worth it. There was too much else going on and it was not worth the aggro.

"It was hard because the *Doctor Who* lobby was quite a fearsome lobby, actually. Though quite why we couldn't all fucking stand up and say, 'Look this programme has come to an end; it's run its course,' I don't quite know. It wasn't just me. It was several grown men who for some reason couldn't. It was sort of like an institutional part of the BBC. There were programmes that become part of the mythology. At the same period, Michael had the problem of moving *Panorama* from its entrenched eight o'clock slot. I later had the problem of what you do with Esther Rantzen and *That's Life!* Things get tired. If one had loved *Doctor Who*, one would have a found a way of doing it. Nobody loved it. Nobody loved *him* [John]. Well, they might have loved him down on the studio floor but up at my level, he didn't have any allies. I didn't really want to help him, that's the truth of the matter and, in any case, he didn't have any intelligent views on the thing. In the end, in everybody's mind, if we couldn't cancel it because of the bloody *Doctor Who* society, we just wanted it to die and sadly he became part of that process."

There was a second key factor in commuting the execution. "Another of the tails wagging the dog," sighs Powell, "is that it was almost entirely paid for by Enterprises. If you cancelled it, you really were going to upset them. What they wanted was something to refresh the catalogue. There was a huge financial imperative."

Drama series and serials manager Marcia Wheeler remembers: "It was made for three and sixpence and half a shoestring and Enterprises put more cash into *Doctor Who* than it cost to make, which was very unfair. He couldn't cancel it without not only losing the programme but the extra money, which he'd then have to rob from somebody else's budget. Every time they tried to kill it, the finance people rose up as one in horror."

Publicly, John never deviated from his story that the show was only ever going to be rested. Strangely, in his memoirs, he put forward the argument that it made no sense to keep him, Saward and the rest of the core team on the payroll "to plan a new series that would never happen" – ignoring the logic that, had the cancellation gone ahead, they would all too swiftly have been out of a job. However, such was the speed of events, and the eagerness of the BBC's top brass to stifle the hue and cry, that cancellation was rapidly rechristened postponement. It was decided that Bill Cotton should telephone the glad tidings to DWAS coordinator David Saunders, who worked as a librarian. "It was a very brief conversation, if you can call it that," says Saunders. "There were already whispers at my work that I had spent too much time thinking about *Doctor Who* and not enough time thinking about Brent libraries. I tried to commit to paper what he said so that I could remember word for word what he'd said."

"We always thought it amusing," says Powell, "that Bill's secretary, Queenie, had called this head of the *Doctor Who* society and the voice at the other end had said, 'Hello, it's Crouch End Public Library' [*sic*] and when Queenie had said, 'Can I speak to Joe Bloggs?' the voice had said 'Oh, he's stacking shelves. I'll go and get him.'"

This sub-Alan Bennett image greatly appealed to John and O'Shea as well, and John even included a version in his memoirs in which they "speculated that David was up a ladder at the time, with another librarian yelling from below, 'David, it's the managing director of BBC Television on the phone,' and the customers all yelling, 'Sssssh!'"

Saunders himself chides, "Yes, most of the time that would been the case but I was actually up in the work area, away from the public. John did say to me afterwards that, 'I've told everybody about this great image I had of you up a ladder researching books.'"

Cotton's subsequent press release was issued on 1st March, couched in the curiously infantile and patronising tone so often adopted by these efforts: "As every follower of *Doctor Who* knows, you can't kill a Time Lord. Today, Bill Cotton, managing director of BBC Television, phoned David Saunders, coordinator of the Doctor Who Appreciation Society to explain the BBC plans... instead of running in January 1986, we shall wait until the start of the autumn schedule and then *Doctor Who* will be a strong item in the mix. We are also going back to... 25-minute programmes. We think that is what the public wants. So does the producer and his team. It also means... that we can run the series for a greater number of weeks." Mr Cotton added: "I am confident that *Doctor Who* has a great future on BBC1."

On 13th March, John gave what appears to be his first interview post the crisis to David Saunders and Patrick Mulkern of DWAS. Mulkern still has the tape and remembers the occasion vividly. "We trotted up to the production office," he says. "JN-T was trying to sound upbeat but smoked non-stop, thrusting each new fag-end into a huge, already brimming bowl. He was quite guarded and would only speak of the 'delay' or 'postponement'. He told us, 'I think the reaction to the postponement of the show has taken a lot of people by

Enjoying the high life on location in Lanzarote for *Planet of Fire*, October 1983

(courtesy: Fiona Cumming)

Hamming it up at a personal appearance for *Doctor Who Monthly*,
summer 1984 *(JN-T collection)*

With Debbie Flint and Wendy Padbury – John as presenter
on BSB's *31 Who*, 1990 *(JN-T collection)*

Ian Fraser, Fiona Cumming, John and Anthony Ainley wow the crowds at an American convention. Jealousy and suspicion would eventually estrange Ainley from his producer *(JN-T collection)*

Smiling in the snow - on location for *Time-Flight* *(JN-T collection)*

Sophie Aldred and John at *The Curse of Fenric* barbie, 1989
(courtesy: Sophie Aldred)

(above left) One of the Brighton "glitterati" –
Michael Jayston and John, 2002 *(JN-T collection)*

(above right) John with protégé David Roden, 1993
(courtesy: David Roden)

surprise, very senior people at the BBC. I'm not surprised at all.' He could smirk about that at least. When we asked him about his current plans, he explained he'd built up a lot of leave, which 'is a constant embarrassment to my personnel officer'. He insisted that the next season would be his last. Then he went on, 'And I can't say why with that tape machine running, but I feel the current situation has not been...' and there he fell silent, but giving us that familiar inscrutable pout and eyelid flutter. Actually, I'd never seen him look so dejected, but then Gary turned up and the four of us went to the pub across the road. We got sloshed on wine and lager and John cheered up massively. The air was soon blue with bitchy tittle-tattle – I remember choking with laughter. That's my happiest memory of being in their company."

Happily for BBC senior management, the press showed remarkably little interest in the cost to licence fee payers of shelving the series just weeks before production had been about to resume. These were considerable and outlined in an internal memo requested by Powell, sent on the same day as Cotton's gushing and (as it turned out) duplicitous press release. As well as paying Colin Baker and Nicola Bryant for the entire series, along with actor Nabil Shaban, who had already been contracted to reprise his role as the monstrous Sil, most of the scripts had been bought and paid for. There were also costs for the transport and storage of the TARDIS console room set, the console itself, various corridor flats and the police boxes. John had chosen his directing team, too, though Matthew Robinson, Fiona Cumming, Graeme Harper and Bob Gabriel were all released from their commitments without any financial penalty for the department. Another potential director was production manager Margot Hayhoe. "He had very kindly suggested when I had done the directors' course that I could direct one of the *Doctor Who*s in the next season and then of course the next season was cancelled. Goodbye to that. They felt the show had had its time."

The grand total for the write-off was £89,471 (£213,000 in today's money).

John had commissioned the first story, *The Nightmare Fair*, from his predecessor Graham Williams. At the time, people were mystified – Williams wasn't a writer on the usual circuit – but in fact it was another of John's acts of kindness. They'd met at a recent convention and, knowing that Williams was suffering from depression, this was his way of doing something constructive to help. Alas for Williams, his story was now abandoned and he had to content himself with the chance to write a novelisation of it. On 7th March 1985, John contacted Brian Turner in copyright to confirm that three of the contracted writers – Chris Bidmead, Robert Holmes and Michael Feeney Callan (who had been a script editor on *Shoestring*) – had agreed to "extend there [*sic*] stories to cover the 25-minute episode, in return for an increase of fee simply to cover the additional minutes. Also all three have agreed to do this without a re grief [*sic* – presumably this should have read 're-brief']." These plans were not to remain in place long.

For many observers, one of the great mysteries is why John and his team, who had been publicly criticised by Michael Grade, were allowed to remain in their posts but were given minimal guidance about what they should now be doing to please their paymasters. "That's what was so awful about the BBC back then," Saward told *DWM*. "No one says, 'We're not happy with this, because...' A reason, any reason, would have given us confidence to plan and move on. We had no feedback from upstairs. I just thought, 'What are we doing here?'"

"John should have been hauled off it," says Wheeler, "and put somewhere he didn't have a history. Nobody had the bottle – the BBC was not, at that time, very good at career management. If I had been head of department, I think I would have tried very hard to get him into light entertainment on a trial basis because I think he would have been very successful."

"It's not as if he might not have been able to turn his hand to other things," observes Pat Dyer, who was John's personnel officer. "But the fact of the matter is that the BBC was very departmentalised at that time. People might have thought he would have done well in variety but you've got to think about what variety was like at that time. It wouldn't have worked. He wouldn't have got in. They home-grew their own people and there weren't that many. People stayed till they retired. It was like an entertainment mafia – they'd all grown up together. In the BBC in the 80s, there was hardly any cross-fertilisation. All these departments had their own way of doing things and their own way of bringing people on. Where was he going to go?"

"I think at the time," continues Wheeler, "Jonathan was very ambitious and tied up in his own agenda. How to say this politely? He hadn't a great deal of management skill or experience."

"There wasn't anybody else around," shrugs Powell himself. "There was no natural line of succession that I could remember seeing. If I'd loved the programme, I would have gone and somehow found a producer. Those were the days when the BBC had begun to take freelance producers but there wasn't a culture where you could ring up a freelance producer and say, 'Come and have a chat about *Doctor Who*, we're looking for ideas' – it very much had to be within the department. I didn't know what to do. I had no ideas. Also, what was I going to do with fucking John Nathan-Turner? What was he going to do? I didn't want him doing anything else because I didn't think he was good enough. You didn't want to give him stuff because you didn't trust him. And the worse the programme got, the less you were going to trust him. I wanted him to fuck off and solve it – or die, really. If he'd solved it, fine. But it had probably gone beyond solving. The only way of resuscitating it would have been to put a new producer on it – but we didn't want to resuscitate it."

Whether or not he sensed this chilly combination of hostility and indifference, John did his best to divine what was required of him now. There was a brief, token meeting, in May 1985, with both Grade and Powell. Grade was critical of Colin Baker's performance and asked that, in future, the programme should include "more fun" and less overt violence. John pitched Saward's idea (which Saward himself later damned as being "more from desperation than creativity") of an umbrella theme to the next season – in which the Doctor would be on trial. The trial idea, turgid, uninspired and fatally undermined by requiring the audience to commit to an over-extended concept, should have been kicked into touch from the first. Instead, it was given the green light, all other scripts were written off and Saward began the tortuous process of finding writers to bring life to his limp concept.

As if the public humiliation of being yanked off the air and run down in public by his own bosses wasn't enough, the latest shock for John and his team was the amputation of his episode count. Again, rumours of this started within a few weeks of the postponement. On 6th April, John accompanied Colin Baker to DWASocial 5, at the Novotel in London's Hammersmith. Before the producer and his star took to the stage, a voluble Ian Levine got there first, addressing a captive audience of barkers. "We're far from safe here, there's a long way to go. Rumours are flying thick and fast. Now is the most dangerous time. We can't prove this, it's only an unconfirmed rumour... the rumour is that when it comes back, they're cutting it down to 20 episodes, which is going to mean a drastically curtailed season. Now I don't want to see that happen. I personally think if this is the case and they give us a short season, it's very bad news. I'm going to urge you now to please write some more letters."

Levine went on to suggest that there were six people who should be the recipients of these letters – Stuart Young (BBC chairman), Alasdair Milne (director-general), Bill Cotton (managing director), Brian Wenham (director of programmes), Michael Grade and Jonathan Powell. "If everybody in this room wrote to all six of these people and got all their friends to do it as well... it would be a help. I hope you will join me in doing that, please."

Levine had heard the story about the possible cut in episode count directly from Saward. When it was John's turn to speak, no doubt already feeling uncomfortable in the circumstances and surroundings, he answered back. He kept his voice smooth but his eyes were flinty. "I was slightly perturbed in a way to hear that shortly before we came up here, which is perhaps why I can feel a sort of wave of tension from you, that somebody has wound you up with stories of one more season and 20 episodes and then it's dead. I think whoever did that is both just stupid and preposterous – *preposterous* – well, it is preposterous when we are giving up Easter Saturday to come along and lay ourselves open to talk to you. Let me tell you that there is no decision on programmes until, at the earliest, July. So for anyone to spread around a rumour that there are going to be 20 episodes at the beginning of April is just lunatic. No decision has been made and that's an end of it. And with regard to the future, I think that the future of the show is secure. And I'm sorry that you were wound up before we came on and I hope we can get this panel onto a more amenable footing. No, I don't want to discuss it further."

His pronouncement triggered a round of applause and there were no more awkward questions. "If you had seen him backstage," seethes Levine, "John stood there all squinty-eyed, 'How dare you? How dare you go and speak about my show? You're in a position of privilege because I put you there. Who do you think you are? It's my show, my show...' Because he was lying and I knew he was lying and I saw my show in danger."

Dominic May, who, at the time, was editing the DWAS newsletter, *Celestial Toyroom*, subsequently "wrote a piece which said, 'Who do you believe?' I could have worded it differently, though. Ian was offensive, taking to the stage and delivering what I always considered to be this Nuremberg rally-type call to arms over the fact the next season was only going to be 20 episodes. He was inciting the fans, which annoyed me. I got it in the neck from both of them. Ian complained to David Saunders and I was made to write an apology to Ian – at the same time I was also criticised by JN-T for questioning the veracity of the producer of *Doctor Who*."

For years, John has been reproached for publicly rebuking Levine and sticking to what have usually been supposed to be his own bare-faced lies. But the truth is more complicated. Even if he was aware of the rumours (and it seems inconceivable that he wasn't), he could hardly scoop his own organisation with a piece of news that was bound to have an incendiary effect (even if the world at large could care less). Besides, at this stage, the paperwork proves that he was still working on the assumption that a full 26-episode run would be required. In a memo to Jonathan Powell and Marcia Wheeler, dated 7th May, he outlined in detail the full proposed filming and recording schedule for a season of five four-part stories and one six-parter. So what happened?

"This would have been in the middle of the offers season," explains Wheeler, "when *everything* was in flux – ideas in and out, episode numbers and target TX dates, film/OB/studio and London versus regional hosting. The offers 'season' started about April, moving to actual budgets by the end of June/July. Remember that series and serials were making about 300 hours of drama a year at this point. A change of plan at that stage would just have come and gone. The argument about episodes (or even survival) may well have continued up to the last minute. Offers wasn't really one decisive moment; various plans for the new financial year would be hatched, very roughly costed, and the head of department would discuss these with the controllers at informal pre-offers meetings. The whole thing was a version of zero-sum budgeting, where each department started with a blank sheet each year (apart from shows running across the financial year end) so everybody overbid, hoping to get more programmes and the money to make them. Matters were not always resolved even at the formal offers meeting, and, anyway, that was only the first stage, as resources meetings followed. Even then, projects could be abandoned or rescheduled through the autumn as deals fell through, scripts failed or something else went wrong. Dead ideas sometimes sprang to life, had a moment and sank back into the primordial slime of the reject pile. Far more ideas were worked up than were accepted, so there was generally a revised allocation after offers.

"Money would not have been allocated to *Doctor Who* until it was agreed at offers, though there must have been a problem with funding at some level, given that the cash cost of making *Doctor Who* was less than the money put in by Enterprises. It was probable that money *was* tight. It might also have been the case that another department had come up with a good idea for that slot, and the only way to fund it was to cut down on *Doctor Who.*"

Postponed, criticised, curtailed, in retreat. "Again, it was a sad time," John recorded in his memoirs. Referring to the careful but illusory wording of Cotton's 1st March press release, he noted: "14 episodes is more than 13, of course, but effectively we'd lost the equivalent of almost half our previous amount of screen time."

He did fight – and this time won – a proposal to record at least some of the next series in Birmingham, noting in the relevant memo: "Having worked as the PUM of the 1977 story which was recorded there, I honestly don't think the studio is large enough for our needs. Although it would be lovely to visit my parents, I don't think nowadays it is a practical idea."

Forced into his least busy year since he'd left school, John, typically, brazened out whatever humiliation and worry he may have felt. He used some of his extensive backlog of leave (paid holiday), travelled extensively, taking his parents on an American tour and attending a string of US conventions. Here at least, it was business as usual and he could be sure of the comfort of an enthusiastic, sympathetic audience. Back at home, he took the surprising decision to take a flying leap – out of a plane. "That's the big story," says Baker. "The Red Devils needed to raise money to buy a new plane. They asked us to do a fund-raising jump. So it was John and I and Sarah [Lee] and Eric Saward, and, because I'd been out with him the night before, Ian Ogilvy. So the Saint and the Doctor jumped together!

"We did our day's training – learning the fall – me overweight, John overweight, Sarah overweight, Eric Saward younger and fitter, being butch and taking the piss out of us mercilessly – 'You're so unfit.' Before we get into the plane, we're told, 'The only way you are going to get out is through that door.' We get up in the plane and the first one to go out is Eric and he turns into this feral creature desperate to save his life. He's scrabbling at the floor, whimpering and begging not to be let out, crying, and saying, 'I can't do it,' as the boot pushes him out of the door. We all looked at each other and thought, 'Even if I'm going to die, I'm not going to die like that.' So we all went out with varying bits of bravado."

As John put it in his memoirs, "I thought, 'I've been thrown out of better places than this and *I'm* not going to be pushed, so I went through the rehearsed procedure with so much statuesque poise that Colin said afterwards that I looked, when framed in that doorway of blue sky, like Claudette Colbert in one of her greatest movies!"

"John had a slightly twisted ankle," continues Baker. "We were all slapping each other on the back. But Eric was very shame-faced. He walked off and didn't socialise with us. He was always very odd after that."

That same summer, Saward had provided Radio 4 with a short *Doctor Who* serial, *Slipback*, (commissioned in a bid to attract some customers to the notorious wasteland of 4's attempts at appealing to younger listeners) and was kick-starting his self-imposed *Trial*. He'd invited two quality writers, Jack Trevor Story and David Halliwell, to join old hands Philip Martin and Robert Holmes but neither could deliver the goods. Meanwhile, having made various premature statements that the two regulars would stay throughout the season to come, John had a change of heart and decided that Bryant's Peri should be sacrificed to make way for a new face who might give his truncated show a mid-series publicity boost. The tension between producer and script editor remained.

"They were very different," observes Sarah Lee, "and I think that was probably good for *Doctor Who*. Eric thought a lot about the stories and characters. He was very bright. They both had big personalities and took their jobs very, very seriously. They both had the programme at heart – they really pushed to do what they thought was good and right. They fought passionately for what they wanted in the programme. They both could be overdramatic at times. But if, as I later did, you work on feature films, you get a lot more hot air than ever went on in that office."

As Christmas came along, John might have been forgiven for feeling relieved to see the back of a shocking and difficult year. But if 1985 had been grim, then both professionally and personally, 1986 was going to prove even worse.

TEN

ON TRIAL

"You can't make something that everyone likes. It's like going on holiday with your family. It's a nightmare – everybody doesn't want to do the same thing. When you're the ship's captain, you have to have the courage of your convictions, don't you?"
Sarah Lee, John's secretary, interview with author, 2012

Since it opened in 1977, Joe Allen's, tucked away in a corner of London's Covent Garden, has been the capital's most theatrical restaurant, its post-show sitting always particularly packed. Whenever you book, at least a few of its tables will be teeming with star turns, the air thick with cries of "Darling!" as Equity's finest gossip or are reunited. Perfectly at home in such surroundings, it was here that John met a young singer, dancer and actress whom he decided would give the wounded *Doctor Who* a dose of Doctor theatre.

Bonnie Langford was 21 years old but already a show business veteran, having made her first television appearance on the grisly talent show *Opportunity Knocks* and swiftly moving on to other high-profile work in *Junior Showtime* (an egregious variety show heaving with stage school brats) and, most famously, playing Violet Elizabeth Bott (catchphrase: "I'll scweam and scweam until I'm sick") in LWT's classy adaptation of Richmal Crompton's *Just William* stories. Her first flush behind her, Langford had reinvented herself as one to watch in the super-competitive world of West End shows. She'd also been in the star ensemble of the BBC's very popular all-singing, all-dancing *Hot Shoe Show*, launched to cash in on the *Fame* phenomenon. With her mane of curly bright red hair, dazzling smile and effervescent energy, she was always "on". Not everyone's cup of tea, she was, nevertheless, right up John's street. More to the point, her agent, Barry Burnett, was a friend and also represented Colin Baker.

"He was out having dinner with Barry and talking showbiz," recalls Langford. "John just loved theatre and showbiz and all that jazz. I just said hello and there were a few niceties and then my agent said, 'John produces *Doctor Who*,' and I said, 'Oh wow, how lovely – I'd love to do that.' I didn't really mean it – I think I just said it as something to say – but he took me at my word.

"I went to meet John in Union House and he gave me a paragraph, literally a paragraph, of this character talking about fitness and carrot juice and he said, 'Do you think you could do that?' and I said, 'Course!' Really, it was as low key as that. There was nothing to read – nothing had been written. The next I heard I was doing *Doctor Who*."

The available evidence suggests that John always intended the new companion – Mel – to be played by Langford. Colin Baker, who'd worked with Langford in a pantomime in 1980, remembers, "A year before, I had said to John something along the lines of 'You'll cast Bonnie Langford next' – I mean, this was way back – and he'd gone, 'Oh no, I don't think so.'"

John devised the character (if you can so dignify the few misogynistic lines he cobbled together) in the summer of 1985. "Melanie is one of those annoying young ladies who is a women's libber at all times, except at moments of great stress when she relies heavily on playing the hard-done-by, downtrodden, crocodile-teared female. [She is] scintillating, fascinating and irritating. She has a mane of red hair... She is heavily into aerobics and health food... and is often heard singing in the TARDIS."

Script editor Eric Saward told *DWM:* "He came in and said, 'I want a companion with red hair.' By this time, I was getting a bit tired and thinking that I really should have left last year and I thought, 'What nonsense is this now?' No thought had gone into it. With all due respect, Bonnie didn't have much of a reputation as an actress. That said, I wrote a piece for her audition with Colin and she was *brilliant*. She read it unseen and she was excellent and I was semi won round by it."

"I deliberately wanted to cast a high-profile artist such as Bonnie," John related in his memoirs. "Not only to capitalise on her enormous talent but also as part and parcel of my attempts to gain publicity for the long-awaited return of the show. I stand by my decision. It worked. The photo of Bonnie and Colin on high wires [at the time, Langford was starring in *Peter Pan* and the photo call took place on the stage] made a tremendous splash."

But here John was deluding himself. After the press got their shots at the Aldwych Theatre on 23rd January 1986, the story certainly ran everywhere but much of the coverage was mocking in tone and the photos, while a marvellous showcase for the lithe Langford, were horribly unflattering to his star. Baker had put on weight during the enforced break and this, his freshly curled hair and the flying harness worn under his heavy costume, bulking it out, all combined to result in unhelpful and unkind comments.

"Of course it was a publicity stunt," shrugs Baker. "Those pictures were awful but I suppose the overriding thing was the pleasure of doing it again with the opportunity to prove that they were wrong to cancel it and to do it as well as we could."

"There was no way I was trying to usurp him," says Langford, "but maybe he felt it was just another thing that he had to deal with. It was difficult. I don't know if he felt differently about me being there. There was an awful lot going on behind the scenes. I thought I should just try to support him. When it came to making the show, he was the main man and I was the sidekick."

Whatever the verdict of press and public, within the BBC, Langford's arrival led to raised eyebrows. "Yes, it's not our finest hour, is it?" says Jonathan Powell. He sighs and thinks about it. "Why would I sit in that office, with all those producers, and 300 hours of drama a year and listen to the likes of Gerry Glaister, who I thought was superannuated and infuriating, and let him strong arm me into doing *Howards' Way*, or someone like Ken Riddington, who wasn't going to set the world alight? Somehow they managed to deal with you and persuade you. John just didn't. He just couldn't somehow."

Whatever his feelings, Powell didn't challenge the casting. "Putting Bonnie in was a bit of a bonkers move," says director Chris Clough, who was in charge of her first six episodes. "She was kind of damaged goods, really, and to put her in was a bit daft, I thought. John didn't play the game as well as he should have done. He should have stepped back and been a bit cannier and buried the light entertainment part of his psyche and worked at the serious side of the show, sharpened it up and not had it so pantomime-y. You could have made something really good."

"They came up with this quite interesting character of Mel," says future script editor Andrew Cartmel, "a computer scientist. Given the set-up of the character, you could have done something very interesting with it but she just wore these garish costumes and became the classic screamer. It played to her existing TV persona – some people hated it and hated her. When you've got Colin in that costume and his companion is Mel, it's camp city from the start."

"Oh my God, his back was up against the wall," says Langford. "He was trying every which way to get the ratings up. He wanted the show to be remembered. Things were awful. I could see that he was stressed and of course I didn't know whether that was how John was anyway. I think in some respects he had me along as light relief. I do keep people jolly and we would talk showbiz.

"It was very tense between him and Colin at that point. I think John kept me purposefully in the dark so that I didn't ask questions but it was quite apparent that it was not a happy set-up. There were times when I did feel that I was being thrown in at the deep end and perhaps being kept in the dark wasn't the greatest thing for me. I couldn't really work out why Colin was quite so angry because I had worked with him before and he had been great fun. I felt it wasn't my business to know. I thought the best thing to do was to go in to work and do the best you could with it."

For superfan Ian Levine, the arrival of bright, bubbly, jazz-hands Mel was the last straw in his disintegrating relationship with John. "Eric told me that he'd cast Bonnie Langford," he says. "Eric was really low. John and I were only just talking after the backstage row at DWASocial. He'd forgotten and it was all over for him but I'd never really recovered from that. I phoned him up in Brighton, knowing full well that Bonnie had been cast and I knew damn well why he'd cast her – for his pantomimes. I thought this was the final insult for *Doctor Who*. He always wanted to know what the fans were saying and what rumours were around. So I said, 'John, you won't believe the latest – you don't want to know because it's so stupid. I told them John is such a wonderful producer, he would never, ever do anything so awful.' He said, 'What is it, what is it, what is it?' 'They're all saying you've cast Bonnie Langford as the new companion.'

"He laughed and said, 'What a silly idea, where did you hear that? Who told you?' I said, 'Well, it's not true – we all know what a great producer you are. You're a man of taste. You'd never have cast her.' I was really playing to him. 'WHO TOLD YOU?' – 'John, why are you so bothered? Anyone would think it was true...' 'Of course it's not true. Who told you?' 'What difference does it make, it's just a silly rumour?' 'WHO TOLD YOU? I demand to know now!!' 'John, you're scaring me now...' and I put the phone down.

"At the time, he was writing this book, *The Companions*. He'd given me the manuscript to check. I started and there were 72 mistakes on page one! I started correcting them and then I thought, 'Fuck this!' He came to the house and said, 'Have you got it?' I said, 'Here you are, John. I don't want to talk to you. Goodbye.' I closed the door in his face and that's the last time I ever spoke to him.'

Even if John had his eye on Langford lending some razzle-dazzle to his future pantomime productions, it was flawed logic. She would never have taken the job. She didn't need to. Although she was appearing in *Peter Pan* and had done her share of other pantos in the past ("They can be a great thing to do, make some money!" she laughs), by this stage her career was principally in big

West End shows and tours. Langford herself rejects the idea out of hand. "I think that's a very foolish thing to say, completely wrong. I think John cast me in order to get the publicity and to lighten up the programme a bit. He did it to get the show to survive. Some people don't understand we're in a world called show business – and business is the longer word. They don't seem to realise that even in talking about it in a negative sense, at least it was being talked about."

The other new lady in John's life at this time was 21-year-old Kate Easteal, taking over as his Girl Friday from the stalwart Sarah Lee, who was leaving to try out as an assistant floor manager in drama plays. "It was quite a plum job," recalls Easteal (who now goes by her married name of Thomson). "I remember at the interview John asking me what my star sign was and thinking, 'That's a weird question,' but obviously that interested him as much as whether I could type. It was whether he and I were going to get on. He was very extrovert, friendly and outgoing. He'd obviously had a great friendship with Sarah and there was a lot to live up to because she was so gregarious and such a good laugh.

"Fundamentally, he had a big heart and when you worked for him, he would look after you. But he was controlling and he didn't like anything to happen without his say-so. He was like the captain of the ship and everything went through him. If he found out something had happened without him being aware of it, that's when he used to turn and snap and be quite unpleasant. I don't think that was related to the drinking – that was just his character.

"An example was when BBC Enterprises sent through a new calendar for the forthcoming year with a note on it saying, 'Can John and Colin both approve this calendar?' They were up at Television Centre so I went up at lunchtime and was in the bar in the BBC Club, waiting for them to come and Colin arrived first so I showed him the calendar. He was flicking through it, looking at all the pictures when John walked in. That was not good news. John was like, 'What's this?' and I explained. He took me to one side and said, 'Why is Colin looking at it?' 'Because he needed to approve it.' 'Yeah but I'm the producer and I see it first.' He was cross with me. I think it was unreasonable and petty but he didn't make a big fuss of humiliating people in front of anybody, like Biddy Baxter used to on *Blue Peter* [where Easteal had worked for 18 months previously]. She was worse and would sweep through the office, telling everybody off. He would just have an outburst. He wanted to be the one in charge. He was prickly like that – it was his show."

But when Easteal's brother died, she experienced his more sensitive side. "He said, 'If you need to have time off, or if you need to be with your parents...' and asked if I had thought about going to this medium because he'd heard about somebody locally and he felt that maybe that would be something which would help me come to terms with it. He could have just said, 'I'm sorry,' and left it at that. But he tried to deal with it in a way that another boss, especially a male one, may not have been able to or wanted to."

Easteal was an immediate hit with John and the wider "family" of *Doctor Who*. Says Andrew Cartmel: "He loved that people would drop in because we had this wonderful, bouncy, charming, delightful secretary that people liked talking to – it made his office a nexus."

Like Lee before her, Easteal was handed significant responsibilities and expected to get on with them. She remembers, "When *The Trial of a Time Lord* was being filmed, John called a press conference to herald the new season, in a hotel out west, somewhere like Somerset. It had been slotted into the lunch break. I was there and when the photos had been taken, John gave me his car keys and asked me to drive Colin back to the location. I was fairly new to the show. I had only just passed my test about three weeks earlier and had never driven on a motorway. It was John's own black Golf GTI that I had never driven before, and he sent me off down the M4 with Colin in the front passenger seat, in full costume. I couldn't believe that John would trust me with his car and his leading man – but he was a bit cavalier like that – I think he sent me so he could stay and have another drink!

"Everything else in the department seemed to be a bit more fluid whereas *Doctor Who* was kind of a law unto itself. John had this stronghold. It was like a separate entity."

Something that struck Easteal from the start, however, was the palpable atmosphere between producer and script editor. "I arrived into a bit of a triangle," she says. "There was a lot of tension all the time. I remember Eric used to come and sit with me and bitch a bit about John and then John would bitch a bit about Eric, raising his eyebrows. They had differences of opinion about the way the show was going. It all ended because Eric just walked out. He had a hissy fit and said, 'That's it, I'm off'. I thought he would probably come back but he just never did. That was it."

It had been a long time coming. Ever since the cancellation, Saward had brooded on the humiliating position in which he now found himself. It was his job to find the material and help to tell the continuing story of *Doctor Who*. With considerable justification, he struggled to understand the apparent schizophrenia of his own management's position. His superiors had traded jibes and criticisms of the show with journalists and broadcasters, while privately demonstrating little interest, support or guidance. Added to this, the increasingly uneasy relationship between him and his producer and the divergence in their respective views of what made good drama or good *Doctor Who* lent a queasy inevitability to what finally played out.

As he struggled with the self-inflicted burden of his flabby *Trial* concept, early aspirations to raise the bar in the writing of the scripts had soon collapsed. The "name" authors, Jack Trevor Story and David Halliwell, had fallen by the wayside. The usually reliable Robert Holmes was struggling with a serious illness. Only one of the original quartet, Philip Martin, had really delivered. Saward turned to his predecessor, Chris Bidmead, to fill the gap but when Bidmead's efforts, titled *Pinocotheca,* finally arrived in the New Year, Saward was first disappointed and then angry. On 2nd February, he fired off a memo to John: "I have now read Chris Bidmead's script three times. I find it boring – gibberish and totally out of character with the first eight episodes of the season, which I now think are working well. The script will not only require an end-to-end rewrite, but also a total rethink – in fact, a new story. Given Chris's personality, commitment to the esoteric and inability to write what was requested of him – a linear, fast-moving, humorous adventure – I think we are looking for a new writer. I strongly suggest that we reject this story and think again."

John supported his decision, though time was now getting tight to find a replacement. In desperation, Saward called in the Johnnie and Fanny Cradock of *Doctor Who,* husband-and-wife writing team Pip and Jane Baker, who, whatever their shortcomings, were industrious and could be relied upon to deliver. As he told DVD producer Ed Stradling in 2006: "I thought, well, it won't be great but they'll do it, and that's where I was at."

Then, on 24th February, the internal post spewed up a memo from Jonathan Powell concerning those first eight episodes, which Saward had felt were "working well". Unlike Powell's one line (and uniformly positive) views of the previous season, this was three pages of closely typed script assassination, aimed chiefly at the opening script by Saward's hero, Holmes. "I do feel that you have quite a substantial problem," wrote Powell, "to which I suggest you address yourself as a matter of great urgency... One of my main objections to the story is the <u>tone</u>. The writer is asking the viewer to believe that the Doctor is on trial for his life and existence. Yet the story comes across as very lightweight and slightly trivial... Some of the subsidiary characters are impossible to take seriously in any sense and this of course dilutes the credibility of the story.... Since the story is unclear, seemingly unmotivated and with rather ill-conceived themes, it is difficult to grasp the relationship of this story to the trial."

Powell went on: "The humour is irritating and counter-productive, the story is confusing and difficult to follow, also it is not clearly established and set up. We are never properly aware of what is at stake. There seems little real reason for the Doctor's involvement."

There was more, along with some suggestions for possible improvement. "I did make an effort reading scripts," says Powell, "and my script notes may not have been brilliant as I didn't understand the programme, really. It was one of those problems I couldn't really solve. I had lots of other things to worry about and I remember thinking I really do want it to go away."

Saward, wounded and thoroughly defensive, began to flail about, trying to salvage Holmes's work. "Maybe he was tired, maybe we were all tired," he told *DWM*. "I think from that moment on we sort of lost our way. Mentally, I'd backed out of it all."

Holmes was also supposed to be providing the concluding pair of episodes, but, overwhelmed by his illness, he stalled. John now asked Saward to take over and provide the final instalment himself, based on everything discussed with Holmes. Wearily, Saward agreed, but, when the Bakers' scripts came in, his spirits sank even lower. "I got up one morning and thought, 'What am I doing? This is mad.' I went to see John and he was very good, telling me to go away and think about it."

On 2nd April, Saward formally resigned, in a letter to Jonathan Powell, explaining, "My reason for this sudden departure is very simple. I have somehow lost credibility with myself. To keep *Doctor Who* afloat, a show that at best is viewed indifferently by management, I have put the best writer (Robert Holmes) the series ever had in hospital and, out of sheer desperation, I am now working with two of the most talentless people (Pip and Jane Baker) who have ever had the nerve to set pen to paper. What's more, I will be expected to 'fix' their appalling drivel so that it will appear less like the pile of trash it is – a task I fear beyond Jehovah himself. Saddens me to leave in such a silly melodramatic way, but I am sick to death of *Doctor Who* and the way it is run."

Powell suggested that John persuade his script editor to return, making it clear that he could offer no replacement. Saward refused but agreed to continue with the task of writing the season finale. A couple of weeks later, on 21st April, he wrote to John: "When I last spoke to you, I had a story that seemed to be working – I'm sorry to say that it no longer is. Strangely, I cannot find the conviction, energy or whatever it is necessary to write this sort of tale at the moment. If, as M Grade stated, this part of the production team (ie me) had become complacent, I would be able to throw any shit down on the page (after all, don't most of the current writers do that anyway?) take the money and run – but I can't.

"As Pip and Jane seem to be liked by their director, I suggest that you ask them to write the last episode. Better still, junk the current episode thirteen and ask them to write the last two – it could in the long run prove easier.

"Thank you for your support and kind understanding over the last few weeks (I sincerely mean that). I wish it wasn't ending so messily (I should never have renewed my contract in March – neither should I have returned after I'd quit!) but I really can't go on. Don't hate me too much – I really would stay and continue if I could. Good luck with the season."

Saward added a telling PS – "A copy of this isn't going to J. Powell, so you can tell him what you like about my departure."

John replied at once. "I'm sorry you've decided that you feel unable to continue script editing the programme and I should like to take this opportunity to thank you for all your hard work, support and camaraderie over the last five years. I shall miss you. However, as you will not have the pressures of script editing, I would very much like you to continue writing episode 14. I accept the problems you mention with regard to writing this particular episode – it's not easy to wrap up all the loose ends of a 14-part serial in 25 minutes and keep the audience enthralled. But I know you can do it. You have always been best able to emulate (Bob's) style. Perhaps rather than rushing at it, if you took another week, you would be able to see the whole thing a little more clearly. I do hope you agree to this proposal and would be grateful to hear from you asap."

Saward agreed but beyond the courtesies and mutual expressions of good will, there remained unaddressed the issue that would finally destroy all trace of any trust, affection and solidarity between the two men. It centred on the final ending of the *Trial*. Between them, Holmes and Saward had agreed on a cliffhanger ending pinched from Sherlock Holmes. In the *Doctor Who* version, the Doctor and his arch nemesis, the Valeyard, would be trapped together in the Matrix on Gallifrey and the series would conclude with the audience in the dark about the Doctor's survival or otherwise. John rejected it out of hand. As he put it, not unreasonably in the circumstances, "I wanted an ending that clearly implied the show was back in business, with no question mark looming over its future."

"There may," ruminates Colin Baker, "have been a certain amount of wanting to aid the downfall of the programme whether conscious or subconscious in Eric's mind when he wrote that."

On 20th May, Saward responded sharply to John's concerns over the final scene. "As with every story we've ever worked on together, you've always wanted a 'pantomime walkdown' as you call it. I've never agreed with this rather old-fashioned way of ending a story, or in this case, the season. I have offered you the ultimate in cliffhangers, which is more likely to have the audience screaming for more, than having Colin cooing into the camera and Bonnie slapping her 'principal boy' thigh. As I've said – you can have your 'walkdown' but I shall require detailed notes on how this is to be achieved."

The previous summer, when I'd spoken to Robert Holmes, his words perhaps give a clue as to the mindset he shared with Saward on the downbeat ending they favoured. "I don't mind, really [if they cancel the show]. A show that's been going that long is terribly difficult to think up a new idea for. I've got this little format ready to bung in the moment I hear it's been cancelled. It would be nice to have a long-running thing, wouldn't it?"

But on Saturday 24th May, in the midst of the squabble about how to resolve the ending, Holmes died in hospital. Saward was devastated, and felt guilty and at least partly responsible. "The story I was told," says Cartmel, "was there had been a lot of pressure on Robert and they'd been working him really hard and Eric was outraged and angry and felt that perhaps John had driven him to his early death. He apparently greatly admired Holmes and blamed John personally. But there was also this huge simmering sea of all these small problems that he'd had with John, which I can understand totally, and this might have been the tipping point. This is just me speculating."

Unable to reach Saward by phone, John had suggested a meeting on either Monday 26th or Tuesday 27th but this did not take place. Instead, on 28th May, Saward's final draft of episode 14 was delivered by hand with a covering letter in which he said, "What I haven't changed – don't start grinding your teeth until you've read the whole note – is the end. This type of ending had been planned from the very beginning. I am also certain that I told you, albeit a long time ago, what was proposed. Even if I hadn't... I think it's stronger, more gripping and gives you the opportunity to take *Doctor Who* wherever you want next season – for it certainly needs to go further than it did this one (as I was responsible for ten of its episodes, I mean that kindly!)

"If you think M Grade will take it off because of what I'm proposing, I think you're mistaken. He'll take it off, if he so chooses, however it ends. You could have "see you next season" flashing in neon throughout the last episode and he would still cancel it. As you well know, it seems to be down to audience figures and his personal whim. I feel in my very bones that your 'walkdown' ending is wrong! It's weak, far too predictable and anyway, we've seen it all before. Neither is it very dramatic. If you don't like my ending – fine. If you want to suggest an alternative – strong, powerful and dramatic ending I will, subject to discussion, happily incorporate it, but not your current suggestion."

The situation now unravelled completely, apparently through hearsay and gossip. On 1st June, Saward again wrote to John. This time there was no attempt to hide his scorn and hostility. "Do you not feel it would be more useful to discuss our difference of opinion privately, reasonably and in a professional manner, rather than you airing it publicly to a group of fans in the bar at

Television Centre? To slag me off to fans, knowing that what you said would be broadcast far and wide in a totally indiscriminate manner, is unforgiveable. Among the many things you allegedly said was your intention to personally rewrite my episode. What makes you think you have that authority? If you don't like my rewrites, we either talk some more (a bit late now) or you reject the script totally and start again. I feel sickened by what you've done, especially after having worked together for so long. I have always been aware of your obsession with the fans – especially the American ones – but I had always put that down to the large amount of money you've told me you earn by attending their conventions. Little did I know that you also opened your mind to them before conferring with the people with whom you work. Does Chris Cluff [*sic*] know that you allegedly said you were co-directing the last episode? As I can no longer trust you, I am withdrawing the last episode."

The letter was copied to Powell. John hurried to reply. "I am amazed... and appalled at the accusations," he wrote. "With regard to the allegation of 'slagging you off' or discussing the script publicly with a group of fans, this is simply totally untrue. Consequently, it is obvious that I have no intention of rewriting your episode. If you had responded to my secretary's attempt to make an appointment to see me today, I would have told you that I'm absolutely delighted with the rewrites and that the only thing I wish to discuss is the end... which Jonathan, Chris and I feel is not yet acceptable.

"The only obsession I have with the fans, as you well know, is that I despise their destructive attitude to those that work on the programme. As you are aware, they always feel they can do better. Consequently, fuelling their fires is the last thing I would ever do. It also goes without saying that the allegation that I was 'co-directing' the last episode is just plain ridiculous. Could you give me a ring as soon as possible to make a date to discuss the end? Rather than being angry about your letter, I am more saddened that you should believe allegations from youngsters whose sole ambition is to muck-rake where there is no muck."

But Saward furiously rejected John's "patronising denial", as he phrased it, suggesting cryptically that he "chew on a name with the initials A.W. [misremembered by John in his memoirs as A.R.] I'm sure it'll bring back tragic memories." It has never proved possible to trace to whom this A.W. refers and Saward claims to have forgotten. The whole mess now descended into a bitter legal struggle. There was nothing John could do to prevent the withdrawing of episode 14 but he fought Saward's attempt to invalidate the penultimate script too. Saward claimed (truthfully) that much of this was his work rather than Holmes's. On 5th June, he wrote to Brian Turner, a senior assistant in BBC copyright: "To make my episode work, I had to rewrite a sizeable chunk. As I wrote the material, unpaid, I am very keen that [the scenes] should not be used in the episode as it stands. I should be grateful if you would confirm, as soon as possible, that the above material has been withdrawn from production."

Brian Turner was on leave so the matter passed to the head of copyright, Stephen Edwards. Edwards wrote to Saward expressing that it was the BBC's opinion that the rewrites on episode 13 had all been conducted within the reasonable remit of any script editor's job. Saward contested this, raging to Powell in a letter dated 16th June: "How much longer must I put up with John Nathan-Turner's abuse, unprofessionalism and now theft of copyright material?"

In the old industry tradition that "shit rolls downwards", Powell ordered John to draft a reply, which he then signed. "I have your letter of 16th June," this read, "which I consider to be grossly defamatory of John Nathan-Turner and the BBC. You would be well advised to consider the legal risks you run in writing in these terms. As Stephen Edwards has already informed you, the BBC considers that the work you did on episode 13 was within the course of your duties under your contract. Accordingly the copyright in it belongs to the BBC. The BBC is therefore free to use it. That is our final statement on the matter."

But if John thought he had seen and heard the last of Eric Saward, he was very much mistaken. Ironically, the next disaster to beset him was largely of his own making. In October 1985, Marvel Comics' failing cult TV and film magazine *Starburst* had been bought by an entrepreneur called Stephen Payne. Payne was one of the founding fathers of DWAS. "I wanted to do an article in *Starburst* about the new series," recalls Payne. "I had rung the production office. JN-T always had a strange way of answering the phone. I'd say, 'It's Stephen Payne here,' and he'd say, 'Oh hello it's Stephen Payne here' – really irritating because it made you feel uneasy. But he was nice about it and arranged for me to have a set visit. Then, as we were getting close to it, he cancelled it for no apparent reason. It left a hole and I felt it was important to cover *Doctor Who*."

Ian Levine suggested that Saward might give the magazine a warts-and-all interview. Saward agreed and Payne conducted the interview himself. "It lasted two and a half hours," he says. "It felt like I was a psychologist that he had got to come along so that he could pour his heart out about what had happened. He was very upset, emotional and really raw about the whole situation.

"I came away thinking 'Oh my God, what am I going to do with this?' Some of it was contentious – facts which weren't verifiable and I certainly didn't want to put out some of the personal stuff – anybody who has fallen out with somebody else can pick holes in the other person and that shouldn't really be shared."

Payne turned to fellow fan Andrew Beech, who was then working as a lawyer. "I went through the manuscript," says Beech, "and there were references which I thought made Eric look rather poorer, delving into private areas which weren't capable of any substantiation."

"Between us, it went through various vetting processes," continues Payne. "I remember Ian Levine wanted a load of stuff left in there that we took out. We cut it down and cut it down. Lastly, I went through it and took out things that I simply thought were not fair – digs and so on." These included sideswipes at Jonathan Powell ("very odd – David Reid wasn't a good head of department but at least you had the idea he was listening..."), Sarah Sutton ("very nice but not very good"), Matthew Waterhouse ("a space prat" who could "never do the same thing twice") and, perhaps most relevant, the complaint that he always had to "sell" any script changes to John.

Luridly billed as "Revelations of a Script Editor", Saward's testimony, seething and bitter, was printed in the September 1986 issue of *Starburst* (published in August). Despite the vetting and the cuts, it was a scarifying piece of verbal terrorism and, leaving aside some bitchy observations about actors (in particular Baker and Langford), its principal target was John. As an article lifting the lid on a troubled television production, Saward's candour and condemnatory tone were not so much unusual as unheard of. "Don't hate me too much," Saward had pleaded in his resignation letter. Now he apparently couldn't care less, blasting his former producer over and over again as "the biggest prima donna on the show", citing the Grimwade row, the fight over scripts, his scathing views on John's choice of directors and actors and making snide comments about the money John was making from conventions on the side. There was also some somewhat disingenuous shifting of the blame for the forthcoming season too. Asked about how the idea for the *Trial* had come about, he replied, "It was as much an 'off the top of my head' suggestion to get things moving. This was July. We'd done nothing for four months." And yet there had been nothing to prevent Saward from getting on with finding some stories or even refining the considerable back catalogue he was left with by the postponement.

Alerted to the story by his old mate in the press office, the wily Kevin O'Shea, John was mortified by the extent of Saward's betrayal and revenge. "I shook with rage," he later wrote. "How could someone I'd worked with for so long say such things? If I was that awful, why had he stayed on the show for five years?"

Asked about it years later, he said, "I was shocked... saddened... angry. And that's pretty much how I still feel."

He considered taking legal action and consulted a solicitor, TJ Smith, who advised: "I must admit that my initial reaction was that any reasonable person reading the article would see it as a spiteful outburst. Be that as it may, some of the statements would appear to be defamatory."

But Smith also advised caution in embarking on any "protracted and expensive court proceedings" and suggested that he consult a BBC solicitor. John referred the issue to Powell, who advised him strongly to let the matter lie and not to make a fuss. "That was good advice," says Powell. "But I probably thought, too, 'Oh hooray, that's another nail in his coffin.'"

Meanwhile, friends rallied round. Director Sarah Hellings hand-delivered a note to him in the studio, which read, "I was appalled to read about Eric's remarks. As far as I'm concerned, if there's anything helpful I can do or say, I'd be delighted. I loved doing my *Doctor Who* and found you a caring, supporting, non-interfering (!) producer who gave me total creative freedom – a good script – and money for a good cast. What more could any director ask?"

Those even closer are still angered by Saward's exposé nearly a quarter of a century later. "I've never met him since," says Colin Baker. "I've always said the reason I don't want to meet him again is that I would hit him if I did. I suppose I probably wouldn't. But I would certainly look at him and I might curl my lip. I'd probably just say, 'Why betray a friendship? What was in it for you?'"

"If I'd got my hands on him on the day he did what he did," says Ian Fraser, "I would have killed him. That's how bad I feel about him. The day that he left that building, I was having lunch with John. We heard that he had gone and we thought, 'Oh,' and went down to his office and he had emptied everything. He'd taken all the scripts and everything and he had no business to, a lot of it was BBC property. We just stood and looked at it and thought, 'Why has he done this?'"

"John felt terribly hurt," says Fraser's wife, Fiona Cumming. "He had trusted Eric and for him to turn round and stab him in the back was a shock. It was a total betrayal by a mean-spirited man."

John never attempted any form of public revenge, wisely realising that he could scarcely refute some of the criticisms and that to maintain a discreet silence (other than bland sentiments of hurt and regret) was the only way to retain any shred of dignity. Had he been minded to do so, there was certainly mud he might have hurled at his nemesis. The surviving paperwork in the *Doctor Who* production files tells its own tales of Saward's particular deficiencies. One running theme is his tardiness with writers, leading to anguished pleas from their agents, like the letter from Glen McCoy's agent, Gilly Girdlestone at Cecily Ware, written on 21st November 1983: "Nearly four months has passed since Glen delivered his script to you and we are still waiting to know whether the BBC has accepted it. I think that Glen has been more than patient. I would appreciate at least the release of the 50 per cent fee due to Glen." A few weeks later, Philip Martin's agent, Sheila Lemon, echoes these sentiments, writing on 20th February 1984. "I do hope you will make a special note of the fact that six months has gone by between delivery of the script and a new request for revisions to add to all the other delays previously chronicled. I would be grateful if you could deal with this negotiation as soon as possible."

There was a tricky situation for John to navigate, too, when Peter Bryant, his predecessor as *Doctor Who* producer who'd become a literary agent, wrote to him on 13th November 1981. "This is a rather embarrassing matter and I am sorry that I have to inflict it on you. Back in August, I submitted the two above named outlines [*War Game* and *The Darkness*] from this client of ours [Eric Pringle]. At that time, Eric Saward, as well as being your script editor, was also a client of ours. However, in the interim, Saward has done a bunk from us, owing quite a lot of commission so our relationship, to say the least, is somewhat frosty. What concerns me is that Eric Pringle's ideas should be properly judged without any bias and since these ideas have been with your office for three months now, I am a little disturbed at not having a considered reaction by now."

Whatever Saward's side of the story, Pringle was the beneficiary of this contretemps. His *War Game* eventually became the well-regarded *The Awakening*, though only after Saward had massively restructured and rewritten the original submission. After the story was shown, a delighted Pringle had sent in a chirpy letter to Saward, enclosing the *DWM* review of the story ("It seems to have gone down very well and I am grateful to you for that!"). Saward passed this on to John, scribbling a terse note to go with it – "As the wrong Eric seems to get the credit for how well the story worked, are we really interested in using him again?"

For every triumph during Saward's time, there was just as much trash. He has since blamed John for refusing to write off more duds and for forcing unsuitable writers on him (usually because they were involved in other projects he was trying to get off the ground). There is certainly truth in both these complaints. But it is not the whole picture. Saward came to the job as an inexperienced television writer, bringing with him few contacts of his own. His naturally taciturn and introspective nature also made it harder for him to nurture relationships with writers, never mind his producer. Two of the most revered stories of the era, *Kinda* and *Snakedance*, were written by Chris Bailey. In a 2003 *DWM* interview, Bailey commented, "I was coming from drama, where the relationship with the script editor is quite important. I can't remember a single discussion about the script. I was used to working closely with a script editor or producer, but none of that happened on *Doctor Who*. I produced the ideas, but nobody would engage with me in terms of conversation. I had no creative springboard. I got back a script revision and quite a bit had been reworked – I'd had no input into it at all. I didn't even know it was happening. And the rewrites were clunky. I phoned the production office. 'This script is badly written,' I said, 'and it's got my name on it. I'm going to rewrite it!' I did a 48-hour rewrite. I couldn't get it back to what it was, though... I remember cutting stuff that Eric wrote, not just because it was gobbledegook, but because it was lame, laboured, fill-time gobbledegook."

The most experienced and respected script editor in the department was Betty Willingale. "I don't think John's judgement on scripts was very good," she says. "They should have widened the net and the script editor should have been the main person trying to get the scripts right. But to stay together for five years was a recipe for disaster. I can't imagine anything worse really. It must have been hell. It's the kind of show that calls out for change." I pointed out that Barry Letts and Terrance Dicks had worked harmoniously for this long on both *Doctor Who* and the Sunday classics. "But they were older and more experienced. They were also better read."

Even if he had declined to comment on Saward's own methods and standards, John might simply have accused his colleague of a fatal inability to say to his face what he was subsequently willing to share with the world, damaging them both in the fallout. As writer and director Peter Grimwade told me in 1987: "Eric's a very sweet man who doesn't want to tread on anybody's toes. I think that sums him up. I think an artist *has* to tread on toes. You've got to grasp these things. The minute you shy away from that, I think you've lost."

That neither man could find some effective way of communicating inevitably had a pressure cooker effect. It also led to the bizarre farce that surrounds the (still contested) writing of *Attack of the Cybermen*. According to Ian Levine, the story was cooked up between himself and Saward. "He'd been told by John that he couldn't write this story and so we had to bring this woman in." The reason Saward could not write two stories in one season was down to the understanding the BBC had established with the Writers' Guild restricting the ability of script editors to commission themselves. The "woman" to whom Levine refers was one Paula Moore (as credited but also sometimes referred to as Paula Woolsey), a former girlfriend of Saward's who apparently agreed to act as stand-in. Levine fumes, "Eric said, 'Everything will come to your address. We'll let you keep ten per cent for using your name and address.' But she kept every single fucking penny. That's why he doesn't speak to her any more. When people phone her up, she has to say that she did write it because she's made thousands of pounds out of it. She didn't write a word of it. Eric couldn't believe it – he was gutted.

"John got suspicious and insisted on meeting her. I went to the producer's booth with Eric at about 6.15 one studio night, trying to tell her the story because she didn't have a clue – she hadn't read it, didn't know a thing about it. We explained the characters motivations and what it was all about. John was easily reassured – he had no idea."

This deceitful subterfuge hardly reflects credit on Saward (perhaps why he has since declined to discuss it) but then nor does the result, a mishmash of fanboy nonsense and macho posturing. But perhaps the most damning indictment of Saward's own lapses of judgement and professionalism came towards the fag end of his *Doctor Who* career, when cast and crew began to wrestle with the undercooked scripts he offered them. "I think I have a logical mind," says Baker, "so I would instantly home in on inconsistencies. And there were plenty of inconsistencies. In order to play this scene with Nicola I needed to know whether the Doctor was being genuine or if the Matrix was lying. I needed to know so I could go for broke with it. So I asked Eric Saward and he said, 'I don't know – Philip Martin wrote that.' So they ring up Philip Martin and he says, 'No, Eric wrote that.' Eric would say, 'Why can't actors just say the lines?' to which I would say, 'In that case, why can't script editors script edit?'"

It was Saward who let script after script go through with pages of wearisome padding in the form of TARDIS scenes chiefly consisting of the Doctor booming and Peri whining. This bothered me enough at the time so I asked him about it when we met for *DWM*. Years later, to other interviewers, he merely blamed the shortcomings of the actress. But as Nicola Bryant was, at this time, ostensibly still a colleague, to me he attempted a different, and unconvincing, defence. "If Peri seems unhappy, you can put that down to me because I think if we all went out there [into space], we'd all be unhappy in a way."

Having decided on an American character, there was also a marked inattention to detail. "The scripts weren't written remotely American," says Nicola Bryant. "I would amend things that I thought were wrong, so I would say meat grinder instead of mincer and 'I don't want to say police, I'll say cop' – stuff like that."

"A lot of the stories from that period were very weak," says Andrew Cartmel, who eventually succeeded Saward as script editor. "You had that dreadful framing story of the trial – John was often the man for the big idea – 'Great, he'll be on trial, it'll be one huge story' but the fact is it was incredibly boring. You have the Doctor standing in the dock and then they'll zoom into the screen for the story to start. It's such a clunky, static, stupid idea. I've always hated anything that demeaned or diminished the Doctor and *Trial of a Time Lord* was a classic example of that – it's like putting a collar and lead on a tiger."

"The trial was a dull motif," agrees Clough. "Absolutely tired. We kept cutting back to this awful set with characters in this ludicrous headgear – nobody could give a damn what was going on and it slowed up the stand-alone story you were trying to tell."

For Saward, his petulance and indiscretion were punished, not by John, but by the way the industry largely turned its back on him. "What a mistake," comments Russell T Davies. "Has he worked since? That interview was gobsmacking – my eyes came out of my head. Awful thing to do, I've got to say. I can kind of understand him letting his guard slip and we hadn't then identified how those magazines can turn around and bite you. He was like the lemming that went over the cliff – and showed us all how not to handle the science fiction press."

Saward has never worked in mainstream British television drama again. "He's still eaten up with it," says Levine, who remained a friend until they too fell out in 2010. "You start talking about it and he gets really cranked up. He'll just suddenly get angry when it all comes back. He's damaged goods, tainted and though he makes trickles off *Doctor Who*, he resents the fact that he hasn't worked on other things. He's very bitter towards John. But Eric didn't let him know how he felt – he would phone me up at 11 in the morning, 'You don't know what John has done this morning,' and he would be on the phone for three hours!"

"He came to lunch at my house two or three times," recalls Baker, "and went out for a walk with us with the dog. All he did was bang on about John. It was the kind of outpouring that somebody who works for somebody would moan about to their nearest and dearest – not to an actor in the programme. I did a lot of trying to mollify, saying all those anodyne things you say, 'Well, he is the producer and you are the script editor and if he tells you to do this...' 'He's wrong!' 'Well, tell him about it.' 'I've told him. He won't listen.' Why would you go to somebody's house, accept their hospitality and then say they shouldn't have been cast in the part? That's why I was so annoyed and appalled when Eric slagged me off in that article."

"Silly bugger," says Bidmead of Saward. "Oh yes, I got his whines. He had Jane [Judge] too. Eric was essentially a writer and I think John just didn't appreciate that sort of thing at all, just wasn't on the wavelength. I think Eric would have liked more feedback and I got the feeling that the essential difference between me and Eric was I wasn't going to put up with this, I was going to make it work. Eric perhaps had a healthier attitude of 'If I can't do it, what the hell, leave it as it is.' So many people's lives were blighted by working on that show. Not just Eric. You get sucked into it – it's a destructive process."

"Maybe Eric's problems are to do with not having done much since?" postulates Sarah Lee. "Perhaps he's blaming *Doctor Who* for things that have happened to him. Well you can't blame a television programme. It's your own bum you have to get off in life. I think, 'For God's sake, shut up. Move on to something else. Write a big hit,' you know!"

"When I moved into my office," says Cartmel, Saward's eventual successor, "it was a mess. I couldn't open the desk drawer – he had turned the key so hard it had snapped off, so we got Mr Mistry, this nice little Indian chap who was the handyman in Union and Threshold House and he came and opened it up for me. Inside was a wine glass with red wine still dried inside it and some shredded paper – it was like the last days in the bunker!

"I think it might have been Kate Easteal who told me about their terrible falling-out, so one day I just asked John about it and instantly he was on the defensive; 'What have people been telling you?' 'Well, it's obvious that things ended really badly between you guys. I just don't want something like that to happen to us.' He said, 'We were doing so many shows in those days, the pressure was constant and we just ended up really falling out.' That was the gist of it."

Just like John, *Doctor Who* continued to define Saward in the years that followed. But, unlike John, he is still alive and so has had many opportunities over the years to amend or revise his views on that era. He decided not to be interviewed for this book but, in his 2006 DVD interview, he commented: "Maybe I said things that should have been left unsaid. I don't resent it or regret it. I would rather have not said some things, it didn't help. It's past. So I'd rather have left it in the past."

John drafted in the ever-biddable Pip and Jane Baker (he called them the Baker twins) to cobble together a finale that owed nothing to Saward's version. The result was widely regarded as risible (though Saward's script wasn't much better, the efforts of a talented man in total burn-out) but it meant there was something to put in front of the cameras. "The first script [the Bakers' four-parter, episodes 9–12 of *Trial*] at least made a bit of sense," says its director Chris Clough. "But the other ones were pretty diabolical. It was all fairly chaotic. I had just had to go along with it and make it work really."

"I remember," says Langford, "during the first producer's run being watched by John and the two writers and we were then put into one of those hospitality rooms – me, Lynda (Bellingham), Colin, Michael (Jayston). We sat there for hours. It got to five, six o'clock – which is unheard of at the BBC – and they wouldn't let us out. They were in conference about the script. Everyone was getting very tense and I remember thinking, 'This is very weird and not a particularly happy set-up'. They were basically trying to rewrite the story. I wondered if this was a flavour of the whole show and I did think, 'Well, this isn't much fun.'"

The whole debacle did nothing for John's standing with his superiors and made a grim mockery of all those proud statements he had made the year before. As he'd told an expectant crowd of fans at the Genesis convention in November 1985, "If something's been off for 18 months, when it comes back it's got to be sensational."

The *Trial* season, the programme's much vaunted comeback, was launched with the expected avalanche of publicity, much of it stage-managed by John. There was plenty of press and high-profile appearances on *Wogan*, *Saturday Superstore* and *Blue Peter*. But the season, launched on 6th September 1986, was a resounding, toe-curling flop. The scheduling didn't help, *Doctor Who* following another over-hyped washout, *Roland Rat: The Series*. Both offerings died a lingering ratings death together. Viewers were bored by the clunky plod of the *Trial*, the confusion in the plotting and the tacky campery of the realisation of all bar the expensive opening shot. Those that did persevere were bemused by a farcical climax, served up with lashings of truly atrocious dialogue. The move to shooting all the location material on tape gave the entire show a cheap and nasty look. "It was hopeless," says Clough, "absolute crap. You got the OB [outside broadcast] unit when they weren't doing football. John wanted you to aim high but there was just no money to do anything. The internal politics of BBC drama obviously had their knives completely out for him but he was a good old-fashioned type of producer who was on it and got what he wanted out of the show. Baker, though, was a bit of a liability. Terrific chap, very good actor and all the rest of it but again, it was all a bit lightweight. It was really ready for a change."

"The unsympathetic character that they conceived for Colin," says Cartmel, "and that fucking costume were just disasters from the off. They really never gave Colin the chance he deserved. Then *The Trial of a Time Lord* was a feeble idea and a boring framework – a complete mistake."

For months, John had been under the impression that this season would finally mark his farewell to the programme. "It had been the most turbulent time on the show for me," he confided in his memoirs. "I was exhausted both physically and emotionally."

"He did ask to be taken off it," remembers Powell. "But you kind of pigeon-holed him and thought that's all he can do and the problem is he can't do it because he's a buffoon. The trouble is, I suppose, from his point of view, is that the worse the programme got, the less good one thought he was. Everybody was in this vicious cycle."

"Knowing Jonathan, I think he thought John was second rate," says Willingale. "And when I say I know what he means, I don't mean that to be anti-John because I believe in horses for courses – I wouldn't have put John in charge of the classic serial, for instance. But Jonathan would appreciate good *of its kind* – he knew about good scripts and bad scripts. They were bad scripts."

Powell summoned John and explained that it had been decided that a new Doctor was needed. John was to break the news to Baker on behalf of the BBC. More humiliating than the cancellation, more painful than Saward's public meltdown, this was and would remain, John's lowest professional moment. In vain he argued for a reprieve. Powell was implacable. Today he still refers to "the disastrous Colin Baker" and explains, "It was another way of grasping at straws and keeping it going. I probably fought for it a bit secretly because I didn't want to lose the real estate. I knew that if I lost the programme, we'd lose the slots so I said, 'OK, we'll throw it a sop and say: Sack Doctor Who and find somebody else' – to give us a bit of hope and a story."

John arranged to have lunch with Baker to break the news in person. But, on 29th October, alerted to the story leaking to the press, he was forced to call the actor instead. "He said, 'I've got some good news and some bad news,'" recalls Baker. "I said, 'Well, let's have the good news,' and he said, 'The programme's coming back next year.' I thought well, the bad news can't be that bad then. Then he said, 'but I've got to recast you, though they want you to come back and do four episodes and the regeneration.' It was like a kick in the stomach. I have no objectivity about my performance but I think I did a reasonable job, with a certain amount of brio. I did my best and I certainly cared about the programme. I just don't think they liked it and they wanted to get rid of John. But then I would say that, wouldn't I?"

Awkwardly, that Christmas Baker was contracted to star in John's revived *Cinderella*, this time in Brighton. "Colin came into the theatre raging about it," says Fraser. "He felt as though he had been hit in the head. The way it was done was dreadful because there was no discussion."

Some have suggested that the honourable thing for John to do would have been to resign. Years later, he allowed, "If it was to do with his [Colin's] performance, then I'm partly responsible..." But there was no resignation, not even when Powell twisted the knife with the news that John was now to produce the next season after all. "I think he was very upset for Colin," says Easteal. "But he wanted to keep going – he wanted to keep *Doctor Who* on air. At the time I couldn't imagine him moving on to produce anything else. He was totally intrinsic to the show."

"He was getting it in the neck from everywhere," sighs Langford, "and yet really he went above and beyond the call of duty keeping it alive. When I was involved with it, there was no backing, no budget – everything was really done on a postage stamp and I think that he found that very, very hard to handle. *Doctor Who* was having to scrape the barrel. We were always pushed for time. We were always having to make it work and it was difficult. I think any other producer might have turned round and said, 'All right, that's the end of it. Bye!'"

Did Baker feel any sense of betrayal that the man who had cast him was cutting him adrift, even if under orders? "Like all of us, when the chips are down, you save yourself," says Baker. "I'd have thought, 'Thank you,' if he'd said, 'No, I'm not sacking him.' Amazingly, the effect on the friendship wasn't that bad, actually. I can imagine some people would feel betrayed. But with something like that, I don't believe in shooting the messenger."

However, Baker did insist on seeing Powell for himself and a meeting was reluctantly arranged for midday on 6th November. "I actually took a recording machine with me," he says. "One of those spy recorders. Of course, he was so defensive. A typical suit. His first reaction was 'Why are you here?' – so I explained, 'Well, I sat in this building with David Reid who said we need you to sign a four-year contract – I was delighted to do so and now you're kicking me into touch.' 'No, no, no we're not.' Whenever I used emotive language like 'sacking', it was 'Oh no we're not sacking you, it's just that Michael [Grade] and I think that the programme needs a new actor.' I said, 'Oh I'm not good enough then?' 'No, no, no, I'm delighted with your performance. It's a very good performance but the programme needs a change.' I said, 'When I'm being interviewed, I'm going to say I've been sacked' – 'You haven't been sacked, we're just not renewing your contract' – 'But you have sacked me' – 'I'd rather you didn't say that' – 'I'm sure you'd rather I didn't say that, but I am going to say that.' He did that routine: 'Think about the effect it has on your career – you don't want to be seen to have been sacked so whatever statement you want to come up with about we've agreed together and you want to go onto other projects, I'd be very happy to go along with that.' I said, 'I'm sure you would but I'm not. The truth is easier to remember.'

"Then he said, 'We would like to offer you four episodes.' They needed a regeneration. I said, 'I'll come back and do the series and leave at the end of it.' That would be worth me saying yes – but I'm not committing myself to four weeks' work next April when I might get a year's contract in something else. 'That's very unhelpful,' he said. We left it with, 'You go away and think about whether you will come back and do those four episodes and I'll go away and think about your offer,' and I never heard another word."

Whatever contempt he still reserves for the clumsy machinations of BBC executives, Colin's enforced exit has not diminished his view of John. "If he'd given me the job and then been hideous, I'd say so," he smiles. "But he gave me the job and I liked him and I thought in terms of caring about a programme, I haven't met many producers before or since who really gave their heart and soul in the way he did."

John's *annus horribilis* finally ended with the slight consolation of ringing cash registers, as Teynham's *Cinderella* starring Colin – with Wendy Richard, Hugh Lloyd and Carole Kaye in support – did superb business. As 1986, a painful, difficult, unpredictable, ceaselessly challenging year ebbed away, John can only have contemplated 1987 with some trepidation. There was a huge amount to accomplish. He needed a new script editor, new scripts, new teams and most of all, a new star.

ELEVEN

BUMS ON SEATS

"The Doctor has never had a better friend and neither have we..."
Gail Bennett, brochure text, PanoptiCon New Orleans, 1985

Twenty-first-century *Doctor Who* generally has two executive producers, one of whom also acts as brand guardian – a title that sounds as if it belongs to a character from the show. The brand guardian has an overview of everything connected to the programme lying beyond what you see on screen. It's the formal acknowledgment that the modern BBC has woken up to the commercial possibilities of the show and its responsibility to control both quantity and quality. The brand guardian doesn't work alone, either – alongside them are a dedicated brand manager and an events manager (who deals with all the programme's public activity), supported by a whole team of colleagues.

In the 1980s, when the word "brand" was unlikely to be used, still less understood, there was just one man within the BBC responsible for the show's life beyond the small screen – publicity, promotion, merchandise and commercial exploitation – and that was John Nathan-Turner. Few would dispute that in these areas he showed real ability and flair. "John was very entrepreneurial," says Lorne Martin, who worked in exhibitions and later merchandising for BBC Enterprises (as the commercial arm of the BBC was known in the 1980s). "He was an honest chap to deal with and incredibly helpful."

Not for John the standard BBC nose-in-the-air attitude to anything commercial and self-publicising. He was a natural showman who revelled in the limelight, more comfortable in the glare of publicity than many of his stars. "He was certainly very unusual in being a visible producer," says Russell T Davies. "That's still a very rare thing. I mean even now you don't get a showrunner who appears in the publicity photos. That's really quite strange. What an old showman! He was just enjoying himself, wasn't he?"

John perfected the trick of pointing at whichever actor he was being photographed with. "It meant they couldn't cut him out of the shot," frowns Ian Levine, disapprovingly.

"The standing in photos with the stars does jar on my brain," admits Davies. "I think, 'Why have you made that photo worse?' and I don't mean because of the Hawaiian shirt! Surely they're less likely to print the photo if it's got the producer in it – they want Colin Baker and Nicola Bryant; they don't want some old man."

John's increasingly high profile inevitably led to bitching back in Union and Threshold House. "I think the fame of it all went to his head a bit," says production manager Margot Hayhoe. "But the point was that nobody else in the BBC was promoting it, so although, yes, it was good for him in a way, it was so good for the department that somebody was keeping things going – and merchandising at Enterprises certainly did well out of John's work."

From the moment he was given his chance to produce the show he loved, John's eyes were alight with possibilities. One of the earliest products to which he gave the green light was a behind-the-scenes book intended principally for libraries called *A Day with a TV Producer*. The end product was a sanitised photo-story version of John's early days as producer, a snapshot of 1980 in amber. On page after page, John can be seen at work, fresh-faced, slim, everything ahead of him. He was always happy to shed light upon the mysteries of production in return for promotion and, as well as books such as *A Day with a TV Producer* and *The Making of a Television Series* (which went behind the scenes on *The Visitation*), he allowed photographers, journalists, TV and radio crews regular access to his locations and studios. He was firmly of the old-school belief that "there's no such thing as bad publicity."

"It always seemed to me," says Peter Davison, "that his extraordinary strength was getting publicity for the show. He would arrange a publicity call and you would have hundreds of photographers for me, Sarah and Janet or standing in front of the police box with a cricket bat or the new companion in their outfits or whatever – he had a wonderful relationship with the press, which meant that every time something happened, we'd be on the front or inside page of the *Mirror* or *The Sun* or whatever it was. When we went away to film in my last season in Lanzarote, he actually invited two members of the press out there as part of the troop. I always thought that his perfect position would have been as some kind of PR man and he did very well for *Doctor Who* in many respects – he kept it high profile."

John had the skill of understanding exactly what tabloid journalists were looking for. They valued a good picture – preferably sexy in some way (one of the reasons his unfortunate female artists were dragooned into wearing such undignified costumes) with a story that might spark humour or debate over the breakfast table. The first of his real PR triumphs happened by accident when it was leaked that Tom Baker was leaving the programme. John and his star were supposed to be publicising Madame Tussaud's new figure of Baker but that was lost in the rush to run with the news that Baker had quit. According to John's friend, Grahame Flynn, on the way to face the press in a cab, "Tom turned to John and said, 'You wait till I get out of the taxi. I'm going to say something that will really rock the papers.' When he wished his successor luck and said, 'Whoever he or she may be,' the press went nuts. John took it from there and that was the sort of thing that he was a master at. Just milk it for everything you can, even if it's a bad story."

"Will the Doctor be played by a woman?" became an old reliable for John, every time the casting came around. He scored with other trumped-up stories around the axing of K9 and the possible fixing of the TARDIS chameleon circuit, with John letting "Her Majesty's Press" (as he called them) in on the "shock horror" news that he was considering changing the police phone box look as he was "concerned" that youngsters were growing up with no idea what these actually were. It was nonsense and everyone knew it, but the press was happy to play along and TV often followed suit. In his drive to give the papers a story, John was helped and inspired by his great friend (another ex-actor), press officer Kevin O'Shea. "They would go for these long drinks," recalls John's secretary, Kate Easteal, "and there was a lot of going into his office with the door closed and a bottle of red wine."

"They'd lock themselves up together and they would be intriguing and plotting away," laughs Andrew Cartmel. "John knew that this guy was important. Other script editors and producers would bitch and moan that they couldn't get any publicity for their shows but John was great at that and understood the importance of it. He cultivated Kevin and acknowledged that he was crucial. Some of John's publicity tactics were not my cup of tea – like in the silver anniversary when he said, 'We've got to have the Queen in it' – but in terms of publicity, it was priceless. When they cast Billie Piper in the new series, a perfect piece of casting and a publicity coup, I thought, 'Ah the ghost of John Nathan-Turner!'"

"I knew that, as well as playing the girl, I was there to do an awful lot of publicity," says Bonnie Langford. "I've never known so many photographs being taken of anything. I've never known so many publicity situations. I did everything."

John kept a beady eye on the cuttings and it was his secretary's job to make sure he saw them all. "I'd worked with another producer called Stephen Gilbert," says Kate Easteal, who worked for John from 1986. "We shared an office and got on really well and had a bit of a laugh. He'd gone back out into the real world, and was writing TV reviews for *The Independent*. When the next *Doctor Who* season was about to start, he rang me up and asked for some preview tapes. And I checked with John and he said, 'Oh yeah, yeah that's fine.' So they were sent with John's blessing.

"When I opened the paper a couple of days later, Stephen had really slagged the show off. I then thought, 'Oh my God, John's going to go mad' – even though I'd asked John, the fact that Stephen was my friend and I'd given him the tapes – I was implicated! I'd asked John for this favour. So when the press cuttings came through, I just ripped off the page, thinking if John never sees it, he'll never know. Then [producer] Caroline Oulton, who'd worked with Stephen and didn't really like him very much, burst into the office later in the day saying, 'Oh, I thought it was terrible what Stephen wrote,' and then he flew out of his office – 'Where's the press cuttings?' I was trying to defuse the situation but it all backfired because he was mad anyway. Stephen had made a personal comment about John ("a man whose passion for his programme verges on the pathological"), which I was really cross about. I ended up ringing Stephen and saying, 'Look, you could have toned it down a bit,' and he was like, 'I'm a TV reviewer, what do you expect me to say? Do you expect me to say: Oh, the show's great because my friend works there? Do me a favour. I'm going to write what I think.'"

As a boy, John had often written to celebrities and collected their autographs. Now he was running his own little dream factory, he adopted a Louis B Mayer approach to casting, insisting on stars in every story, certain that this would bring in floating viewers curious to see a famous name in a different context. He was always on the look out for a "name". "I remember going to a press launch in St Christopher's Place," says Langford. "Sylvester and I were there – and Roger Daltrey was there too. He was desperate to do *Doctor Who*. He wasn't just saying it like I did when I first met John. Can you imagine if Roger Daltrey had been in *Doctor Who*? The Who meets Who. It would have been fantastic. John would have bent over backwards to try and make that work. He loved his celebrities and it did become very much a sort of cult thing to do for actors playing bizarre characters."

When stalwart British film actor Richard Todd was cast in *Kinda,* John contacted David Platt in BBC programme acquisitions: "I feel sure there is mileage in a Richard Todd feature film season around about this time. I am sure we could both benefit from this."

His decision to clad the regular cast in "uniforms" rather than allowing them to change from story to story was all because he was thinking of their potential in product terms. When Janet Fielding joined as Tegan, he even commissioned a West End hairdresser to create an expensive style for her, in the hope that it would instigate a fashion and become a talking point for the female audience. Sadly, the result turned out to be more of a "hair don't". (Fielding likened it to having a dead rat stuck on the back of her head.) He might have been better off addressing the antediluvian treatment of women in the actual stories. "Nobody gave a shit about whether girls were watching it or not," says Fielding, simply and to the point.

"He was obsessed with the *look* of *Doctor Who,*" says Davison, "the costumes and everything that was – and I don't mean this in a bad way – slightly *superficial.*"

John spent much time and energy on his stewardship as the guardian of all things *Who,* often to the irritation of his script editors and directors, who sometimes found they had to join a queue before they could gain his attention for their needs. Although their frustration is entirely reasonable, all the extra-curricular activity was part of John's job, too. A bewildering array of products had to be approved by him and him alone – toys, confectionery, wallpaper, ceramics, badges, clothing, games, books, annuals, posters and magazines. His eye fell upon fanzines, too (though these were unofficial and not part of his remit). In the pre-internet days of the 1980s, there were scores of these, some grubby, malnourished efforts that lasted just a couple of issues, others glossier, more ambitious and, as time went on, increasingly professional. John devoted time not just to reading these but to granting interviews and arranging set visits. Perhaps they were an additional form of ego massage but his naturally generous spirit was at work, too. Relations with the fan press remained remarkably harmonious. Apart from his long battle with *DWB* (documented elsewhere), only one other fanzine really caused a headache. The *MLG Megazine* was produced by the Merseyside local group of the DWAS and, true to the cliché of chippy Scouse humour, was brimming with childish in-jokes and near-the-knuckle sarcasm and sneers.

Unfortunately, without the guiding hand of a proper editor, these grew steadily more offensive. Many personal jibes were aimed at John in particular ("Vaseline sales plummeted by 50 per cent when John Nathan-Turner took a recent holiday in Spain... the dagos are pretty greasy anyway.") but in issue 9, a supposedly amusing comment was made about the recent death of Colin Baker's son, Jack.

"When a child dies," says Baker, "that is the worst thing that can happen. There is nothing worse. It alerted me to the world I was entering, that there are people who feel they own the programme to such an extent that they can say and do what they like – even resorting to making a joke about me digging my own child up to get publicity. It was very unpleasant. It put me off Liverpool – I never went anywhere near it for years afterwards."

John had already complained about the content of previous issues (especially the puerile references to sex and the habit of reproducing photos of *Who* actresses in topless roles or publicity shoots). Now he contacted David Saunders, the then DWAS coordinator, to demand action. Saunders responded in a letter dated 19th August 1985, which dissociated the society from the magazine and assured him, "As of this month the 'zine is defunct." On 23rd August, several of the DWAS executive attended a meeting in John's office, where he made clear that this kind of rogue action might bring legal action and the withdrawal of all support from the production team and cast. The immediate casualty was a planned DWASocial in Liverpool. But it was a thankfully rare breakdown in good relations between the fan press and the programme itself.

As for Baker, he became the chair of a charity set up to raise awareness about cot death, which had claimed his son's life. "2300 babies were dying a year when it happened to Jack," he says. "When I resigned, it was down to 300. Over 20 years that's 40,000 people alive today who otherwise might not have been. Indirectly his short life has achieved something."

Doctor Who Magazine, published monthly by Marvel Comics, was officially licensed and effectively the show's shop window, especially during the off-air months. John was billed as consultant, which meant that, ahead of the press day, he was sent every issue's copy for official approval. As one of the magazine's main feature writers, I soon got used to his sometimes seemingly random decisions to excise passages or question content with the infamous "blue pencil". It was rather like having your answers marked by a teacher without always knowing the questions. Once he so butchered my preview for the story *Vengeance on Varos* that the planned two-page feature had to be compressed into one. Editor Sheila Cranna was not best pleased but even she couldn't see what was wrong with some of the passages he'd cut, such as this controversial segment (!): "Predictably, the [Sil] costume and make-up combined proved extremely hot and constricting for Nabil and between takes somebody always rushed up with a small electric face fan to try and cool him down a bit."

Later, he seemed to relax a little and by the time I was reviewing season 24 (and struggling to find positive things to say), he allowed a much more critical tone to enter the reviews. Or perhaps he'd given up and stopped reading them?

At times, he could be surprisingly prurient, phoning me to question the inclusion of a two-part piece of padding on the various Fantasy Males and Females who'd appeared in the show over the years. "Keep it clean, OK?" he urged, as though I was planning to write pages of utter filth instead of a lot of tongue-in-cheek blether about some (depending on what tickled your fancy) eye candy. As with most people who had regular dealings with John in a professional capacity, there was no way of predicting how he might be – sometimes generous, helpful and constructive – at other times, rude, snide and obstructive. He once insisted that I interview his secretary, Sarah Lee. "The readers will be interested," he said, in a tone that dared me to contradict him. A few days later, I met Lee in the Wood Lane wine bar often frequented by the "front office", Albertine. She was sparky (if a little patronising) and did her best to talk up the typing, filing and answering the phone into something I might write about. I did my best too, but *DWM* editor Alan Mackenzie decided to dig his heels in and refused to run the piece. "I've had enough of John Nathan-Turner," he growled, though he did pay me, as he realised I'd simply been caught in the crossfire. At one point, John offered Marvel his own "producer's column" and they were interested until it became clear he expected a fee for the job. "Outrageous!" laughs Russell T Davies. "Totally against the rules."

This may now be so, but John belonged to an era when there were far fewer guidelines floating around the BBC about what was and wasn't acceptable. Producers could make good money on the side if they happened to be lucky enough to work on a show that generated spin-offs. Biddy Baxter and Edward Barnes scored a small fortune from the huge sales of their *Blue Peter* books (alas, by the time I was writing them, it was a modest one-off fee as staff were no longer permitted royalties) and those making lush documentary series did equally well from tie-in titles. John was no author and his *Doctor Who* books (*The TARDIS Inside Out* and *The Companions*) were slim volumes of largely inconsequential waffle. Quality was no barrier to these or to some of the even more questionable publications for which John smoothed the way. *Travel Without the TARDIS* purported to be a guide to *Doctor Who* locations throughout the UK. It was written by Jean Airey and Laurie Haldeman – American fans who happened to be acquaintances of John. That might have been OK if the text had been accurate or interesting.

The most blatant cash-in, however, remains *The Doctor Who Cookbook*, compiled by Gary Downie and, with hindsight, fascinating because it captures "the court of John and Gary" at its peak, just before Michael Grade and Jonathan Powell ruined the party. It's as camp as you'd expect, with daft recipes ("Kipper of Traken", anyone?) and a running commentary from Gary, which authentically captures his gossipy, trivial line in chit-chat. John contributed Hawaiian soup (a noxious-sounding concoction of prawns, double cream and tins of chilled Vichyssoise soup) and a sickly coffee and chocolate drink called "No Comment Nectar".

Even at the time, cynics suspected that the cookbook was a way of validating Downie's inclusion as a guest at conventions. At some of these, he held "Anyone Can Dance" sessions, in which he hectored overweight American fans with inevitably embarrassing consequences. "He managed to inveigle himself into the programme in a way that I didn't think was completely ethical," comments Peter Davison. "The idea of him sitting there and signing autographs kind of rankled," agrees Colin Baker. "We had no option about contributing to that cookbook, of course. 'Gary's doing a cookbook – do you mind giving him a recipe?' And you'd do it for John. We tolerated Gary for John but I never understood why John tolerated Gary."

For all the tat he let through the net, John put new merchandise near the top of his agenda and rarely refused a licence (one exception was *Doctor Who* darts as he worried that in the hands of children these could lead to injuries). "John always went that little step further than other producers," says Martin. "For instance, loads of people wanted to license *EastEnders,* and Julia Smith [the producer] was very difficult to work with. It was a nightmare because each agent thought that whichever actor they looked after was more important than the other ones and they all wanted different royalties. That's where John was good. He would have gone to all the agents and said, 'Look, we'll give them all a ten per cent royalty' or whatever. Julia wasn't really interested in merchandising – she was doing a programme but John could see the PR side. It was keeping his programme alive – it wasn't on every week of the year like *EastEnders.*"

When BBC Enterprises arthritically clutched at the emerging home video market, John, never backward in pushing himself forward, cheekily suggested himself as a presenter in a prototype for the kind of video compilations he later produced for BBC Worldwide (as Enterprises were renamed in 1995). On 9th March 1983, he sent a memo to the editor of programme adaptations. "The fans of the programme throughout the world are longing to see selected gems from old *Doctor Who* programmes. Consequently, I suggest a one-off or series of tape/disc presentations including excerpts from the 118 stories still retained in the BBC Archives. I suggest I am responsible for the selection of clips (eg first appearance of Hartnell, first appearance of Daleks etc) and present the package as, due to my regular appearances at *Doctor Who* conventions both here and in America, I have become something of a celebrity figure among the fans. As you know, I am very keen to promote the programme throughout the world and this would seem, together with <u>your</u> enthusiasm for the project, to be an ideal approach."

The project progressed a little further into a proposal for *Doctor Who – The Hartnell Years* (John screened the two hours of clips he'd compiled for it an American convention in July 1983) until it foundered amid clearance issues. That same year was the series' much trumpeted (thanks to John) 20th anniversary. In November came his great coup, a 90-minute special, *The Five Doctors*. More than any other contribution he made, this captures both the very best and the worst that John had to offer. The big concept, the sheer ambition (much grander in scale than *The Three Doctors*) and the absolute determination to pull it off were typical examples of his finest qualities. He persuaded an impressive array of talent to appear, although Tom Baker eluded him, playing a drawn-out game of "will he, won't he?" with John, perhaps as an act of revenge for being eased out of the series just two years earlier. Meanwhile, *Radio Times* produced a glossy souvenir magazine to coincide with the special and mark the anniversary, compiled by the unfeasibly named Gay Search. There was a full-page photo of John in his "womb" and he got Ian Levine the gig of writing a potted history of the show, although there was then an unseemly squabble over Levine's credit. John deleted this, keen to keep his 'superfan' in the shadows, but it was reinstated by *Radio Times* editor Brian Gearing. Ironically, John hoped that *The Five Doctors* would be his own swansong to the series but the go-ahead for the special became conditional on his producing another season.

Alas, having achieved so much, John let his attention lapse on the actual execution of his epic. This was demonstrated especially by the choice of director. Earlier in the year, John had met the series' first director from 1963, Waris Hussein, at a party and, typically, excited by the press opportunity this full circle appointment would offer, asked him to take charge. Hussein stalled and weeks went by before John sought a definitive answer. Hussein finally turned him down in November 1982. Next John offered the job to one of the most admired directors from the show's past, Douglas Camfield. This was a good choice, but Camfield was reportedly affronted to be asked so late in the day (in any case, he was booked to direct the serial *Missing from Home*). With time running out, John turned to faithful old Peter Moffatt, whose availability in the autumn of his long career was scarcely an issue and who, faced with a sprawling cast, could be relied upon to keep the turns sweet. John himself contributed some second unit directing, thoroughly enjoying himself in shooting a sequence of Cybermen being massacred.

Unfortunately, Moffatt had little understanding of the show itself and, although his work was never less than professional, in the sense that he covered the action and came in on budget, his directorial vision was often limp and lacking in atmosphere or menace. The consequence was that while one can admire many aspects of *The Five Doctors*, Moffatt's artistic interpretation isn't one of them. There were a number of plainly embarrassing misfires and some poor casting.

The special transmitted in America two days ahead of its UK slot where it was subsumed into the BBC's annual Children in Need appeal on 25th November. Although this was entirely down to a change of schedule from BBC1, it incensed some British fans, who were also irritated because every major *Doctor Who* star was spending the anniversary as a guest at the showcase Spirit of Light convention in Chicago. "It was massive," recalls the man in charge, Norman Rubenstein, an attorney by trade. "It just sort of kept expanding and expanding – we didn't expect it to be as vast as it turned out. We had serious estimates of attendance – the low end was 7,500, the top end 12,500 – somewhere between the two was the actual figure."

Rubenstein had been at Longleat, scouting for talent, and was "somewhat surprised to see how it was run. They certainly shouldn't have underestimated to the extent that they did. I just think they were out of their depth and they saw it happening and didn't know how to rectify it at that late stage. We learnt to quadruple whatever we thought the attendance would be and schedule for it."

"Chicago featured heavily on my passport," John confided in *DWM*. "The most memorable visit must be the 'mega' convention of 1983. It was so odd, yet strangely moving watching *The Five Doctors* transmitted on the actual anniversary, together with most of the cast."

By this time, John was already a familiar face on the American fan circuit. His adventures and achievements across the Atlantic are an important part of his story. They started soon after he took over from Graham Williams as producer. When *Shada* was pulled, Williams decided to accept his invitation to one of the very first *Doctor Who* conventions in the States. He took Tom Baker with him and they received an ecstatic reception. As John told *DWM* in 1991, "When Graham returned, he brought back with him a film of some of the event, which we viewed together at one of the BBC Lime Grove viewing theatres. The film was fascinating. I felt honoured to be associated with a programme that instigated such terrific response and enthusiasm. I couldn't wait to attend a United States convention myself."

About a year later, he made his debut at a convention in Tulsa, Oklahoma, taking Peter Davison, who had yet to appear on TV, with him. For John, American fandom – predominantly female, noisy, effusive, quick to praise and slow to criticise – was a welcome break from much of the British counterpart, which was predominantly male, socially uneasy, inhibited or hostile. "They didn't like us at all," says Ron Katz, who headed the Doctor Who Fan Club of America. "The fans in the United States were all dressed up in outrageous costumes, having a great time. You could be at a Whovian festival and you could hear the hum of joy. You would go to England and they were all dressed in black and they were all very quiet and serious – male-dominated and it seemed like nobody was having any fun. I kept thinking, 'What in hell are they doing here?' – I felt like an African American in 1950s Alabama."

Even if he spent most of his time in hotels, John loved the travel and blossomed in the constant party atmosphere that so many of these conventions generated. Expenses and, often, a decent fee, only added to the allure. "I think he made a lot of money out of them," says Andrew Cartmel. "The whole thing was a bit of racket," says Marcia Wheeler, manager of drama series and serials. "But, on the other hand, there was definitely a call for it. There was an industry."

By 1983, John was flying back and forth to America, burning the candle at both ends and keeping up an exhausting schedule. Frequently jetlagged, he would sleep in his office and take shortcuts such as getting Gary to read a new script to him in the car on the way to work.

"There was never secrecy from him about the conventions," says his personnel manager Pat Dyer. "He never hid it and he got permission. I think it gave him great happiness going over there. They idolised him and he always used to come back with the most flamboyant shirts I've ever seen!" While it is true that these trips were always signed off by John's management, he was less scrupulous about admitting the amounts of money that were routinely changing hands.

Early on, John realised that the existing American fan club, NADWAS, led by the forbidding Barbara Elder, wasn't fulfilling its potential. "She could have been one of the bad guys on *Doctor Who*," laughs Ron Katz. "Very negative, very dykey."

"W3 we called her," sniggers David Saunders. "The Wicked Witch of the West. John got back from America and we met in the pub for the monthly business meeting and he said, 'Barbara Elder doesn't do a good job. I want you to get rid of her – and if you don't, there'll be no more news for you.' I had to write to her and tell her. Of course, she was absolutely furious about it – she stamped her feet and disappeared in her own whirlwind."

John was backing a different horse – the emerging Doctor Who Fan Club of America, run by Katz, a young businessman, and his friend and colleague, Chad Roark. At its peak, the DWFCA would boast 50,000 members. "As a businessman, John was a very smart guy," says Katz. "He could walk into a situation and assess it in five seconds flat and put his hand on the pulse of nearly everything that was around him. I had a great deal of respect for him."

As well as running the fan club, Katz had been making good money from a range of *Doctor Who* T-shirts, which he'd tried to license from BBC Enterprises to no avail. "I knew that we were guilty of copyright infringement but after getting pushed off and laughed at by people at BBC Enterprises, we realised that those guys were idiots. It probably wouldn't be them that would catch us but we were going to get caught some day. So Chad and I saved 10 per cent of everything we brought in. At StarCon in Denver who walks up to my booth but JN-T. He was very nice and quizzed me about a lot of stuff and then, as only JN-T could, very quickly changed, and said, 'You're guilty of international copyright infringement.'

"So I said, 'So sue me – what's your problem? You wouldn't be here if it wasn't for me.' We bantered back and forth – he had brought a gentleman from BBC Enterprises with him who was supposed to be the heavy – Roy Williams – but actually he was a decent guy. We sat and talked and he said, 'Well, you're going to have to sign a contract with us.' I said, 'That's what I've been trying to do.' I had documented every phone call, shown him every letter and fax I had written to BBC Enterprises and said, 'We've got nowhere – we really want to be your licensee.' JN-T liked me and what we were doing and he helped – none of this would have happened without him. He said, 'Make this deal. Don't break this deal.' We negotiated a contract that was very favourable to us. I faxed it to my lawyer and I said, 'I want you to rewrite this completely – everything that's for them, I want it to be for me.' A complete 180-degree flip-flop on what they're asking. He did – and when I gave that to Roy Williams, he looked like he was very studiously reading it and then he just signed it. It was a *joke* but, by the time the convention was over, I gave him the money there and then. They were just thrilled."

"BBC Enterprises – a misnomer if ever there was one," chuckles Colin Baker. "It wasn't the beast that Worldwide is now. Now if the BBC said they weren't doing it any more, Worldwide would go ballistic – they've finally worked out what a property they've got."

"BBC Enterprises was a little behind the times," agrees Katz's main rival, Norman Rubenstein. "Medieval, I would say. I started negotiating with them and flying out to London and in addition to the merchandising, it was their idea for us to run a huge convention for the 20th anniversary. Anything like that had to run through JN-T at the time. He was genuinely a very nice person. He had a fantastic sense of humour and really, really cared about the series. That might have been his one fault – caring about it a little too much. He wanted to leave his mark. He bent over backwards to take fans seriously. Whether or not he would intend to take them up on the various things they felt strongly about, at least he was always willing to listen to them."

John worked like a Trojan to help build the show's profile in the States. Episodes were shown across the country by public television – PBS – and these regularly held "pledge drives" to raise money from fans to keep the series on the air. Acting as a kind of unofficial BBC ambassador, John escorted actors from the show to take part in these "begathons" as they were known off camera. He became the ringmaster for the US convention guest circuit. "If we wanted to get anybody," says Katz, "all he had to do was make a phone call and it was done. That was worth its weight. He was the real pulse of *Doctor Who*. I would have to pay him and Gary and they were frankly not the draw that Peter Davison or Lis Sladen would be. But once he was here, he became his own little folk legend – the fans loved him; he was famous for his Hawaiian shirts and he was quite articulate and great-looking and lots of fun. John would walk into a room and it would light up. He owned the stage and he became a hit. Towards the end, he *was* a draw."

"I would see him occasionally," says Matthew Waterhouse. "He did absolutely love them – he told me it was because he'd always wanted to be an actor – and he loved the performance element. He was very old school – much more Danny La Rue than Ben Elton. I did watch him do panels and he was very skilled at them. He told jokes and they applauded him and he began to see himself as the Gene Roddenberry [creator of *Star Trek*] of *Doctor Who*, at least for the duration of the convention."

John himself said that his favourite moment from these years was "entering a John Nathan-Turner lookalike contest and coming fourth!"

"I think he was a very frustrated performer, really," says Sylvester McCoy. "That's why he loved conventions because they allowed him to get up there and show off with the rest of us."

"He sold himself wonderfully well on that convention circuit," recalls Davison, "and he was always wonderful fun to do them with."

One characteristic of many US conventions was a celebrity cabaret with the stars performing some kind of party piece. "Some of the actors were concerned," recalls Rubenstein, "that a certain segment of American fandom sometimes failed to fully grasp that they were professional actors acting a role.

We came up with these cabarets as a sort of response to that. I approached John and said, 'What do you think?' and he thought it was wonderful. It worked because then fans were able to see them not as the Doctor or Tegan or whatever, but as actors. The first year John basically stage-managed the whole thing for me. The second year he said, 'You're going to do it now.'"

John, who was usually the compere, charmed even the most reluctant of the guests into taking part. He had his own spots, too, acting as stooge to Jon Pertwee (whom he called OMP – short for "Old Mother Pert") and performing a double act with Janet Fielding in which they insulted each other with aplomb. One of these routines was performed to the tune of *I Remember It Well* and went as follows:

John: You signed three weeks to *Doctor Who*
Janet: I stayed three years to upset you
John: Ah yes, I remember it well
Janet: I started work, you gave the hint
John: You didn't read the smaller print
Janet: Ah yes, I remember it well. I shivered with the cold
John: In costumes far too rich
Janet: But I was good as gold
John: You lying....(at which point Janet clapped her hand over John's mouth)

"We were all expected to do something," actress Wendy Padbury (who played 1960s companion Zoe) told *DWM*. "I was sitting in JN-T's hotel room, moaning that I didn't have a 'party piece' and he gave me that look he does, then looked at a suitcase on top of his wardrobe, then back at me and said, 'Wendy, do you think you could fit in that case?' I thought perhaps he'd had too much laughing water but I went and sat in the case anyway and he said, 'Right, I know exactly what we can do.'

"Come the cabaret, John was on stage and announced that he'd be bringing a friend on to say hello to everybody. He went off stage and came back, lugging this suitcase with him, and told the fans to shout loudly to get his friend to appear. After a few minutes shouting, he opened the case and pulled me out, put me on his knee and did this ventriloquism act, which went down a storm."

"I remember John once sang Bette Midler's *Big Noise from Winnetka*," says Langford, "and I think it probably summed him up. He loved it."

"He was Mr Entertainment," smiles Sophie Aldred.

"They had such fun," says Lynda Baron, whose daughter, Sarah, was John's secretary. "They went to New York for a big convention and were booked into a very smart hotel, on something like the 19th floor. Because her name was

Sarah Lee, everybody thought it would be funny to send her a Sara Lee cake so when they arrived in this hotel suite it was full of cakes. John thought it would be very sweet to share them with New York so they spent quite a lot of time just frisbying them out of the window!"

"I did get to know him much better at conventions," Lalla Ward (companion Romana) told an American radio show in 2002. "There was far more camaraderie and fun than we had time to have when we were in the studio itself. Then one began to see what an incredibly good-humoured, good-natured, easy-going, kind person he was too – just really fun to be around."

As soon as a new cast member joined the show, John would whisk them off to meet the Whovians (as American fans often called themselves). Colin Baker was "trundled out for a convention in Miami before I'd even known what my costume was, let alone shot anything, which was bizarre. John and I had codes at conventions. There was one which, if introduced loudly in our conversation, meant you wanted rescuing from a barker!"

"The first thing I did was to go to a convention in America," adds Bonnie Langford. "I had seen no script. At the time, *Doctor Who* wasn't on and we had no YouTube or DVDs to be able to tap in to. So I really was entering into it blind. John did look after me a bit – we had such a laugh.

"We were given these pseudonyms so that the fans didn't call our hotel rooms without permission and I was Judy Garland. My mother had come with me – and she was Gwen Verdun [a celebrated Broadway star] – and I said, 'Well, at least you're alive!' My agent was trying to get hold of me and when I phoned him after a few days just to say 'Hi,' he said, 'Where the hell have you been? I've been trying to get hold of you!' And I said, 'Oh, you needed to ask for Judy Garland!' and he nearly dropped the phone!

"John came on all the panels with me because I had nothing to say. I'm quite good at bluffing but my God that was really pushing it. Obviously, the fans wanted to know everything and I think they thought I was being very coy and discreet, playing my cards close to my chest – but actually I didn't have any cards to play. All I could say was, 'I'm sure it's all going to be marvellous!'"

"I got the job on the Monday," laughs McCoy, "and on Thursday, he flew me out to Atlanta. That was my introduction to it and I was gobsmacked, completely, utterly gobsmacked. I will never forget arriving at this university and there were tall young men wearing Tom Baker's heavy coat and scarf and it was a heat wave. I thought, 'These people are completely mad.' Then there were ladies who wandered around dressed up as Leela, wearing tiny little bits of chamois leather over their private bits – but these women were built like Michelin men and they wobbled. I just thought, 'What is this? It's completely out of my ken!' But Americans are so loving and when we did the convention, John turned to me and said, 'My God, you've taken to this like a duck to water'"

"I'd never seen anything like it," says Sarah Sutton. "It was phenomenal, terrifying, exhausting. If John hadn't been there, I would have really floundered. You got paid – often in dollars. He dealt with all that – it came through him."

The fact that John often acted as "broker" or agent for cast members led to a gradual but inexorable breakdown in his relationship with Anthony Ainley. In the end, just the mention of the man's name was enough to make Gary Downie spit in disgust. Ainley was an eccentric, fond of asking female fans to call him "Uncle" and giving them sweets from his pockets. Wealthy in his own right, he was unusual among actors in that he represented himself. He began to suspect that he was being underpaid for convention appearances and that John was siphoning off the available cash for himself.

"You know, Anthony Ainley, God bless him, was a pissy little guy," says Katz. "From the very, very first, he always felt that he was getting cheated. There are people in life that are natural born victims and he thought that everybody was out to screw him. In my book, Lis Sladen was the biggest draw for a companion. I paid her more than any other and I paid Ainley as much. He told me later that we paid him more money in one weekend than he made from the BBC as the Master. He still felt that he was getting screwed. He wanted to make as much as Tom Baker or Peter Davison. He was bitter about that and always pissed off that John got anything – 'He's just a producer.' 'Yeah, he is *the* producer.' You run into those guys in life. It's unfortunate."

"Anthony Ainley was obsessed by the idea that John was making money and not giving it to him," adds Colin Baker. "It was absolute rubbish. I sat down with him and he said, 'John's on tens of thousands and so are you,' and I said, 'No. I'm not.' I was honest with him and he just wouldn't believe me."

"He was certainly better paid than John was," confirms Rubenstein. "If he thought he wasn't, that was in his own mind."

John, always sensitive to hostility, used Ainley less and less and in return, during interviews, Ainley rewrote history by claiming it had been Barry Letts's idea to cast him and losing no opportunity to make a snide remark about "Nathan". "It was a vicious betrayal of JN-T," believes writer Gary Russell. "I have nothing but loathing for Ainley – one of the most despicable men I have ever met in my life. He was absolutely horrible. Vainglorious and like so many of the stinking rich, all he cared about was screwing money out of people."

"I had no idea of the depth of the hatred between the two men," comments Grahame Flynn. "In February 2001, I produced a three-day convention in Coventry at which both John and Ainley were guests. We scheduled the whole event so they never had to appear together but, during an autograph session, I was suddenly aware of raised voices. They were having a blazing row in the middle of the room. I got the stewards to usher the attendees out and close the doors. John and Ainley were totally oblivious. 'Nathan, I will never forgive you,' Ainley was shouting.

"I waited until a break in the argument and quietly said, 'Gentlemen, I don't think that this is the right time and place. Do you?' They were red with rage, perspiring and breathing heavily. They both turned and looked at me. I maintained my ground. I was the producer here. Both men suddenly looked like naughty schoolchildren. 'Yes, of course,' said John. 'Sorry, Grahame.' They left the room via separate doors."

The Ainley situation was unusual. John was good with artists and conventions allowed him to develop his friendships with them. Naturally, he had his favourites and one of these was Patrick Troughton, the actor who'd played the second Doctor. On 28th March 1987 Troughton died on the job at an American convention in Columbus, Georgia. John used all his contacts and experience to deflect any potentially unwelcome press interest, managing the delicate situation with sensitivity and flair. He persuaded BBC management to pay for a *Doctor Who*-biased wake in the great actor's memory. This took place on 15th April 1987 at the Bridge Lounge in Television Centre. John invited everyone from close family and friends to principal cast members such as Jon Pertwee, Peter Davison, Colin Baker and Troughton's co-stars in the show, Michael Craze, Frazer Hines, Deborah Watling, Wendy Padbury, John Levene and Nick Courtney. From within the BBC he asked Jonathan Powell, Graeme McDonald, Shaun Sutton, Innes Lloyd, Paul Stone and Renny Rye (who had, respectively, produced and directed Troughton in *The Box of Delights*), Jane Morgan (a drama producer from radio), Barry Letts and Terrance Dicks. From outside the BBC, the guest list included former producer Peter Bryant and the American fan who had been with him when he died. Again, it was John at his best – kind, thoughtful and doing what he could to protect both the show he loved and an actor he admired and liked.

In the summer of 1988, there was a challenge of a more personal kind when his former script editor turned sworn enemy Eric Saward began a series of formal complaints about the screening of *Doctor Who* stories in America. Saward claimed that these were shown in flagrant breach of copyright and demanding compensation. Getting no response from BBC copyright, he elevated his correspondence to managing director Paul Fox. "Over the last four months," he wrote, "I have written several times to both Stephen Edwards and Tom Rivers of your copyright department asking for an explanation as to why

[John Nathan-Turner] has been able to supply tapes .. written by myself and many others... to fan conventions. As they have not bothered to reply, I am now forced to write to you.

"John Nathan-Turner's activities cannot be seen as innocently supplying tapes to promote the show he produces. American conventions are organised by businessmen (Ron Katz, Norman Rubenstein and others) to make a profit... John Nathan-Turner, a BBC staff producer, has also been paid large sums to attend these conventions. And when he does, he has taken along copyright material to be shown to an audience who had bought tickets to view it. Does he have the BBC's permission to do so? If so, why won't your copyright department answer my letters? If not, when will I and others be paid for the use of our materials?"

This finally galvanised Tom Rivers (deputy head of copyright) into a careful three-page response, in which he sought to close down the debate, claiming that the tapes fell under the acceptable category of a "trapped audience" – in other words, that having paid to attend the convention, a guest was not then required to pay for the chance to see old episodes too – so that there was no case to answer. Saward wasn't having any of this and on 21st June sent his own three-page missive, refuting Rivers's arguments and sneering that "conventions are commercial. Please don't tell me John Nathan-Turner took tapes to conventions to simply promote his show. He took them there for the purpose of making money. Doesn't sound like a 'BBC legitimate publicity' to me. Now, surely, it's time to pay those who created the shows he so kindly abused? ... If I do not have sensible answers to all my questions within five working days, I intend to make this issue public."

The exchange rapidly escalated to include the BBC's head of personnel, Glynne Price (who spoke to John about it) and the various craft unions, Equity, BETA, ACTT and the Writers' Guild. "I remember there being a bit of a smell around all that stuff," says controller of BBC1 and John's former boss, Jonathan Powell, disapprovingly. When I asked both Ron Katz and Norman Rubenstein if they had relied on John to supply them with tapes, both were unequivocal. "I really didn't need John to do that for me," says Katz, "because I had my sources in the UK. I never asked him to do that, and nor did he advance it."

"We would ask the BBC for episodes to show," says Rubenstein. "BBC Enterprises knew about it and we were given them and I don't remember there being a charge for them."

Eventually, a compromise was reached and the BBC paid compensation. "They were stonewalling like crazy," says another ex-script editor Chris Bidmead. "In the end, I got seven grand or something to sign a nondisclosure thing and all that bollocks. I think one or two other writers had a similar deal."

By this stage, the American fan bubble had burst. A combination of the postponement and pruning of the show in Britain and a suddenly more aggressive approach from the BBC's US distributor, Lionheart, damaged Katz and Rubenstein's big fan organisations so badly that they could not recover. "Whatever was happening in the UK," says Katz, "*Doctor Who* had a bright and big future in the USA in many, many ways. We were very shocked – it was really a blow to us and we didn't understand why they would do that. It was just stupid to throw water on that flame."

"It would have kept growing," agrees Rubenstein. "It was extremely popular in the United States and we were very shocked at the sudden turnaround from the top of the BBC – they decided they were sick of the series and, by hook or by crook, they were going to shut down *Doctor Who*.

"I think the final betrayal was in 1986 when my group and Ron's group were told that there was going to be this huge meeting. We were going to work through all differences and try and work together to promote *Doctor Who*. BBC Enterprises asked us to come up with our marketing plans and we came up with a highly detailed business plan. My understanding is that Ron did as well – we didn't get to see what he had done and vice versa. We felt very good that the BBC was finally going to take charge and coordinate to everyone's advantage. There was certainly enough market place for us all to do rather well. Then they hit us with a 90-day notice telling us that they were going take over the whole thing themselves.

"That was the end of it for us. We felt that we had spent months of effort and gave them lots of marketing ideas and they said, 'Thanks very much, we're going to take what we want from that and do it all ourselves. It's been nice knowing you, goodbye!' John and I lost touch rather suddenly at this point – he basically asked, 'Don't put me in the middle of this.' But I look back on it all very fondly – it wasn't a lucrative endeavour in the end – every single penny I had went back into the company. At the end we were left holding the baby."

"Lionheart got very greedy," agrees Katz. "They couldn't have cared less about the fans – they thought they were just a bunch of freaks. Everything they did was second rate. For myself, I was travelling a lot and working very hard, promoting the fan club, the series and PBS. I would be in an airport and I would hear, 'Hey, there's Ron,' and I got a little creeped out with that and everybody touching me. So I turned my back and walked away from it."

Many people believe that John could, would and perhaps even should have found his future Stateside. "He had the right type of personality that would have gone over in Hollywood," believes Rubenstein, "certainly in television. He could have done well."

"He could have in a heartbeat," says Katz. "I was always miffed about why didn't he go to New York or LA. He had ties there – he certainly had the moxy to do it. He could have been cynical and dark but he wasn't – he was kind of like a fan who was more American than British. But on the other hand, he was the ultimate Brit – I'm sorry that the British fans weren't like him."

"One of the reasons John never finished up in America," explains close friend Fiona Cumming, "is that he would never give up on the responsibility of looking after his mum. She had to go in a home and he wanted to be close by."

John's affection for the States and for American fans never waned. He continued to attend conventions and later, cruises, in which fans paid to travel alongside stars from the series. In 1988, writing to apologise for being unable to attend the leaving party for an old friend in the press office, Peter McArdle (whom John called Pina Colada), he explained: "I will be away on an all-expenses-paid, first-class cruise around Florida and Mexico – with 100 *Doctor Who* 'barkers'. (There's always a catch!)"

BBC apathy and incompetence may have temporarily derailed *Doctor Who*'s American invasion but there is no doubt that John helped to lay the foundations for what is happening there today – a thriving market reinvigorated by the rebirth of the series which he never lived to see.

"John saw the importance of making inroads into the America market," says Cartmel.

"He was absolutely ahead of the game," says Mark Strickson. "I've enormous respect for him. Britain is a small place. John thought internationally and that's what saved *Doctor Who*. It now seems the simplest thing in the world to say, 'We've got to sell it to America,' but there was nobody in the BBC who really, really got that. What he did was really simple – he made it profitable. He made it make money for the BBC. They could never ignore *Doctor Who* again."

TWELVE

PRESUADED TO STAY

"I saw him in reception around the time the series was ending and I said, 'What are you up to these days?' and he just said, 'Guess!'"
Bob Richardson, interview with the author, 2012

If 1986 had been John's *annus horribilis*, 1987 was year zero – a new beginning forced on him by politics and circumstance. In the wake of Eric Saward's departure and his own conviction (based on what he'd been promised) that the 23rd season would be his last, nothing had been done to commission any new scripts. Hastily, John recruited his writing acolytes, Pip and Jane Baker, and they got to work scribbling an opening four-parter, *Strange Matter*. The Baker Twins had been around since the year dot but John's new script editor was an industry ingénu. Twenty-eight-year-old Canadian-born Andrew Cartmel was tall, bespectacled and softly spoken. He was a computer science graduate working for a software company in Cambridge but had a lifelong ambition to write and had managed to secure himself an influential agent on the basis of some unproduced scripts. This agent, Richard Wakeley, recommended him to John, who liked the earnest young man. The final hurdle was an interview with Jonathan Powell who approved too, so the job was his. But if Cartmel had been under any illusions about the status of *Doctor Who*, they didn't last long.

"I'd been interviewed by the chap who ran children's drama [Paul Stone] too," he remembers, "and there had been a feeling I might end up there because I got along well with him. So I told him, 'I've now got a job at the BBC,' and he said, 'What is it?' and when I said *Doctor Who*, he said, 'Oh well, never mind.' I thought it was odd, and amusing, because I was delighted to get the gig. But that was the kind of attitude. Inside the BBC, it was reviled. We were like the idiot relative that they try to keep locked up in the attic – a bit of an embarrassment."

Over the next three years, John's partnership with Cartmel helped to heal some of the wounds left by Saward's betrayal. Perhaps inevitably, his sharp reversal of fortune had somewhat mellowed John. Shorter seasons meant less pressure too. Cartmel was, in his way, a kindred spirit – just as driven, he brought fresh energy, focus and ambition to the job. Professionalism and creative ambition were qualities to which John always responded, unless they posed too much of a threat to his own status. But Cartmel was laid-back and considered and, while he occasionally had to fight his own corner, he usually won his producer round. Scripts had never been John's strong suit and he was relieved to find he'd stumbled across someone with no shortage of ideas. Unlike Saward, Cartmel was also able to attract and nurture a raft of new writers who shared his vision for *Doctor Who*, although, in fairness, he had fewer slots to fill.

"Trying to keep the script sensible and a little bit scary and truthful at the same time was always problematical," says director Chris Clough. "He assembled a very young team who were really quite exciting and they got some big themes in there. That was a positive element. He did well, Andrew – he kind of subverted the Eric Saward regime, which I thought was not very good. John left him to it a bit. I think he was tired of the show."

"When Andrew came on, immediately there was a huge difference," agrees fellow director Andrew Morgan.

"John wasn't deeply involved with the scripts," says Cartmel, "but he had an overview of them – in broad strokes he had a lot of influence. If I hadn't delivered the goods, what he would have done first would have been to interfere a lot more – if my way hadn't shown results."

"Andrew and John were like chalk and cheese," says Sophie Aldred (who played Ace). "God knows how they worked so well together but it was a very good relationship. Andrew managed to speak to John quite honestly in ways that other people couldn't. I think what John respected about Andrew was that he really knew what he was doing and came up with good ideas. OK these new writers were writing scripts that were too long and needed cutting, but they took it in an interesting new direction."

"Andrew was very precise," says John's secretary, Kate Easteal, "about what he thought would work with the scripts. John would have respected that. I think he rated him."

"I kind of kept him at arm's length," Cartmel explains. "I didn't go out boozing or socialising with him off the job. He and Eric had been as thick as thieves and I realised that was a really bad combo. Not just because John was gay and I was straight and he was an alcoholic and I was, by comparison, a teetotaller but also because I knew if you're working with people under a lot of pressure and you hang out with each other off-duty too, you're going to get sick of each other."

Cartmel did experience an echo of the infamous Grimwade row, when he inadvertently took a group of writers and some of the cast to lunch without including his producer. "It happened once and after that, I just made sure he was always copied in," says Cartmel. "He was usually too busy to come anyway. He was oversensitive and a bit paranoid but in his position that was justifiable. He was a very sensitive guy and his feelings were hurt if he didn't think you liked him and wanted him along. And he also would have wondered, what are you up to – are you intriguing against him? That institutional thing. He was under enormous pressure. You couldn't have more of a pressure cooker show than *Doctor Who* when it was rolling.

"Then his family life was a fucking disaster zone – he used to shoot up to Birmingham every Friday as soon as we wrapped – deal with his father who'd had a stroke and was in hospital ripping the tubes out of his arms and trying to walk out, deal with the mother who was also a complete horror show and then come back to resume the show on Monday morning. Christ, that poor guy was stressed out. We were aware of that but he wouldn't moan – he was a real trooper – he was a 'Come on, we've got to get on with it and be cheerful' kind of guy.

"But I don't see him as a tormented man," continues Cartmel. "Really, John loved life and loved being who he was. He just wanted everything to be lovely and happy and everyone to have a great time. The trouble is that would also involve him necking down endless amounts of booze, trying to sleep with any number of extras and doing a certain amount of drugs. Everybody knew what he was doing. It was not conducive to professional work if you were that much of a party animal."

The big priority was to secure a new leading man. Powell suggested Ken Campbell, whose reputation was forged on a career as a subversive actor/director in experimental and fringe theatre. John found Campbell alarming and unsuitable. His preference was for an actor with the memorable stage name Sylvester McCoy (his real name was Percy Kent-Smith – John tended to call him Kent). Ironically, Campbell had helped to get McCoy started in the business and shared some of the same anti-establishment credentials. On television, McCoy had been in the cast of imaginative children's shows *Vision On* and *Jigsaw*. McCoy recalls his first impressions of John as "a curly-haired teddy bear in a red room full of *Doctor Who* paraphernalia. A pair of underpants with Tom Baker's face on them stood out, I remember! I learnt early on that if you go to an interview or audition, wear something unusual because people remember you. So I arrived wearing a Panama hat. He said, 'I love the hat,' – and I said, 'Well, if the hat stays, so do I.'

"Normally, you go into that kind of interview and do half an hour of charm at the most and that's it. When I went in, it took two hours. By the end of it, I was digging deep down into my bag of charm to find anything to keep him on my side. But I must have done somehow."

Powell was uncertain, feeling that McCoy might lack the necessary gravitas or range. He felt that Baker's Doctor had been a "clownish" figure and the last thing he wanted was a successor cut from the same cloth. He told John to hire a casting agent, now a ubiquitous part of the process but then a novelty, and to hold screen tests for the shortlist. "I think I said, 'Get a casting director,' because I didn't have the first clue about who to get to play Doctor Who," he says.

"They didn't think I could do the serious stuff," says McCoy. "That was the principal concern. And John, bless him, fixed it – because he was going to get who he wanted, come what may, and those bastards upstairs weren't going to get in his way. He told me that they wanted Ken Campbell and he said, 'No, Ken will frighten the children!' He would have made a great villain, Ken. What he did was get two other actors [Dermot Crowley and David Fielder], smashing actors, but wrong for *Doctor Who* and manipulated it that way. It was fixed."

The screen tests were recorded in the tiny Pres B studio at Television Centre on 18th February 1987. Cartmel wrote a script and John asked Janet Fielding to play opposite the three candidates. Andrew Morgan, who'd signed to handle the first four-parter, directed. "Others weren't so sure about Sylv," he says. "John tipped me the wink and said, 'This is the man I want. Make sure you shoot him properly.' And he was the best. Dermot Crowley was good but I don't think I felt secure that he would come up with the goods every time."

"Sylvester was a very intelligent choice," believes fellow director Chris Clough. "I thought he took it into much more interesting places – and having a physical comedian as well was a nice thing to play with. The costume worked well, too."

McCoy was announced to the world at large on 2nd March 1987. "It was easier when Sylvester came in," says Bonnie Langford, "because he was the new boy. I remember John asking me about him because I had worked with him in *The Pirates of Penzance* – and I said how lovely he was. Colin and Sylvester are very different people. Sylvester was the Doctor, too, but we were a partnership and I welcomed him in."

"Compared to other television jobs," recalls McCoy, "John was incredibly generous in allowing me an amazing amount of freedom. I definitely felt that he was on my side all the way through. I was working with very creative, off-the-wall people, prepared to try something. There was a feeling of us against them – them upstairs."

John worked out a new production system, which would remain in place for the next three years. He divided the season into three – two four-parters and a block of six, each made by a self-contained team. The six-episode block would then be subdivided into two three-parters, one shot entirely in the studio, the other entirely on location. It was the perfect example of John's continuing skill at making a little go a long way, squeezing the scant resources at his disposal to deliver maximum results on screen. It made the most of his reduced episode count, so that the four contrasting stories still gave some semblance of an overall season with different shades of style and approach.

While John was working to make the best of a bad job, his bosses, were, as ever, undermining his efforts. For the next three years, the programme would be placed opposite British television's most consistent ratings big-hitter, ironically John's favourite show – *Coronation Street*. "Moving it against *Coronation Street* was just a way of throwing it away really," admits Powell, "because in those days nothing got an audience against it. Michael [Grade] wasn't interested. When I became controller of BBC1, I kept it there because you couldn't put it anywhere else. By this time, it had got into a cycle of diminishing returns. I wasn't going to fight for money for it. I still didn't know what to do with it."

"Michael Grade was a master scheduler," says Marcia Wheeler, manager in drama series and serials. "He was scheduling it to death."

"It must have been awful," ruminates Russell T Davies. "The moment we brought *Doctor Who* back [in 2005] it was at the top of the agenda. We used to work like hell behind the scenes to keep it at the top of the sixth floor agenda. It's vital to be at the top of everyone's list. To make it despite that absolute lack of interest, I think the man achieved miracles. It must have been so dispiriting to go in to work and not even have people comment on it. I bet his colleagues didn't even watch it. You could just tell that was the atmosphere at the time."

"There was no support really," confirms director Alan Wareing. "Jonathan Powell didn't give a shit. Now *Doctor Who* is big-time again and all it needed was a little bit of TLC and money, really."

As might have been expected from the speed with which it was thrown together, McCoy's first year was, at best, erratic. The first story, retitled *Time and the Rani*, was a less than auspicious start, a bonkers script stuffed with the

Bakers' trademark verbosity and laden with the unlikely (but unintentionally hilarious) conceit that a middle-aged Kate O'Mara could pass herself off as Bonnie Langford, in ginger fright wig and identical garish costume. "It was very last minute," says Morgan, "and it wasn't very good. Because I didn't know anything about special effects, I was sort of bullied by the visual effects department and told under no circumstances could I move the camera during effects shots.

"On the plus side, the designer was great, mad as a snake and pissed all the time but a real talent – he came up with these wonderful designs. He had rows all the time because he didn't care about health and safety. But Pip and Jane were a nightmare to work with. It was a loser from the beginning really. I finished it and felt 'I'm not proud of that piece of work' – I really mucked it up. It was one of the worst jobs I ever did."

The second story, *Paradise Towers*, directed by Nick Mallett (whose real name was Vic, hence his nickname of NickVic), suffered from crude design and a toweringly awful performance from guest star, Richard Briers, while the final pair of three-parters were the experimental *Delta and the Bannermen* (which John christened *Delta and the Diddymen* in homage to its guest star, comedian Ken Dodd) and the more traditional *Dragonfire*. This was let down by a stupidly literal cliffhanger to episode one in which the Doctor, apparently for no reason, clambers over a railing to dangle in peril above a vast chasm of ice. I was in the studio while this was being recorded and could not understand why no-one was aware of the obvious idiocy being played out in front of their eyes. By then, I was losing patience with *Doctor Who* – and so was Bonnie Langford, who made her final appearance in the same story. "There was nothing to grab hold of," she says. "At first I was very earnest and conscientious and tried every which way to find something of meaning, when really I should have just said the lines and got off. Which I did in the end. I would approach things differently now, I really would. My agent at that time used to turn round and say, 'Well, darling, at least you're busy.' I say nothing more. To me it was just a summer job. All my memories of it are me doing very little, being over the top and it not being exactly my best work, to say the least."

In her place came a young actress with no television experience – Sophie Aldred, who overlapped with Langford on *Dragonfire*. "I think John worked a lot on instinct," she says, "and probably he knew as soon as I walked into the room that he was going to hire me. He just went on a hunch. So I was booked with the understanding that it might continue. It was extraordinary, looking back. I never had a screen test – it was just those two readings at Union House."

John did sound out McCoy, too, who gave Aldred his thumbs up. "JN-T told me I'd got the job after the first studio day," she continues, "when they'd eyed me up and down with the camera. He came down, lit up a fag and said, 'Well, we're up for it if you are,' and that was it."

But Aldred had a rough start with her star-maker. "I had this cockiness of youth but I was very insecure. *Dragonfire* was fine because I didn't really have much contact with John. He came for the producer's run and everybody was bowing down to him. If he'd had jodphurs and a megaphone it would have made sense. Now I think it was completely an act. It was simply that he needed to show who was boss to get the job done. He was a real presence.

"When I came back the following year, I wasn't particularly happy because I was given very little direction. I was craving some feedback from John – 'That was good, well done' or even, 'That was rubbish, do it again.' But he was very much a figure in the background – he would stand by the monitor breathing down the director's neck. In those days, I wanted to be liked and I remember going home crying to my boyfriend and saying, 'What have I done?' I felt that he was very aloof and not communicating with me at all."

Matters reached a low point during the location shoot for *Remembrance of the Daleks* (1988) in London's Hammersmith. "We were in this enclosed space and I am not very good with cigarette smoke and John lit up a fag and I said to the floor manager, 'Do you think that there's some way that John could maybe not smoke because it's making me feel awful and I've got to do this big sequence?' I saw him go over to John and John immediately and very ostentatiously took out his pack of fags and lit one. It was all testing, I think. Later on, I remember walking past him with Karen Gledhill [who played Allison in the story], and we said, 'Night, John,' and he said, very pointedly, 'Good night... *Karen*.'

"I think he really didn't get me at all at first. I was this ex-radical feminist theatre student from Manchester University. They'd had to get me to shave my armpits – they were, 'Oh My God! What's that up her sleeves?' By comparison, Bonnie and Kate O'Mara and those camp old ladies in *Paradise Towers* [Brenda Bruce and Elizabeth Spriggs] were absolutely John's cup of tea."

It was during this time that I bowed out of *Doctor Who*. I'd left university in the summer of 1987 and joined the BBC the following year. For four years, I'd been churning out thousands of words of waffle every month as the main feature writer for *Doctor Who Magazine* and I was bored and restless. As the programme lurched from one crisis to another, it no longer felt like a very positive association. I disliked many of the creative decisions being taken, which meant I had to feign a previously genuine enthusiasm. Many interviews were tinged with bitterness or bitching (which obviously we couldn't print). There was a new editor at *DWM*, too, and we cordially disliked each other. It was jump or be pushed. The fact that I now had a proper career on which to focus my energies and ambitions helped. I was making the transition from onlooker to participant.

When I joined studio management (as John had done all those years before), I learnt that the BBC's system was to start you with a few weeks' "trailing". As the word implies, this meant that you accompanied the scheduled floor assistant on a show and shadowed their every move. Sometimes, they, or an indulgent floor manager, might let you actually do something yourself – perhaps collect the cans and talkback boxes from the sound gallery before the start of rehearsals (and take them back again at the end of the day), mark up the chalk board at the studio entrance or even (butterflies in your stomach) do some actual cueing of artists. They started you on the easy stuff – *Grandstand* (where I spent some of the most boring days of my life) or *Kilroy*. I progressed to *Top of the Pops*, sitcoms and children's drama, and wasn't far from going solo, when I came in one morning to look at the new "sheets" containing what was coming up.

To my absolute horror, I saw that I'd been scheduled to trail Louise Percival (who was lovely and one of the most welcoming of my new colleagues) on *Doctor Who*. I tried to get out of it but my allocator refused and was understandably confused. "I thought you'd be pleased – you said you like drama and we don't do so much now." I could hardly tell them I was a fugitive barker. As the days passed and the time grew closer, I felt nemesis approach. I felt sure that John would clock me at once, demand an explanation, suspect a plot and have me humiliatingly ejected. Worse, I worried that he might make trouble with my new department. I fantasised about throwing myself on his mercy and pleading that I wasn't (and never had been) a spy and that I didn't even like the programme any more. Spot the flaw in that argument.

Studio day dawned and with a sick feeling in the pit of my stomach, I went to work. The story was *Remembrance of the Daleks*. In some ways, it was fascinating to be "on the inside", albeit so fleetingly. I was immediately impressed with Andrew Morgan's calm, authoritative direction, especially as there was a huge amount of material to get through. Sophie Aldred quickly spotted me – I'd met her several times for *DWM*. Always warm and friendly, she didn't bat an eyelid to see me lurking about with a headset on, clutching a camera script to give me an aura of purpose. The day went on and on. It was like playing a one-sided game of hide and seek. Several times, I ducked out of John's way and carefully avoided walking in front of any cameras lest I be spotted on the monitors in the studio gallery. I was kept busy too, getting teas and coffees, herding walk-ons about and liaising with make-up and wardrobe (which translates as nagging them to get artists out onto the floor).

During the evening recording, in classic *Who* tradition, tension mounted as a daunting number of pages remained to be recorded before ten o'clock, mostly in one set – the operations room. Sylvester McCoy began to struggle with his words – the sheer volume he had to retain, I suspect. Then it happened. Pamela Salem and Karen Gledhill had been cleared and sent to make up to de-wig and take off their slap. Suddenly, Simon "Sam" Williams grabbed me and, as I'd been feeling so furtive all day, I yelped slightly. He looked momentarily thrown and then, dismissing this, whispered that he wanted me to help him play a joke on the "girls". Horror gripped me and I wanted to plead, "Not me, please – pick on someone else!" but he was bossy and not in the mood for a chat about it. "Go in and tell them there's been a mistake – a fault on the tape – and that they've got to be back on the floor and ready to go in five minutes. It'll be funny.' How I hated him then. But there was no escape.

Reluctantly, I began to slink towards the double doors that led to make up and wardrobe, hoping Williams would get distracted and the moment might pass. But he was watching me all the time and when I looked back a second time, nodded his head sharply in the direction of the doors with an exasperated expression as if I must be an idiot child. The red lights were on and a scene was being recorded, so even opening those heavy hinged doors was agony – the slightest creak might bring disaster upon my head. I was picturing the scene as John discovered who was at the bottom of this stupid practical joke – the trailing floor assistant, the lowest form of studio life and a barker to boot.

I crept inside and did my best but I was too terrified and hesitant to be convincing. Salem and Gledhill saw straight through the ruse and carried on wiping off their base. I was red in the face but relieved and didn't even care when I turned to see the lanky Williams looming in the doorway with an expression that didn't bother to disguise his disgust at my comic ineptitude.

When the recording ground to a halt, behind schedule despite the frantic pace of work, Louise thanked me and asked me to take back the bundle of headsets. I was walking down a fire lane towards the steps that led upstairs when I spotted John coming the other way. He looked straight at me and I wondered if this was it – the moment I would be confronted and accused. But it turned out I was building my part. As he walked past, he just said, "Thanks – see you in the bar" and it occurred to me that behind my bundle of cans and wires, I must have been more or less incognito, camouflaged as a junior crew member. It was my last professional encounter with him.

To Aldred, John remained an authoritarian figure throughout her first months with the show, unilaterally choosing what she felt was an unflattering publicity card. "Not even my mother recognises me," she told him. He also refused to pay for late-night transport following studio recordings. "I wouldn't have sent my leading lady back on a late-night train to Lewisham," she observes, wryly.

It was only during the Dorset location shoot for *The Greatest Show in the Galaxy* that Aldred finally bonded with her producer. "The crew and the cast would always be in hotels together. This is typical John – he did create the most fantastic ensemble, it was like something by JB Priestley [a playwright famous for ensemble cast productions]. He got wind that *Rockliffe's Babies* were filming nearby and said, 'I know, let's have a skittles match in a nearby pub.' So we challenged them and went to this lovely pub in the middle of the countryside. For some reason, I ended up sitting at the bar with him and we chatted. I think we just took the piss out of each other – it was humour and me getting on his wavelength – finding out about each other. We were very different – I didn't drink – but when I got to know him, I discovered that he was lovely and humble – a great guy who knew exactly what he was doing."

It was his saving of *The Greatest Show in the Galaxy* (the title was John's) that represents JN-T in his element. During that summer of 1988, Television Centre was discovered to be riddled with asbestos and its studios had to be closed down at short notice. Across the BBC, production was thrown into disarray. Some programmes adapted better than others – *Wogan* was transmitted from main reception and *Blue Peter* from its garden or Lime Grove down the road (which also housed the evacuated *Tomorrow's World*). But *Doctor Who* was a full-scale drama and the options seemed limited, especially as, entirely for political reasons (what other reasons are there for BBC management?), the director-general had decreed that in-house productions were not permitted to out-source themselves to non-BBC facilities. Briefly, *Greatest Show* was cancelled but John fought the system with all the knowledge and guile he'd absorbed over the past 20 years. He was determined to avoid another *Shada* and the non-event of a ten-episode season. Finally, he prevailed, thanks to designer David Laskey's brilliant suggestion of shooting all the studio interiors in the car park at BBC's Elstree studios. The fact that much of the story was set within a circus tent was fortuitous.

"The BBC had written it off," says director Alan Wareing. "It was John that insisted that he found a way. JN-T just lived and breathed that sort of situation – for him that was what it was all about. He was a fantastic bloke. I loved the guy, I really did.

"The girl that I had been given as the production manager [Susanna Shaw] on *Greatest Show* walked out on the first day of shooting in the car park at Elstree and, lo and behold, Gary [Downie] turned up to take over. We were supposed to say, 'Thank you, Gary, it's wonderful that you could come and do this,' but, to be honest, actually my heart sank because he was pretty useless really."

Gary quickly managed to fall out with the designer, flouncing off the set and having to be sweet-talked back by John. It was hardly professional but Gary was now being scheduled on the series more regularly. "I liked Gary," says fellow director Chris Clough, "but he was quite moody and he could get queeny, which got in the way when you're a production manager because you've got to let these things sort of slough off you. I felt his heart was in the right place – you just had to watch the rough edges. It was easier on *EastEnders* but on *Doctor Who*, it was awkward because he was John's partner. You just had to make it work and tiptoe around Gary sometimes. He did wind John up. There was a lot of, 'This isn't right and that isn't right' – he would take agin people and shove the knife in. Whereas John was very easy and went with flow quite a lot. His 'produce-orial' style was very good because he knew the business backwards, knew his budget, managed people extremely well, and he was a very likeable personality to have around on the set."

Over the McCoy years, John booked the same core set of directors again and again. The only one-off, Michael Kerrigan, was nominated by Andrew Morgan, himself unavailable to return for a third time. "John said, 'It's such a hard show to do,'" recalls Cartmel, "that if he found anybody who could do it, he tended to stick with them. He had a point there. There were all the demands of a science fiction show, so much stuff to shoot, with all the effects, weird costumes, weird make-up, people in masks, all on a shoestring budget and the terrible short fucking schedules we had. A lot of the most talented directors just couldn't do it physically. If he could find someone who could do it physically he would use them again, even if, maddeningly, they would steamroller over every nuance, as a number of those directors did."

"Tight budget and tight shooting schedule – it was hard work," says Wareing. "He wouldn't allow you to go a minute beyond wrap and was very aware of making the programme for the budget. He was on location by the monitor all the time. I've been directing for a long time and I can't think of another show where the producer is by my side all the time. It wasn't that he didn't trust me; it's just that he wanted to be there, to see what was going on, to be part of the sharp end. That was what made him tick. Other producers only come out for lunch! He was a bloody nuisance at times but he did it for all the right reasons. He wore his heart on his sleeve and what you saw was what you got."

I asked Chris Clough, who later became a hugely successful and award-winning producer on cutting-edge shows like *Skins*, what, if anything, he had learnt from John. "Trust. Get the talent absolutely on side, zhuzhed up and part of a company. That makes a tremendous difference. He schmoozed the cast very well, looked after the crew very well, always parties, always drinks, very generous with drinks and his dosh – always buying rounds. Everyone who worked on *Doctor Who* enjoyed it. He hid any worries he had – he was a very positive producer."

But whatever his accomplishments, there was nothing he could do to stem the rising wave of open hostility to him within the pages of Gary Leigh's high-selling and increasingly glossy fan magazine *Doctor Who Bulletin*. Season 24 was – and remains – the least watched and most criticised season of all. Fuelled with news fed to Leigh by disgruntled but well-informed "fan glitterati" such as Jeremy Bentham (ex-*DWM*) and Ian Levine, *DWB* regularly carried banner headlines like "89% of fans want a new producer" and "JN-T Must Go Now". "I found some of the articles hurtful, to say the least," John admitted in his memoirs, although he also claimed that it flattered his ego to be such an integral part of the magazine's content. "I remember my secretary saying with outrage one day, 'The new *DWB* has arrived and you're not on the front cover! You must be slipping!'"

"He was really deeply hurt about *DWB*," says close friend Stephen Cranford. "He kept saying, 'They don't know who I am, they don't know me.' It was a campaign aimed at his job, but done personally. He went through a lot of shit and had a lot of hate mail."

"That was horrific, that magazine," says Russell T Davies, before admitting, "I used to find myself buying it every month – I couldn't look away. But it was monstrous. If you did that now, someone would step in."

Attempts were made to do just that. In 1986, visual effects designer Mike Kelt invited *DWB* along to his workshop. Leigh planned a lengthy, picture-heavy feature. "JN-T found out and went ballistic," he recalls. "They placed an injunction on me using the pictures. My solicitor said, 'They can't do this,' and got in touch with the BBC solicitor. They had to admit that what they had done was basically to try and scare me – they had no grounds. I ended up getting a £500 payment from the BBC in damages and I had to sign something to say I wouldn't mention this to anyone."

Later that same year, John appeared on the BBC's viewer feedback programme *Open Air*. Not popular with staff, this was the latest device devised by the Corporation to eat itself alive – a tradition that thrives to this day. Many producers refused to cooperate (often the wisest course of action, as the level of debate was rarely rational or balanced) but John agreed to face the wrath of a small group of highly critical fans whose cheerleader, the gravel-voiced presenter Patti Caldwell, didn't bother to hide her own bewilderment about the appeal of the programme.

In 1987, hardcore fandom's general dissatisfaction grew louder as they reacted to dire stories, declining ratings, the sacking of Colin Baker and the arrival of Langford and McCoy. Andrew Beech, new co-ordinator of DWAS, contributed a carping article to the *Daily Mail*, which seemed steeped in spite, though Beech claims otherwise: "John didn't know I had done it because it had all happened very much at the last minute. While I stand by the thrust of the argument, some of the phraseology had been tweaked, which made it even more pointed. It was terribly well-meaning – making positive suggestions as to where things might be improved. It was badly received because he wasn't expecting it or the harsh terms in which it was expressed. The article was published on the day of a convention that they [John and McCoy] were supposed to be coming to and they didn't show. The expression I heard second-hand was that it did seem rather foolish to bite the hand that feeds."

Beech subsequently made stringent efforts to heal his rift with both John and McCoy (to whom Beech composed a four-page letter of explanation) and was eventually forgiven (though John continued to refer to him as Andrew Bitch – "every word a lash"). "Within a fortnight I actually called him up and arranged to meet – just the two of us. He was clearly not very happy – I had an opportunity to explain what I had been trying to do – and what had been changed. And that he should blame me rather than the society. That meeting cleared the air and it was pretty much over and done with. One of the good things about him is that once he had formed his assessment of what had happened, he moved on completely."

When BBC2's *Did You See..?* decided to run an item giving another critical voice to fandom, this time John declined to take part. Shortly afterwards, however, *DWB* launched Operation Who, a co-ordinated attempt to force change – specifically, the removal of John from the series. On 9th December, BBC solicitors wrote to Leigh demanding an apology for remarks of a "malicious nature", which might be seen as damaging to the producer's "personal and professional reputation". Leigh, never afraid of a fight, was delighted and simply published the correspondence, along with his view that it would be "morally wrong" to offer an apology. He noted, too, that JN-T had chosen not to take personal action as it would be damaging to him. This was a snide reference to

Leigh's unique form of personal protection, provided for him by Ian Levine, who had switched sides with such a vengeance. "I had an old answerphone," explains Levine, "and John once called and said such damning things, things he shouldn't have said, about something sexual I'd set up for him, that I kept the tape. When I got the word back from Andrew Beech that they were going to sue me and Gary, I let it be known that I'd got this message and if he dared to sue me, it would get out and he would be finished. Because I'd been so badly treated I behaved equally badly in return. I made a terrible comment to one of those magazines about him being like a cancer and I regret it terribly.

"The show had become quirky, oddball and weird. In retrospect, apart from *Time and the Rani*, they all have some merit but, at that stage, it was not the kind of *Doctor Who* I wanted to see. Because of my personal feelings about JN-T, I was looking for the bad and ignoring the good. Gary Leigh kept urging me to write anti-JN-T stuff. He had been virtually raped by them – he considered it to be rape at the time. I think it affected him very badly and gave him a skewed viewpoint. He was very bitter about it."

Certainly, Leigh harbours no regrets about his prolonged and passionate anti-JN-T campaign. "No, not at all. It always pissed me off that John said I was being personal," he says. "Well, he was being personal when he propositioned me as the producer of *Doctor Who*. I wasn't offended – I just wasn't prepared to drop my pants for an exclusive. People have commented about how horrified they were by 'personal attacks' but these people don't realise the context in which those attacks were made. He didn't really have grounds to complain because his personal life *was* his professional life. There never were boundaries – he brought it all on himself, unfortunately, by blurring the lines. For all that fun and charm, he had a split personality. A lot of the traits that John displayed were sociopathic – taking the credit for other people's work. I think he was led a lot by Gary Downie – the two of them were a toxic cocktail.

"A lot of people say, 'Oh, he loved the programme and was committed to it,' and that's why he stayed so long, but equally it fed his ego and was a useful additional source of income that probably dwarfed at some points his salary as producer. It was a nice little earner for him. I think there was a fair amount of fraud going on, though it's very hard to prove. We had another legal tussle in 1993 when I got a threatening letter from John's solicitor about personal attacks. Basically my lawyer – and I had a very good one – said it's all fair comment and they had no grounds.

"It infuriates me that people are rewriting history," continues Leigh. "No matter how harsh or aggressive people may have thought I was to him, it was fair comment. I wouldn't change anything I did. *DWB* gave me a vehicle to voice my anger and bitterness about something I loved so much."

In Matthew Waterhouse's 2010 memoir, *Blue Box Boy*, he alludes to Gary Leigh as "the kind of muscular gay man who goes to clubs in army fatigues. He launched a fanzine exclusively devoted to whinging about John, pages and pages of vicious bile." He goes on to say: "Things ended unhappily for the boy. He had a huge mental collapse and his psychiatrist instructed him to apologise to everyone he had ever treated badly. So he went to John and begged his forgiveness, which of course was granted."

This seemed a fascinating development, if true. I asked Leigh about it. "I have not read his book," he comments, "but if Mr Waterhouse is implying that this person is me, then he is clearly still living on the planet Alzarius! For the record, I have *never* worn army fatigues, I have *never* had a mental collapse or seen a quack and I absolutely have never begged JN-T for anything as I stand by everything I ever said. [It is] about time fantasists and sycophants like Mr Waterhouse and the revisionists of the JN-T era got the reality check they deserve."

"That horrible little magazine played absolutely into the BBC political hand," comments Clough. "It was hugely negative. The *Daily Mail* and so on would always quote one of these fan magazines and then you'd have Michael Grade wading in. The whole thing had a very negative emotional effect on all of us – you felt hung out to dry."

"It was grist to the mill to those in the BBC who didn't really want it," agrees McCoy. "There were certain fans who were very vitriolic. John couldn't shield me from that – I saw it and heard it. There was this ongoing attack on John and therefore I was also getting some of the flak. That was natural, I suppose, but annoying. You just wanted to swat them like flies. It was a very small cliquey bunch who thought if it wasn't going to their way, it wasn't going to be anyone's way – let's destroy it. Fans who wanted to bring it down and in a sense they did, after a while."

One of the most persistent contentions aired in the pages of *DWB* was John's quote, year after year, that he had been "persuaded to stay". It was glib and infuriating and also untrue. There was no persuasion about it. John was stuck with *Doctor Who* and *Doctor Who* was stuck with him. "We were on the same floor," remembers veteran producer Joe Waters. "I used to like John – he was always full of enthusiasm but I know he was always very disgruntled because they wouldn't let him do anything apart from *Doctor Who*. It's the way I got typecast with *Dixon of Dock Green*. But I was lucky because Jack Warner was so old it had to be ended. If not, I'd still be doing it. John was always very upset because it didn't matter what he put up, they wouldn't do it."

Frustrated, he looked sideways. On Thursday 26th May 1988, John reported to room E616 in the East Tower of Television Centre. He'd been shortlisted for the job of executive producer in children's programmes, and the role at stake was to act as head of drama. *DWB* rumoured that the outgoing incumbent, Paul Stone, had been offered *Doctor Who* but there is no truth in this (Stone actually took early retirement). John's interview was conducted by the formidable head of children's programmes, Anna Home, but, as she points out, "I was much more interested in people who were breaking new ground rather than things that had been around for a long time. One wanted somebody with a broader perspective on where we might go from there."

John continued to try to get other projects off the ground, cajoling close *Who* colleagues into working with him on proposal after proposal. With Andrew Cartmel, John put forward a TV version of a book by Derek Tangye called *A Gull on the Roof*. "It was a Gerald Durrell-type thing," remembers Cartmel, "about this guy living in a farmhouse in Cornwall. It was one of a series of books – they were really lovely – and they had animals and the countryside. John and I went down to see Derek Tangye and he was looking at John like he was a creature from outer space. So I let him know that my girlfriend loved his books and he was clearly thinking, 'Thank God, it's not a coterie of homosexuals who've come from London to destroy my beloved literature.'

"I said, 'Let's get [Ian] Briggs to do it,' because he was the best writer we had in terms of creating characters well-rounded on the page. He turned in a script which John loved. It would have been a really good series. John submitted this to the powers that be and they just turned him down flat. It contributed to the breaking of his heart."

But Cartmel also recounts that it was around this time that John was offered a potential escape route from *Doctor Who*. "John went upstairs to talk about future projects and was really excited," he says. "This was the time of *Gull on the Roof*. He came back down and you could see he was simmering with fury. He said, 'They offered me *Bergerac*. I said I'd only do it if I could fire John Nettles and change the location from Jersey.'"

"I have never heard this story before," says Marcia Wheeler, then the manager of series and serials. "That sounds like malicious gossip to me. The only other possible explanation is that it was a jokey way of saying he didn't want to do it; that is *just* plausible, but unlikely. John was a lot of things but not *stupid*."

It has proved impossible to locate the source of this offer, if indeed it was made. Neither Powell nor his successor Peter Cregeen remember it (the other contender, Mark Shivas, is dead) and the then producer of *Bergerac*,

George Gallaccio, also thinks it is suspect. But Cartmel himself remains adamant. "It's clear to me that John had a conversation with someone about this and told them to take a running jump. The point was he'd gone in with his own agenda, hoping they'd give him the thing that he wanted to do. At a convention years later I said to him, 'Remember when you turned down *Bergerac?*' and he said, 'You know what? I was too arrogant. It was the wrong decision.' It wasn't a fantasy. It did happen."

Alan Wareing remembers: "John said to me, 'All I've got on my CV is *Doctor Who*' [this became a refrain with others too] and *Doctor Who* at that time had become a bit of a joke. I felt sorry for John because I think it destroyed him in the end. He was dedicated to the BBC in his way and he had the talent but maybe not in drama. He should have been in light entertainment. At a different time in a different place, he would have flourished. If he'd been allowed to produce something showbiz and razzmatazz-y, he would have been hugely successful."

"That *Doctor Who* baggage probably coloured a lot of the reactions to the other things he put up," believes Wheeler. "It was like wearing blinkers."

"John had tried to move on and do other things," recalls production associate June Collins, "but they sort of said, 'If you move on, we'll cancel the show.' I can't imagine anyone else there at the time doing it as well as he did it. It was one of the most successful shows in terms of doing it in the time and money."

"When I worked on *Blue Peter*, Biddy Baxter was like the programme," says Kate Easteal. "No one could imagine *Blue Peter* without her and yet it survived her by a long, long way. In the same way, when I was working on *Doctor Who*, it was like John is *Doctor Who* and you couldn't imagine another producer or John doing anything else."

"I felt really sad and sorry for him," says Clough, "because we'd go off and do other shows and come back and he was still labouring under it. He knew that he was being sneered at by the other producers and the whole department and the men at the top."

"The problem is that somehow John Nathan-Turner became more than a producer of *Doctor Who*," says Jonathan Powell. "He became *Doctor Who*. There was something in him that found his identity in the programme so you weren't really arguing with a producer about 'What shall we do?' – you were arguing with a person who represented himself as the programme. The dynamic of it was that *he* became the problem and not the programme. He used to go off to all those conferences and presumably he was treated like a Time Lord – 'Oh, there's the great man,' whereas in fact he was just another BBC producer doing not a very good programme and making, frankly, a bit of a hash of it. Not completely his fault because what was he going to do with no budget and no support from anybody?"

"I think that tells you more about Jonathan than it does John," says Wheeler. "He should at least have given him a go on something else."

"I will always take issue with Jonathan over that," says his predecessor, David Reid. "My own view is that if you were the head of department and you didn't like someone, you didn't let them know it. Your job was to get the best out of them and give you what they can give you. I never believed it was my job to produce programmes that only I like or appreciated. Indeed, I always saw my role as encouraging others to go with their own passions. My rationale was that even if I wasn't on John's wavelength, millions were."

"I don't think Jonathan Powell ever understood popular drama," believes Wareing. "He was more interested in Dennis Potter and the upper end. During the routine playback, he used to sit there with a disdainful look on his face, cleaning his ear out with a paper clip while watching your programme."

"You'd walk into his office with your producer," adds director Michael Morris, "and Powell would plug the cassette into his machine. Then he'd walk around the office, tidying up. At the end of it, he'd say, 'There you go' – and he hadn't watched it. He didn't care. The sort of popular stuff I was doing he wasn't interested in. It had to be of the *Tinker, Tailor* ilk for him to be interested."

"He missed out on *Darling Buds of May*," recalls his long term secretary, Sarah Lillywhite (now Cheetham). "That was offered to him and he always said that turning it down was one of his biggest mistakes. He missed the boat on that by being slightly antagonistic to what he called family entertainment."

"He once told me that police series were finished," chuckles producer Ron Craddock. "There's nothing to say to that, is there? I don't know what he thought would replace it. One assumes he had other ideas."

"The department had to do stuff across the board," points out June Collins. "Also the snobby stuff cost a load of money. I wouldn't trust Jonathan Powell as far as I could throw him, myself – too smooth for me. A lot of these people were just there for their own good. With John, you got what it said on the tin."

"I have to say," counters personnel manager Pat Dyer, "I never found Jonathan to be anything other than absolutely fair about his staff. He'd help people more than you'd ever know – and he'd never talk about it. It's one of the things I respected him for. I was very taken by the fact that when staff were in trouble – whatever that trouble was – someone finding they were HIV-positive or hitting the bottom of a drinking curve – he wasn't the person who'd say 'Get rid of them', he would say, 'What can we do to help them?' Because Jonathan is quite a reserved man, people had an impression that he was quite cold. When you got to know the private man, you found that he was much more charitable and kind than people gave him credit for."

"He was quite a prickly customer," says Sarah Lillywhite. "Not easy. He lived on the edge slightly and he was always, always under pressure so if somebody came in at the wrong moment, he could let rip and be very cutting. He had too many things to think about and he could be very unapproachable because of that. It was a huge workload. He knew he had his faults but he had a great sense of humour too. You didn't mind working for him because he was interesting to work for."

In December 1987, Powell once more climbed the ladder, suddenly succeeding Michael Grade as controller of BBC1. In drama he was followed first by Mark Shivas and then, from April 1989, by Peter Cregeen. "I didn't think the scripts were very good," says Cregeen. "The production values weren't good either. Judging it against other product that was around, it looked tired and slightly amateurish. It wasn't getting big audiences – they were of a size where there was no point in keeping it going without really grabbing it by the horns and saying, 'OK, new producer, new writers. Let them go away and dream up a way of making this show and then let's argue whether we can get a lot more money for it.' That wasn't what I felt was the best route to go down at that time."

"Regarding the scripts, fuck him," responds Cartmel, "and as for it looking amateur, give us some money then."

But Alan Wareing is less defensive. "John cajoled me into doing a *Doctor Who* in that last year, which I wish I hadn't done. I said to him at the time, 'I don't think it will work.' If there was a criticism of John, it was that he couldn't see beyond what he wanted to do. It was called *Survival* [the final transmitted show of the classic series] and the idea was good and the script worth realising but not on the time and budget the BBC was offering him. The end result was rubbish, absolute tripe, and should never have been allowed. It was just shit, really."

Although it had been a long time coming, and despite John getting the go-ahead to option McCoy for a possible fourth series, throughout 1989 there was a sense of inevitability about the end of *Doctor Who*. "We did this last scene that gave a finality to it," recalls McCoy. "I didn't really know it had been dropped until later in the year. John called me and said, 'I'm phoning you up to tell you I'm sending you a letter,' and I said, 'Oh, gosh, yes' – 'I'll tell you what's in it' – 'OK' – so he told me that the BBC were going to put it into hiatus. A word I hate – it's a horrible word.

"I wasn't that surprised because Jonathan Powell had taken over Michael Grade's job and we knew that Powell didn't want it. In that last year, although things were really working well as far as the programme was concerned, and the stories were very strong, you got the feeling John wanted to be somewhere else. It was sad towards the end."

McCoy phoned Aldred, who was rehearsing her children's show *Corners* at the North Acton rehearsal block. "It was before mobiles came in," she says, "and there was a call for me in the little production office. It was Sylvester and he said, 'Are you sitting down? I've got some bad news... *Doctor Who*'s not going ahead next year.' I was on an option for half of the next season but I was kind of hoping that they would say, 'No, stay!'

"John wrote me a letter but not with whys and wherefores. And I was really pissed off with him then because I thought the least you could have done was to give me a call and talk to me about it. But only later did I really realise what he'd been going through and I think he was probably too upset to call me."

"At the time," says Cregeen, "I don't think many people believed that what I was actually saying was that this product, which is of immense value to the BBC for all sorts of reasons, needs a break, if it's going to have a further life. One of the other things that happens, when you get a new broom like me coming into an organisation, is that obviously you wanted to bring people in to do things that were exciting you, to create a new era rather than just inheriting what was there already. We were also in the early days of having to commission a certain amount of programmes from the independents. Initially I had a target of 25 per cent and that rose to 40 per cent. I think the BBC would have thought *Doctor Who* was unsuitable to take outside so that was a factor.

"There was this whole offers process and I said, 'I don't really want to offer that this year.' Jonathan just accepted it, if I remember correctly. I don't think there was a huge amount of discussion over it."

"Peter Cregeen says it was his decision to drop *Doctor Who*," says Cartmel, scorn in every syllable. "Well, allow me to say this – if so, it's the first recorded instance of him ever having made a decision."

"When I think back," says Powell, "I think it was a cruel process, because we – Michael Grade, Bill Cotton and all the others – never had the courage to cancel it in the first place. If I'm brutally honest, the real truth of the matter is that we just let it die, quite slowly and painfully. He became so associated with it, you were letting him wither on the vine and die as well. It was just suffocation. Quite a personal process, born out of bureaucratic inactivity, a lack of inspiration, a lack of leadership from people like myself who should have cancelled the programme or taken him off it. But because everyone was so cross about it and so defeated by *Doctor Who* and it was so unwanted, it was really like everyone just turning their backs. It was very BBC. It makes me slightly squirm now."

"Shame on them," says Russell T Davies, with feeling. "It's interesting that he admits to that now but I suspect it's with a certain grandeur. It's a fine phrase that we collectively turned our back – but they abrogated all responsibility for a programme that was loved by a lot of people. Imagine if a head of drama in today's BBC said, 'I'm turning my back on that,' and that went public. You'd be kicked out of the job and quite right too. He gave his attention to *The Barchester Chronicles* or whatever was going to win him a BAFTA and let me tell you, 30 years later that stuff isn't coming to bite you on the arse but the *Doctor Who* stuff is. Your sins will find you out!

"I'm on a soap box but I just think it's appalling that he can be so rude about his own member of staff. If you're the employer, you have a duty of care. He clearly exhibited none then and he doesn't exhibit any now. He's got off the hook too long, that man – being that dismissive about his own member of staff. I don't think the duty of care stops when someone is dead. I think you have a duty of care to your employees for life if you're a proper, responsible boss. I'm ashamed of the way he talks about him."

Cartmel was swiftly moved on to the hospital series *Casualty* but for John, there was no such sponsorship or encouragement. His paperwork reveals increasingly desperate last-minute struggles to parachute himself into another project. The numerous ideas he submitted included a proposal to revive the *Bunter* stories he'd so enjoyed as a boy ("presented as a period comedy of manners"), a Stephen Wyatt series called *The Cat Club* (a pilot of which was commissioned by head of comedy Robin Nash but came to nothing), and something called *Black Curtain* ("I hope you like it," he wrote simply in the accompanying note). Another offering was *Stage School* (aka: *That's Entertainment*), following "the careers, lives and frustrations of a group of young people training for a life in the 'business', set against the machinations of a new headmistress who intends to move the school forward to cope with current trends in the entertainment industry".

All these were rejected. "There wasn't anything there at the time that I thought was right for him," says Cregeen. "He needed a really original challenge but the number of shows that you could actually get off the ground was not particularly high. All the time the money in the drama field was being cut, too."

"He had a tough time," says John's personnel officer, Pat Dyer. "Labelled with *Doctor Who* – that was all they thought he could do. Jonathan thought that part of *Doctor Who*'s unravelling was due to John Nathan-Turner. At the same time drama was going, 'We don't want any staff producers or directors, they really ought to be all freelance.' A lot of people made that transition to freelancing but they probably had a wider CV at producer level – it was difficult if you've been born and bred in the BBC."

"They were short-sighted and couldn't see that his talent didn't only lie in doing *Doctor Who*," says Collins. "Quite honestly, anyone that can manage those resources, the numbers of people, on the budget that he had, has got to be good."

"John was BBC through and through," says Wareing. "I don't think it ever occurred to him that there was a life for him outside."

As the weeks went past, John was left alone in the once busy production office now transformed into mausoleum to a dead series. He applied for the job of managing editor at BBC Radio Sussex but wasn't even shortlisted. On Valentine's Day 1990, he was called to a meeting with Pat Dyer, who broke it to him gently that he was going to be made redundant. "Thank you for your help and sympathetic wisdom," he wrote to her later. "Redundancy was the only option," says Dyer. "Everybody understands redundancy now; there's no stigma attached but then it was a tainted word. 'I'm being fired for not being good enough' – that's how John felt about it. He was very upset and he showed that. Whatever you say to people when they are made redundant, it's almost like bereavement – first of all there's shock, then you get very, very angry about it, then you come out the other side.

"But you didn't give people a golden handshake if it was a performance issue. The redundancy package was a good one – very generous – and you got a lot of time to start to make your contacts outside. Is that the kinder thing to do? To be honest, I thought that yes it was. Often it pushed people to do something else with their lives."

John worried whether *DWB* might have had a hand in the demise of the series and, by default, his own livelihood. He raised the issue with Dyer who responded on 1st March 1990: "Mark has now confirmed to me that there is absolutely no connection at all between the *DWB* letter-writing campaign and the decision to change direction with *Doctor Who*. The decision was mooted internally well before the campaign. I do hope that this puts your mind at rest, at least on that front."

On 3rd May, John received a formal letter from Dyer via the internal post informing him of his "dismissal from the BBC on grounds of redundancy", giving him one month's warning and three months' contractual notice. John spent his final weeks on the staff tidying up his affairs, writing letters, undertaking useful computer courses and looking for work. Among others, he approached Yorkshire TV with *Starlets*, a vehicle for Jessica Martin (one of the guest artists on *The Greatest Show in the Galaxy*, who had since become a friend), but this was rejected by David Jackson, Yorkshire's deputy controller of entertainment. He said the idea "disappointed" him and "would be impossibly expensive".

John declined the offer of a leaving party, informing Cregeen: "On reflection, I've decided I'd rather leave in a quieter fashion. It suddenly occurred to me that these parties have a dreadful finality about them and, after all, I do hope to return."

He never did. "He was exactly the kind of person the hatchet was designed for," says actor Chris Guard. "That was the tragedy. Those kind of people are in short supply now – people who are prepared to put themselves on the line for what they either truly enjoy or believe."

John's last day in the drama department was 31st August 1990. Despite his wish for no farewell celebration, some friends and colleagues surprised him with one anyway. It was "eyes and teeth" all over again and one can only guess at his real feelings during this impromptu party. Having undergone a similar experience at the end of my decade on *Blue Peter*, I recognise that leaving dos are a necessary process for others to feel that they have done the right thing and given you a proper send-off. But when you are not leaving of your own free will and you're saying goodbye to a programme you both love and resent for everything it has demanded of you, your pleasure is a performance and great is the relief when it's all over. I have a hunch that it was like this for John, too.

His "womb" had been stripped and car-loads of scripts and memorabilia removed to the houses in Brockley and Brighton. John was officially an ex-producer and on his own to face the world and what remained of his career.

THIRTEEN

NO COMMENT

"[The BBC] never forgive those they have betrayed..."
Robert Muller, *Talk of Drama* (1998)

When made redundant by the BBC in 1990, John had only just turned 43. He was a comparatively young man and the remaining decade or so of his life would be punctuated by attempts to relaunch himself professionally, to find a new and satisfying outlet for his abilities away from the all-encompassing universe of *Doctor Who*.

A few months before he left the BBC, he wrote to Steve Phelps, the editor of *31 West*, a daily magazine programme being produced by John Gau for fledgling satellite station BSB: "Together with reporter Shan Lloyd, I have just completed a series of items called 'Glitz and Bits' for Radio Sussex. The items are based around light-hearted showbusiness gossip. We have become something of a minor cult in Sussex, as we wear Evening Dress for our broadcasts (whatever the time of day) and this produced a great deal of press interest... Radio Sussex has approached us with regard to another stint of 'Glitz and Bits', the Nigel Dempster and Hedda Hopper of the airwaves... I wondered if you had had the chance to consider us as guest presenters on *31 West...*"

"They used to review what was going on at the local theatres, what was in the press and stage – local actors and what they were up to," recalls close friend Stephen Cranford. "Shan had been a very high-powered Fleet Street investigative journalist but she was now a hopeless, chronic alcoholic. I dare say they contacted the editor and let's face it, it's not hard to get something like that on local radio."

"He'd get little jobs in Brighton radio," says Sylvester McCoy, "and you thought, 'He shouldn't be doing this.' He was abandoned by the BBC and it wasn't made easy for him to do other work. I really did feel sorry for him. We all knew that there was this terrible frustration but he never discussed it."

31 West were not, as it turned out, interested in John's speculative offer but BSB were planning an entire *Doctor Who* weekend and, after a few planning meetings with John as consultant, they asked him to join their presenting team. By no means a natural, John still managed to trump the two professionals lined up beside him, Debbie Flint and Shyama Perera, who looked bemused and occasionally gormless throughout much of the undertaking. It was his first job after leaving the BBC and it set the tone for what was to follow – much as he wished to move on, the reality was that it was *Doctor Who* that continued to pay the bills and keep him busy. While he was still working on the BSB weekend, to no avail he tried to interest John Gau in a series about famous variety acts, called *Funny Man*. "It is a project very dear to my heart," he wrote, adding "I am most keen to work in the independent sector."

During those long, frustrating months when the series had finally been dropped and he was still staff, he had been allowed to do some moonlighting for BBC Enterprises. Now they offered him a series of contracts closely involving him with their burgeoning range of video and audio releases. Among these were some extended versions of stories, although here John was largely hoist by his own petard. His previous insistence on wiping extraneous material meant that a potentially rich seam soon ran dry. A story exploited in this way was *The Curse of Fenric* and in John's memoirs, he noted: "I insisted director Nick Mallett be involved also and we did all our preparatory work together, re-inserting as much as possible, adapting the soundtrack and adding the small amount of new music we could afford. We did the edit and agreed to dub the show somewhere off Oxford Street. However, Nick didn't turn up to this session and has never to this day told me why."

One man who could have told him is Mark Ayres, a fan whom John had given his first big break as a composer in 1988 [on *The Greatest Show in the Galaxy*]. Ayres had scored *The Curse of Fenric* and was keen to be involved in the extended version. "Nick Mallett and I had got together and had a curry, going through the whole thing and what we would like to do with it. A couple of weeks later, I got a call from John saying, 'Come for a meeting – we've done the extended edit – now we can talk about the music.' I then had a phone call from Nick saying, 'Please don't get your hopes up, it's not what we discussed.'

"What John had done, on the cheap, was literally take the broadcast version and cut in a few extra scenes. I went through it with him and said,

'Basically, you need about five minutes of new music and the rest of it I can do by modifying or re-cutting what I've already done.' The following day, having thought about what was involved, I let him know I could do it for £600. John said, 'Fine, I'll pass this on.' He gave me a date for the dub and I then did the work. A couple of days before the dub, I got a phone call from Enterprises saying, 'Your price of £250 has been agreed.' I said, 'That's not what I suggested and for the amount of work and time I'm putting into this, I think that's a bloody good deal.' 'Oh no, the producer's told us it's £250.'

"I rang Nick Mallett and told him this and he was absolutely furious. He said, 'I'm pissed off. This is not what we wanted to do – you're being taken for a ride. John's done it his way. I've lost complete heart.' The following morning I turned up for the dub but Nick didn't. John was quite cross about this so I told him Nick wasn't very happy. Nick and I kept in touch and then he stopped answering his phone. I heard via the grapevine that he'd died [from an AIDS-related condition]. I rang John and said, 'I've just heard that Nick's died.' And he said, 'Yes, I went to the funeral,' and I said, 'Why didn't you tell anybody else?' That was John being John. He could be incredibly callous and unpleasant but he did give me a big chance and was willing to get things done on a budget. He had a hell of a lot of strengths."

John's output at BBC Enterprises was prolific if largely undistinguished. He churned out a series of tapes devoted to each Doctor, a version of *Shada* (with links provided by Tom Baker) and audiotapes of missing episodes with narration (clumsily written by John) to fill the gaps. "There was a night," remembers writer and then *DWM* editor Gary Russell, "when John [Ainsworth, Russell's partner at the time] and I went round and had dinner. Then the other John and Gary put on *The Tom Baker Years* tape. It was before it had come out and the reason they'd asked us to go round was that they were absolutely rubbish at actors. They knew the one thing I can do is spot an actor a mile off. So I'm sitting there saying, 'That's such and such,' and every time a name came up, one of them went, 'Dead', 'Gay' or 'Had him'. It was a fun evening but also very maudlin because they hadn't realised how many people in the industry they knew who they were saying 'dead' to. Both of them were getting quite sad. It led to a conversation about how many writers, directors and actors from their time had already died."

John's continuing association with the now defunct series infuriated his old enemy, Gary Leigh: "There was no work for him anywhere else," he mocks. "His reputation in the industry was such that he couldn't get a job even with the start of all these new channels. When he became overseer of BBC video and audio, I thought, 'This is it. This is war.' He'd not just seen *Doctor Who* off the air, he was now buggering up the commercial stuff."

Leigh's widely read fanzine *DWB* launched a remorseless new offensive to oust John. "There was a letter-writing campaign to dislodge me from my continued involvement at the fringes," John recalled in his memoirs. "Most of this mail ended up on my desk."

"There were some quite rabid fans out there," says David M Jackson, who became John's boss at BBC Video. "We protected him from some of that and felt sympathetic because whether or not you felt he'd done a good job, he'd done what was expected of him. He bore the brunt of a lot of blame for *Doctor Who* having been de-commissioned and he felt that very keenly, I think, and was resentful. I think we were a bit of a bolt-hole for him. He was very keen to come up with things which would please fans and be commercial. All of them did pretty well."

Much of the criticism from fans focused on John's understandable decision to prioritise video projects in which he could have some hand, writing and directing links. Perhaps these helped to assuage the pain of the increasing pile of returned formats, ideas and job applications but it is true that many of them were surprisingly amateurish efforts. BBC Video turned down his proposal for a compilation tape of drag acts, which John called *Dragged from the Archives*. "He shot some stuff for this," comments Jackson, "and we looked at it but it was so awful. You weren't talking Lily Savage. *Doctor Who* at that time was pretty niche but this was very, very niche."

Away from Enterprises, Teynham Productions (the company John ran with Gary and their old friends Fiona Cumming and Ian Fraser) organised a successful series of *Doctor Who* lecture tours around the UK. John also made a pilot for a sci-fi magazine show, intended for a prototype on-demand service called BBC Select. *The Space Station* was presented by Sophie Aldred and lawyer and DWAS co-ordinator Andrew Beech. "He got me to go and read for it," says Beech. "I think he was always very much on the lookout for new talent and to give people a chance. I still remember one note that he gave me, 'There are two distinct sides to your personality – I don't want the lawyer Andrew, I want party Andrew.' He gave me a bit of an insight into my own personality, which I was aware of from then on."

The Space Station stalled and, after a couple of years, the well of work from BBC Enterprises ran dry too. In John's memoirs, he makes a barbed but slightly veiled reference to his departure, which centred on the proposal to make a straight-to-video *Doctor Who* adventure for the programme's 30th anniversary. Claiming that he first pitched this idea in 1990, John goes on to write "There were the usual hiccups but I kept pushing the idea throughout 1991 and 1992. Imagine my surprise when, late in 1992, the then number two at Home Video announced that there was indeed to be a five Doctors story and that *he* was going to produce it! He asked me if I'd be his script consultant. I declined, to put it mildly, and my contract was not renewed as had been the norm."

David Jackson (in fact, John's boss by this stage), the man about whom these lines were written, tells a somewhat different story. "He'd been drinking and, after lunch, he came into my office and started yelling and bawling. I didn't even bother getting up from behind my desk. He did allude to the special but I didn't give this any credibility because we had spent a lot of time talking about it, plotting and planning. He had been part of the discussions and he thought it would be logical that he would be asked to produce. This was never on the cards. Even if we'd thought he was creatively the right person, it wouldn't have been sensible from a commercial point of view. If we had done it, it wasn't intended for broadcast, it was a straight-to-video idea, intended to be a sort of present to the faithful fans. His name on it was not going to be attractive.

"He decided that I was the author of his downfall simply because his contract wasn't being renewed. That was because there was nothing else for him to do. He felt that he'd been badly treated which I thought was a bit unfair. To come f-ing and blinding into my office was a bit daft of him because I'd been a colleague and a supporter but it was also typical of his kind of behaviour. He seemed to fall out with everybody. Eventually, he blew himself out and went away. We didn't speak again."

"There was a degree of sadness to John," says close friend Grahame Flynn. "He was a wounded man. He'd worked very hard for the BBC and now he was doing the odd little video thing and I think it was, 'Who else is going to take on this bloody show?'"

"He had spent years stuck in a cul-de-sac," says director and close friend Fiona Cumming, "and he felt as though he was bashing his head against a brick wall."

"You had a feeling things were not going to work out well," says director Chris Clough. "When he packed in the show and the BBC, where was he going to go? He gave a lot of his life to them and he hadn't got himself another niche."

It wasn't for the want of trying. "He'd worked very hard," says another director Alan Wareing, "and was quite a creative bloke in his way but his CV was worth nothing. He and I bought the rights to this book once. I'd worked with this PA on *The Bill*, Susan Lewis, and she'd written a book – holiday reading pap. It took off and she'd given up TV to carry on writing. I approached John and we bought the option on the rights for a year. It would have been a mini-series. He went over to America to see somebody about money and waited hours and hours, you know like you do, and it never went anywhere. But even if you come up with a good idea, in this business, that's just the start of your problems."

He tried to use what contacts he had and inevitably this meant colleagues from his many years on *Doctor Who*. "John came to see me in every production and in cabaret," says actress Jessica Martin. "He was looking for other projects and he believed in me as a performer. There was a proposal for something set in the 50s in the British film industry – a bit like *Hi-de-Hi!* but about the Rank charm school. People used to see it on the top of desks of executives like David Liddiment [who worked at Granada and then the BBC]. John was not wanted any more by TV and I felt that was a reflection of things I stood for as well – I felt his pain, if you like."

"I got some letters from him," says director Matthew Robinson, who was producing children's drama *Byker Grove* at the time. "I won't call them begging letters but they were certainly letters about coming to work with me up in Newcastle. I remember hearing that he was pretty depressed."

Janet Fielding, who had played Tegan, had now undertaken her own career change, ceasing to act and becoming an agent. "He phoned me and asked me to represent him," she remembers, "and I said no. I said no because I knew that I wouldn't be able to resurrect his career. Producers really have to create their own thing. There was nothing I could have done for him so it was going to be a no-win situation for me. All I could do was fail and then I would have failed him. He had kind of missed his time and place. He was a spent force."

Andrew Cartmel disagrees. "If you'd given John a show and a budget, he would have done it. He was very good. He could make stuff. His personal taste was to do very camp, showbiz crap – I call it crap because I don't like it but other people love it. But if he had been a hired gun doing something that wasn't to his taste, he would have done you a bloody good job on it."

"John never stopped coming up with ideas," says his close friend David Roden. "How good they were, well... some were great. There were all sorts of things. He tried a game show set on an aeroplane where passengers move up and down the seats, which he got Des O'Connor to agree to present. They pitched that to ITV and ITV weren't interested. I worked with him on an idea for a science-fiction drama series called *ACTUAL Reality*. ACTUAL stood for Advanced Computer Terminal Undertaking Assessment of Life. It was *Doctor Who* in a virtual reality setting – people got lost inside this computer and went on different adventures. We got in front of a chap called Ed Pugh [a contemporary of John's in studio management] at Granada and they paid to develop it for a bit. Then suddenly they decided it wasn't quite right for them. I found it very sad at the time. He was paranoid that he would never ever work again."

His old friend Anita Graham, who worked extensively in the theatre, tried to recommend him as a director to impresario Mark Furness (with whom

John had worked as adviser on the *Doctor Who* stage play in 1989). "I knew John was a terrific theatre director but Mark said, 'Oh no, I think I want to go with somebody who's got a track record.' People wouldn't use him. He had some good ideas for quiz shows, too. He never really laid his soul out but one thing sticks in my mind. He said, 'I worked there for all that time. I've sent them so many things. *Everything* I've sent can't be rubbish, can it?' I don't think he ever got over the rejection and I don't think anybody would."

Despite the let-downs and the euphemisms for 'don't call us, we'll call you', again and again, John persevered. He applied for the role of series producer on *EastEnders* but was not even invited for interview. Chris Clough, who worked extensively on the soap, believes, "It had got into miseryville and John might have kept it lighter and more enjoyable viewing."

But Peter Cregeen, in charge of series and serials, felt differently. "I don't think he would have been ideal. I thought that *EastEnders* at that stage needed grabbing hold of. It needed someone grittier not showbiz."

Cregeen's predecessor, David Reid, roundly dismisses this view. "*Of course* he could have produced *EastEnders* and made it sing whatever tune anyone wanted. It simply needed the trust and will of those above him."

When, in 1995, CBBC launched a new drama series called *The Biz*, John caught his breath, so similar was the idea to his own *Stage Door* proposal, pitched a few years before to the same department. Fiona Cumming recalls, "That was his idea and then suddenly it turned up but with no reference to John."

As *The Biz* went into production, John was invited to lunch by an old acquaintance called Nick Handel. Handel had played drums in the band of John's 1972 panto *Emberella*. Now he was the editor of the BBC's annual fundraiser, *Children in Need*. He suggested that John might produce a special mini-edition of *Doctor Who* to mark the programme's 30th anniversary and form a highlight of the 1993 telethon. The result was *Dimensions in Time*, which grew into a two-parter, episode one screening during *Children in Need* and the conclusion in the following day's edition of *Noel's House Party* (then the BBC's top-rated Saturday entertainment show). The story featured a bizarre kaleidoscope of characters from the programme's glory days mixed up in a plot that deliberately confused their chronology. Also involved were assorted members of the *EastEnders* cast. The villain was the Rani (once more played by Kate O'Mara) and her sidekick Cyrian (named after Sir Ian McKellen, for whom the role was intended) was brought to life by a young Sam West. The son of two of Britain's finest actors, Timothy West and Prunella Scales, he was here for the ride as he'd been a fan as a boy.

The big gimmick was that the production was made in 3D and this meant giddy camerawork to go with the nonsensical plot. It was written by John's star student, the youthful David Roden. "John never seemed to me interested in character," says Roden. "He was interested in plot. There's a huge difference. *Dimensions in Time* is a plot and I wouldn't write it like that now or even approach it like that."

The director was BBC staffer Stuart McDonald who had a thorough grounding as a cameraman and vision mixer but whose experience lay in live magazine and entertainment shows. This made him the perfect choice for *Children in Need* but a less obvious candidate for a drama, even one as bastardised as this. "John was really keen, for some reason, that I directed," recalled McDonald in a 2010 interview with Ian Levine, intended for a documentary about the project.

"John didn't want Stuart McDonald at all," contradicts Roden. "He was foisted upon us. John kept saying, 'He's not a drama director' – he wanted to do it himself. There was a massive personality clash."

"It turned into a very high pressure situation," agrees McDonald, "and a situation of conflict in some ways because the whole purpose wasn't really to do another *Doctor Who* episode, it was to do something in 3D. It was terribly frustrating for John because he never really accepted that this was, in the main, a 3D demo and a *Doctor Who* special secondarily – he wanted it the other way around. In a way, I admired him for that – as a good producer when you care about your show, that's a good thing to do but he got more and more angry and more and more distressed. But he didn't listen to the original brief and didn't want to give any quarter to his territory. I was doing my best as well and there was quite a lot of friction there."

The friction wasn't helped by John's insistence that Gary act as production manager. "At first," continues McDonald, "he was terribly helpful but then he'd take notes from John. I remember once he said, 'We've got to get on – we've got to leave room this afternoon for the stuff that John wants to do. Kate O'Mara must leave by ten past one.' So I said, 'Oh, I didn't realise that.' 'She must, she must.' 'Well, OK, I'll go and have a word.' 'Are you doubting me?' 'No, I'm not doubting you. I'm just going to check.' I went to over to Kate, who I'd worked with on *Triangle* and who I knew very well and said, 'I'm terribly sorry, have you got to leave by ten past one today?' 'Oh no, darling. I can be here all afternoon.' So I suddenly realised there was another agenda and I was being given misinformation. I'm sure that Gary thought that was the right thing to do, to side with the producer, but it was the wrong thing to do because producer, director, artists, everyone on the set are a team effort. There were all kinds of difficulties in that direction. John was very authoritarian, old-fashioned and strict. He got more and more annoyed at virtually everything that I did. We had to edit various sequences in Munich to optimise the 3D and eventually he wouldn't even go on the same flight as me.

"It was sad that he was so tricky to deal with. The last thing I said to him was, 'You know, John, I'm sorry that it's ended like this with us falling out over what we should be doing with it because you've worked so hard on it. You've done such a brilliant job to get the whole thing together.' It has to be remembered that, without him, that show would never have happened. It would have been impossible to pull the favours and get people to do stuff without John's input."

By the mid-1990s, as far as *Doctor Who* was concerned, John was a spent force. For a time, he withdrew from conventions, sick of the scornful looks and the criticisms that followed his appearances. He was no longer "the producer", in charge of all things, someone to be listened to, looked up to, admired and feared. Instead, he was the man who had killed the programme and a spectre at the wake. However, whatever bitterness or blame he may have felt, he couldn't stop himself from caring about the show. "I bought a video called *The Doctors*," remembers Grahame Flynn. "It was a documentary about the series. I was at John's and we started watching it and there was a bit where Peter Davison and Strickson, or Stricko as John called him, had obviously had a lunchtime beer or three and were talking about the show and every other phrase was, 'It's shit.' John got visibly upset and then very, very angry. His view was that there are things that you might think but you don't say them in a public forum. He felt that they'd betrayed the show and logically him, as well."

In 1996, the BBC announced that *Doctor Who* was coming back, in feature-length form (with American funding), hinting that a series might result from this pilot effort. The star was a hot young actor called Paul McGann. Flynn again: "I remember driving John and Gary to an event at the *Doctor Who* exhibition at Llangollen. The guest for the day was Sylvester McCoy. When it finished, John asked me to drive Sylvester to the railway station. Sylvester was in the back of the car and JN-T and I were in the front. It was rather quiet. Sylvester suddenly said, 'Do you know today is my last day as Doctor Who? Paul takes over tonight. The Seventh Doctor dies today.' His delivery was calm, understated but full of emotion. By the time we got to the station we all had tears in our eyes. We hugged Sylvester goodbye and his Chaplin-esque figure disappeared. John found moments like this very moving. He was a very sensitive man.

"He'd managed to get hold of a preview copy of the film. He used to watch TV lying on his belly on the deep white pile of the living room carpet, chain-smoking, with a glass ashtray nearby absolutely overflowing. He hated the story and, more than anything else, the whole idea of the Doctor being half-human. He loved Paul McGann's Doctor and the production values but he was very pissed off too, saying, 'But they've got money and time.' He always felt that he'd been left to go on with it and that nobody really cared. But he said, 'You know what, Gray? If this fails, at least I will not be known as the man who killed off *Doctor Who*.'"

When John had been forced out of the BBC, Gary had remained behind, working principally as a production manager on *EastEnders* (hence the decision to use Albert Square for *Dimensions in Time*). But this didn't remain a bolt-hole for long. "The BBC clearly wanted to make Gary redundant too," recalls David Roden. "He kept refusing to take it so they kept giving him really shit jobs to try and piss him off. At one point he was loaned to the National Film and Television School as production manager on a student film where he was treated really badly and had an awful time. In the end John persuaded him to take redundancy and Gary immediately went to work for [producer] Mike Dormer on *The Bill* who he was great friends with."

Gary's old promise "I can get you a part in *EastEnders*" became "I can get you a part in *The Bill*" but he wasn't there for long and this marked the end of his television career. But, unlike John, he was bullish about this and decided on a complete career change, retraining as a psychotherapist. For a man not renowned for his powers of empathy or discretion, it might have seemed an unlikely choice. "He didn't see it as a strange move at all," says Marcia Wheeler, a former colleague from series and serials. "I remember talking to him about this at a party and he said he'd always had an instinctive idea of why actors behave in the way that they did and that he'd now learnt the theory about it and knew at an intellectual level why they did."

"Gary used to meet clients at the flat they had in Teynham House," says Stephen Cranford. "They set up one of the rooms overlooking the sea. He was very, very discreet – 'I've got a client' was all he would ever say."

"Gary could suss people out very, very quickly," believes close friend Barry Hannam. "He'd size people up and was very intuitive."

"Gary was emotional on the inside," believes another friend, Mark Jones. "For someone who came over as brash, he was quite empathic. My wife and I went through a trial separation and he was very supportive. He would listen and ask questions and then he'd say, 'Do you know what, Mark – *unprofessionally* I would say that you should bloody well man up and go back to your wife!' That's what I did and we're still together – all our issues were external ones. The Gary I knew was so insightful and intelligent – sitting down and listening to people's problems as a psychotherapist, doing hypnotherapy as well, seemed the perfect career for him."

John, on the other hand, was still floundering. He had high hopes for a children's series called *Big Step*, the adventures of a benign giant in a generic fairy-tale land, to be narrated by Tom Baker. This project came his way from his old mate at Enterprises and exhibitions, Lorne Martin. "Jim Francis was another pal of mine," continues Martin. "He was a freelance visual effects designer and was doing an advert where they used a giant. We decided it would make a cracking idea for a children's series, all told in voiceover so we could flog it abroad. I'm not a producer so I contacted John and he jumped at the idea. We worked out 13 storylines, shot a test at Shepperton Studios which John directed and I tried to hawk it round and get people interested."

Viewing the pilot, even allowing for the rapidity with which children's programmes can date (especially those trying to use the most advanced techniques), it is hard to imagine anyone pumping serious money into such an undernourished concept as *Big Step*. Then and now, children's content is one of the toughest and most competitive international markets and, bluntly, the concept, scripting, imagination and execution are just not in the league necessary for success.

Cold-shouldered by television, John kept his hand in with corporate work, pantomimes, revues and charity shows. One of these, called Friends of Dorothy, raised a large amount of money for the Terrence Higgins Trust. "He was always getting phone calls and going to meetings and trying to launch new things," says Stephen Cranford.

But David Roden witnessed how the constant round of professional rejection affected John. "I think the more depressed he became, the more he drank and the more he drank, the more depressed he became – it's a horrible vicious circle. I have nothing but praise for Ian [Fraser] and Fiona [Cumming] – they were rocks in John and Gary's life."

"I first met him in 1994 and he was a huge drinker," adds Mark Jones. "Every time he went out of the room and came back, his glass was full again."

John belonged to an era in which some TV professionals routinely consumed massive amounts of alcohol. Many of his onetime colleagues were hardened drinkers – men like Bill Slater, Geraint Morris, Graham Williams, Peter Moffatt, Tom Baker. Even his eventual nemesis, Jonathan Powell, later became an alcoholic. Staff director David Sullivan Proudfoot regularly drank himself into oblivion (and had to be removed from the job of re-editing *Genesis of the Daleks* for its 1982 repeat as a result). "I used to drink Kalibers at lunch," recalls former script editor Chris Bidmead, "trying to meet John bottle for bottle. I did try. It was all totally fucking stupid because what a marvellous opportunity the BBC was at that time and to some extent I pissed it away. But I think John pissed it away in spades."

"What we used to do," remembers director Chris Clough, "was meet in the Bush [the pub near Union and Threshold House] about half twelve and then drink through the afternoon. I was there with him. You'd think, 'Oh shit, it's five o'clock,' and go back and do half an hour's work and then come back down for another one. There was quite a lot of heavy afternoon drinking. It was a bonding exercise – it was all pretty positive really. You had to have a certain sort of stamina."

"My goodness," agrees Nicola Bryant, "during my time on *Doctor Who*, I've never drunk so much. Every time he got me a drink it was a vodka – I don't think I was allowed a soft drink. I remember once bribing a barman because I just could not keep up. I said, 'Every time somebody orders me a vodka and diet coke or a vodka and orange, just bring me the soft drink.' It was just huge amounts of alcohol, all the time."

"They were very heavy drinkers," says Barry Hannam. "They really, really did like to party. I could never keep up with them. If I ever went to their house for a drink, I'd end up nursing the same drink all night long, just topping it up with a bit of tonic or lemonade or whatever. You just couldn't drink like them two."

"People who drink like that," ponders Andrew Cartmel. "What happens is they can be very ebullient when they're on the way up but when they're in their hangover phase or sobering up, they can have really bad tempers. He was a man under enormous pressure and he was a heavy drinker – drink doesn't improve anything in people's psychology."

"He drank like a fish," says Alan Wareing. "The Bush at lunchtime was absolutely heaving with BBC drama people. At North Acton [near the BBC rehearsal rooms] at the Castle, you couldn't move. John spent an absolute fortune – he was a very generous person. All the things that you mustn't do to prolong your life he did constantly."

"You could see the same hard drinking gangs propping up the BBC club bar more or less permanently," says Marcia Wheeler. "Drinking destroyed many careers as word got around and work fell away."

"It was a drinking culture," admits BBC personnel manager Pat Dyer. "Drama had an arrangement with the BBC doctor to get the worst cases into an alcoholic clinic in Ealing. It was treated as an illness. You had three times to dry out."

John never needed to avail himself of this service. However, it was, perhaps, a curse rather than a blessing that, for years, he managed to drink so heavily and escape the obvious penalties. "He was such a good social drinker," says actress Janet Hargreaves. "He never got aggressive like Gary or slurry like Nick [Courtney]. He was just always his pink-faced ebullient self."

Sophie Aldred remembers "going for a fantastic meal with John, Gary, Mike Tucker [visual effects designer – John referred to him as Tricky Fucker] at a funny, down-at-heel Italian restaurant. Mike, silly boy, was trying to match John drink for drink and he slowly slipped under the table. John never appeared drunk at all."

"I think he held it pretty well," agrees John's secretary, Kate Easteal. "I wouldn't say he got particularly aggressive or sleepy or anything like that. Maybe he used to mellow a bit in the afternoon but generally you wouldn't be aware of it."

"I never, ever, saw John once the worse for wear in a professional situation," says actor Mark Strickson. "He saved his drinking for when he knocked off. But he was binge drinking on a regular basis after work. He wasn't a miserable or violent drunk, he was a happy drunk. I was also in those days a happy drunk. We were very similar people in that sense. There was something between John and me – I'm driven in the same way he was. You could party all night so long as you were there in the morning, knowing your lines with your costume on, on time, in place."

"John would party hard," says Grahame Flynn. "But he was quite a sickly man and it wouldn't take a lot for him to be ill."

"He always said he didn't feel quite right," agrees Anita Graham. "I think he always felt that he had something wrong with him. I don't think he felt that he would make old bones."

During the 1990s, John suddenly started to go grey and from now on, he had his hair carefully and regularly coloured. He had an operation to remove a non-malignant cyst from behind one ear. The effect of this was to pull up the skin slightly on one side of his face and, typically, he joked that he'd had a mini-facelift and only needed to get the other side done to match. "That was actually a very tough operation," says fan and friend Stuart Money, "because if they'd hit the carotid artery, it would have been goodnight Vienna. He was very lucky to get out of that. At that time, Jon Pertwee was still alive and, very generously, he said, 'Why don't you take JN-T and Gary away and have a week in the house in Majorca?' which we did. John recuperated there. He was very tired but in great spirits."

It didn't help that John's parents, for whom he had always felt such filial responsibility, now began to become more of a worry and burden. Kath Turner's mental health, always fragile, deteriorated so that she was more or less permanently confined to a specialist nursing home. "She was very quiet," recalls Barry Hannam. "She could go so within herself so that no matter what you did, you wouldn't get any joy from her at all. Every year, they used to take Christmas up in the car to John's parents. They would do everything for her and she would just sit there and pretty well say, 'Is it time to go back to the nursing home yet?'"

"There would be times when I would meet her," says David Roden, "and she would be perfectly reasonable and lucid. He brought her down to see pantomimes. He adored her. He used to speak to his parents every day. His dad would call him and he would call his mum. Some days he'd phone and she wouldn't speak to him. Other days they'd be on the phone for ages. His dad was one of these really funny broad Brummies. He used to phone John and talk about his bowel movements, or lack of, and just make John howl."

"I once phoned up his dad," laughs Sylvester McCoy, "and said, 'Is John there? I need to speak to him.' He said no, so I said, 'Can you tell him Sylvester McCoy phoned?' so he said, 'All right, yeah.' When John got in, his dad said, 'Oh, Sylvester Stallone phoned!'"

Despite a serious stroke, Sam Turner continued to live alone in the family home in Birmingham. Because he was now less mobile, his bed was moved into the living room. "One day the TV caught fire," says Roden. "Somebody had to carry his dad out of the house – and he was a big, fat guy. He only just got out in time."

"He was only saved," explains Stephen Cranford, "by the fact that they'd lived in the house for years and years and had re-wallpapered it endless times so that in the same way that if you try to burn a book, you only char the edges. All those generations of wallpaper actually prevented the fire taking."

John bought yet another flat in Teynham House, this time on the ground floor, hoping to be able to move in his parents. "It never actually happened," says Fiona Cumming. "Even the ground floor at Teynham House had steps up to it and there was no way that Sam could manage that."

Sam Turner finally died in 1996. "John had been at Shepperton Studios," recalls Stuart Money, "working on the *Big Step* pilot. I remember saying to him, 'John, your phone's off charge. Always keep it on charge because you need to be able to reach your dad – it's the only way to keep in touch.' Bugger me, it's just as well I did. Next morning, I'd gone to work and he phoned me at the office about nine o'clock and said, 'Stu, thank goodness you told me to keep the phone on charge because my dad died last night.' He was absolutely devastated."

"I was with John when he got the call to say that his dad had died," says David Roden. "Gary answered the phone and it was the home help who they paid to come in and get Sam out of bed. They'd let themselves in in the morning and found him dead in bed. John was very deeply affected. They immediately decided they were going to go up there – so they dropped me off at the station – but John just literally wouldn't talk. He just cried a lot and chain-smoked non-stop."

After his father's death, John decided to move his mother to a nursing home in Brighton. During these difficult and sometimes downright bleak years, it was John's many and various friendships that made the biggest difference to him and allowed him some emotional expression beyond the boundaries of his life with Gary. "He was very caring," asserts Stuart Money. "He would find no effort in spending three hours on the phone cheering me up. When I used to give speeches at commercial events, he'd write them – it would be the work of a moment. You'd give him a bit of background and the personalities involved. He was a wizard at that."

John became especially close to actor Nicholas Courtney, who, over many years, had played the Brigadier in *Doctor Who* but who only became a true intimate after John had left the BBC. "I think alcohol had something to do with it," says Sylvester McCoy. "Nick was a gentle, lovely man – you couldn't help but like him."

"Nick was a famous drinker, of course," says Janet Hargreaves. "He adored John and it wasn't an affair, Nick was straight. I think they shared very jolly times, a sense of humour and an innate and absolute love of the business."

"John was a terrible old gossip and so was Nick," says Stuart Money. "They'd retire to Broadcasting House in the afternoon but they'd both want to ensure they got back home for *Coronation Street*, which was so sweet."

John helped Courtney through what he called his "black holes" or periods of depression. "He would call a lot," recalls Grahame Flynn, "and John was very supportive."

When Courtney remarried, John was best man. It was Courtney who cleared the way for John to become friendly with Tom Baker, too. During his turbulent final year with the programme, Baker had resented and despised John. But, over time, and nurtured by Courtney's mutual affection, John's loyalty, offers of work and convivial personality cemented a real bond between the two men. "John and Gary used to go out and have real benders with him," says Barry Hannam. "They'd come back and they couldn't stand and they'd be full of what a wonderful night they'd had with Tom."

There was a bond, too, with another of his leading men, Sylvester McCoy. "We became great friends," he says, simply. "He was a warm, rounded human being, so it was easy to get on with him. I'm a party animal as well, so we had a lot in common. We liked people and we enjoyed a good time."

The catch remained Gary. Because of his uncompromising attitude, earlier, longstanding, friendships were lost or jettisoned in fits of pique, jealousy or misunderstanding, apologies left unsaid. "I didn't socialise with them until after I left the show," points out Janet Fielding. "While I didn't see a different side to Gary, John was a lot kinder than I'd supposed. I was living with another actor called Michael Percival. John didn't like him. It was mutual. There was a massive falling-out one night. We were round at Jane Wellesley's, who was a big friend of John's. Michael just went for Gary and had a real go at him. I thought, 'Oh Christ!' and dragged him away. Who knows why guys do that? It's just meaningless aggression. That was it – it was just easier to drop out of that network of people and that's when I lost touch with John."

Jane Wellesley's own friendship with John and Gary had endured for nearly 20 years when it, too, came to an abrupt end. "I had moved out of London and had a house in Lymington [in Hampshire]. John and Gary were spending every weekend in Brighton. My then partner and I didn't get to see each other very much because he was working. But over the August bank holiday weekend of that year he was going to be down in Lymington. Then John and Gary rang up and they wanted me to go to Brighton. I thought, 'I just can't face that road along the south coast on a bank holiday weekend.' Particularly when it was one of the only two days I had to see Al. So I think they took umbrage at that and really, I heard very, very little from them after that. You'd send them a Christmas card and get nothing in return. I was really quite shocked because we had been friends for such a long time. Basically, they just dropped me like a hot potato."

The most bruising fall-out was with David Roden, the young man who had first approached John at one of the Teynham lectures. Throughout the 1990s, they had remained close and when, in April 1998, Roden got the job as manager of the Elgiva Theatre in Chesham, he didn't have far to look for a source of money-spinning, bums-on-seats shows. He set up a meeting with John and Gary, as the theatre's technical manager, Tristan Collett remembers: "We talked about a bunch of ideas ranging from ladies' nights, *Doctor Who*-related things and, of course, panto."

Collett was 26 at the time. "I was very excited to meet him – I'd been a sci-fi nerd as a kid and he was a legend as far as I was concerned. A lot of the technicians were wary but he knew what he was doing and could produce any show to a high standard.

"The first thing we did was one of these ladies' nights – a load of male strippers basically. He got a friend who was a drag queen to host it. It was extremely controversial for a little town-council-run, 300-seat theatre but we knew we were going to make a lot of money out of it and it was a big success."

Roden asked them to follow this with that year's pantomime – a production of *Aladdin*. "Richard Franklin [who played Captain Yates during the Pertwee era] was in it," he says. "It was very bare bones and traditional but it did exceptional business and the council were very happy."

There was, however, some tension, the result, Roden believes, of John's deeply ingrained, old-school attitudes and approach. "It wasn't unmanageable but John would get very uptight very quickly in a working environment. I always put it down to the way the BBC had been run – by dragons and ogres, very hierarchal. It was all about empire-building. That old-school BBC way of doing things was already, at that time, ten years out of date. I think that was one of the reasons why the BBC wanted shot of him and everybody of that ilk."

"The main problem," adds Collett, "was that John had been used to having a lot of people running around and sorting things out for him and not questioning anything. He could snap his fingers and get whatever he wanted – there was a lot more money in *Doctor Who* than a small council-run theatre. It's a completely different world. I'd always do my best but if it wasn't possible, then he didn't want to hear that. There were many examples. They were both frustrated and angry."

"It was a brand-new theatre," says Roden, "only open a couple of months and he had frustrations with that which weren't his fault. John wasn't used to working without screaming and shouting at people but, saying that, he could be incredibly nurturing and mentoring as well. Gary choreographed. That's when I noticed that the drink was an issue. We'd arrive at nine in the morning and Gary would go over to Sainsbury's directly opposite and pick up a bottle of vodka and a couple of bottles of Tango and he would bring those over to the theatre. They would sit there at their desk right in front of stage – the vodka would be in a bag under the table. John would chain-smoke his way through his Dunhills and Gary would pour the vodka under the table. That would go through to lunchtime and then they would take the entire cast – but not the crew – to the local pub. Usually, John and Gary would have a bottle of wine between them – if not more – and they would never eat – and then they would do an afternoon's work. At six they'd go back to the pub. When the show opened they would turn up half an hour or an hour before the matinee and stand at the bar. Go in and see the show, take drinks in with them – go to the pub after the show and give notes. Some of the younger cast were scared of them."

"They had high expectations and I actually quite liked that," says Collett. "But there's an impatience and aggression which comes with alcohol. John was pretty much drunk from morning till night and so was Gary. There was inappropriate language in front of the children. It was very difficult to manage."

Given the commercial success of *Aladdin*, it was unsurprising that the council wanted more of the same the following year. Despite his misgivings, Roden invited John back and, this time the production was *Mother Goose*. "Perhaps because the show was more technically demanding, the atmosphere was worse," he says. "A couple of weeks before the show opened, a scandal was narrowly averted. We had one boy in the show who was about 14. Gary had been working with this boy on his own and I had a complaint from the mother. I don't know whether anything happened but I had to launch an official investigation."

Tristan Collett remembers the incident well. "My girlfriend was working there at the time and had to comfort a young lad who was changing under the stage. Gary, who was down there with him, made a pass at him. It put this boy off theatre for life. David spoke to the parents of the kid and they were very cool about everything – they shouldn't have been – if I had been the parents, I would have let him have it. Gary was predatory. It was really unpleasant."

Roden was in a very difficult position. "John said, 'How can you do this? We're your friends. You've known us for years.' I said, 'I'm really sorry. I'm manager of the theatre. I've had a complaint made against Gary. I have to investigate it.' There was some talk of it being passed on to the police. But within a day the complaint was withdrawn. I don't know why. I knew what Gary could be like but I wouldn't have credited him with that. That was a major turning point in my relationship with them – I don't think they felt I was on their side."

When the show opened, there were still a lot of residual technical issues that John wanted to address. "During the press night," remembers Collett, "he ran up from the auditorium to the control room, poked his head in and started asking for the music to be louder. It was already deafening but he was going deaf, you see. Then I had David coming up and saying, 'We're having complaints that it's too loud.' I said, 'Look, I've got John saying make it louder, you're telling me to make it quieter,' so David said, 'Do what I say and I'll deal with John.'

"John used to get very frustrated with follow spots not happening on time – mainly because he'd changed his mind. He'd yell 'Lime' very loudly, which is the old-fashioned term for follow spot [derived from the word 'limelight'] and of course the young technicians hadn't got a clue what lime meant. He had a different training and was a lot older than us. It was a clash of cultures."

"There was one morning," recalls Roden, "when John had called the technicians in early before a matinee at one o'clock. I got a phone call from my technical manager saying, 'Can you come down here? We've got a bit of a problem.' As I walked into the car park, I was greeted by John and Gary. They wanted to get in first. They said, 'Your staff are morons. They're idiots. They can't do anything right.' Then, almost as an aside, John said, 'Oh and by the way, I may have smashed a plate.' I went inside and my technical team were sitting in the scene dock smoking. I've never seen them so angry."

Collett takes up the story. "Things hadn't been going as fast as he wanted. He just exploded out of nowhere in the middle of the auditorium and picked up the nearest thing to him – which happened to be a plate – and threw it at the wall of the set in frustration. As he did that, my then girlfriend Emma [Wilson] was coming in to work, through that door. It smashed to pieces right next to her head. Everything went silent – he was red in the face and still fuming so I got the entire crew away from the situation."

"Basically," grimaces Roden, "they said they weren't going to work with him. I called my boss – the town clerk – and he said, 'Ask John and Gary to go back to Brighton for a couple of days. Take the heat out of the situation. Let me take some statements and sort it out.' So I asked them to leave the theatre. It might as well have been a nuclear bomb going off in Chesham. John said, 'You can't refuse me entry. Are you refusing me entry? Are you refusing to let me deal with my show?' I said, 'If you do, we won't have a show.' They went. I can only imagine what the journey was like – with Gary driving and winding up John. On the way home, John wrote me a really awful note on the back of an envelope and stuck it through my letterbox. He'd scrawled, 'We've been your friends for years. This is the way you treat us. You've betrayed us. It's our production.' And so on.

"What should have happened in a reasonable world is that I would have had a meeting with John and Emma. He would apologise and maybe see the rest of the technicians. Because it was John and Gary and they were their own worst enemies at times, they refused to apologise or meet the technicians. They didn't like playing the game. John was very icy when I said, 'We need to sort this. Will you come up to meet me and the town clerk, Mike Kennedy?' He agreed to this. Gary wanted to come too but I said it wouldn't be appropriate. The meeting was perfectly reasonable. John asked that he be allowed to finish the work and we agreed, with a certain amount of pre-requisites. But that was it for our relationship."

When the show's run concluded, there was the ritual of the "get out" (when the sets are dismantled and everything is cleared to make way for the next production). "During this," says Roden, "Gary had a go at me – 'You've treated John really badly.' There was a lot of 'Don't you know who he is? I'll never forgive you for what you've done.' I didn't hear from them for a while and then about three months later, out of the blue, I had a phone call from a friend of theirs called Brian Ralph in Brighton. He was an old queen – a real 1960s throwback – it was 'varda' this and 'dolly' that. He said, 'Hello, daughter, how are you?' We had a bit of a chat and I couldn't work out why he had called me. Towards the end of the conversation he said, 'Give John and Gary a call. They miss you.' I don't know why but I just sensed that I was on speaker phone and that they were there. I said, 'Do you know what, Brian? I won't. If I had behaved in one of John's studios the way he behaved in my theatre, he would never have forgiven me. They're the ones that need to apologise to me.' That was it. Never heard another word. I did see them at a couple of *Doctor Who* conventions. John was fine and we had a chat but Gary was just vile – 'Get away from him. He doesn't want to talk to you.' Had it not been for Gary, I think we would have been fine but Gary never let the slight go."

Tristan Collett still works at the Elgiva (which has since been rebuilt on a different site). "They were good quality shows and they did make money," he acknowledges. The story of the plate-spinning producer and the production from hell "still gets told to this day. The imitations of John are still happening."

One friendship that did endure and was to have great significance for both John and Gary was with their hairdresser, Barry Hannam. They'd met on holiday in Malta, around 1982, when Hannam had just turned 30. "We was in a restaurant," he remembers. "I was with two friends and them two were on their own. John always said that Malta is where he'd met his first love, and he was showing Gary round the island. We just got speaking. It was a very strange evening. We took them to a gay bar – they didn't know where any of these bars were. We stayed up all night, ending up in a bar just round the corner from where they were staying. Then Gary drove us into Valetta [Malta's capital] and we went to the flea market and had a full English breakfast accompanied by large brandies!

"Because I was a hairdresser, they said, 'Oh, you must come and do our hair.' You exchange numbers with people you meet on holiday but you never expect to meet. I lived in Tooting and they had a house in Brockley. They phoned me out of the blue to go over there. I went and did their hair and had a good night. John was one of these people who always turned a light snack into a banquet. They were just very good fun. I've never had any interest in showbusiness and some of the stories they used to come out with were very funny. We just stayed in touch and got friendlier and friendlier."

When subsidence affected their house in Brockley, John and Gary had to move out to allow for repair works. Rather than rent somewhere, Hannam suggested they come to stay with him. "They was claiming off the insurance for the accommodation, though I never charged them," he confides. "But they was extremely good to me. When I got into trouble and had a tax problem with my businesses, I was moaning about it, just letting off steam, while I was doing somebody's hair. It was around Valentine's Day. The post came. My customer said, 'More Valentines?' and I replied, 'Yeah, I should be so lucky!' and she said, 'Well, it sure as hell won't be a cheque, will it?'

"When I opened it up, John and Gary had sent me a cheque for £5000 to help me out. I never ever cashed it. I just couldn't believe it. They were so kind. They were the one constant in all my friends. I knew I could rely on them 100 per cent. I'd only have to phone up and say, 'Can I do this?' – 'Oh, OK.'" Hannam was to have ample opportunity to repay their kindness.

In 2000, Big Finish Productions invited John to record an audio version of his memoirs. "We'd asked him to direct audio plays for us but he didn't want to," explains Gary Russell, then working for the company as a producer. "It was not his forte and he didn't understand it. When we went to see him and said, 'Would you like to do your memoirs on audio?' he said yes in about two and a half seconds."

The memoirs had started life in 1996 as a series of articles for *DWM*, commissioned by the then editor, Gary Gillatt. As he subsequently explained in the 350th edition of the magazine "I felt [we] needed an in-depth after-effects interview with JN-T. There was no way he was going to do it without being paid but...that would have set a precedent so I decided to pay him to write it. He wasn't the most fluid writer..." Gillatt led him through the process in detail, sometimes meeting John in London or Brighton to run through the material or sending him several pages of questions and notes, detailing points John might consider addressing. A first draft was submitted on typewritten foolscap pages, which were then rewritten and sent back to John for approval. The series eventually grew into many more instalments than originally intended. Gillatt's big challenge was not trying to get John to remember what had happened but to say what he felt about what had happened. There was sometimes a battle to steer the account away from 'safe' themes, like frocks and wigs and parties, and into franker territory. "Each conversation was combative," Gillatt recalled. "His absolute watchword in life was loyalty. People were either loyal or disloyal and if he thought you'd crossed that line, he'd fix you with a beady eye and say, 'You've made an enemy for life.' You could talk him back but he was a stormy human being."

Writer Stephen Cole abridged and adapted the original articles for the audio recording, which took place in a London studio over the weekend of 16th and 17th September 2000. According to producer Nick Briggs, John wasn't on his usual form. "He drove me almost bonkers that day," he comments. "Fluffed almost every sentence." Gary Downie did not accompany John to the studio and Gary Russell echoes the sentiments expressed by others when he remarks, "John was always at his best when he was alone. The ending was all new and when he recorded this, he was crying."

The new millennium brought another test for John's fortitude when Gary became seriously ill and was diagnosed with cancer. "It was a tumour on the pelvic bone," says Hannam. "The treatment was awful and left the whole area right across his genitals completely red raw. For a camp old queen, he was such a brave man – a real tough South African."

Terrified that Gary might die and leave him alone, John began to drink still more heavily. "I saw a real change in his personality," says Stephen Cranford. "For the first time, he was getting very, very drunk and becoming quite nasty – not necessarily to me. He was always ill – gout was a common problem. He was always off to the loo and he would always look very red and quite bloated."

"John had started drinking himself to death," believes David Roden. "He couldn't live without Gary and wanted to go first."

"He would get very down," says Barry Hannam. "Depression obviously went through the family. Nothing big was entering his life – nothing was moving."

Having endured weeks of painful, humiliating and aggressive treatment, Gary entered remission. But there was little to celebrate. John's drinking had gone too far and now he was really ill himself. Finally, he turned his back on alcohol and gave up smoking and he did both cold turkey – quite an achievement for a man with a lifetime's addictions. There were occasional lapses but, as Stephen Cranford remembers, "He said, 'I'm on the wagon – I'm not having any more.' He started to go quite yellow. He knew he was never going to get a transplant. He told me, 'I'll never get that far.'

"We had a conversation," says Grahame Flynn. "He said, 'You do realise that I am going to be very low on the list of priorities.' I think there was a realisation that things were very serious. Every time I saw him, he would always say the same thing. 'Promise me that you will look after Gary.'"

"John was optimistic," believes Mark Jones. "It was about the time George Best got his transplant and buggered it up by carrying on drinking – Gary used to get absolutely furious with rage over that."

"He was vituperative about him," agrees Fiona Cumming. "By this time, Ian and I were working in Denmark at a European film college, so we weren't seeing them so frequently. John let us know that things were serious. He was fairly philosophical about it. He was on a waiting list for a transplant."

As 2001 came to a close, John's beloved mother, Kath, whose mental health issues had caused her such anguish for so long, finally died in her nursing home. She was 79. On 28th November, John emailed Grahame Flynn: "It's 4.30am and I can't sleep. My mom passed away at 1.30am this morning. We were with her at the end. She is at peace now. I shall miss her, of course, but she didn't suffer – just went to sleep and didn't wake up. Gary had his hand on her brow and I was holding her hand when she went."

Amazingly, given the state of mind he must have been in, he still found room in this email to give Flynn, who had himself been unwell, some characteristic advice: "I'm so sorry to hear that you're poorly... Try a hot toddy mixed with Horlicks before bed – seriously – better than tablets. Remember – when the going gets tough – the tough get going."

The funeral had to be arranged while John himself was going into hospital for a series of gruelling tests. On 8th December, he again emailed Flynn: "It really was unpleasant, though luxurious surroundings. I have to take things very easily. The consultant wants me to take a nap every afternoon and go to bed early every night, so I think they suspect something very serious. I am waiting to hear when I see the top liver specialist in London... We are going to Barry's (our hairdresser) for Christmas. As Mom is no longer with us, we shall travel to his lovely house on Christmas Eve and stay till Boxing Day morning at least. It will be good to be away at this time – the first Christmas without Mom. I have given all her clothes and dress jewellery and bits to the Martlets Hospice shop – as she had a lovely wardrobe, it's nice to think others are getting some benefit – in life she was a very generous woman."

"There were about six of us that Christmas," says Hannam. "I think they went through about eight bottles of vodka. It was hysterical but then John went very quiet and said, 'I'm going out for a minute' – Gary took no notice. John just wanted go and walk round the church at the top of the next road. He'd taken himself there one day and met the vicar – and I don't think it was because he was religious in any way. Having just lost Kath and knowing his own health wasn't that great, I think he found comfort in it in some way."

It was to be John's last Christmas. Less than six months later he too would be dead.

(left) Working on *The Pallisers*, John attained
rapid promotion, 1973 *(JN-T collection)*

(right) The woman he loved – with Liz Rowell on
How Green Was My Valley, 1975 *(courtesy: Liz Rowell)*

Never happier than when in the kitchen, November 1974
(JN-T collection)

John and Gary, Brockley, November 1974. They were together
for nearly 30 years *(JN-T collection)*

(above left) Downie the dancer, April 1974. *(JN-T collection)*

(above right) Even the lamps were camp... *(JN-T collection)*

"Knickers with the knockers", budgie smugglers and Jackie P. Time off during
The Two Doctors, August 1984 *(JN-T collection)*

(above left) Short shorts ahoy! John in Lanzarote for *Planet of Fire*, 1983
(courtesy: Fiona Cumming)

(above right) "I felt really comfortable hugging him..."
Colin and John, 1984 *(JN-T collection)*

His Girl Fridays – with secretaries Kate Easteal *(left)*
and Sarah Lee *(right)*, April 1986 *(courtesy: Dominic May)*

Not quite a BAFTA – John with an international science-fiction award for
Doctor Who, 1983 *(JN-T collection)*

Receiving his "Fans' Producer" award from Paul Zeus of DWAS,
July 1982 *(courtesy: Stephen Payne)*

King of all he surveys – John oversees Longleat, April 1983

(courtesy: Paul Vanezis)

He called her Miss F, she called him God. Janet and John in cabaret

(JN-T collection)

Gary and John with Patrick Troughton at an American convention, 1984. It was John who persuaded Troughton to join "the circuit"

(JN-T collection)

Relaxing *Dynasty*-style in his hotel room
(JN-T collection)

(above left) Party time in the office *(courtesy: Kate Thomson)*

(above right) John at work in his "womb" *(JN-T collection)*

Normally "eyes and teeth", a rare pensive moment caught on camera
(JN-T collection)

John and Gary
(courtesy: Grahame Flynn)

FOURTEEN

...IT'S WHERE YOU FINISH

"We were talking about the lifelines on our hands. My lifeline goes all the way down. John's ended very high up and Gary's didn't go much further. We were saying, 'Oh my God, you're going to die young...'"
Ian Levine, interview with author, 2012

Up in the mountains, just a short distance from the flashy tourist mecca of Benidorm, lies the old Spanish town of Finestrat. The streets wind round the mountainside and the houses have a Moorish influence, many of them painted in bright jewel colours. Now that John was finally free from parental responsibility, it was here that he planned to spend the rest of his life with Gary. But this wasn't the story of two wealthy gay men contemplating early retirement, and Finestrat meant much more than a place in the sun. It was supposed to be a whole new beginning, the start of fresh opportunities and the drawing of a line under *Doctor Who*.

It began with a holiday, the destination suggested by their close friend and hairdresser, Barry Hannam. "I love Benidorm," he says. "I always have done. The chap that lived next door to them, Jimmy McFauld, owned the White Swan, one of the biggest gay pubs in London. Jimmy had bars and property out there and he told them about this village that he lived in, Finestrat. So they go and then they see a place there which is like a theatre..."

John and Gary decided to buy a three-storey house there but it was the possibility of owning and running their own theatre that was the real attraction. The plan was to renovate the place and do seasons of shows to attract the army of British ex-pats and tourists in the area. "By this time," says Hannam, "John was quite ill and his mind wasn't as sharp as usual. It was a tiny little village and they never would have got an audience there. It would have been a money pit."

"John rang me up," recalls their friend Grahame Flynn. "He was really excited. 'We've got this theatre. We're going to invest money in it and we want you to oversee the renovation of the building and produce the first few shows. We'll pay you a retainer.' He thought it would be really popular with people out there. I think it was a pipe dream. My partner Jeremy and I talked about it at length – and I was sort of tempted."

Whether or not it was pie in the sky, for John, Finestrat represented the future. It was something to dream about, plan for and focus on beyond the depressing day-to-day struggle with debilitating illness. Throughout 2001, he used everything that needed to be accomplished to distract himself from a failing liver and the sadness of his mother, dwindling away in her nearby nursing home. "It was all about downsizing," says Grahame Flynn. "They sold Brockley and were getting rid of the Brighton flat. It was 'What are we going to do with the rest of our lives?'"

On 11th December 2001, John emailed Flynn: "I see Dr Cairns the consultant with the biopsy results on 18th. On January 2nd (and a happy new year to you too), I see the liver specialist in London and Gary sees Dr Hale in Hove for the first follow-up remission check. On 4th he sees a specialist for results of the analysis on a suddenly appearing mole which was removed a few weeks back. And I thought you got all these problems when you were old, not when you're in your late thirties!!!"

"I have been approached by an independent TV company to produce a new series – first draft scripts available in January and pre-production starts September 2002. So I must concentrate on getting well..."

Alas, this project soon went south, as John explained in a follow-up email on 2nd Feb 2002: "This constant delay with tapes and scripts whiffs a bit... When I suggested we regularised the situation, everything's gone quiet. Strange that. I may be wrong – let's hope I am."

In the same email, he was full of news about all the jobs he'd been having done, both in Brighton and London: "A new door on the sitting room... Yesterday the baby grand [Gary was an accomplished pianist] went away to be French polished, today buying a new cooker and a smaller spin-dryer. Wednesday coming, we're having the skirting boards in the sitting room replaced. Friday a ceramic tiled floor laid in the kitchen. Monday 11th cloakroom ceiling lowered and tiled floor to ceiling. A new loo (goodbye pink!) and smaller washbasin. New double glazed windows... New French windows for sitting room..." And so it went on, with the poignant postscript: "All this is not meant to appear boastful – I am so excited. The quack said I should find something to occupy myself but not too taxing. So that's what I'm doing – all those things I've always been too busy to do before."

John was also planning for a big event that August – a party to celebrate his 55th birthday and his 30th anniversary with Gary. "Everything was building up to this," says Flynn. "So there was lots of decorating in the house. They had the most awful 1970s burgundy bathroom with matching red carpet that went up the side of the bath. That was all stripped out. The lounge carpet was removed and the floor boards waxed. The old carpet would move when a draught ripped through the house. The first time it happened, I thought I had drunk too much vodka and was seeing things!"

"John was always talking about his party," smiles their friend Stephen Cranford. "'I've ordered this and we're going to do this... I've bought some furniture for the garden. I want you to come round and help me put it up.' I remember him saying, 'For years, I've been saving for a rainy day and it's now that rainy day.' He was trying to tie up loose ends and put things in place. Someone had bought them an engraved crystal vase with 'John and Gary, 30 years' and this was on the mantelpiece. But of course they never made it that far."

John was doing his best to follow his doctor's instructions and go to bed early. Unfortunately, this meant he often woke in the early hours, killing the dead time before dawn by writing emails and watching TV. It was the reason he was wide awake when some old friends decided to phone him in the middle of the night, as Janet Fielding remembers. "Sarah Lee, Peter Davison and I had been out at Soho House [a private members' club for London media types] until about three thirty in the morning when we went back to Sarah's place. We were drinking more wine – it seemed like a good idea at the time – and we decided to phone John and find out how he was."

"It was Janet's idea!" laughs Peter Davison. "We were amazed he was still up. He seemed very pleased to hear from us and he told us that everything was fine."

"Little did we know," adds Fielding, "that it was the last time we would ever talk to him. I was so glad that we'd got pissed that night and phoned him."

On 15th March 2002, John travelled to Shad Thames in London to make what was to be his only appearance on the BBC's *Doctor Who* DVD range. It was for a feature on the making of *Resurrection of the Daleks*. The producer was Paul Vanezis, though, true to form, John nicknamed him Paul Veranda. When John arrived, by cab, Vanezis immediately noticed that he "looked quite upset and nervous. He was bright yellow. Even the whites of his eyes were yellow."

It was pouring with rain, so shelter was sought in Le Pont de la Tour, a nearby restaurant. Vanezis offered John a drink. "I'll just have some water," he replied. Then he told Vanezis that he had problems with his kidneys and needed an operation. "When he said it, I thought he was going to burst into tears. It sounds awful to say it, but I could smell death on him."

On the evidence of the rushes, this interview is a masterclass in "eyes and teeth". Sometimes, John fluffs his words and then gets furious with himself. He goes out of his way to give Vanezis and Peter Finklestone, the team behind the camera, what they need. There are flashes of humour and bite and, at one point, dared to reveal something that no-one knows about the story, he shares some malicious gossip about one of his leading actresses. No matter that he'd got his facts wrong, it was a sign of his undiminished mischievous spirit. When the interview was finally at an end, he got up and said, more to himself than anyone else, "Told you I could still do it..."

At the time, away from his work on the DVD range, Peter Finklestone was a GP. He had immediately spotted the seriousness of John's condition. "I spent 40 minutes alone with John," he says. "His mind was on his mother and how much he missed her. During our chat, he realised that I wasn't taken in by his story of having problems with his kidneys. He said, 'I've seen the doctors and they're hopeful I can get a transplant and then it'll be fine.' He stopped in mid-sentence, sort of shrank into himself slightly and said, 'I'm not fooling you, am I?' I said, 'I'm a doctor. I've had quite a lot of experience. I know things are not good.' We didn't go into specifics but we made this connection. It was almost like I was a priest in a confessional. The doctors had levelled with him. He knew he was dying and was lying to spare Gary the guilt because John had started to drink so heavily with the stress of Gary's cancer. He shared his honest fears and feelings with me that he couldn't even share with his life partner. It was humbling and I felt privileged, though slightly awkward. He said, 'You won't say any of this to anybody, will you?'"

Finklestone kept his word but warned Vanezis, "If you want to do any more with him, you've got three months."

Vanezis had already spoken to John about recording a commentary on one of his stories. John was enthusiastic about starting with *The Leisure Hive*, his very first story as producer. Now Vanezis spoke to Tom Baker, alerting him to the situation with John's health. "Of course I'll be there," he said. Vanezis also lined up actors Laurence Payne and Adrienne Corri to participate. To make everything as easy as possible for John, it was suggested that the commentary be recorded in Brighton. "Once I'd got everything in place," remembers Vanezis, "I rang John. Gary answered. He said, 'John didn't like that interview. He doesn't want it to be used. It's just not him.'" Vanezis did his best to reassure Gary that the piece would be carefully edited so that John wouldn't look bad, offering to show it to them before it was signed off. When he got the chance to ask Downie about the proposed commentary, he was told that John was in hospital."

On 20th March, John saw his consultant, who put his name down for a liver transplant. "This will happen later this year," he emailed Flynn, "within six months. [There's been] no appreciable change in me since July 2001. Don't breathe a word. Don't want to look an idiot or get OTT sympathy as it makes us both worse. Life in state of flux but making good decisions."

The final deterioration, when it came, was rapid and brutal and, ironically, apparently triggered by something trivial which had happened when John and Gary were last in Finestrat. "It got terribly hot there," says Flynn, "and Gary said that when it got too hot, they would actually sleep up on the roof. I think it was then that John got bitten."

This bite, on John's leg, swiftly became infected. "I think his whole immunity had gone," says Hannam. "The poison was within him. He got blood poisoning that you or I would fight off with great vigour and no particular problem. But because his liver and other organs were so damaged, he couldn't fight it."

Mark Jones, another friend, works in the medical profession and explains, "Slowly but surely, he began to deteriorate from that moment. It's like cascade failure. When one thing's not working, it has a knock-on effect to another and so on and so on."

His legs became swollen and blistered and had to be dressed and re-dressed. Despite the considerable pain he was in, John insisted that he still attend the Battlefield convention, which he'd agreed to appear at in Coventry over the weekend of 30th and 31st March. "We'd arranged for a wheelchair," says Grahame Flynn, who was one of the convention organisers. "When I met him, I remember trying to keep a stiff upper lip because I was totally shocked – he was very gaunt and even the whites of his eyes had gone yellow. He rang my room and asked if I'd go across and help. It was the first time I saw his legs – he'd got all these blisters and Gary and I re-bandaged his legs. It was absolutely horrendous. He was in a lot of pain but he would keep smiling to make people feel relaxed."

Bizarrely, John wasn't the only guest in a terminal condition. Stunt man and actor Terry Walsh was also obeying the old theatrical maxim of "the show must go on", despite the fact that he was dying from lung cancer. "[Terry] had told me that this was to be his last event," says Flynn. "He was so ill we found him collapsed in his room and then he had to go to hospital. I found myself dealing with this and I made a really big error on the schedule. John had looked at his call sheet and had assumed the final panel was a solo affair. In fact, he was scheduled to appear with a group of actors including Colin Baker. Nobody was there to production-manage it because we were getting Terry off to hospital and so John assumed that he was on his own. He was ill and a little bit odd in his head. So the lights go up and he goes on and he doesn't really know what he's doing. He starts talking and I think the other people who were going to be on with him suddenly realised what had happened and they went on and joined him and sort of held his hand. But there was no structure to it and I am absolutely mortified that that was his last appearance."

"I was concerned for him," says Colin Baker, who was also attending the convention. "I am truly sorry that my only memory of the last time I saw John was that he didn't look at all well."

"They were due to go back out to Spain to recuperate," says Flynn. "He looked me in the eye and said, 'I love you, Gray.' He had never said this to me before. As I went back to my room, I felt my eyes welling up. Something told me that I wasn't going to see my friend alive again."

Rather than return to Finestrat, John was admitted to hospital, keeping the news a secret from all but the very closest friends. "I saw him the day before he went in," says Mark Jones. "I'd done graphic design at college and he'd asked me to produce the lettering for the theatre in Spain. I phoned him in hospital and he said, 'Mark, can you email the graphics over to Gary please?' I said, 'But you're in hospital! I haven't even started because all this has kicked off.' He went, 'You wanker! Do it, do it now!' He was desperate to make sure Gary was occupied, you see. I remember spending that night doing the graphics and emailing them to Gary. I figured that, as long as John knew I was doing it, he wouldn't think about it and worry."

"I went to see him in hospital," recalls actress and friend, Jessica Martin. "I didn't think for a moment that this was it. There was no question that he wasn't going to come out and thrive."

"I went to see him a couple of times with Tom [Baker]," says former BBC Enterprises man Lorne Martin. "He was in a private room, very posh and, though he looked terrible, he was never down – he always made sure when you went there that you were looked after."

But the cellulitis infection was steadily worsening. John's right foot turned black and there was a partial amputation in an attempt to get rid of the dead tissue and stop it from spreading further.

"He then deteriorated very quickly," says Cranford. "They had got me to put in a new kitchen and John was determined to see it and come home one final time – this would have been April. Gary told me that he literally staggered in, glanced at it, said it was great and then collapsed on the sofa. He was really very, very weak and in great agony and I think Gary knew that he was going very, very soon."

"He came home for a weekend," says Lorne Martin, "and then he was rushed back in."

"I got a call from Nick Courtney," says Grahame Flynn. "He said, 'John's in hospital.' 'Right, I'll come up tomorrow,' I said. Later that evening I got another call from Nick and he said, 'You need to come now.' But I couldn't because I'd been drinking."

"We came down from Scotland to support Gary," says Fiona Cumming.

"John had been moved into the high dependency unit," adds her husband Ian Fraser. "He wasn't conscious."

There was nothing to be done. With the Frasers and their local priest Father Martin Morgan (who had conducted John's mother's funeral just a few months before) by his side, Gary was asked to make the agonising decision to turn off the machines keeping alive the man he loved. "The biggest crisis in my life," he called it when he talked to *DWM* in 2003. "I had to give permission and I had to watch them do it because that's the law. Thank God we'd talked about it. We'd always said that whoever went first... Neither of us wanted to ever be a vegetable."

"We were told that once the machines were switched off, it wouldn't take long," says Cumming. "We stood there for about the next two hours."

Fraser recalls, "One of the nurses said, 'Keep talking,' because the last thing to go is the hearing. He'll be able to hear you.'"

"Gary told me that he sat there talking to him, saying, 'Your hair's grey now. You'd hate that but actually you look lovely with it.'" remembers Anita Graham, one of John's oldest friends.

"We spoke to him and to Gary," says Cumming. "John had such a will to live and all you could think was, 'It's *all right* to go.'"

John Turner, professionally known as John Nathan-Turner, died at 13.30 on 1st May 2002. He was 54 years old and the death certificate gave a twofold cause of death: multi-organ failure and alcoholic liver disease. Despite his months of ill-health, the news was greeted with incomprehension by many of his friends and colleagues. BBC News online, *The Guardian* and *The Daily Telegraph* all carried obituaries but, before the tributes and re-appraisals could begin in earnest, a wave of shock travelled throughout the worldwide *Doctor Who* community.

Actor Matthew Waterhouse was living in America when he stumbled across the news in a weekly digest edition of the *Telegraph*. "I bought it on a whim," he says, "opened it up and there was his obituary. I remember mentioning it to Peter [Davison] and he was amazed that John had actually *got* an obituary!

"I'd been in touch with him a year or so earlier when I wanted to move to America. He wrote a very nice letter for my green card application. I sent him a thank you letter. His death was a big shock. It was really weird – this person who was very important in my life, who I would never have thought of as approaching death, suddenly popped his clogs. I felt sad that I hadn't seen him again."

Anita Graham was also living in the States at the time: "I didn't realise how ill he was. I'd had a Christmas message saying how Gary had been ill but was better now. Then I got the news that John had died. It was just awful. He was my oldest friend, the only person from that period I'd kept up with. You go through all the regrets – it's like half your life's gone."

"I just sobbed," says Carol Snook, an old friend from series and serials, "because he was such a lovely man. You don't forget the happy times."

"I was very sad," agrees Ron Katz, who ran the Doctor Who Fan Club of America. "Still am. Even though we lost touch, I know that he was a lifetime friend of mine. We had intellectual and intimate conversations. He was a great man and a great friend. If I go somewhere after I die, I know John will be there."

"It was such a terrible time," says Grahame Flynn. "John always had music playing in the house but now it was silent. Gary and I just sat in the darkness talking."

According to Mark Jones, "before he died, John made lots of phone calls making up with people he'd fallen out with."

But these didn't include a call to his one-time leading lady, Nicola Bryant, from whom he remained estranged. Like Waterhouse, she found out that he had died by reading about it in a newspaper. "I was upset and I did cry," she says, "but I was probably at least as upset that there was never now going to be an opportunity to make it right between us. Colin knew how much I had suffered and I remember him saying that if Gary had gone first it would have been different. He felt that John would have apologised or we would have reached a place where neither one of us needed to say anything. But it wasn't possible. I think Gary felt jealous because John adored me. He used to refer to me as 'his girl' – 'Isn't my girl an angel? Isn't my girl lovely?' It was 'My girl, my girl, my girl.' Certainly when I worked with Gary, he gave me a hard time. I can still do the routine from that panto, that's how hard I had it drummed into me, which really is kind of weird.

"It was terrible that I couldn't go to the funeral but I thought if I go, there might be a scene. That wouldn't have been right because it was his day. I did actually say to Colin, 'What do I do?' He said I should stay at home, so I did."

The funeral was held at Brighton's Woodvale Crematorium at 12.45 on Thursday 9th May. It was, by all accounts, an extraordinary and unusual service. "It was huge," says Fiona Cumming. "We arrived in the car with Gary and as we turned in to the crematorium, cars were all the way down either side. Gary said, 'I don't believe this.' There was an enormous crowd, so many people that not everyone could sit down. It was incredible."

Sylvester McCoy and Sophie Aldred both wore Hawaiian shirts in tribute to their late pal and producer. Andrew Beech of the DWAS organised a floral tribute and placed a TARDIS key on top of it, which was later pinched, presumably by a barker whose grief didn't exceed their acquisitive urges. Among the flowers, one wreath bore a shaky hand-written label which read "From the Time Lords". Gary Leigh, whose *DWB* had remorselessly hounded John for years, sent a bouquet. "You don't wish what happened on anybody," he comments. "It was very sad."

Another of John's most vocal critics, Ian Levine "phoned up Andrew Beech and said, 'Should I come to the funeral?' He said, 'No – Gary would never forgive you.'" Levine did as he was advised and stayed away.

"There were people dressed in *Doctor Who* costumes at the base of the hill," remembers American fan John Frank Rosenblum. "There was a bevy of beautiful young men there, too – God give him credit for that. Hard to say that one of my most amazing memories of my friend John was his funeral but it was."

"It was amazing," says Ralph Wilton, a former colleague. "More like a most wonderful show, a *Night of the 100 Stars*. There was Biggins and June Brown. As we went in, there was an Elvis Presley lookalike singing, 'Maybe I didn't love you...' I thought, 'Hello, this is going to be like no other funeral that I've ever been to.' It was a joyous occasion. He was so well loved."

"It was a really fitting end," says director Andrew Morgan. "It brings tears to my eyes to think about it – it was such an emotional thing. The old vicar was as camp as arseholes, the whole thing was just wonderful. John would have absolutely adored it. He was genuinely loved – I have nothing but good vibes when I think about him."

"It was very celebratory," agrees Jessica Martin. "Not maudlin at all. Fabulous. And it struck me that what an honour it was for him to extend the hand of friendship to me."

"He always used to say, 'I want a really big finish,'" recalled Gary Downie. "We always used to end our shows with *It's Not Where You Start, It's Where You Finish*. At his funeral the vicar said, 'This is a song that John and Gary used in their shows. Most of you know the words, so if you want to sing along...'"

The crowd of showbiz mourners needed no second bidding, as Ralph Wilton remembers. "That awful bit where the coffin slowly slides into the distance and the curtains draw round it. Well, we were singing *It's Not Where You Start* and Dora Bryan and Carol Kaye actually tap-danced down the aisle – it was just amazing."

"People were clapping and cheering in a bloody funeral," says Grahame Flynn. "It was unbelievable."

"One of their shoes went off during the high-kicking," chuckles Fiona Cumming, "and there was lots of laughter. As they were dancing, the curtains closed around the coffin. Gary said afterwards, 'I wondered if we should have pulled the curtains back again and given him an encore?!'"

"I'll never forget those two old hoofers dancing," laughs Sylvester McCoy. "It was the funniest thing and it kind of summed up his love for all that. 'Oh my God, they've upstaged John' – but, no, John would have loved it, two old ladies up there, dancing away."

"It was so apt," agrees actress Sarah Sutton, "so John – so them. I remember going home to my parents and saying, 'I've just been to the strangest cremation.' My mum thought it was wonderful."

"When we all came out of the chapel," adds McCoy, "we were still laughing and there was another group going into another chapel and they were all sad. It was weird. Colin and I immediately had to do a photo shoot for the local paper and we were standing there – the usual showbiz 'eyes and teeth' – and I suddenly thought, 'This is a funeral, we shouldn't be doing this!'"

But, as Gary told *DWM*, "A woman came up to me and said, 'Ooh, Gary, how can I tell people that I've enjoyed a funeral?' You couldn't have paid more respect to John than that."

A few weeks later, on 3rd September 2002, a "service of celebration for the life of John Nathan-Turner" was held at St Paul's Church, in London's Covent Garden. Popularly known as "the actors' church", this was the theatrical profession's venue of choice for the best memorials in the business. The service was led by Reverend Mark Oakley and started with the hymn *I Danced*. Other music included John's favourite Dusty Springfield number, *I Only Want To Be with You*, Eva Cassidy's *Time Is a Healer* and Bonnie Langford singing Robbie Williams's *Angels*. "Gary phoned me and asked me to sing something," she says, "and I suggested that. We talked for hours. He was broken-hearted – oh, he was so broken. It was just so sad. I don't know how I sang it."

Just like the funeral, the church was packed with showbiz pals, friends, fans, long-lost colleagues and loved ones. "I met up with people I hadn't seen for a long time," says one-time production associate June Collins. "John would have thought it was great. It was just like him – fun."

"Everybody turned up for John's memorial," says veteran script editor Betty Willingale. "He had been very, very popular about the place and I think it's telling that he was liked very much by the production secretaries."

"It wasn't what I was expecting," admits Jane Wellesley, a close friend from John's early days in drama. "There were loads and loads of people that you knew. It was slightly bizarre but great fun. Sylvester McCoy played the spoons."

"I did," he admits. "When we were doing one of the early shows, we were on location and he organised a party one night. I did my party piece, nicked some pudding spoons and played them on Bonnie Langford. He thought that was great and said, 'My God, we've got to have that in *Doctor Who.*' I said, 'You must be joking?' but he wasn't and we did, so it became part of my thing really. So I put on a Hawaiian shirt, went to his memorial and played the spoons."

Veteran actor Hugh Lloyd, one of John's Brighton crowd, wrote and performed a special tribute: "John's feeling very pleased with himself at the moment," he began. "It's the first week in September and he's already cast his first pantomime up there. And what a choice of cast he's got! And he hasn't had to deal with agents – well, there aren't any there! So here goes:

Principal Boy: Oscar Wilde

Principal Girl: Liberace

Dandini: Freeman, Hardy and Willis – well, they're expert shoe-fitters

Baron Hardup: Nelson D Rockefeller (John couldn't find Robert Maxwell)

Buttons: Al Capone (he leads the communal singing with "All together or I'll shoot")

Speciality act: Hannibal and his elephants

Dancers: a German group – the Attila Girls

Stage Manager: St Peter – Well, he's all right but John's already made him move the gates twice!

Scenery: Leonardo da Vinci – Michelangelo's livid so John's letting him do the PR for the show

Costumes – by Angels

Lighting – by God. Well, it's a sure way to get a perfect black-out.

And finally, in the orchestra pit, that well-known all-girl band – the Henry VIII sextet."

There were tributes, too, from Nick Courtney, Colin Baker, Louise Jameson and Tom Baker. "Everybody was sitting down," remembers Grahame Flynn, "and suddenly the doors bang open and Tom Baker walks down the aisle. He looks round and says, 'Ah, *this* St Paul's...' It was very funny. Nick Courtney was a devout Christian and read *Do Not Stand at My Grave and Weep* by Mary

Frye. Then Tom stands up and says, 'John's dead and he won't be coming back.' It was very powerful stuff."

"Tom Baker said something I loved," says Anita Graham. "That everyone was saying, 'It's what John would have wanted.' He said that the reality of what John would have wanted was 'for me to be where he is and for him to be here!'"

"It was such a great celebration of his life," sighs Sophie Aldred. "A camp knees-up. Exactly what he'd have wanted it to be. It was really positive, not at all depressing or down."

The final words in the order of service proclaimed simply, "Remember yesterday, look forward to tomorrow, live for today."

As anybody who has been bereaved will tell you, the immediate weeks after the death of a loved one are, to some extent, cushioned by the adrenalin of everything that must be organised and sorted out, as well as by nature's emotional anaesthetic, a kind of numbness that prevents the pain from being totally overwhelming. To a concerned onlooker, this can seem to be an indication that a person is coping or even that they haven't taken the death as badly as might be expected. It is, alas, a false assumption, based more on hope than grim reality. Grief is a cold and lonely place. Usually that helpful numbness starts to wear off just at the point when, if you are lucky enough to have them, the carnival of friends and family move on. No matter how well intentioned they may be, necessarily they must return to their own lives and priorities. For Gary, hardly had the laughter and applause began to fade from St Paul's, than he began to discover the bitter truth of this. The months after John's death were bleaker still as he was forced to confront the sad reality that most of their social circle had been there because of John and not him. Even if he had always suspected this (and he did), to be proved right must have given him a peculiarly bitter kind of satisfaction. His own parents were dead and he no longer had contact with either of his brothers, following a sordid feud over their mutual inheritance. Rows of this kind are so often the cause of a final breach where family relationships have been historically difficult and conducted at long distance.

"When John went," observes Ian Fraser, "Gary lost his life basically. Although he did spend a lot of time trying to get himself together, he was just shattered by the whole thing. Totally bereft."

"He said, 'Now the producer is dead, nobody phones,'" recalls Stephen Cranford. "When they were both alive, the phone was always ringing. It was a very busy, social, thriving house. When John wasn't there any more, about three quarters of that stopped."

"After John died, everyone deserted Gary," says Barry Hannam. "All John's so-called friends, it all stopped. Tom Baker was one – they was very close to him but when John died, Gary never heard from him again. There were only a few of us who stayed loyal to Gary – Ian and Fiona, Mark Jones and Lorne [Martin] was very, very loyal – a lovely, good man."

"It was clear that he thought, 'Now that John's gone, nobody will want me,'" says DWAS coordinator Andrew Beech. "We made a point of still inviting him to events that we did and he did come along."

In the months and years after John's death, his professional legacy began, inevitably, to fall under the microscope in the form of interviews, articles and, increasingly, in the commentaries and mini-documentaries recorded for the BBC's DVD range. Emboldened by the fact that it is impossible to libel the dead, some took their chance to settle a few scores or distract attention from their own deficiencies with a few carefully chosen words about the late producer. The mistakes and disasters were his and the achievements and accolades were thanks to others and often attained, it was implied, despite his involvement.

As people became more candid within the pages of *DWM*, Gary, as loyal to John dead as he had been in life, was keen to set the record straight. He contacted the magazine and, no fools, they sent Ben Cook, the latest in their family tree of fresh-faced eager beaver reporters, to interview him in Brighton. "We leapt at that opportunity," he says. "When I went up to do the interview, he had copies of the magazine with him, which he highlighted to mark the various interviews he wanted to comment on. In typical Gary Downie style he grabbed the opportunity with both hands. A lot of what he said I didn't agree with and there are bits in the interview where I pick him up on what he said but it's what he had to say."

The results were splashed over two issues of the magazine and accurately capture Gary's sometimes illogical train of thought as he set about him, issuing snubs, denials, reproaches and scorn. "What I hate about the fans," he blasted, "is that they all think that they can do it better. They're working at Tesco service tills or as warehousemen, but they all know how to produce the show better than John."

He branded Anthony Ainley "a big, dictatorial bully", Peter Davison "boring", theorised that Eric Saward "probably thought he should have been producing the show" and suggested that the show had been cancelled by Michael Grade ("Arrogant... boring... a grey blob in a grey suit") because of a personal vendetta between Grade and Colin Baker. This one stuck and still does the rounds, the story going that Grade was a great friend of Baker's first wife, the actress Liza Goddard. "The divorce was acrimonious," Gary told Cook, "and she moved into Michael Grade's house while she was getting over [it]. Michael Grade was determined. He did not want Colin Baker working for the BBC."

"Michael was a great friend of Liza's," concedes Baker himself, "and Liza's friends did tend to take sides. But I've always said that story is ludicrous. I really don't think it was anything personal. I remember seeing Grade interviewed by Clive James when Grade was at London Weekend. They were talking about the BBC and James said, 'Maybe you'll work at the BBC one day,' and Grade said, 'The BBC is too tough a nut to crack,' – and I paraphrase – 'It's still churning out tired old stuff like *Doctor Who* and *Come Dancing*'... so all you can say is he was consistent. To say it was because of Liza is nonsense, I think."

Nearly a decade later, for me, the most poignant part of the interview came at the very end. "[John] hated the show in the end," claimed Gary. "I can actually say that. He loathed the show. He loathed it because the fans, as far as he was concerned, no matter what he did, they didn't like it. You'd get interviews with actors and writers and everybody running him down. Narcissistic, egocentric people.

"There will never be another producer like John."

Despite his obvious anger and grief, the leopard stayed true to its spots and Gary didn't miss the opportunity to make a hopeful pass at Cook: "Well, yes," he admits, somewhat awkwardly. "I was young and beautiful all those years ago. I made my excuses."

Very little was cut from his outpourings and, in its way, the Downie interview caused a minor sensation, though nothing on the scale of the Saward *Starburst* debacle. "It's the sort of interview that I wonder whether we'd be able to get away with now," Cook acknowledges. "I'm pleased that we gave him that opportunity."

"That would never have happened if John had been alive," believes Grahame Flynn. "He would have been very annoyed. But it gave Gary a way to vent his spleen and have a pop at absolutely everybody he could."

"People say that gays have all the worst traits of a woman," observes Lorne Martin, somewhat prehistorically. "He would definitely go off the deep end and was very protective of John – but he was a decent bloke."

Surprisingly for a man whose professional reputation was grounded on his extreme efficiency, especially where money was involved, John's financial affairs were something of a mess. "When Gary was going through John's stuff," says Stephen Cranford, "he found dozens and dozens of pay cheques from the BBC that hadn't been cashed. Many were out of date. They were silly little cheques like royalties from a video and they all had to be sent back to be reissued. Their house was in a right pickle – if you wanted to find something, it would take you a long time. That's very rare for a gay couple!"

"I'd done a documentary in 2000 all about K9," recalls fan turned producer Paul Mark Tams. "John had appeared in it and, after the funeral, this cheque arrived in the post from Gary saying John never took the fee you gave him. That was typical of John – he'd done it for the love of it and to help me out and he didn't want to take money off me. It was so sweet and upsetting. I've still got that cheque to this day."

Despite the chaos in the paperwork, John had left his partner an unusual and thoughtful legacy, intended to help sustain Gary in the first months following his loss. "When John knew he was dying," explains Cranford, "he started leaving notes hidden in the house. He would order things and weeks after he'd died a parcel would turn up with a ring for Gary or something else that John had bought for him."

Although Gary was naturally the chief beneficiary of John's will, this was before the changes in the law that ushered in civil partnerships for gay couples. Consequently, after John's death, Gary was confronted with a significant inheritance tax bill on what he understandably considered to be their joint estate. This rankled with him for what remained of his life. "Gary kept saying to the estate agent, 'Make the valuation as low as you can,'" says Cranford. "He also withdrew very large amounts of money and hid them so they wouldn't be counted. He just told the officials, 'We had gambling debts and I've paid them off.'"

He also continued the process of downsizing started the year before, taking a bilious view of the accumulated *Doctor Who* material. "The BBC are getting nothing out of me," he snarled at Grahame Flynn, who recalls that Gary then "wanted me to load all the tapes into boxes with a view to taking them to the tip. To scupper this, I put all the tapes into the biggest boxes I could find so he couldn't move them on his own. Over the following weeks, I would find the odd prop or item ripped up in the wicker basket in the sitting room. Gary did give all the scripts to the BFI but he was a bitter, angry man."

The theatre in Finestrat was abandoned. "I talked him out of it," says Hannam. "So he bought this little house out there instead, which he loved."

Hannam began to assume more and more importance in Gary's life. "John had been my friend, the one I'd sit and talk to. After he died, Gary became a whole new person to me. All this come out about his dancing and his career. He used to sing to me, 'You'll never get away from me.' He hated being on his own and just gradually started staying with me more and more. We got on well, we used to go out, go to a few of the pubs. I just sort of adopted him, really."

"Gary used to have these really vivid dreams," says Stephen Cranford, "that John appeared in. He'd say, 'I met John last night in my dreams and we had this conversation,' and I'd say, 'It was a dream,' and he'd say, 'No, it was a vision – I know what I know.'"

"Gary was very spiritual," says Grahame Flynn. "One night I stood on the landing and actually heard him talking to John in his sleep. I was filled with compassion for this monster."

"Gary used to dream about John all the time," agrees Hannam. "When he was coming back from Spain, he stopped in France, near Limoges and John appeared to him at the side of the bed. When he come back, he told me that John had said it wouldn't be long before they was together again."

In 2005, Gary's cancer returned. "I'm convinced it recurred because of the stress and devastation," says Fiona Cumming. This time it spread fast. Two major operations removed most of his bladder and intestines. His weight plummeted. "I got this email saying we hadn't spoken for ages," recalls Anita Graham, "and, 'I'm ill now but I'm not going to do anything about it – it's champagne all the way!' I emailed back but I never heard from him again."

It was obvious that Gary was dying. Grahame Flynn says, "I contacted people from his past and said, 'Look Gary's terminally ill. It would be nice if you got in touch.' Tom Baker used to write little cards and Gary would revel in them. But Tom later told me, 'Gary never replied or picked up the phone when I called.' One day I was in Exeter and my mobile rang. It was Danny La Rue [for whom Gary had worked as principal dancer] – 'Hello dear, it's Dan. It's very good of you to write to me about Gary. He was one of my greatest admirers!'"

But despite the years of friendship, what Mark Jones calls the "genuine love" between Flynn and Downie, eventually it disintegrated in an atmosphere of mutual recrimination. "We were making a replica of Tom Baker's scarf," explains Flynn, "as part of this display for a convention we were planning. I was also doing some research for Gary as he was going to put some stuff in an auction at Bonham's. So I said, 'I know a bit about the history of the scarf, there's been various repairs – can I borrow it?' 'Yes, you can.' Then about a week later I get a telephone call saying, 'Have you got the scarf?' 'Yes.' 'Why have you got that?' 'Because you let me borrow it – we were doing this research.' I took it back at the weekend."

"He let Gary down very badly," counters Hannam. "Gary was very fond of him but he was just a user. Gary wasn't silly. When Grahame said, 'Oh, you were so high on the morphine that you didn't know what was going on,' I said, 'Gary, you may have been a bit drugged up but you didn't have amnesia!'"

Flynn continues, "I found out that subsequently that there was this implication that I'd nicked it – which really, really hurt me. Jeremy, my partner, whose judgement wasn't clouded, said to me one day, 'If John was here and he saw what Gary had put you through, do you think he would have asked you to keep your promise to look after him?' In my heart, I knew the answer was no. I wrote a long letter where I put down years of bad experiences. I printed it off, signed it and addressed it. Then I thought about what John would do and ripped it up. But I never rang Gary again and, of course, he never rang me."

Hannam was now Gary's full-time carer. "When the cancer came back, I think their relationship changed," ventures mutual friend Mark Jones. "They became so close. Gary had been really fucked off at the amount that had to go on tax after John died. When gay marriage came in, he and Barry used to jokingly say, 'We're both spinsters. Old and crusty, we've had the loves of our lives. If the gay marriage comes in, we'll get married and that'll be that.'"

"As he became iller and iller he relied on me more and more," says Hannam. "Then he said, 'I think the tax man has had enough money. I think we should do this civil partnership.' He'd already put the house in Spain in my name."

The ceremony was swiftly arranged and took place on 22nd December 2005. "I know that he only held on for that," says Hannam. "He said, 'I know this isn't a proper marriage but you've made me quite happy,' and he told other people – friends of mine – that I'd given him an extra year of life. We was never what him and John had. We were close but not like that.

"The moment that that was over, he just give up. He just couldn't take any more. He'd had a uroscopy and a colostomy, he was in such a mess. It just was awful. We couldn't go out very far – it would take so much preparation. He had trouble sitting. He absolutely loved cars and the funniest thing was when he got a mobility car, a Chrysler Cruiser with hands control. He said, 'Oh I can drive this easily,' and then we nearly mounted the pavement and knocked someone over. He just got out and laughed – and he could make people laugh, even though he'd nearly killed them!

"The sense of humour was still there right to the end. The last thing he said to me was, 'Will you get me a hamburger?' He loved those instant ones that you just put in the microwave. I got one and took it to microwave it in the little hospital kitchenette. I went to his bed – and he was in a coma. He just wouldn't wake up – and he was a very light sleeper – so I knew it was a coma. I stayed there till about two in the morning. I'm on oxygen for 16 hours a day so I said to the nurse, 'I'm going to go home for a few hours – I'll be back at eight o'clock.' As I left the following morning, they phoned to say he'd passed away."

It was the 19th January 2006. "When he died," says Cranford, "it wasn't 'How awful for you, Barry.' Everyone, including Barry, said, 'He's back with John.'"

The funeral was simple and low-key. None of Gary's family attended. "Apart from Barry and myself," says Mark Jones, "and some of the young chaps, there was an old friend, Brian Ralfe, June Brown, Chris Ellison, Fiona and Ian. But there weren't really that many people. No fuss, no messing – exactly what Gary wanted. The vicar stood up and spoke for 20 minutes and told us what no one knew – about the money they'd given abroad to Ethiopia and stuff, helping to have a church rebuilt and sponsoring children. They'd never mentioned a word of it – this was John and Gary. Barry asked me to speak – so I spoke, and I said, 'The only stories I could retell, you couldn't actually say in a church!' I added that the world's a little bit empty without John and now even more so. I said he would be forever loved and missed."

Over at *DWM*, an obituary posed a problem, as Gary Russell remembers. "The editor said, 'We've got an Anthony Ainley situation – no one is willing to write it because no one has got anything nice to say.' So I did it and was quite honest and then got criticised afterwards because it hadn't been a lovely, fluffy piece."

In final defiance of the taxman, Gary Downie left everything to Hannam. "They were hoarders, John and Gary," he says. "Without Fiona and Ian, I would never have got that house cleared. They are lovely people. I left Fiona there for about five days and she did so much. I didn't realise that John and Gary were so comfortably off. I couldn't have done half what I've done since, all the travel and buying another house in Worthing."

John and Gary's formidable *Doctor Who* collection remained to be dealt with. Some of it was unique and of historical importance, some was ephemeral and kept but for the sake of a skip. Before his death, Gary had sold some of this strange hoard, including props, paintings and scripts. Stephen Cranford was trusted to sort through what was left and the piles of tapes, photographs and paperwork. "All of John's *Doctor Who* collection came to me when Gary passed," he says. "I returned a lot of it to Peter Crocker and Paul Vanezis, the DVD restoration boys. They had been chivvying away at John and Gary for years and they just kept saying no. John was open to it but Gary just wanted money. 'How much?' he'd say. There was loads of it in the garage. It was racked out with stuff – as producer, John was always being sent samples and he had loads of those. I could have sold it all for an absolute fortune. Peter and Paul came round and we went through everything. They knew what was important."

"There's been a lot of grandiose assumption in fandom about John's tapes," says Peter Crocker. "There's no good evidence that anything was kept other than by chance, with the possible exception of a U-matic copy of the first hour of Davison's first studio session for *Four to Doomsday*, which seems too significant to be a random chance survival."

There were stacks of VHS tapes which John or Gary brought home to recycle. Some survived intact, others were partially recorded over but, in this way, some rare material was uncovered. Also salvaged were various early edits of some shows, a lengthy studio recording from *Earthshock*, effects film from *State of Decay*, the missing master soundtrack and film inserts for *The Five Doctors*, which have since been returned to the BBC, and the master titles (on 35mm film) for seasons 17 and 18 and for the *K9 and Company* special. There was a lot of material from the McCoy era (although much of this was still retained by the BBC) and from John's work at BBC Worldwide. "A real smattering," as Vanezis puts it.

"I did destroy some tapes and papers," says Cranford, "personal stuff that when you looked at it, you went, 'Oooh, OK...' but which everybody has. I could have binned a lot of stuff that I didn't. I wanted it to be kept so it's a truthful record. Perhaps it was my policeman's side – this was evidence. He'd kept it, after all. Why had he kept it? I think they knew that I would do the right thing with it."

Gary had lived just long enough to see the BBC re-embrace *Doctor Who*, at last paying serious money for its production and promoting the results with spirited aggression. The show's return, masterfully spearheaded by the brilliant Russell T Davies, was a *coup de théâtre* bagging undreamt of audiences in this multichannel era. Ever since, *Doctor Who* has remained a staple yet cherished part of BBC1's strategy. The show is protected, supported and believed in, perhaps as never before. So what would John have made of all this hoopla? According to Mark Jones, "Gary (who thought it was great) told me that John would have said, 'That's no different to what I was doing!' I said, 'Come on now, it does look a bit more expensive,' and he replied, 'That's just technology today!'"

"He knew it would happen and be a success again," says actress Lynda Baron. "He said, 'They'll live to regret it. It's ridiculous – a no-brainer.' Television seems to have fallen off the rails a bit. It lacks JN-Ts. You can't have a world of proles – you need mavericks like him. It's all gone corporate, led by clones and accountants."

"He would have been dead jealous of the money," laughs Sylvester McCoy. "So he would have been frustrated in one way but also incredibly pleased that in many ways a lot of what we were putting into effect has carried on. You can still see the connection between 20th-century Doctors and 21st-century Doctors because of him."

McCoy's co-star, Sophie Aldred, is of the same mind. "If you watch *Survival* or *Ghost Light* there are shades of what's happening now," she says. "The dark, mysterious Doctor who wasn't just the Doctor, not just a Time Lord or a hobo in space – that's his legacy too. He would have loved David [Tennant] and Matt [Smith] and Karen [Gillan] – and all the gay references."

Matthew Waterhouse takes up the theme. "It's interesting how many of the things they do now were initiated in his era – the attempt to have *Doctor Who* companions slightly more complex in terms of character. Less overt than on the new series but it is there. There are episodes I've seen that have reminded me of something John might have commissioned in the Sylvester McCoy era – really quite strange and dreamy. I think in fact in some ways his influence on the new programme is much deeper than people might assume. I think he would have loved that it had come back and was really, really successful."

"I don't think he'd be surprised at all," says actor turned producer Mark Strickson. "You get an amazing product if you have that kind of money. OK, you have to be creative as well but you can't drive a mini and beat a Formula One car."

"He would just be so jealous," thinks Andrew Cartmel. "It would gut him really. He would have said, 'We could have done that, if they'd given us half a chance,' and, in a sense, we could have, had he stood back and allowed the correct talented people to do the creative stuff. He would never have stood for Catherine Tate – he would have said, 'Get rid of that old trout and get some totty on there!'"

"I look at it," says John's one-time secretary, Sarah Lee, "and I think he would have loved the casting. Look at the performances of the current couple of Doctors. They are so John, aren't they? It's definitely going in the direction that he would have liked to have taken it. He would probably love to have knocked on a few front doors and said, 'There you go, you see, you were wrong.' I suppose there would always be a hint of sadness for him because *Doctor Who* is going on and doing things that he would have loved to have done. It might have haunted him a bit. He did love the show."

The only key creative figure who has worked both on the classic series (as the pre-2000s era is now known) and the current show is director Graeme Harper. "I think he'd have loved the new *Doctor Who*," he says, without a moment's hesitation. "I think he would have said, 'That's exactly what I wanted to do but nobody gave me the money.' When I was invited by Russell and Phil Collinson [the producer], by the time I had done the first block, they were the same as him and he was the same as them – exactly the same – the difference was they did it 20 years later."

I spent months journeying through John's life, trying to see him as others had done, as well as myself. I spoke to scores of people who knew him far more intimately than I did, lovers, friends, friends who became enemies and implacable critics. I was curious about the emotions he still provoked and this led me to ask what some of these people would say to John, if, hypothetically, he were to return to them for a matter of a few minutes only. One last time.

"The hairs went up on the back of my neck when you asked me that," says Grahame Flynn. "I would thank him for what he has done for me since he died. He taught me that you have to go out there and do stuff. If you've got something in your head, you've got a dream, go and work for it. And I'd give him the biggest hug you'd see in the world."

"I'd say, 'God, we miss you,'" says Ian Fraser.

"...and didn't we have fun!" adds Fiona Cumming. "There was so much fun and so much laughter. We love talking about him."

"I'd say, 'How dare you die so young!'" says Barry Hannam, succinctly.

"I'd say, 'You should have taken *Bergerac*,'" wisecracks Andrew Cartmel.

"I'd just go up and give John a big hug," says Stephen Cranford. "I think about him all the time and I still miss him hugely. He was such a profound mentor to me. I wanted to get into broadcasting. He coached me, said he would represent me, encouraged me to do hospital radio and get voice training. He wrote scripts for demos for me and helped film them. I would love him to see what I am doing now. If he could look over my shoulder, I think he'd be proud of me."

This is a sentiment shared by Mark Strickson. "I think John would be very proud of me because I did learn a lot from him. Most of all, I'd say thank you. And I'd buy him a drink."

"I'd say, 'Here's a very large vodka and diet coke,'" laughs Stuart Money. "There's nothing in the fridge but plenty in the freezer. Now entertain me and I'll entertain you until four o'clock in the morning."

"I'd say, 'Tell me another story,'" says Mark Jones. "No matter how crazy the story was, I believed it. They inspired me. I miss them both. They were funny and blunt and outrageous – honest and great fun."

"I'd say, 'Let's have a laugh over old times!'" suggests Gary Leigh. "If he's learnt anything in the afterlife, he'd have learnt from his mistakes, hopefully!"

"I think I'd just be very pleased to see him," says Peter Davison. "I don't hold any bitterness about him at all."

"I'd give him a big hug," says Bonnie Langford. "He was adorable. He had a big heart and he cared so much about the show."

"I'd just want to hug him," echoes Nicola Bryant. "Let him know it was OK. I forgive him because I don't think he really knew what he was doing. I do feel fiercely loyal to John. That in itself I've been analysing – it's very interesting. I'll always owe him for changing my life."

"I'd say, 'Let's go and have a vodka and tonic and chat about the way *Doctor Who* has gone," suggests Sylvester McCoy.

"I'd give him a big hug," counters his predecessor, Colin Baker, "and we'd have a scream. I'd tell him, 'You came back as Russell T Davies!' I still miss him. There are odd occasions where I think, 'Oh I must tell John that.' It's usually a bit of scurrilous gossip. I liked him, warts and all and felt about him a bit like I would a brother."

"Oh I think we'd have a lot of laughs," says Sarah Lee. "And lots of champagne. I can't see that things would be very much different."

"It would be great," enthuses Sophie Aldred. "I would throw my arms around him and say, 'Thank you for giving me this opportunity – all this amazing travel, meeting all these incredible people, my career. Thanks for putting your money on a complete unknown from the back row of the chorus in *Fiddler on the Roof*. For having that hunch, huge gratitude to him."

Some, like Jessica Martin, are more directional. "I'd say to him, 'You know what, John? Go to the fringe and find all the drag queens you can and put on the most fabulous show. Show them what you can do.' He would get a second wind and get rediscovered."

"I'd say, 'Get your finger out and do that show you've always wanted to do,'" says actress Jacqueline Pearce. "You've got people that would climb on board with you immediately – myself being one. Do it – fulfil yourself – be a producer again, do it your way and fuck 'em!"

"He was very unusual for BBC producers," says actor Chris Guard. "His delightful campness, his fearlessness, his absolute determination to drink and smoke more than was good for him. He was one of those mavericks who thought, 'This is life, we're not worrying about tomorrow, we're worrying about the job we're doing and how best to do it.' I know that might sound a little bit romanticised but I honestly think that was the case with him. I remember him firing on all cylinders, warts and all – and I think, 'Well, that was a life worth the living.' It was a real fucker that he died but the biggest fucker was the changes at the BBC, which signalled the death of that kind of person."

"As much as the booze, I think what killed him in the end was that they stopped him working," conjectures Andrew Cartmel. "He was a workhorse. That was his biggest addiction really. He wanted to make stuff. When they pushed him out into the cold, that eventually killed him. It was just so sad. It wasn't only that he was dead, but that he had been destroyed – diminished to nothing. I suppose it's classic tragedy because it wasn't as though it happened instantly and his own temperament and decisions were also to blame. He determinedly continued in the wrong direction. He'd worked long and hard over many years to dig himself into that fucking hole."

"I think he had a broken heart, really," says Jacqueline Pearce. "I think what happened with him was *Doctor Who* broke his heart. It was very, very fucking cruel. It was appalling and he deserved far better than that."

"The BBC does not come out of it well," says actress Clare Clifford. "It was wickedly done – he was left looking like he'd failed. It must have been like being stabbed. He might not be dead if it hadn't been for that."

"He was dedicated to the BBC in his fashion," agrees director Alan Wareing. "In a way, they destroyed him."

"One of the reasons I feel very badly for John," explains Ian Fraser, "is the way the BBC shut him out. I could not believe that they could do that to someone who had so much talent. There was no way that he could just sit at home and do nothing."

"It is shameful that an organisation the size of the BBC could find no way to make use of his undoubted, though maybe wacky, talents and unbounded energy," comments former head of series and serials, David Reid.

"The BBC was his everything," says Janet Fielding. "You don't get to be a producer when you're 32 by being an idiot. I really disagreed with him on lots of things but also I was fond of him. He was a great character in so many ways."

"I thought he was shoddily treated at the end," adds director Andrew Morgan. "It was just shocking that he ended up pissing his life away in Brighton. He was actually a very good producer, all the nitty gritty stuff worked well. If he had a weakness it was in the scripts, which weren't that good. But he was underrated."

"I think John was very influential in keeping the brand alive," argues Bonnie Langford. "He felt that there was a future to it. In a way, he empathised with those fans – he really did want to keep the show going not only because it had such a long history but because he loved it and loved doing it."

"I think," says Matthew Waterhouse, "that partly there's a loyalty to him because, by the end of his time on *Doctor Who*, he was being shunted aside and treated so shockingly badly by people at the BBC. This sort of narrative crept in that he was rubbish and he couldn't do anything. It just wasn't true. A lot of his period running *Doctor Who* was very, very good and always genuinely interesting, even when it wasn't always working. In Sylvester's run, there's a lot of really inventive, interesting stuff. This idea that it was really good and then Nathan-Turner came along and it's all bollocks is crap, completely untrue and unjust."

"He was a great talent," says director Graeme Harper. "People loved working with him and being in his aura – he was absolutely charismatic. He brought you into his secret den of iniquity. He said it as it was. If he thought something was wrong, he would say so and wouldn't mince his words. If he didn't like you, you weren't there. He was so enthusiastic and that's what I think is sometimes missing today – the enthusiasm from the producer and director.

If you can't drive the bloody thing, nobody else is going to do it. Both at the BBC and ITV, I've worked with some producers who shouldn't have been there. He was the epitome of what a producer should be – who cares about the people who are part of their show. He was a *real* producer."

EPILOGUE

In the picturesque village of Rottingdean, a Victorian lychgate forms a handsome entrance to the church. St Margaret's has been here since the 13th century and it stands imposingly within a graveyard of lush green grass. The Pre-Raphaelite artist Edward Burne-Jones is buried here, as is 20th-century novelist Angela Thirkell and the music hall entertainer, GH Elliott. On a flint sidewall, you can find a simple stone tablet engraved with the words:

> IN LOVING MEMORY
> KATHLEEN IRIS TURNER 19.11.22–28.11.2001
> JOHN NATHAN-TURNER, 12.8.47–1.5.2002
> PRODUCER OF DOCTOR WHO
> AND PARTNER
> GARY DOWNIE-PINKUS 17.7.40–19.1.2006
> ALWAYS LOVED ALWAYS MISSED

It is in this quiet corner that the ashes of all three were scattered. It seems fitting that, in death, John remains so closely linked with the two people he most loved in life.

There are gravestones at St Margaret's that date back hundreds of years. Some are so old that the names are now illegible. But even if this fate eventually awaits John's memorial, elsewhere he will never be forgotten. That's because as long as new generations are born, people will still care about *Doctor Who* and be charmed by its magic. All over the world, on screens great and small, from cinema-sized to tiniest mobile device, John Nathan-Turner's legacy will continue to enthral audiences, to annoy, amaze and amuse them. In this way, the little boy from Birmingham with the stars in his eyes has ensured his own peculiar, particular immortality.

ADDENDUM

EYES AND TEETH

Culled from my diary, emails and letters, this is a chronology of the writing of the book, the circumstances which accompanied its publication and the reactions which followed.

2010

24th June 2010 *Richard Marson diary extract*

Ordered Matthew Waterhouse's *Blue Box Boy*, his memoir of his time in *Doctor Who*. I know I shall find this interesting on various different levels. I vividly recall interviewing Matthew in the boardroom at Marvel's shabby Queensway offices back in the eighties. When he first arrived, he was clearly nervous, and the start of the conversation was somewhat stilted, his eyes darting from side to side before offering wary answers. He soon warmed up, however, and began to talk intelligently about his experience of stumbling into *Doctor Who*. After the euphoria of getting the part, it hadn't taken long for reality to bite. By this stage, Tom Baker's behaviour was out of control, and he evidently bullied more or less everyone around him, including Matthew. There was pain in the implied rejection of his eventual departure too, crying in a flower-filled cab on the way home from a lacklustre BBC send-off. I wonder how frank he will be at this distance of time? That's always the drawback of these *Doctor Who* books, they rarely talk about the individuals concerned as real human beings trying to get by in a difficult, contradictory, profession. It is all kept remorselessly bland with the same old tired, convention-friendly anecdotes with rarely a laugh at the ridiculousness of it all. If nothing else, working in television is *supremely* ridiculous, and yet no one in the *Doctor Who* world seems to have captured this aspect yet, still less brought to life what seems to me any kind of truth about the ramshackle process of making the programme which I observed, like Matthew, as a teenager myself.

1st July 2010 *Email from Tim Hirst (publisher) to Richard Marson*

Thank you for your order – it's a great book. Obviously I'm aware of you and your career (I've been a *Doctor Who* fan and reading *DWM* since about 1982). If you ever want to write a book, please let me know!

1st July 2010 *Email from Richard Marson to Tim Hirst*

When I saw that Matthew Waterhouse had written a book, I wanted to support it – he was kind to me back in the day and I always thought he got a very raw deal at the time. I'm looking forward to reading it. Funnily enough I have been toying with a couple of ideas for *Doctor Who* books – one is based on looking back at the years I worked on *DWM*, the studio and location visits, the interviews and the various controversies... hopefully funny and thoughtful. The other is more straightforward in that I'd love to tackle a proper biography of John Nathan-Turner, assuming I could canvass enough people willing to talk frankly and fairly about him and perhaps trace what if any family are left.

Let me know if either of those have any interest.

1st July 2010 *Email from Tim Hirst to Richard Marson*

Both books would be of interest, especially the JN-T biography

2nd July 2010 *Email from Richard Marson to Alistair McGown (friend and* DWM *writer)*

I've been asked by a guy called Tim Hirst (Hirst Books – know him? Know them – mainly *Doctor Who* actor memoirs?) if I'm up for writing a book for him. I've suggested a serious biog of JN-T and he's keen. But it would be a fuck of a lot of work cos I'd want to find out more about John's early life and career as well as bring a fresh and fair slant on what came later. Of course so many of his circle are dead and gone... but I'd be interested to hear your thoughts. Getting the contacts won't (hopefully) be the hard part – it will be the colossal process of interviewing, cross-checking, going back etc... but I must say I do fancy the idea.

2nd July 2010 *Email from Alistair McGown to Richard Marson*

I asked someone who had had vague dealings with Hirst and he said, "Yep, lovely bloke but ... the company tends to be Hirst doing everything himself. Hence the weak covers, poor typesetting and general air of cheapness. He won't pay for designers or anyone professional like that." Is he paying the writers? I genuinely don't know! So tread warily. A good JN-T biog would be fascinating.

4th July 2010 *Email from Richard Marson to Andrew Pixley (researcher and writer)*

I've been asked by Tim Hirst of Hirst Books (know him? know them? The autobiographies of various *DW* people) whether I am up for writing a book for them – and I suggested a biography of JN-T – which they are very keen on. However, if I embark on it, I would like it to be as frank, fair and wide ranging as possible (obviously) and I am going to need the key interviewees. Of course the available pool is dwindling in any case as the Grim Reaper calls.

If I do go ahead, I will try especially hard to find out more about John's early life and career and this will be a challenge as I'm guessing both parents are dead (he was an only child I think) and of course Gary has gone too.

5th July 2010 *Email from Biddy Baxter (producer) to Richard Marson*

Glad to hear you may be writing John Nathan-Turner's biog. My only memory of him was not as a floor assistant or an AFM but dealings I had with him when we were featuring the series on the programme. K9 in the studio, loads of Daleks, etc., etc. He was always pleasant and co-operative. Even though *Doctor Who* was wildly popular he didn't under-estimate the value of the programme being featured on *BP*!

7th October 2010 *Email from Tim Hirst to Richard Marson*

I wondered whether you'd had any further thoughts on your JN-T biography?

7th October 2010 *Email from Richard Marson to Tim Hirst*

Well, I am still interested – and compiled a list of possible interviewees but was waiting to hear from you and hear your thoughts! I guessed you were probably mighty busy hence the lack of a nag from this end.

Anyway, I think it would take a while to research (i.e. to do it well rather than just a cuts job – can't see the point of that). I have made some preliminary contacts and ascertained that I could access his papers in the NFA. I'd want to try to track some people who knew him when he was younger and on the way up. And also to weave in some of my own memories and experiences from that time.

Let me know what you think – and what kind of timeline/schedule you had in mind.

At this point the project foundered. I began to hear worrying stories about how Hirst Books was run and decided that they weren't the right people to work with. Life was also busy with other work, mainly for the BBC, including an unforgettable trip to Afghanistan for a series which sadly never happened because of the enormously complex and difficult logistics involved. But the idea stayed in the back of my mind and every so often, I would flirt with getting it off the ground again. Early in 2012, I was coming to the end of a wonderfully nostalgic six-month stint producing and directing a 90-minute documentary [Tales of Television Centre] *for the BBC celebrating Television Centre, which was due to be closed in 2013 for redevelopment. This amazing building, in which I, like so many others, had shared some of the most interesting and exciting years of my career, had been John's workplace and playground too and the thought of telling his story appealed even more. Immersed in so much nostalgia, I realised the book might be more than just John's narrative. It could be an allegory for the changing BBC and for the many creative and extraordinary people who became victims of that sometimes savage evolution. But I didn't allow myself to get too fanciful; I realised that the principal market was going to be* Doctor Who *fandom and, at that point, the publishers with the most consistent record in that field seemed to be a company called Fantom Films. I'd bought a couple of their books in the past;*

the sadly unfinished Barry Letts autobiography and, as a present for a former BBC colleague, the autobiography of film cameraman Fred Hamilton. Now I looked at some of their others too. In terms of design and layout, they were all fairly basic but the content was what mattered most and they clearly let their authors write the books which they wanted to write, which was important to me. So finally I decided to pitch JN-T once more. Just as I was composing the email, and, given how things turned out, by some strange coincidence, I had an email from someone else getting increasingly involved in this thriving niche market . I'd first met Matt West the previous October when he had interviewed me for his book on the Audio Visuals Doctor Who stories. We had hit it off straight away and stayed in touch.

2012

9th March 2012 *Email from Matt West to Richard Marson*

The rather ghastly direction the *DWM* thread is taking on Roobarb's [an internet forum] at the moment makes me wonder – given any more thought to that JN-T book?

9th March 2012 *Email from Richard Marson to Matt West*

Yes, I am going to do it, I think. Dive into the research.

9th March 2012 *Email from Richard Marson to Fantom Films*

I'm getting in touch as I'm wondering whether, with your impressive track record of *Who* books, you might be interested in one I have been thinking of researching and writing for some time? It would be the first biography of the late John Nathan-Turner – focusing mainly on his *Doctor Who* career but with a highly personal angle, attempting to illuminate the man from those who knew and worked with him.

I've written several books before – on *Blue Peter* and *Upstairs, Downstairs* – and for four years in the mid-80s was the regular features writer on *Doctor Who Magazine*.

Do let me know if the project sounds of interest to you and then maybe we can talk it through.

9th March 2012 *Email from Dexter O'Neill (Fantom Films) to Richard Marson*

Yes we would be interested. Any chance you could put together a short breakdown of the areas of research, what your aims are, research materials et al.

12th March 2012 *Email from Richard Marson to Dexter O'Neill*

As promised, my outline thoughts on how I would go about researching and putting together this biog.

I should explain first that it started life after an approach to me from Hirst Books – but I withdrew once I realised that their set-up wasn't really going to be able to cope with the books they'd already taken on. However, it does still seem to me a sound proposition – a biog of *Doctor Who*'s longest running producer, attempting to cast some light on the man before and after, as well as during, his extensive *Doctor Who* career, to explore why he seems to polarise opinion to such a degree – and aiming to explain how he saw the world and how this affected the way he worked and the many key decisions he made.

I'd need to go through the surviving JN-T papers held at the NFTVA in Berkhamsted and I'd also contact his old school to see if I could trace any contemporaries that way. I don't think there is any family left – but I would investigate.

Among the key interviewees, I would certainly aim to talk to the following: the Doctors with whom he worked (TB, PD, CB and SM), the companions (esp Janet Fielding and Sophie Aldred), Eric Saward and Jane Judge, Sarah Lee (the latter two his secretaries), Chris Bidmead, Andrew Cartmel, Fiona Cumming (among other directors), Ian Levine (who can also put me in touch with some of JN-T's non-*Who* friends), his bosses at the BBC – esp Jonathan Powell and David Reid and some of the key fans – David Saunders, David Howe, Gary Russell. I'll also ask RTD for his perspective.

I would also, of course, draw on my own (sometimes bizarre and even alarming) personal encounters with JN-T between 1983 and 1988.

The book – which I'd like to call *THE MEMORY CHEATS* (or perhaps *STAY TUNED*) – would be candid and revealing, without being salacious and would aim to present a range of perspectives on this important and controversial figure in the history of *Doctor Who*.

I think the research and interviewing would take about 6 months – on that basis, I'd aim to have the manuscript (of between 60-80,000 words max) completed by the end of the year.

I hope this gives you some idea of what I've got in mind.

14th March 2012 *Email from Dexter O'Neill to Richard Marson*

Many thanks for the detailed email – much appreciated. Here follows a rather rambling email, as I'm catching up on all sorts of loose ends today and have yet to get my brain into gear.

Barry Letts' *Who & Me* and Fred Hamilton's have been very successful, so we know that autobiographies of production crew will and can work. The only thing that puts us on the back foot is that it is a biography rather than an autobiography, and if memory serves me right JN-T did write and record his own memoirs. But having said that, I couldn't say we as an audience know who the guy is, so it has legs.

Just a couple of thoughts off the back of my head is that I would like one of the conclusions to the book to be a re-evaluation of his time on the show; he really was twenty years ahead of the time. Particularly on his stunt casting and character development, stuff which gained him negative press, but is done all the time in the new series. Also, it would be nice to investigate the items he left behind, lots of film reels etc - you don't know what sort of information can be gleaned from this...

We are currently looking for books for next February onwards.

14th March 2012 *Email from Richard Marson to Dexter O'Neill*

Yes, John's own memoirs were very selective, alas and not really indicative of the man and how he ticked. It's one of the reasons I think there is a gap in the market. That and the fact that I think there is a great story to tell here – lots of light and shade, ups and downs.

I would imagine that this would be the prime opportunity to re-evaluate his contribution to the show. I'd certainly chat to the guys who went through his estate – I know various interesting items were found as a result.

By Feb – do you mean you are looking for a book to publish in Feb or one to commission then? As I said, I'd expect to do a lot of interviewing and research for a really decent biog.

14th March 2012 *Email from Dexter O'Neill to Richard Marson*

We are currently looking to print and release books from February 2013, so delivery would need to be the beginning of December – so that would give you 8 months.

16th March 2012 *Email from Dexter O'Neill to Richard Marson*

Well – here are the terms of the agreement; let me know if you have any questions. I would want to meet up with you in a couple of months to discuss the project; and would want to see some preliminary work over the next three months just so I can keep of track of the project and make sure we are both on the right track.

27th March 2012 *Richard Marson diary extract*

Ian Levine is willing to 'spill the beans', as he puts it. In return he wants me to buy him a slap-up dinner in a restaurant of his choice. Now that I've finally decided to do this book, there are so many people to contact, so much research to do, that I'm more than slightly daunted. I realise how little I actually know about John's life before or after *Doctor Who*. Meanwhile, trying to think of the right title has been frying my brain and driving me crazy. I mean, realistically I know the title doesn't really matter yet but somehow I think once I christen it properly, this will help make the whole project feel more defined and real, rather than the abstract concept it has been for so long. When I first thought about it, I was going to call it *The Memory Cheats* but I've gone off that. It's more of a chapter heading. Instead, I'm going to suggest *Totally Tasteless: The Life of John Nathan-Turner*. Just thinking that with the right garish cover that would really stand out, especially to anyone not immediately familiar with who John was. It's suitably tongue-in-cheek, with a touch of the pantomime about it. And I think that it might inspire the designer to come up with a cover worthy of John and his passion for all things bright and sparkly. I distract myself by day-dreaming about what the finished book will look like, how it will feel in my hands, and then it's back to reality. There is *so* much to do and somehow it has to fit in around the day job.

2nd April 2012 *Email from Eric Saward to Richard Marson*

Thank you for your enquiry. I am sorry to say I do not have the time to talk about John Nathan Turner. Good luck with your project.

2nd April 2012 *Email from Richard Marson to Ed Stradling (TV producer)*

I've just had a 'no' from Eric Saward. His views on JN-T are not exactly shrouded in mystery. I was more interested in whether he viewed things at all differently at this distance of time – i.e. his views of doing the *Starburst* interview now etc etc.

2nd April 2012 *Email from Ed Stradling to Richard Marson*

Eric has almost nothing good to say about JN-T, and gets massively criticized every time he talks about him negatively. I think overall he would rather not talk about it, but he's prepared to do so on the DVDs because he's being paid a fee! Not entirely surprised he's not prepared to help with a book interview. Still there are always DVD interviews you can review and quote from. He's pretty much said it all in those.

2nd April 2012 *Richard Marson diary extract*

Left Television Centre soon after 7pm and drove up the M40 to Hanger Lane, to the restaurant where I've arranged to meet Ian Levine. I was early so I sat in a corner with a glass of red wine. Ian arrived at 8.20pm, flustered by his own lateness and full of apology. It's been years since I last saw him. He is bossy with the staff, who indulge him as he is a regular here. He immediately insists on us being moved to a back room where we can talk in peace, away from a family party who are having a raucous good time nearby. I say 'where we can talk', but it is a struggle to interrupt the flow as he off-loads the bitterness and resentment of years. It was impossible to keep him to any kind of timeline or chronology, it all just spilled out wherever the anecdotes took him. I virtually had to shout him down whenever I made an attempt to direct or focus the flow. He ate the way he talked, almost without interruption, and seemed offended that I stuck to two courses. There is no filter with Ian and he doesn't deal in shades of grey – everything is his way or no way – but he is not a hypocrite or a dissembler. What he says, he not only plainly means – he actually feels, and feels deeply. He is ridiculously opinionated but it is not quite the one way traffic you might be forgiven for taking it to be – he is anxious to be heard and understood too. There is an obvious vulnerability beneath the bombast. He rejects any suggestion that he may be on the autistic spectrum. As we got up to go, he hands me a pile of DVDs, copies of the various *Doctor Who* projects on which he has lavished thousands. He has been talking pretty much non-stop for three hours but his parting shot is accusatory: 'We've only scratched the surface!'

10th April 2012 Richard Marson diary extract

My last day on *Tales of Television Centre*. Quite a cocktail of emotions. I wandered down to the deserted *Blue Peter* garden, which is so full of ghosts. It's in a sorry state now; asset stripped with the sunken garden filled in. But the tree for the year 2000 is still there. I don't stay long, it's too depressing. There are so few people left in the building now and it is unnerving to walk past the parade of empty, abandoned offices. Lots of stuff to do today but managed to fit in a first chat, on the phone, with Fiona Cumming. She was cautious, protective towards John, to whom she and her husband had become a surrogate family. I wasn't really treating this as an interview, more a chance to state my credentials and intentions, allow her (and her husband Ian Fraser) to make their own judgement about how much they wanted to talk to me, and what they wanted to say. I explained that I'd first met them back in the eighties when I had been a teenage reporter on *DWM* and went to interview Fiona in their Brighton flat. She had been a total darling then, a softly spoken Scot with no pretensions to being a great director, happy to be regarded as she judged herself – a competent 'jobbing' director. I gave her my guarantee that she could see everything I eventually wrote – indeed, explained how I would welcome this from all the main contributors as it helps with the balance and perspective. It's the same technique I used on the TVC documentary, quoting interviewees back to each other, in the hope of achieving a more 'joined-up' tone and giving the whole film a conversational flavour. I think the same conversational flavour would work well in the book, and it would be a neat fit with the gossipy nature of John himself.

11th April 2012 Christopher H. Bidmead Tweet

Just finished being interviewed by a delightful chap, Richard Marson, for his upcoming book about John Nathan Turner. I got coffee & cake.

11th April 2012 Email from Matt West to Richard Marson

Bidmead's announced your JN-T book for you

11th April 2012 Email from Richard Marson to Matt West

Has he? Well, it's not a secret!
Lots of work to do though, to fit in around other projects

12th April 2012 Richard Marson diary extract

Spent a long day in the NFTVA archive at Berkhamsted, wading through all the JN-T paperwork which Gary Downie deposited here after John's death. It's a bit of a mess, not properly catalogued, but there are is some fascinating material all the same. I'm laughing out loud at some of the bonkers programme ideas he pitched. Don't suppose these did much for his reputation with the management. A case where less would definitely have been more.

16th April 2012 Richard Marson diary extract

Doing some development work for BBC Factual Entertainment, based in the uninspiring Media Centre, up the road from TVC. The Controller of BBC One is keen for development to come up with projects to revive the careers of Rolf Harris and Anneke Rice. Painting celebrities with their pets is the best they have come up with so far. I am not inspired.

30th April 2012 Richard Marson diary extract

Lunch at the Television Centre club to interview Gary Leigh (once Levy, editor of *Dreamwatch Bulletin*) for the book. He is very friendly and polite. Also quite nervous. But he is articulate and soon warms to his theme. He's clearly not forgiven John for what Gary considers to be his continual abuse of power, and for both John and Gary Downie's various attempts to neutralise the baleful influence of Leigh's fanzine *DWB*, and to seduce Leigh himself.

1st May 2012 *Richard Marson diary extract*

Met Patrick [Mulkern] for lunch. We sat on the benches outside the Media Centre and shared memories of John, Patrick chortling at the impressions of John's characteristic drawl I've dusted off from my repertoire. Mark Thompson, the DG, strolled past and I told Patrick how he had been crossing the doughnut (inner circle) at TV Centre when we had been filming the interview with Brian Blessed. Blessed had just been talking about the way the doughnut created the perfect acoustic, carrying the sound everywhere within the vast circle. We had to pause to let Mark Thompson exit the shot and when I explained to Blessed, he beamed and then shouted at the top of his famously booming voice, "The Director-General is a cunt!"

After work, meet up with my old mate Gabby (Jonathan Powell's wife), who drives me to the big house they share in Acton with her sons from her first marriage and his daughter from his first marriage. When I arrive I'm greeted first by their excited puppy, Blue, and then shown into Jonathan's study. He appears a moment or two later, smartly dressed in a suit and toying with his Blackberry. I don't tell him (perhaps I should but it feels too squirmy) that he was one of my early television 'heroes' – as a boy, I loved so many of the dramas he produced before he moved upstairs into management. These days he is a senior academic at Royal Holloway College, lecturing in the field about which he knows so much – television drama. Gabby deposits a tray of tea and biscuits and leaves us to it. It wasn't a promising start, with Jonathan claiming not to remember anything, but I could sense that this was just a defence mechanism. I bet he remembers every detail. But talking about *Doctor Who* is clearly not a prospect he relishes so it takes a while to get going. Then, gradually, he finds his voice and there turns out to be plenty to say, despite the occasional moment when he pauses and stares suspiciously at the little digital device I'm using to record this. In the end, it is all riveting stuff; there was obviously some anger and resentment, also a continuing bewilderment about why anyone intelligent should care about something like *Doctor Who* (though he is scrupulously complimentary about the contemporary revival – "but we didn't have people like that, who understood it and could do it and deliver," he says) and ultimately a degree of poignancy; he regrets the institutional cruelty of the way John was treated, and of which he was a part. It was, as he says, all a long time ago and Jonathan has had his own disappointments and personal battles since then. He is older, wiser, more compassionate. It's been a fascinating evening and it is Gabby I have to thank for persuading Jonathan to open up like this.

3rd May 2012 *Email from Richard Marson to Dexter O'Neill*

The interview with Jonathan Powell was brilliant. Very, very interesting and frank.

I have a title for you. Hope you like it. *WHO WAS JOHN NATHAN-TURNER?*

3rd May 2012 *Richard Marson diary extract*

The *Sun* have picked up on the various mentions of sex and drugs on the premises in *Tales of Television Centre*. Other papers predictably jump on the bandwagon and follow suit. Usual press office panic but once they are reassured that no one has been libelled and everyone has 'confessed' to these sins voluntarily, in a spirit of happy reminiscence, everyone calms down. Meanwhile, over in scheduling, some bright spark has suggested lumping the words 'Lights, Cameras, Action!' on the front of our already long title. I point out that in any case this is meaningless as it is a film rather than television term. Good old *Radio Times* (in the form of Patrick) save the day by saying that they are going to press with *Tales of Television Centre* and scheduling now back down "to avoid confusion in the listings."

6th May 2012 *Email from Dexter O'Neill to Richard Marson*

RE: *Who Was John Nathan-Turner?*

I like the title, but I would worry that the *Who* pun is a well worn one. Plus Michael E. Briant has done the same with the title of his autobiography released this month. Perhaps using his initials JN-T would have more of an impact, with a subtitle including his whole name?

9th May 2012 *Richard Marson diary extract*

Have joined Twitter. Apparently this is modern and the right thing to do. Post a photo of myself standing by a balcony on the roof of TV Centre. Gethin Jones texts me: 'You look like a budget version of Kate Winslet in *Titanic*.'

15th May 2012 *Richard Marson diary extract*

Tales of Television Centre screening at the BFI. A wonderful celebratory evening, with so many familiar faces – Sarah Greene, Katy Manning, Jeremy Swan, Babs, Dee Dee and Ruth from Pan's People, plus so many former staff colleagues and friends. It was packed to the rafters. I did a Q and A afterwards and then there was a party in the green room (with a meal to follow) at which Margot Hayhoe, once a Production Manager in drama, sought me out with some programmes of the pantomimes John produced in the 1970s. I was really touched she had gone to so much trouble and we had a brief chat about him. He was so well thought of in the years before he became a producer. Margot told me that he genuinely cared about his crews, wanted them to work hard but have a good time, too.

17th May 2012 Richard Marson diary extract

Tales is pick of the day in most of the press. Twitter goes bonkers during and after transmission. There is a lot of love for that old building!

18th May 2012 Email from Jonathan Powell to Richard Marson

I watched your film last night and thoroughly enjoyed it. Naturally I appreciated the fact that you had been good enough to retain some nice bits of my interview, but over and above blatant self-interest, I found the whole film really absorbing. Fabulous archive – I had never seen the Busby Berkeley tap dancing sequence before – and I was so impressed by some of the material you found – goodness knows how you dug it out. You seemed to me to manage to avoid all the pitfalls of making such a piece and produced something which was an affectionate, amusing and fitting tribute.

18th May 2012 Email from Russell T Davies to Richard Marson

Oh that documentary was absolutely spellbinding! What a wonderful piece of work, it had me hooting with laughter, and then crying at the end. Wonderful, wonderful, wonderful. And it brought back so many memories. Ah, golden days.

18th May 2012 Email from Richard Marson to Russell T Davies

I am in the early stages of researching a biog about John Nathan-Turner – a one-man Greek tragedy – at some point, perhaps you would have a chat with me about him – would love to include your thoughts about him.

18th May 2012 Email from Russell T Davies to Richard Marson

Blimey, a JN-T book would be a wonderful thing. He is tragic, somehow, isn't he? And he's very much the story of Old TV and New TV. I so wish he'd been around to have seen the success of new *Doctor Who*, I think he would have revelled in it. We would have carried him shoulder high!

19th May 2012 *Email from Colin Baker to Richard Marson*

First of all my congratulations on a superb programme about TV Centre – I got quite emotional about the loss of such a peerless facility and to recall so many memories of times spent there between 1970 and 1986. Practically every director, producer etc that appeared I knew or had worked with. Wonderful programme.

Anyway yes, insofar as my imperfect memory will be of use I would be more than happy to commemorate my dear and much missed friend JN-T.

21st June 2012 *Richard Marson diary extract*

Drove up the Westway with Patrick as we had both been invited to Ian Levine's 60th birthday party, being held at the same restaurant in which Ian had unburdened himself to me a few weeks ago. A huge table with an extraordinary mix of people from Ian's different worlds; music, *Doctor Who* and family. "Ooh," said one camp soul loudly, "there are hardly any women here." The equally camp man next to him piped up. "And the ones who are here aren't women, they're carers…"

Ian himself was loving every minute and kept introducing me to more people who he thought I should talk to for the book. Shortly after 11, I asked Patrick if he'd had enough. "Half an hour ago," he replied, wearily.

27th June 2012 *Email from Richard Marson to Dexter O'Neill*

You were quite right about the first title – too familiar. I have a new suggestion and this one I really like – hope you will too!

PRODUCER: *The Life and Scandalous Times of John Nathan-Turner*

What do you think?

27th June 2012 *Email from Dexter O'Neill to Richard Marson*

I'm going to be honest and say I'm not keen on that title either; I really do think that the title needs to have JN-T involved somewhere as that's what 99% of people knew him by – having said this, I think perhaps we should await till we see the text as a title will no doubt become apparent.

27th June 2012 *Email from Richard Marson to Dexter O'Neill*

I take your point re: title (sometimes emerging from the text) – let's brainstorm it more – it always helps when the right one emerges.

Other than trying to do my best to bring to life John's early life and career, which has never been covered before, I'm aiming to try to bring the man alive, with all his complexities and contradictions – examine why he divided opinions so sharply, explain the relationship with Gary and its significance (and issues relating from it), explore some of his famous (and infamous) decisions, conceits and prejudices, his relationship with fandom here and in the States, the background of how the BBC operated at the time and how it changed and how this affected him. There will also be stuff about his life following *Doctor Who* and his eventual decline and death, plus the legacy of the man – why he continues to matter.

I will also weave my own connection in there, my years on *DWM* and involved in fandom of the time, my dealings with John and Gary and my own subsequent experience of how the BBC works.

In terms of structure, I think it should only loosely be chronological – it may be a better read if the chapters are divided into themes which cover issues like 'sex', 'politics', 'controversy', 'star power' and so on and so forth.

My aim is to continue to immerse myself in the interviewing and research until the start of August when I will begin the manuscript.

28th June 2012 *Richard Marson diary extract*

Lunch with David Roden [writer]. Now working for BBC drama. He's charming and completely frank. Later, a telephone interview with Matthew Waterhouse, who lives in America these days and who laughs like a drain when I suggest that he was dared to do the 'web' scenes in *Castrovalva* with a visible erection. This has been a fan myth for donkey's years and it does seem like something which might have amused John. "That's a fabulous myth," he exclaims, "completely untrue but I like it." He is very interesting and perceptive, I think, about John, and enough time has elapsed for him to access the obvious pride and affection he has for the stories in which he appeared.

9th July 2012 *Richard Marson diary extract*

Another long day with the JN-T archive at Berkhamstead. Disinter some horrendous US convention photos in which everyone looks wildly drunk and distinctly seedy.

10th July 2012 *Richard Marson diary extract*

To BAFTA in Piccadilly to meet Andrew Morgan for a drink and to record his memories of John. AM is a very witty man; he'd just had lunch at Wagamama's and said, "They served me a plate of something that looked like ebb tide at Shanghai." He's a solid bloke, looks like a veteran rugby back, with a high colour and a booming laugh whenever something amuses him, which is often. He loved working for John and enjoyed the technical challenges of doing *Doctor Who*. We chatted about Jonathan Powell for a bit. "Do you know?," says Morgan, "It was my idea to dramatise the Mapp and Lucia books. I took them to Jonathan who rejected them on the grounds that they were too camp! Talk about missing the point...." Andrew had wanted Penelope Keith as Lucia and Prunella Scales as Mapp (Scales did eventually play the part in the LWT version). Beneath a stream of funny anecdotes, there was a reservoir of compassion and understanding too. He has known so many self-destructive types during his long career, it goes with the territory and he is illuminating about John the alcoholic. When we finish it is dark outside and pouring with rain. He has a small umbrella with him and we make our way towards the tube, huddled together under its inadequate shelter.

11th July 2012 *Email from Dexter O'Neill to Richard Marson*

I think your blurb and bio are excellent. I am gagging to read the book! I shall be officially announcing the title in the next two weeks.

15th July 2012 *Email from Richard Marson to Dexter O'Neill*

It's JN-T mayhem here – interviews and info piling up. Which is good.

I've mapped out a plan for 12 chapters of approx 6,000 words a piece plus a short intro.

16th July 2012 *Richard Marson diary extract*

Jeremy Swan texts me with a contact for Paul Stone, who I'm trying to trace for the book. "I must warn you, however, that I haven't heard anything from him in a long time. At our age, silence is not golden – but sinister..."

19th July 2012 *Richard Marson diary extract*

Tea with June Hudson in her tiny basement flat. She plies me with cakes bought from a nearby bakery. The whole place is crowded with interesting souvenirs of her long career, both as designer and actress, and she is a wonderfully engaging eccentric of the type that the BBC used to hoover up and keep gainfully employed for years. She loved John (it was mutual; he was deeply interested in "frocks") and talks about him fondly though without blinkers; she didn't approve of everything he did. She agrees to paint a special cover for the hardback edition. I'm there a couple of hours and I find our encounter life-enhancing and come away full of tea, cake and hope.

21st July 2012 *Richard Marson diary extract*

To Sheffield to this Fantom signing, where they have arranged for me to talk to Sarah Sutton and Clare Clifford. We huddle in the back of the little shop where the signing is taking place. This is the first time I have met Dex and Paul, the guys who run Fantom. Dex is small, round and very friendly. Paul, taller, thinner and less so, more waspish in manner. But they gossip cosily about the old actors and actresses who provide their bread and butter and obviously love what they do. We discuss the title again. They don't like *Page Turner*, not obvious enough. I suggest *JN-T: The Life and Scandalous Times of John Nathan-Turner*, the 'scandalous' being an obvious 'lure' but the placing of it with 'times' being significant; in other words, the 'scandalous times' refers to all the dramas John had to navigate during his *Doctor Who* years; the cancellation/postponement, the enforced sacking of Colin Baker, the Saward *Starburst* interview, the *DWB* 'JN-T Must Go' campaign etc. Dex and Paul like it. We are in business – a title we all agree on *at last*. The interviews go well; both women are on form and Clifford worked with both John and Gary on *Angels*, and for a time knew them socially, so that is a real bonus.

24th July 2012 *Email from Richard Marson to Dexter O'Neill*

Are we agreed on the title btw? – in other words – JN-T – The Life and Scandalous Times of John Nathan-Turner

24th July 2012 *Email from Dexter O'Neill to Richard Marson*

Yes – agreed :)

24th July 2012 Richard Marson diary extract

Interviewed Sophie Aldred at the British Library. She had a lot to say, and has offered me photographs and so on. As lovely as ever. John gave her a pretty tough time at the beginning but once they bonded, they got on famously. How could you not get on famously with Sophie?

28th July 2012 Richard Marson diary extract

Drove to Birmingham to sort through John's photographic archive and make selections. Struck me as profoundly melancholy that all this intensely personal stuff has ended up in the care of virtual strangers. John had so little in the way of family, and Gary was estranged from his, so their family were their friends. And when the friends didn't want stuff, they passed it on to fans, in whose care it now resides.

29th July 2012 Richard Marson diary extract

Spent much of the day wading through back issues of *DWM* from the eighties. I've not seen these in years. Staggered by how much drivel I wrote, but there are good bits here and there. It is powerfully nostalgic and not all in a good way. A pall of depression sets in long before I am done.

2nd August 2012 Richard Marson diary extract

Lengthy telephone interview with Fiona Cumming and Ian Fraser. They have been wonderful, sending photographs and taking a close interest in everything. Their grief has necessarily diminished over time but talking about John and Gary now and they become emotional as they talk about John's terrible decline and death.

4th August 2012 Richard Marson diary extract

With Patrick, to the party for *DWM*'s 450th edition. Various *Who*-lebrities milling about, including Steven Moffat, Mark Gatiss, Louise Jameson and Sophie Aldred again ("How are you getting on?" she asks me. "There's so much to do, I'm trying not to think about it – just totter on day by day!" I tell her). Long chat with Andrew Smith, mainly about his fascinating career in the police force. He wants to return to writing, having had early success on *Not the Nine O'Clock News* and, of course, *Doctor Who*.

5th August 2012 *Richard Marson diary extract*

Drove to Television Centre to be filmed for Russell Minton's DVD documentary about *Doctor Who* and TVC, and also because he has very kindly said I can take the opportunity to chat to his key contributors, Peter Davison, Janet Fielding and Mark Strickson. The eighties dream team! A bonus was that the whole thing was being presented by my old mate Yvette Fielding, who I hadn't seen in ages. She is still a terrible giggler. We reminisce about how she lived in fear of Biddy during her first year on *Blue Peter*. She was only a teenager and horribly homesick. Russell, whose day job is in BBC entertainment, is old school (and sensible) enough to have booked a proper make-up designer and so we all sit in the TC6 make-up room gossiping merrily. Janet accuses me of making her look "horrible" in *Tales of Television Centre*. "Oh yeah," say I, "that was the general idea." There was a busy schedule, but Russell had scheduled the gaps I needed to record separate interviews with each of the actors. After lunch, went to Blue Assembly with Peter Davison but a couple of minutes in, the battery on the voice recorder inexplicably cut out and so I had to flee to the make-up room, grab my car keys from my bag, race up to where I'd left the car in the multi-storey car park and retrieve some fresh batteries. Ten minutes later we resumed and I tried to seem outwardly calm while fighting the strong urge to throw up from all that unexpected and frenzied exercise on top of lunch.

13th August 2012 *Email from Ian Levine to Richard Marson*

I think that one day this book that you're writing will get made into a major feature film.

There's no other situation in television history quite like it – you only have to watch the documentary *Trials And Tribulations* [Ed Stradling's documentary on the *Trial of Timelord* DVD release] to see that. I don't think any other TV producer ever in history was more unsuited to the job. It makes Ed Wood look tame. Even recently, watching the extras on *Timelash*, where they all blame the bad acting on JN-T taking them away from rehearsals to do a convention in Chicago, followed by his pantomime, causing the TV show itself to suffer, I was shocked. And even Colin Baker, who normally defends JN-T, was critical.

19th August 2012 *Richard Marson diary extract*

Call from Andrew Pixley to say that Ian Levine has posted online that I'm doing a "hatchet job" on JN-T and that he, Andrew, is posting to contradict this. I don't look at these online forums and Andrew advises me not to start.

20th August 2012 *Email from Richard Marson to Dexter O'Neill*

Please hold off on issuing any official statement about the book or its title – I am involved in complex negotiations with a couple of potential interviewees and Ian bloody Levine has potentially buggered them up by claiming online that I am planning a "hatchet job" on John. As you know, it's a small world and this has caused trouble.

Equally as you know, I am absolutely not planning a hatchet job – rather a proper complex biography that doesn't shirk the difficult bits and controversies – but is also fair and compassionate.

Ian's characteristically unguarded comments did cause concern in various quarters. That same day I received an email from Colin Baker outlining his reservations about what Ian had said and, in consequence, declining my invitation for an interview. I responded with a lengthy email explaining my goals and the work that I'd already done, stressing that this was certainly not a "hatchet-job". The following day, Colin replied "Okay, you've convinced me."

25th August 2012 *Richard Marson diary extract*

Drove to High Wycombe to meet Colin Baker in a hotel. We got drinks and sat in a corner. He was absolutely fascinating, and, I think, absolutely honest. We were talking about a period in which he experienced the most terrific highs (getting the part of the Doctor) and the worst possible lows (the death of his son, Jack). He plainly still feels the injustice of how things turned out for him, though he is admirably loyal to John, who didn't fall on his sword when ordered to give Colin his notice. I wonder why he didn't. I suppose because it was so exactly what 'the men upstairs' wanted and John couldn't bring himself to give them the satisfaction.

27th August 2012 *Email from Colin Baker to Richard Marson*

It was a great pleasure to meet up with you – and it is a tribute to your relaxing interviewing style that three hours passed so quickly. I apologise once again for keeping you waiting at the beginning.

I am glad you feel that you got some useful stuff and will be happy to answer any further questions you may have.

*11 **September 2012** Richard Marson diary extract*

Meeting at Television Centre to discuss the *Doctor Who* characters we (Chris Chapman, the director, and I) want to use in this CBBC documentary I'm exec'ing about a deaf boy who is mad about the Doctor. Edward Russell (*Doctor Who* brand manager), rocking a polka dot shirt of which John would certainly have approved, met us and took us to a little room where we were presently joined by Caro Skinner, one of the current *Who* execs, small, dark and constantly texting until, after a few minutes, she sits down and we begin. This is the first time I've met her and Edward gave me a blush-making introduction. "Russell loves Richard, and so do we." I try to look suitably modest. Caro, clearly used to the hyperbole of telly folk, nods politely through all this spiel and then gets on to business. Use of the characters we wanted (Daleks and K9) is rapidly green lit. Our request to shoot a cameo with Matt Smith is not quite laughed out of the door but clearly isn't likely to happen. "His schedule is a TOTAL nightmare," sighs Caro, with feeling. We are not surprised but if you don't ask, you don't get. During the closing pleasantries, I told them both about the book and Edward's eyes lit up. "Oh, I can't wait to read that," he enthused.

*12th **September 2012** Richard Marson diary extract*

Meeting with Dex so that he can see the photos I've selected so far. He tells me that Janet Fielding is fighting cancer and also describes the incredibly depressing circumstances around Mary Tamm's recent death. This all has a very lowering effect.

*18th **September 2012** Email from Dexter O'Neill to Richard Marson*

All ready to announce tomorrow – just need one more thing from you – can I please have a quote – something about your agenda (if that's the right word) in approaching the book... something which says you are going to be open and frank, but in a positive nature – something to whet the appetite...!

*19th **September 2012** Email from Richard Marson to Dexter O'Neill*

How's this?

'John was a fascinating character who had a huge and enduring impact on *Doctor Who*. My biography, which tells the full story of his life and career, aims to be open and revealing, complex and compassionate. Along the way, I've been often surprised, sometimes shocked, occasionally saddened and frequently amused....'

19th September 2012 *Email from Dexter O'Neill to Richard Marson*

Great – all up and live now. First orders rolling in!

25th September 2012 *Email from Dexter O'Neill to Richard Marson*

You will be pleased to hear the book is the fastest selling we have had in the past two years.

4th October 2012 *Richard Marson diary extract*

Spent a long time discussing this emerging Jimmy Savile story with my exec, Anne. She was a researcher on *Jim'll Fix It* back in the eighties and said she learned very quickly always to carry lots of files about with her, or Savile would insist on grabbing her hand, kissing all the way up her arm. Vile man. Naturally, we invited him to contribute to *Tales of TV Centre* last year. Now heartily glad that he declined.

8th October 2012 *Richard Marson diary extract*

Waiting on the plane to fly to Monte Carlo, where are to film an interview with John Cleese for this documentary about the business of comedy. Just as I'm about to turn off my mobile, it rings. "Is this Richard Marson?" says an unfamiliar voice. "Er...yes," I reply. "Who's this?" "John" – and so much do I now associate John with JN-T, whom I know to be dead, I am momentarily confused and only just stop myself from saying "John who?" when the voice clarifies. "John *Cleese*." He was phoning to check all the details for the filming and invite me round for a drink before we shoot the interview – old-school professionalism.

20th October 2012 *Email from Matt West to Richard Marson*

Miwk has had a remarkable first half-year. We've only been trading for 6 months and we've trebled my forecast.

Wishing you no end of success with the JN-T book. Fascinated to read the final product. That hardback has to have a Hawaiian shirt dustjacket.

On an unrelated note, I've been following this Jimmy Saville stuff and was thinking, just a few months earlier and this would likely have made *Tales from Television Centre* a heck of a lot less joyous!

22nd October 2012 *Richard Marson diary extract*

Panorama on Jimmy Savile. Nauseating stuff and almost defies belief that he got away with it. Many of the shots of TV Centre were taken from the rushes of the documentary, which have been archived. Horrible to see them used in this context and to think how differently the poor victims must feel about the place.

23rd October 2012 *Richard Marson diary extract*

Telephone interview with Nicola Bryant. Her friendship with John came to a truly horrible end, and as she described this, she got increasingly upset. She said that she knew that once the account of how he spat in her face was "out there", she would be asked about it for the rest of her life. But she didn't retract.

28th October 2012 *Richard Marson diary extract*

First chapters finished and sent off to the publishers and various contribs.

7th November 2012 *Email from Dexter O'Neill to Richard Marson*

Just finished reading Chapter 2 – utterly fascinating and compelling. It says a lot about his personality and take on life – that he can embark on a three week holiday and splitting up with your partner on the plane out!! It's vivid and you have built the characters that you can imagine how Gary would have reacted to it!!!! (sic)

7th November 2012 *Fantom Films Tweet*

Just read the first two (rather excellent) chapters from the forthcoming JNT Biography by @richardmarson2 – you are in for a real treat!

7th November 2012 *Email from Fiona Cumming and Ian Fraser to Richard Marson*

We enjoyed the first chapters of the book, and found out much more about the first years than we had ever known.

It makes fascinating reading and the balanced picture you have portrayed by many different friends and not-so friends gives an insight into JN-T that sits well.

I would take issue with Mark Jones on John's culinary skills. I've seen Mark happily woofing down meals in Brighton with no complaints!

The Liz Rowell episode comes over with tact and caring. Eventually they remained good friends and worked together after a period of time. I think I sent you the Lanzarote crew photo outside the hotel which has Liz in the front row on the RH.

We found Gary changed a great deal after John died and came to the conclusion, that he had always felt insecure and in disbelief almost that John had chosen him. He could be quite jealous of anyone getting too close to John.

We look forward to the next chapters and are in awe of your energy.

10th November 2012 *Richard Marson diary extract*

The Director General, George Entwhistle, has been forced to resign (having scarcely started the job) as a result of this *Newsnight* scandal. The madness of this constant blame/apology/resignation culture. Don't see any newspaper editors resigning for the pernicious lies they print daily, nor for their collusion in Savile's use of charity and PR to protect himself. So much hypocrisy.

11th November 2012 *Richard Marson diary extract*

Phone Ian Levine to talk him through the sections in which he is quoted or discussed. It's a long call but, though he is practically frothing at the mouth at some of the things people like Paul Mark Tams have said about him, he asks for nothing to be cut or changed.

15th November 2012 *Email from Dexter O'Neill to Richard Marson*

Just a quick email to say I have read Chapters 3 and 4, and found them to be extremely interesting! Especially love the contextual colour – I think it is very easy for us to have a hindsight view on John and the BBC – but you manage to get the reader into the right mindset for consideration of JN-T!

[Later same day]

Chapter 5 read! LOVE the title. Just fantastic, intriguing stuff, all the information is cleverly handled.

16th November 2012 *Email from Brian Spiby [former BBC drama department manager] to Richard Marson*

I must say you have skewered JN-T precisely. I can vouch for all of the facts (and most of the opinions) you have recounted. It's a very accurate – warts and all – picture you paint particularly of John's career up to his appointment as the producer of *Doctor Who*. Obviously our paths diverged when I became a producer and I was no longer so close to him as I had been but his subsequent troubles on *Doctor Who* were well-known throughout the Department. On a personal level it was fascinating to see how many of the people I used to work with are still at large. I am sure the book will be a great success.

20th November 2012 *Email from Dexter O'Neill to Richard Marson*

Just a quick email to say I have completed reading, up to date!

I do think we have to be careful that certain comments aren't taken in isolation without the context of everyone else's and your commentary – which people will evitable do (sic). but we can discuss this in detail tomorrow!

All good stuff, where are you at in the grand scheme of the book – I must have had 40,000 words? Half way?

29th November 2012 *Email from Fiona Cumming to Richard Marson*

Re: Chapter 9

What an interesting episode!

The machinations of what was going on behind scenes now make sense to me! I had a phone call from John telling me that the show had been cancelled and the Wally K Daly script I was due to direct would not go ahead. It was completely out of the blue and I didn't take it in properly. "Have you signed your contract?" he asked, which I had (it was honoured). He then explained it wasn't just that script but the whole programme. Unbelievable.

Jonathan Powell certainly shows himself in an unflattering if I suspect true light. John had tried on many occasions to come off *Doctor Who* and move on to another programme, but was told he was indispensable to the programme. The result being that when the programme went he was totally dispensable. It was such a waste of a very talented man.

Ian Levine had such an encyclopaedic knowledge of *Doctor Who* that JN-T thought of him as a friend and did rely on him with reference to fandom. Once IL overstepped the mark and thought of himself as in charge the split between them was inevitable.

My Ian has read this and agrees.

3rd December 2012 *Email from Richard Marson to Eric Saward*

I'm fast completing my biography of John and, once again, I wanted to invite you to contribute.

I've tried to represent your viewpoint from existing sources but there is naturally no substitute for a direct quote.

If you'd still prefer not to talk to me (either in person or over the phone – or even answering a few questions via email), I shan't bother you again – but I did want to reiterate the invitation.

Eric Saward did not reply to this email

8th December 2012 *Email from Andrew Cartmel to Richard Marson*

Many thanks for letting me look at this.

First off let me say I think it's really well written, lively and vivid and magnificently researched – it brings it all back, and also tells me things I didn't know.

I only scrutinised sections in which my name was mentioned; forgive me, but pressure of time imposed this approach. So if I'm cunningly referred to, not by name, in the text you better tell me!

I've gone through with track changes on in Word and made some minor changes and corrections – mostly trying to clarify what I wanted to say.

I've also changed the description of myself from 'geeky' to 'bespectacled'. I trust you won't object.

Please look at my changes and, if there's anything you're not happy with, kindly drop me a line and we'll fashion a compromise.

I very much appreciate being kept in the loop.

Here are the chapters back again. The preface is included for completeness' sake, but I didn't make any alterations to it, just the four chapters.

Good luck with the book. It deserves to be a considerable success. Let me know if I can help with a quote for it.

9th December 2012 Email from Richard Marson to Andrew Cartmel

Well, thank you – both for the very positive comments overall, which mean a lot, and for taking the trouble to hone your own contributions – an unexpected bonus.

9th December 2012 Email from Andrew Cartmel to Richard Marson

It's really good stuff. I love the chapter titles!

10th December 2012 Email from Richard Marson to Patrick Mulkern (*Radio Times writer and friend*)

I am finally there.

It's been a really emotional day (family shit) – perhaps the right day to get to the end of this.

I'm pleased with it. It made me cry! (but anything does that sometimes)

11th December 2012 *Richard Marson diary extract*

Commentary recording for the *Business of Comedy* with Eddie Mair, from Radio 4. He is excellent, total pro, makes good suggestions, also very funny. We walked back to the TVC multi-storey car park together and he asked what I was doing next. I told him about the John book, never thinking he would have a clue who I was on about but turns out that Eddie is a bit of a *Doctor Who* fan on the side, and he knew exactly who John was. He grilled me about the book until we reached our cars and then said, "You've got yourself another sale," as we said goodbye.

12th December 2012 *Richard Marson diary extract*

Watched *K9 and Company* for the umpteenth time. Amazed how much enjoyment I get from this.

16th December 2012 *Email from Andrew Pixley to Richard Marson*

Thank you very much indeed for the last two chapters of your magnum opus. I had the opportunity to read these last night, and I am delighted to say that I am now sure that this is one of the very best books I've ever read. And I don't mean *Doctor Who* books – because it isn't that really – but books in general, and biographies in particular. This is up alongside Harry Thompson's work on Peter Cook, or Mark Lewisohn's piece on Benny Hill or the Humphrey Carpenter tome on Dennis Potter.

It is a massive skilful and talented piece of work which does justice to an amazing man.

20th December 2012 *Email from David Reid to Richard Marson*

Your book about John is, I think, quite wonderful on many, many levels. Initially I was fascinated by your motivating reason for writing the book – two guys slaving away to keep fresh shows the BBC had essentially come to lose interest in at vaguely similar times. The fact that you met John (and how and when) – adds an amazing kind of spice to why you are so determined to tell his story.

However, for me your book goes way beyond this and in the story you tell (and how you tell it) it becomes gripping, fascinating, appalling – and, by the end truly moving.

It is written with such energy and gusto that I defy anyone who starts reading to put it down. This, allied to your immaculate research makes the whole utterly trustworthy from beginning to end.

There were aspects about John and (definitely) Gary's life that were probably truly reprehensible. I admired enormously the way you did not duck a single issue but brought things out into the open in order to draw conclusions that were very well argued and, I felt, entirely fair and convincing.

I suppose I am mildly biased because of when I was at the BBC but I also greatly admired your ability to conjure up the atmosphere and *mores* of the times. The whole thing – to me – felt 'spot on'.

A pretty good test of a writer is do you tell the reader exactly what he/she wants to know at the moment he/she wants to know it! I'd say you pass with flying colours.

27th December 2012 Email from Fiona Cumming and Ian Fraser to Richard Marson

Recovering from Christmas Rush, pre and post, and thought I'd better get back to you as I know the book is due out in March.

Chapter 12

During this period I was working in ITV and so the connection with John and Gary was more social than work but I was aware of JN-T's feeling of a conspiracy against him. Ian was working as Production Manager on several *Who*s so I'll leave him to say a few lines.

I would like to point out that Susannah Shaw was not allowed to walk off *The Greatest Show*, Gary was sent to supervise her so she stayed on. However I got a call from John asking me to supervise her for the run of the show and Gary went back to TC to go on to *EastEnders*. I don't think that was the reason but I did not discuss it with John.

Richard, you and I must have worked together when you were working with Louise on *Who*. Ian.

Chapter 13

By this period Ian and I were working in Denmark, keeping in touch by phone and seeing J and G in the summers when we came home for the long break. The consumption of alcohol had always been a feature but I never saw JN-T drunk. It must have been a case of constant topping up in order to function.

There is a quote from Barry Hannam, after Nicola Bryant's quotes on bribing the barman to serve her soft drinks, which comes earlier in the chapter than the explanation of who Barry is, which might not make sense to those who don't know him. Barry was a lasting friend who was totally outside the *Doctor Who* group and set-up, who gave them both a refreshing outsider's look at life.

In the para about follow spots on *Mother Goose*, John would yell "Line" very loudly, is a misprint for Lime. The young technicians hadn't a clue what lime meant.

Chapter 14

During this period Ian was in Estonia and I was in Scotland where we had moved after returning from Denmark but there was constant contact each week and we knew that the health issues were paramount. The cruellest thing on a personal level with them was that Kath died in the November, giving the pair of them freedom from responsibility and it was only five months later that John died.

When I was clearing up in the Brighton house I found *The Radiant Way* among John's possessions. It was the first schoolbook to teach a child reading and I recognised it immediately as I too had learned to read from it ten years earlier than him. I still have it.

We both still miss the pair of them and have enjoyed reading the draft of your book. You've given a very rounded version of how the regard John was held in differed so widely. Please let us know if we can be of any more help.

Happy New Year!

31st December 2012 Email from Sophie Aldred to Richard Marson

Am loving the JN-T chapters; completely addictive – scurrilous, fascinating, hilarious and naughty – I am sure it will all put an enormous cat amongst the pigeons. Just wish he and Gary were around to read it! Loads of love

2013

10th January 2013 *Email from Richard Marson to Dexter O'Neill*

Here you go... preface, all the chapters, the acks, photo guide and captions, note and back cover blurb. Happy reading!

10th January 2013 *Email from Dexter O'Neill to Richard Marson*

All received!

Well done – I'll give it one more read over while I am off next week, and then get it to the typesetters!

11th January 2013 *Email from Grahame Flynn to Richard Marson*

I must say that this is a wonderfully balanced account of my old friend's life. Warts and all!

12th January 2013 *Richard Marson diary extract*

Off to the BFI for the first of this year's monthly 50th anniversary [*Doctor Who*] screenings, starting with, naturally enough, the opening story, *An Unearthly Child*. The green room was packed. Had a chat with Clive Doig, who is always funny and irreverent and then William Russell, who said that he never thought he would live to see the 50th anniversary. But he seems much younger than his years and as sharp as a tack, even in this noisy environment, with all kinds of people competing for his attention. Edward Russell bounds up and asks if I'll sign his copy of my *Upstairs, Downstairs* book. Mark Gatiss also very sweet and complimentary about it and I say I hope they'll both like JN-T too. A chorus of knowing laughter. Caro Skinner joins us. She is very friendly indeed – and knows how to work a room all right, but there is nothing perfunctory about it. She has a refreshingly direct manner and is truly charming about the way she darts neatly from one conversation to another. A natural born hostess, I'd say. The story itself is a magnificent piece of work, given its age. I am in awe of what they achieved.

22nd January 2013 *Email from Louise Arthur* (The Culture Show researcher) *to Dexter O'Neill, forwarded to Richard Marson*

I am working on a *Doctor Who* special for *The Culture Show*. Presented by Matthew Sweet, the programme will be broadcast on BBC Two in 2013 and will look at the cultural significance of *Doctor Who* – how cultural change made *Doctor Who* and how *Doctor Who* changed culture. We will argue that the show is a product of fifty years of extraordinary social change and unprecedented uncertainty, and explore how the teams who created it produced a unique body of work that reflects the anxieties and trials of the changing times. In turn, we'll argue how the show has become a cultural force in its own right, the innovations and originality of its music, design and storytelling reverberating through the decades, feeding the imaginations of the cream of British creative talent today.

I am keen to talk to Richard Marson about John Nathan-Turner and *Doctor Who*. I know you are publishing Richard's book on this topic in a couple of months and wonder if you could put me in touch with him. As we will be filming between February 4th – 17th, it would be great to be able to chat to him on the phone as soon as possible.

28th January 2013 *Email from Jude Ho* (The Culture Show producer/director) *to Richard Marson*

I'm directing *The Culture Show* special on *Doctor Who*. Thank you very much for talking to Louise! Think you'll be a really great contributor in the show.

I hope you don't mind me asking, but our Execs are a little worried about JN-T and his sexual activities!

We've been talking to ed pol [Editorial Policy] in the wake of Jimmy Saville and we're keen to double check a few things. In an ideal world I'm not especially interested in telling the JN-T story of him having sexual relationships with the fans as I don't think it's relevant to the Cultural significance of *Doctor Who*. However everyone is keen to exercise caution post-Saville and to make sure the BBC isn't going to be accused of a cover up, etc. Our ed pol adviser is keen to know the following which will help us work out if we need to mention it in the programme.

1) What was the extent of JN-T's sexual relationships with fans?

2) Is there evidence they were below the age of consent? (over 21 until 1994, when it was lowered to 18. Lowered to 16 in 1997)

3) How substantial is the evidence that JN-T had relations with the fans? How widely known was this at the time? How widely known is it now?

4) Is there definite proof that he had sex with fans?

5) Was there any evidence that these relationships were not consensual?

Look forward to hearing from you

28th January 2013 *Email from Richard Marson to Jude Ho*

Perhaps you could give me a call to chat about this?

29th January 2013 *Richard Marson diary extract*

In Marks and Spencer when the phone rang. It was a researcher from *The Culture Show* wanting me to send her a copy of the book. I declined but said I was happy to speak to someone from Editorial Policy, if that would be helpful. A while later, the series producer called me back and also pressed me for a copy – "even if under embargo". Didn't like his approach at all. Went from smarmy to aggressive without passing go. "Otherwise we may not be able to feature the book on the programme," he told me. "That's fine. You're not transmitting till November, are you?", said I. "Plenty of time to read the book when it is published. We can talk then, if there is anything to talk about."

Some time later, I was again called, not this time by anyone from *The Culture Show* but by the head of the department which makes it, Music and Arts. He asks if I will contribute evidence to the Dame Janet Smith investigation. I explain that late last year I actually had been consulted about *Top of the Pops* and the relative layout of dressing rooms here and at the Television Theatre. But that was in relation to Jimmy Savile, which was surely the remit of the committee? Apparently, they are also looking at the culture of the BBC at this time, for context. So I agree to speak to someone involved.

When I do, I relate what I think is relevant about the culture of the times – in terms of liberal drinking, sex on the premises etc – but I'm clear that I found nothing about John to put him in the same category as Savile. He was no better or worse than many of his contemporaries, emphatically not another Savile.

1st February 2013 *Richard Marson diary extract*

Dex came to St Albans to meet and talk through everything that's outstanding. He was 45 minutes late so I sat in the cafe drinking coffee and reading the newspapers. When he arrived we talked though a possible approach for publicity and I handed over all the photos and the cover artwork June Hudson had painted specially. Exciting to think that we are getting so close now. He ran through various events he wants me to take part in. "I'll do whatever you need," say I. An easy booking, that's me.

4th February 2013 *Richard Marson diary extract*

A grim start to the week. An email from Colin Baker declining to write the foreword for the book and outlining his various objections to what I've written. He was apparently hurt by some of the comments that others have made about him in the text. I'm really sorry he has taken it this way. I liked him so much when we met and was expecting some notes or tweaks, a negotiation, not this complete rejection. I wrote a careful and detailed response and then, a short while later, took a call from Dex. He ummed and ah'ed and slowly stammered through what he wanted to say but it was horribly obvious what he was leading up to. And so it turned out. He said that he had felt a bit uneasy for some time (a secret he kept well) and that he now didn't feel that they were "the right publishers to support your book". Apparently, it had been Colin's email (sent to us both) that had tipped the balance. They are understandably scared of upsetting him because they make their living running events with cast members. If they went ahead, incurring Colin's displeasure, not only would he withdraw from these, but might encourage others to boycott the business too. I did my best to stay calm, although I felt really furious at the feeble expression of so much weakness. Talk about mixed messages. Only last week, when we had met, Dex had been all smiles and encouragement. But even as we were going through the details of the divorce, I was thinking, "What now, where next?" – I immediately thought of Matt West, who had always been interested in the book.

We'd met when he interviewed me for his history of Audio Visuals and I had liked him at once. His dark sense of humour and cynical world view appealed to me. There was nothing fake about him whatsoever. And he has a roster of interesting books, though I hate the name of his company – Miwk. What's that all about? Not good to have a company name that you can't even pronounce easily. Still, that's the least of my problems right now. It's time to get emailing and work out a rescue plan.

Colin's email put forth his position in detail. In the main, his concerns related to the recent Savile revelations. He believed, not unreasonably, that the book would attract unwelcome media attention despite the lack of any evidence of paedophilia on John's part. He lamented the fact that British law makes it impossible to libel the dead. However, he did not request any changes, cuts or amendments to the significant contributions he had made to the text.

4th February 2013 *Email from Richard Marson to Colin Baker*

Naturally, I was sorry to read this but I am grateful that you took the trouble to explain your feelings.

My own view is that 'de mortuis nil nisi bonum' cannot apply to any serious or rigorous history or biography – that would result in mere hagiography (and what is the point of that?) There are many painful aspects to John's story – but my aim was always to produce a complex, detailed, thought provoking and yet compassionate account of his life. I believe I have achieved this.

I'm sad that you were upset by some of the comments made about you by other contributors. I think readers will only be sympathetic to you and the hand you were dealt, as I am myself. Any negativity is there as a necessary reflection of the motives and opinions of other key players and I am sure will be seen as such. You are a good actor and a good man, who was served an impossible hand.

Again, thanks for reading the book and giving me your reasons for declining the invitation to write the foreword.

4th February 2013 *Email from Richard Marson to Matt West*

As you'll know, I've written a biography of John Nathan-Turner.

Despite a contract and the completion (to their apparent delight) of the work, Fantom Films, who were lined up to publish it, have now decided to withdraw.

They feel unequipped to deal with the probable scale of press interest and they are concerned that they may upset some of their convention guests (the bread and butter of their business).

I am (naturally) keen to find the right home for the work, which I'm really proud of.

4th February 2013 *Email from Matt West to Richard Marson*

Good grief! I'm rather shocked by that.

Could you send me the manuscript? I'll look at it with Phil (our proofing/editing guy).

I can't imagine there's anything in there that would scare us as events aren't really our thing. But even so, surely things can't have been said that are so bad they'd upset current cast and crew?

As you know I'm incredibly excited about the book, my order was in months ago. I'd be delighted to chat it over.

5th February 2013 *Email from Matt West to Richard Marson*

Christ, Richard. I'm blubbing like a little girl here. This book is everything I'd hoped it would be. Totally unbiased and just … appropriate.

I don't know if you ever saw Robert's rejected cover [the one ultimately used for the Miwk edition] but I rather like it. Dex wanted to use an image from *Time Flight* but it's not great quality.

There's something about the showbiz smile of this one (a passport photo of John) that I like. What do you think? Nice silver-embossed signature as well of course.

5th February 2013 *Richard Marson diary extract*

All day long the rescue plan flourished. Matt has much better ideas about design and actual craft. He seems to genuinely care about all the details.

6th February 2013 *Email from Matt West to Richard Marson*

Refunds have gone out from Fantom and we've been besieged with re-orders!

11th February 2013 *Richard Marson diary extract*

Marc Sinclair texted to ask if the book had been cancelled, saying that this is what he had heard from Eric Saward!

17th February 2013 *Email from David Roden to Richard Marson*

I've read it now. Oh my god, I wanted to read the rest of the book. Beautifully written, Richard. And so many things I didn't know, and stuff I'd forgotten – either deliberately or just from the passage of time. It's interesting how pretty much everyone says the same things about the two of them.

I think it's also incredibly moving – a tragedy in so many ways. The awful way in which the BBC rid themselves of both John and Gary, and the deep lack of loyalty displayed. Times were clearly changing at the Beeb, and obviously John and Gary were so clearly part of the 'Old Guard'.

It was a very hard read – and reduced me to tears on several occasions. Such a sad end.

It's great to have been part of it, and I will be intrigued to hear what the reaction is.

Well done, matey!

28th February 2013 *Richard Marson diary extract*

Starburst interview published online. A flurry of texts, tweets and emails as a result. It's not a piece of journalism – just a Q and A, and I cringe at some of my phrasing and waffle, which hasn't been judiciously edited or tidied up in any way.

At home with John and Gary, July 1973
(JN-T collection)

(above left) and right) P.U.M.'s the word – shooting *All Creatures*
(courtesy: Les Podraza and David Crozier)

Producer at last – shooting *The Leisure Hive*....

(JN-T collection)

.....and *Logopolis*

(JN-T collection)

(above left) Eyes and teeth *(courtesy: Dominic May)*

(above right) Producer as Star; at the Stoneleigh Town and Country show, 1984

(JN-T collection)

Convention circuit, Tallahassee, March 1985

(JN-T collection)

Who's who? New Orleans, July 1985

(JN-T collection)

Sharing the limelight – *(L to R)* David Saunders, Colin Baker, John

(JN-T collection)

(above left) Cinderella, January 1982 *(courtesy: Dominic May)*

(above right) Making the point, 1984 *(JN-T collection)*

Panto stars, January 1985 *(JN-T collection)*

Two views of John's office

(JN-T collection)

About to pull – New Year's Day, 1991

(JN-T collection)

(above left) Have Dalek will travel – en route to Edinburgh
to promote WH Allen – August 1985 *(courtesy: Dominic May)*

(above right) On holiday in Crete, 1989 *(JN-T collection)*

(above left) Straight to video, 1992 *(JN-T collection)*

(above right) Wedding guests – Fiona Cumming and John *(ccourtesy: Fiona Cumming)*

Flying the fag, New Orleans, July 1985

(JN-T collection)

2nd March 2013 *Ed Stradling on Facebook*

I think there is an increasing tide of opinion that this year is not the best time to publish the book, and I suspect that will view likely be reflected in any licensed media. There are two issues, firstly concerns about the salacious content of the book (with which I have no sympathy), and secondary concerns (which I do sympathise with) about tabloids picking up the story and turning it into bad headlines for *DW* and the BBC. Which may or may not happen. And obviously it's massively in Matt's interest that it should! In Matt's shoes I would absolutely go ahead and publish the book – which is brilliant by the way. But if I were in charge of an oft-tabloid-quoted-BBC-licensed magazine, I'm not sure I'd give it much coverage.

3rd March 2013 *Richard Marson diary extract*

Matt and Mark arrived to shoot the interview he suggested a while ago. The idea is to put this online to answer most of the obvious questions and make our intentions clear. One of the first conversations we had was about the approach to publicity. We both agreed that we didn't want to let any of the tabloids anywhere near it. Other than the genre press, we are thinking that *The Guardian* and perhaps the other broadsheets (if they don't think it is beneath them) are the only credible newspaper options. Matt has a watermarking security system for the review copies which means he can trace where they end up, which will be useful. He's keen to avoid copies getting into the wrong hands.

3rd March 2013 *Email from Matt West to Richard Marson*

I still don't think tabloid interest will actually generate sales. It'll generate web hits, but outrage alone won't sell a book about a *Doctor Who* producer to someone who's not a fan.

I have however been wondering about sending a copy to *Gay Times* for review. Any tabloid chatter will have an unpleasant homophobic subtext to it. Why not get the gay readership on-side to defend it? They're far more reliable than *Who* fans.

3rd March 2013 Email from Richard Marson to Patrick Mulkern

Looks like *DWM* will be boycotting the book!

3rd March 2013 Email from Patrick Mulkern to Richard Marson

That shows better than anything how they're obliged to operate. I bet they all drooled over it with envy. A *DWM* boycott will prob have negligible impact on sales. Maybe the kiddies' mag, *DW Adventures* will big it up.....!

4th March 2013 Richard Marson diary extract

The book has gone off to print!

10th March 2013 Richard Marson diary extract

Matt texted to say that *SFX* have given the book a five star review. Apparently this has already stirred up a reaction online. Amazing that so many people feel confident to go out there and voice very strong opinions about something they can't have read yet. I think this is testimony to the feelings still inspired by John himself and take it as a compliment to him and his enduring power to divide fandom.

11th March 2013 Email from Matt West to Richard Marson

The Guardian have come back and confirmed they are running a review shortly and it looks like Paul Laity is handling it himself.

I'm going to simply ignore the emails from the tabloids, just as I've ignored a lot of the other review requests. One interesting one was Den of Geek which I noticed came from a Hotmail address. I asked them to confirm the guy requesting the copy was doing so on their behalf and they said they'd never heard of him. Oh, internet. You're so … fucking annoying.

11th March 2013 Email from Matt West to Richard Marson

Guardian have asked me to forward a review copy to <drumroll please> Matthew Sweet.

Always nice when our customers review our books. I think he's already ordered it

11th March 2013 *Email from Richard Marson to Matt West*

He's also presenting the *Culture Show Who* special who phoned me a couple of days ago, desperate for a copy which will inevitably circulate upstairs at the BBC.

The Culture Show say they still want to interview me but once they've read the book!

13th March 2013 *Richard Marson diary extract*

Matt has had a flood at home, causing massive damage and effectively putting him out of action at what is turning into a very busy time. He's apologetic and highly stressed.

14th March 2013 *Email from Josh Halliday* (The Guardian) *to Matt West*

Is *The Guardian* the only newspaper with a review copy? We're keen to run our review (which has already been written) but I've been asked to see if there's a standalone news story to run alongside it, which I just started this pm. I'm speed reading the book as we speak.

14th March 2013 *Richard Marson diary extract*

Frantic calls from Ian Levine; that Matthew Sweet had been on the phone to him last night asking if Ian has had his lawyer read the book – with particular reference to the section where Ian is referred to as acting as John's pimp! Sweet has genuinely put the wind up Ian, talking about the possibility of criminal action. "The thing is," Ian shouts in my ear, "It's all TRUE!"
I reassured him that I thought it was fanciful in the extreme to think that Ian would be the subject of any legal action. Who from and on what grounds? Not sure what remit this Sweet man (John would have nicknamed him "Sour" in a heartbeat) thinks he is operating under – thought his job was to write a review not stir the shit with the contributors.

Meanwhile, poor Matt is having to move to a hotel for twelve weeks while his flooded house is repaired. "I'd say it never rains but it pours..." I venture. He cuts me off. "Too soon" he says and we laugh in a savage kind of way at the bad luck and timing of all this. We kept in touch throughout the day as it seems that *The Guardian* are now treating the book as a news investigation rather than a review. In between the various calls and email, I'm contacted by CBBC and asked if I might be interested in exec'ing a documentary series about cheerleaders. Oh the crazy world of showbiz.

15th March 2013 *Email from Louise Arthur* (The Culture Show) *to Richard Marson*

Just wondered if you have a firm publication date for the book yet? We are keen to set a date for the interview with you.

15th March 2013 *Richard Marson diary extract*

Patrick called. He'd been to the press launch for the new *Doctor Who* series. He'd had a chance to talk to Matthew Sweet, whose attitude was all "this hurts me more than it hurts you". He told Patrick he thought that the book wasn't very well written ("like a fanzine"), although he commended the depth of the research. He remarked that *The Guardian's* lawyers were "jumping on chairs" about it and added that the BBC were in "a right tizzy" about it too.

17th March 2013 *Twitter direct message from Matthew Sweet to Miwk Publishing*

BTW, as you probably know, the *Guardian JN-T* review was held back for a week – probably the most lawyered book review it's ever published!

18th March 2013 *Email from Ed Stradling to Richard Marson*

There is a feeling of antipathy towards the book in what might be regarded as the senior fan press. I think you can expect a negative review from Matthew Sweet and I believe that *DWM* have decided not to run a review of the book at all, which strikes me as a strange decision but I think the alternative would likely be another negative review.

Clearly there are a lot of people who simply don't like to see a senior *DW* name dragged through the mud like this. These are people whose opinions I would normally agree with but they appear to have come to the decision that it's a bad book, a decision that's all-too-easy to reach if you find the subject matter distasteful or if you've already taken the view that such a book should not have been published.

I can only assume that these people don't find the workings of the BBC drama department in the 80s as interesting as I do.

18th March 2013 Email from Richard Marson to Ed Stradling

I didn't see the book as dragging anyone through the mud but then most of the revelations within it are not a shock to me.

I do think there is a lot of hypocrisy and humbug involved in some of the opinions which have so far been fed back to me – but it was ever thus!

19th March 2013 Email from Matt West to Richard Marson

Daily Mail been on to us today. Told 'em to fuck off. Politely. I'm working 7 days a week while we're getting out of the flood situation. Biddles printed the dust jackets today. They seem to be on track.

20th March 2013 Richard Marson diary extract

The *Daily Mail* have been trawling the online *Doctor Who* message boards, where some very inflammatory stuff has been posted, none of which has anything to do with what's actually in the book, but which is potentially very damaging for certain individuals. They again contacted Matt for a comment but he refused to co-operate.

Private Eye have run a story suggesting that I've written the book as an act of revenge against the BBC. Bleedin' strange way of going about it, if so, especially given the amount of work I am doing for them.

21st March 2013 Email from Josh Halliday (The Guardian) to Richard Marson

Hi Richard ... can you remember whether it was Gary or John who asked in the BBC Club bar: 'Have you ever had two up you?'

21st March 2013 Richard Marson diary extract

To Television Centre for the big closing night party. I've been invited as the guest of the Director of Communications. I got there early and spent some time in reception chatting happily to the lovely Joan Stribling, one of the tribe of super talented make-up designers that the BBC dispensed with in the 1990s. Quite unprompted, she mentioned working for John Nathan-Turner and what a party animal he had been. Studios 4, 5 and 6 had all been tarted up as vast corporate party spaces. I've worked on so many programmes here, it's the background for some of the most intense experiences of my life. Can't bear the thought that it's all going to be swept away. So instead of letting sadness get the better of me, I focus on all the familiar faces milling about. The air is full of the cries of recognition. "Darling! It's you!" People I haven't seen in years. Wendy Hutchinson, PA on my first big studio directing job. Women like her were the absolute rocks of the BBC – quietly calm, deeply supportive and ultra professional. We reminisced about the first music number I directed – D:Ream's 'Things Can Only Get Better'. To this day, if I hear the opening bars of that song, my stomach flips over. In another corner, I spy the wolfish and brilliant camera supervisor Roger Fenna, who used to glide about the *Top of the Pops* studio on the big crane camera, a man of utter charm. I avoid the floor manager with the unkind nickname of 'pig in a wig' (the wig is present and correct tonight, and it struck me as odd all over again why anyone would choose such a vivid shade of red). We are told that we are free to explore anywhere. Nowhere is out of bounds. Like giddy children on a school trip, small groups of old friends form and set off on their own individual adventures. My group wanders the basement and ground floor first, peeping in at the dressing rooms (including the one I once had to show Diana Ross into, only to discover that a previous occupant had left the sink clogged with sick) and then we make our way to the observation rooms on the second floor where you can peep into the studios below. I spent hours in these back in the 1980s, watching *Doctor Who* rehearse and record. We check out the canteen and then head to the fourth floor, to the BBC Club, which is heaving with a night of last orders. I've just accepted a large glass of red when my wife texts to say that a reporter from *The Sunday Times* has turned up at the door. Then a message from Matt to say that the *Mail* have offered pots of money for the serialisation rights. Neither of us remotely tempted. These messages interrupted the warm sense of nostalgia and I left the club and returned to the studios. Some of my group caught up with me there and said, "We're going to explore the East Tower...coming?" But no, I wasn't coming, I was going. I had had enough and couldn't shake the melancholy thought that this fabulous building was just being squandered and thrown away by the usual suspects who have fucked up so much already. This wasn't a party, it was a wake.

22nd March 2013 *Richard Marson diary extract*

On the way back from the gym when Mandy called to say that the press were ringing at the door. I snuck in via the side door and we ignored more frantic ringing. This is what they do – pester you until you can't bear the noise any more. They'd tried our next door neighbours, too, who were utterly bewildered by their attentions. Turned out to be the same girl from *The Sunday Times* who had showed up yesterday, and a smartly suited man from the *Sunday Telegraph*.

22nd March 2013 *Email from Grahame Flynn to Richard Marson*

It is no surprise that the book has been picked up by a National. SEX and *Doctor Who*!! Christmas!! I have been contacted by a couple of John's old friends who saw the *SFX* review and were very upset. I have calmed them down but saying that the book is well researched and balanced. I have maintained throughout that consensual sex between adults is not a crime. The only difficulty for some people is the age of consent. Many young gay guys of my generation were technically breaking the law between the ages of 16-21 when our straight friends were free to have 'fun'! It seems ironic now that the government has agreed and many thousands of people are having old convictions quashed. The world is changing. I know that John wasn't a paedophile but he did try it on with young adults. That was my experience.

22nd March 2013 *Email from Chris Chapman (TV producer and friend) to Richard Marson*

So, do I sense a storm brewing? :-)

23rd March 2013 *Email from Richard Marson to Chris Chapman*

Not co-operating with the press with result that I've had the *Times, Mail* and *Telegraph* all come to the door two nights running, ringing away for hours. Madness.

Matthew Sweet's review (*Guardian* was only paper we agreed to send a copy to) didn't help in that it focused on 2 of the 14 chapters. More of an article really. But heigh-ho. Looking forward to (rational) people being able to judge for themselves. A couple of John's closest friends have been in touch and said lovely, reassuring things about how fair, balanced and, ultimately, poignant it is. But the British always obsess on sex!

Staying out of the snow and watching *The Three Doctors* by the fire!

23rd March 2013 Email from Chris Chapman to Richard Marson

Watching *The Three Doctors* by the fire seems a much better idea than talking to the press!

I was surprised by how focused Matthew's piece was – I find articles like that odd, where it talks about how there will no doubt be a fuss, but in fact it's kick-starting the fuss itself!

24th March 2013 Email from Matt West to Richard Marson (and all other Miwk authors)

Good morning all.

Dropped Richard a line this morning but thought we may as well all assess the damage.

Not bad really is it?

There's still the *Mail* to come which I suspect may be waiting for the new season premiere next weekend, but frankly I have no time for anyone that reads the *Mail* so any carping or moaning that comes from it doesn't bother me.

Guardian and *Times* have been OK but actually haven't demonstrated much of a surge in sales – nowhere near as much as the genre magazines did. I think this rather proves the point that only *Doctor Who* fans care about *Doctor Who*, especially 30 year old *Doctor Who*. I also see Richard's doorstep buddies get a name-check at the end of the *Times* article. We should send them a Christmas card.

Ed Russell has been on again for a review copy ('can you bike it over in the hour?' – no I fucking can't! If we did YOU'D send a bike, why should we pay?).

24th March 2013 *Richard Marson diary extract*

A man from *The Sun* came round while I was in the bath. Stuck my head out of the bedroom window to ask what he wanted (as if I didn't know). He was very cheery and upfront, "We want a story to knock the BBC". I told him that I didn't and wouldn't be commenting. At the fag end of the evening, someone tweeted tomorrow's *Mirror* front page. '*Dr Who* Sex Scandal' it screamed. John pictured alongside Colin Baker. Poor Colin. It is a hideous piece in which I sound like some bleating ninny.

24th March 2013 *(Late) Email from Richard Marson to Matt West*

The *Mirror* cover isn't great is it? Fuckers.

25th March 2013 *Email from Richard Molesworth (writer) to Richard Marson*

I don't know if you're hiding from – or massively embracing – all the publicity your impending JN-T book is getting, but if it's the former, then I just thought I'd drop you a few words of encouragement, and let you know that I'm soooo looking forward to reading your book. I'm slightly – no, massively – staggered that some elements of fandom seem to be in a state of shock about the elements of JN-T's life that you've covered and which have been reported in the reviews and previews so far. I guess I just didn't realise how insulated the majority of fans were to JN-T's ways. It makes me realise how privileged I was to know the man, despite his flaws and imperfections.

That all just makes me admire even more the even handedness you appear to have approached the subject.

26th March 2013 *Email from David Roden to Richard Marson*

Well, you've caused a bit of a fuss, haven't you?

Bloody hell, Richard, I didn't think your book would provoke the massive reaction it has done. Unbelievable. I just hope the reaction to the more unpleasant elements in it don't overshadow what is clearly a beautifully written and diligently researched book. Has there been much response from people involved in old *Doctor Who*?

26th March 2013 *Email from Richard Marson to David Roden*

Well, I'd say the tabloids did that!

None of them got review copies and I wouldn't speak to any of them so they just lurked on the genre websites and lifted quotes from the *Guardian* and *Starburst* reviews/interviews.

26th March 2013 *Richard Marson diary extract*

The *Mail* are still aggressively pursuing every possible angle. They've phoned Matt numerous times, getting progressively shirtier. A producer from Radio 4's *The Media Show* got in touch to invite me onto this week's edition. I spoke to her and stressed that I'd only be interested if they were willing to consider the whole book and not just the bits that the tabloids are trying to get their teeth into. I also asked Eddie Mair (with whom I worked at the end of last year and a thoroughly good bloke) for his advice and he seemed to think it would be a good idea. So I agreed and we sent off a copy of the book to the programme.

The books should be back from the printers by the end of this week, and will start going out at the start of next week. The sooner the better.

27th March 2013 *Richard Marson diary extract*

Set off to Broadcasting House, where I'm to do this *Media Show* interview. They originally said it was going to be live but then asked me to come in an hour earlier so that it could be pre-recorded and played in. I was taken up through the famous maze of corridors in BH to the tiny studio, where the presenter, journalist Steve Hewlett, sweating in his shirt-sleeves, gave me a flinty welcome, not bothering with any pleasantries. There was no mistaking the hostility and I thought, "This is going to be tricky". He ran through the script which was going to introduce me and was scornful when I objected to *DWM* being described as a 'fanzine'. "It's the officially licensed, commercial magazine." "Bit of a mouthful, that" sneered Hewlett. He also seemed completely incredulous that I was still working for the BBC, following my dismissal from CBBC in 2007, and that I'd done a lot of work for them since then. I patiently ran through the various credits and they were cross-checked, as though I'd be making them up. Thank God the thing was pre-recorded. We had hardly got started before Hewlett put it to me that I had known all about the Jimmy Savile scandal when I started to work on the book and that wasn't this really just an attempt to cash-in on that and get my own back on the BBC? At this point, I said "Can we stop?" "You just did," snapped Hewlett. There was a tense moment before the producer came in from the little gallery. I pointed out that I could absolutely prove that the book was being worked on months before anybody knew about Savile. There was a delay while this was confirmed. No apology but we were off again, this time with the offending accusation left out. Hewlett then asked me why I hadn't responded to the Dame Janet Smith letter requesting for people to assist with their investigations. Because they were investigating Jimmy Savile, not John Nathan-Turner, I responded. Again, the point was grudgingly conceded. During another pause I asked Hewlett, "Have you actually read the book?" "Excerpts," he replied dismissively. And I thought, "Yeah I can guess which bits too."

When the recording was over, Hewlett casually admitted that he was good mates with Richard Deverell. This apparently rather random comment must in fact have been perfectly deliberate, as Deverell was my boss when I was forced to leave *Blue Peter* in 2007. "Then shouldn't you have declared an interest?" I said, as my parting shot. It didn't make me feel any better.

Listened to the transmission. Immensely relieved that the most offensive sections had been edited out (as well as my explanation of the thinking behind the wretched title). But really it had been a lucky escape because if it had been live, as originally intended, it really would have been the proverbial car crash.

28th March 2013 *Email from Stephen Payne (magazine editor) to Richard Marson*

Just heard your interview on Radio 4 *Media Show* and wanted to say I thought you handled the questions, and came across, very well.

29th March 2013 *Richard Marson diary extract*

Matt arrived with a car loaded to the rafters with boxes of hardback books for me to sign. They look really lovely and I couldn't be more thrilled with them. Matt has done me – and John – proud. He is bright and funny and has all his own shit to deal with on top of all this palaver with the book, but he hasn't once faltered or expressed doubts or regrets. He has been a genuine partner in the whole project since he took it on, never a feeling I could say I had with the previous outfit. We have visitors and Niamh, the 4-year-old daughter of one of our friends, watches me sign dedication after dedication. Presently she asks, "Why are you scribbling in all those new books? That's naughty!" Then she takes a closer look and comments admiringly, "That's joined-up writing...."

2nd April 2013 *Email from Richard Marson to Russell T Davies*

You'll not have missed the circus around my JN-T book. Tabloids furious because we only let *The Guardian* have a copy and refused all their offers (silly money). Course they ran stories anyway and I was hauled onto R4's *The Media Show* to face the music. I hope the circus will now have moved on and then perhaps the book can be judged on its merits or otherwise – as an in-depth biography which covers some difficult and challenging issues.

Anyway, would you like me to send you a copy?

2nd April 2013 *Email from Russell T. Davies to Richard Marson*

I saw the coverage, and though you defended yourself wonderfully. You can hardly speak a word about anything without being pilloried for it these days – which only means we must speak louder and more often! I hope you're all right and haven't received too much flak personally.

God, I'd love to read it! Though I'm happy to wait for a hard copy once it's been printed, is that okay? It'll sit proudly on my shelf. I can't wait to read it, it sounds remarkable.

2nd April 2013 *Email from Richard Marson to Russell T Davies*

Always a voice of reason – RTD for DG or PM or Head of Social Media or something...(cut to RTD fleeing to Rio...)

Thank you. A few haters got through – including a charmer who declared himself pleased that my son had died! Thank God for therapy eh? There's so much damage and dysfunction out there. Thankfully not all mine!

I'll get a copy off to you pronto

2nd April 2013 *Email from Russell T Davies to Richard Marson*

Dear God. Someone said that?? Christ in heaven. Well, nothing could be more sour and miserable and lost than that man's soul, so let's be happy that we're not him.

3rd April 2013 Email from Mark Ayres to Richard Marson

I have now read it, and I think it's an excellent, fair book. If not always an easy read. Now, I cannot claim to have been one of John's close friends, but I did work with him for a few years. And this book makes sense of a heck of a lot of things that happened. It also makes me wish (perhaps bizarrely, I don't know...) that I'd got to know him better. I think I now do. So... thanks.

5th April 2013 Email from Richard Marson to Matt West

As for Fantom, it's an ill wind and all that. I can't say how impressed I have been with the work you guys have put into this book, especially given the time frame and many other pressures (especially you Matt, of the crumbling homestead) you've been under.

I love how much you care about detail and quality – that you've worked so hard to deliver ahead of even the original deadline – and that you so clearly believe in the book itself. That means a colossal amount to me.

6th April 2013 Email from Louis Barfe (writer and researcher) to Richard Marson

Am loving the book. Even to a not-we, the BBC detail is fascinating. All this current inappropriate behaviour stuff bothers me. In my single days, I tried it on with any number of women. As I get older, I see there can be a very fine line between a flirt, a try-on and something more sinister but I think a sense of proportion has been lost.

6th April 2013 Email from Richard Marson to Louis Barfe

Well, that's lovely to hear. You won't be surprised that yours is an opinion I truly rate.

I share your concerns about the blurring of the issues around sex in the workplace. We seem to have entered an age of new Puritanism and censure which sweeps all before it and makes rational debate nigh on impossible.

Remind me to tell you the full saga of going onto the *Media Show*, where thank Christ it was (at the last minute) changed from live to a pre record. They'd been sent a PDF but no one seemed to have read it, least of all Steve Hewlett, the interviewer. I had to stop the recording twice. Maybe I should have taken the 40K offered by the *Mail* for rights to the thing and just gone over to the dark side!!!

7th April 2013 *Email from Louis Barfe to Richard Marson*

As I listened, I thought Hewlett sounded clueless and as though he had an agenda. Funny, that. I saw him on *Newsnight* at the height of the Savile thing and he was floundering. Supposedly an expert, but I'd have respected my local butcher's opinion more (and by God, does he have opinions). 40k from the *Mail*? Bloody hell. Actually, that would have been hilarious. They buy it up for serial, thinking there's going to be filth and bile on every page. "Hang on, most of the people are saying he was a lovely bloke, and there's an awful lot about marking out rehearsal room floors with coloured tape," asks Dacre, "Is that some sort of poof euphemism?"

14th April 2013 *Email from Kate Easteal (John's production secretary) to Richard Marson*

Many thanks for sending me your book. I've started reading it and think the research is brilliant – I'm really enjoying it. I don't know how you found all those people from John's early years, but it's all very interesting to me.

I heard you being interviewed on Radio 4 and read Matthew Sweet's comments. It seems there was so much more going on at *Doctor Who* than I was aware of at the time, both within the department and off-shore. I'm feeling a bit naive – but then again, I was young at the time so probably only saw what I wanted to see and was too polite to ask questions (and of course, John and Gary must have been discreet in front of me). I'm sure your research will paint a much more complex and complimentary picture than Matthew Sweet suggests – I can tell that already.

I'm really looking forward to reading other people's reminiscences of John and getting to know the man all over again. When you write about the nicknames he had for everyone, that made me laugh because I'd forgotten that. He always called Marjorie Cooper (a Management person in Series & Serials), Brunehilde, because she was large and Germanic-looking. He was mischievous like that.

14th April 2013 *Email from Russell T Davies to Richard Marson*

Oh, it's arrived, in its beautiful Hawaiian shirt jacket! Oh my eyes. It actually took me a few seconds to work out what it was! But thank you so much. And a lovely letter from Miwk, what nice people they are.

I'm going to read it as soon as I can! I'm a little scared of it!

20th April 2013 *Email from Russell T. Davies to Richard Marson*

Oh Richard!

That book is extraordinary. The ending is devastating. Oh, what an end to a life, it's genuinely tragic. All those hopes and dream poisoned and rotted by alcohol. It makes me even more appalled with the BBC – no duty of care for the man, not a hint of compassion anywhere.

But that's a great piece of work. I have read it in two days flat, I couldn't stop. It's so extraordinary, to find those schoolboy friends. The girlfriend! It's then quite extraordinary when you, Richard, actually enter the picture – defending your honour with a copy of *Timelash*, I was hooting! I've never seen a biographer enter the story like that, it was brilliant and invigorating.

And the picture painted of Gary Downie is ferocious – what a shame JN-T never escaped his shadow. I spent a lot of the time wondering what he'd have been like, if he'd got away. And yet, and yet… that's easily said, because the relationship was his own choice, in the end.

I must say, those upper echelons of fandom come out of it terribly. Terribly! Those monsters. God, I'm glad I stayed away from all that, I'd have murdered them.

That really is a major piece of *Doctor Who* history, and the history of an entire industry. An entire age, really. As these accusations go on, I can't help wondering if we're living in a witch-hunt, or undergoing a form of justice; I genuinely don't know. Your book captures that confusion perfectly. I suspect none of us would come out of it well, to have the details of our lives laid bare, and yet it's irresistible, when we can read someone else's!

But in the end, I think the book is clear – we have to forgive JN-T. He did little wrong, except get a bit too horny a bit too often, with a bit too much power mixed in. And, yes, okay, with some horrific lapses in professionalism. (I'm far more alarmed by his treatment of Nicola Bryant than by a frantic blowjob in the office!) But that ending, that ending… Oh, he didn't deserve that. And I think, by writing about it, you have made something elegant and even beautiful out of such a wretched mess. And I think that's very kind of you indeed. This book says a lot about JN-T, but it says a lot about your good and kind heart, too.

20th April 2013 Richard Marson diary extract

Set off to London for the latest of these BFI anniversary screenings (*Robots of Death*). Lunch there first with Patrick, Ralph Montagu and Patrick's colleague from *Radio Times*, Mark Braxton. All very relaxed and pleasant. Edward Russell comes over and exchanges in a barrage of small talk. Think how very odd it is that he never once refers to the book, despite this being the first time I have seen him since all the fuss and bother. Eventually he rushed off as "I need to find Steven". When I saw the BFI's Justin Johnson, he grinned and said "You're brave to show up! We're thinking of shining a spotlight on you." Just before the programme started, we bumped into the ever-smiling Peter Ware from *DWM* and a nervous-looking man who turned out to be writer and fan Jonny Morris. Morris had recently written an ambivalent but on the whole fairly complimentary blog about the book, for which he was told off in public on Twitter in schoolmarmish tones by a hoity-toity Nicola Bryant. She has been sounding off about the book (despite not having read it), saying that it is amateurish. Morris didn't seem pleased to see me, visibly squirming while I thanked him for the nice things he had said.

Robots of Death delivered the goods all over again. Such an enjoyable story and so well made. There was an on-stage panel with Tom Baker afterwards, the great man using a stick to make his way up to the platform. Of course I know he is an old man now and shouldn't be surprised somehow the enduring image of these *Who* actors is always of them in their prime. Which is kind of wonderful, I suppose – that strange immortality. Baker didn't give much of a fuck what he said or who he offended back in the day and being in the twilight years has only accentuated that. He was very funny. I was pleased that his references to John were perfectly in step with what I'd included in the book. They'd hated each other to begin with and then, years later, a real friendship had formed, partly as a result of John's loyalty – he was one of the few producers with whom Baker worked who continued to offer him both employment and hospitality.

21st April 2013 *Richard Marson diary extract*

Despite misgivings, decide to email Nicola Bryant to at least give her the opportunity to vent directly, or make any points she wants to, because the snide digs she has been indulging in on social media are unfounded when she also professes not even to have read the bloody thing! My own theory is that she used the book as an opportunity to vent her spleen about the hideous spitting incident that ended her friendship with John and, at some level, she is now shooting the messenger. It was her choice to put that saga in the public domain but maybe there's a twinge of conscience about the wisdom of doing so and she's transferring the guilt/anger/or whatever negative feelings she's experiencing onto the book. Or maybe I am over analysing.

24th April 2013 *Email from Stuart Denman* (Newsnight) *to Richard Marson*

So, following on from my email last night, I'm working with Shaun Ley planning a *Newsnight* film to mark *Who*'s 50th, but which we'd aim to broadcast next month. With the programme's success and popularity now a given, it's hard to imagine a time when it wasn't celebrated. But we'd like to take a look at the period when it struggled to keep going. From the end of the 70s when rampant inflation ate into its already modest budget, when TV sci-fi was left exposed by cinema successes such as *Star Wars*, and throughout the 80s when the programme's multi-camera studio set-up was becoming increasingly old-fashioned. Yet, the programme was still a big earner for the BBC, despite being held in contempt by many of those in charge of the corporation at the time.

As you've just written about the man who had to steer the programme through those years and worked at the BBC when it was undergoing significant changes, it would be great if we could talk to you. (I appreciate that your biog is more about JN-T the man.)

Please let me know if you'd be interested in getting involved.

26th April 2013 *Email from Fiona Cumming and Ian Fraser to Richard Marson*

Back from Denmark after a fraught journey there. JN-T's book went with us and proved riveting. The photos were well chosen (although I met Ian Levine around 1980 and can't remember him ever looking that good) and made happy memories.

I fully endorse Russell T Davies' thoughts. It was such a shabby way John was treated after all he had given. Fandom certainly behaved badly but I cannot get past the behaviour of the upper echelons of BBC and their lack of care. For a Head of Department to have so little humanity and be as vituperative (even all these years later) as Powell is mind boggling.

The honesty shown throughout your assessment of his life is heart warming to those of his friends still left. I do hope that reactions after publication look at the whole rounded story which you have drawn with empathy and understanding. Ian and I are glad that we were able to contribute in a small way to a book you should be rightly proud of.

1st May 2013 *Email from Saul Nasse [TV executive and former editor of* Tomorrow's World*] to Richard Marson*

Finished your book last night. It was really compelling – particularly as it worked for me on three levels: as the *DWB*-reading fan; the acquaintance of JN-T; the TV type. It is of course a terribly sad story, and the sheer weight of testimony you brought together was amazing. Did you ever try to speak to Colin Rogers? I knew him quite well when he was at the BBC World Service Trust, and he was John's immediate boss for some time – he was the first person I ever heard talk about John's promiscuity. The thing I felt reading it was if he was around now he wouldn't have got so sozzled or shagged as much as it just ain't an industry for that these days – so he'd have survived physically. And also if he'd been producer for RTD or SM he'd have been extremely effective. With their budget of course. There's a bit of an irony that John survived all that sex without getting HIV but was destroying his liver at the same time.

I started the book nervous about the thought I'd be quoted in it, but by the end really wished I had been. Aside from the drinking and the sex I saw every side of

JN-T in my dealings with him. In the end, as every bit of advice he gave me was spot on, he has my respect.

1st May 2013 *Richard Marson diary extract*

Today is the 11th anniversary of John's death.

Ian Levine is on the phone. 'Steven Moffat hates you,' he blasts into my ear.

This is not news, I tell him.

3rd May 2013 *Email from Jude Ho* (The Culture Show) *to Richard Marson*

We are very keen to pick up an interview with you. However, needs to be once your book has been published. Is the publication date still 31st May? And is there a press copy available yet?

5th May 2013 *Christopher H. Bidmead Tweet*

This JN-T book of @richardmarson2's is deeply researched, full of surprises, and is turning out to be the best read of the year so far.

6th May 2013 *Email from Christopher H. Bidmead to Richard Marson*

It's a hell of an achievement, and I'm in awe of the evident work you've put into this.

IMHO Miwk's made a bold and entirely sound business decision to run with this book of yours, and I'm sure they're onto a winner. There's no question in my mind that *JN-T* deserves to go mainstream.

7th May 2013 *Christopher H. Bidmead Tweet*

There's definitely a movie to be made from @richardmarson2's JN-T book. Could we get @rickygervais to play the lead?

15th May 2013 Peter Harness (writer) Tweet

Brilliant book, by the way. Many congratulations. And I do in all honesty think it would make an excellent movie.

15th May 2013 Richard Marson diary extract

To NBH for this *Newsnight* interview. Met by Stuart Denman in reception and taken straight down to make-up and then onto the studio floor. It's all green screen. Interviewed by Shaun Ley, who is very pleasant and naturally well-informed as he's a true fan. Seemed genuinely interested in the saga of what went wrong with *Who* in the 1980s, though I admitted that when they first got in touch with me, I had thought this just a ruse to get me in to talk about the dirt. But no, I was building my part; they really were keen to explore the 80s as far as the programme was concerned, though it does seem an odd item for *Newsnight*. Then again, who am I to judge when I think of some of the bizarre stuff I agreed to cover on *Blue Peter*. Not least devoting nearly a whole show to *Doctor Who* way back in 1999, long pre the revival. This is what fans do – we keep the flame alive, however we can! Anyway, the interview went very well. Afterwards, Shaun did tell me that one or two actors (I guessed who!) didn't want to contribute once they were told I was involved.

20th May 2013 Christopher H. Bidmead Tweet

I'm serious. There's a movie here, and #MichaelWinterbottom's the one to make it.

29th May 2013 Email from Tom Spilsbury (editor DWM) to Richard Marson

I've just seen the DM, thanks for getting in touch. I'll have a think about reviewing the book - I do feel it's a tricky one as I know the BBC brand people got very worried about it, and although no one has told me NOT to review it, I'm still a little wary. But I'll give it a bit of thought.

29th May 2013 Richard Marson diary extract

Gloomy news. Biddles, printers of the book, have gone into administration and won't honour the 3rd print run which was due next week. Nothing I can do about it, but it is frustrating.

30th May 2013 Email from Richard Marson to Tom Spilsbury

Thanks for giving this further consideration.

At the risk of boring you to tears, I suppose this matters to me not because I'm desperate for more column inches (I can hardly complain on that score!) but because there seem to be so many misconceptions around the book and the intention in writing it – most of which don't actually focus on the content, which even Matthew Sweet in his somewhat sniffy review admitted contained 'admirably dogged research'.

As you will know, these projects are done for the love, not the money. I really felt there was something to explore here, a story worth telling, to which I had something meaningful to contribute and my ambition was to write something readable but 'grown up' – in that it wouldn't duck the issues when examining in detail the behind the scenes life of such a high profile and troubled TV drama.

For *DWM* to avoid all mention of the book just seems, well, a bit odd, really. Slightly Stalinist, I suppose. Other *Who* books have contained material which some might find uncomfortable – and this is usually flagged up and dealt with sensitively and appropriately by you and your team. I feel sure you would get the balance right. Perhaps one approach might be to get a 'guest' name in to write about it – as you've done with people like Andrew Cartmel in the past.

Ultimately, however, I do completely respect that it is your decision.

There was no response to this email and for over two years, DWM *studiously avoided all mention of the book, or the related public controversy and debate, which made their review of the 50th anniversary year in particular a bit of a nonsense. It wasn't until the spring of 2015 when Miwk were to publish my next biography, about the producer Verity Lambert, that the lengthy fatwa was finally lifted. The piece promoting Verity was presented with a separate section devoted to the JN-T book and the resultant fall out, neatly legitimising its mention and inclusion in future issues. In August 2016, the magazine printed an interview with Peter Davison in which he accused me of trying to draw a parallel between John's activities and those of Jimmy Savile. As this was precisely the opposite intention of the book, I asked the editor, Tom, to print my response, which he did:*

Surprised (but not delighted) to see Peter Davison's comments about my biography of JN-T in the latest issue of DWM. *One of its key conclusions was that there was absolutely nothing Savile-esque about John. At the time of publication, making that clear was particularly important and three years later, it bears repeating for anyone else who clearly hasn't read the book..*

During our lengthy chat concerning this, Tom reiterated that it had been his decision not to run a review of the book back in 2013, although he did admit to having forwarded his PDF review copy to Steven Moffat. In hindsight, this made the frantic requests from BBC Cardiff for a copy seem rather odd as evidently the show runner had one all the time.

15th June 2013 *Richard Marson diary extract*

Driven to Manchester by Matt to the Fab Cafe (ironic name if ever there was one; it's a dark and dingy place) to promote the book. Am-dram microphone arrangement and the guy interviewing me was already very quiet so that didn't help. But *Starburst,* who organised the event, have been very supportive so I do my best, sitting on a stool like a poor man's Val Doonican and fielding questions. Sold and signed a good few books. One man was buying three copies – one to read, one to keep pristine and one to flog on eBay! Meanwhile, Edward Russell can be found on Twitter asking for everyone's approval of his 'sexy' new look.

16th June 2013 *Richard Marson diary extract*

To Leeds for the next event. Asked to pose for a photo alongside a big blow-up of the cover. I should, of course, have done the JN-T 'point' to the man himself, but this didn't occur until too late.

22nd June 2013 *Richard Marson diary extract*

Drove to Ian Levine's birthday dinner in Ealing. A distinctly 1970s Eastern European feel to the venue. "May I have a Bellini?", I asked the unsmiling woman behind the bar. "No," she said, simply. Ralph Wilton, very sweet ex-BBC production manager cornered me and, perfectly charmingly, asked why I'd described him as a "camp old queen" in the book. I said that I hadn't, but had actually quoted Ian who had used the term. Ralph pouted a bit but didn't really seem too upset and continued to chat very amiably about the good old days at TV Centre. "Darling, it was such a fabulous time, wasn't it?" he said, waving his hands around. Eric Saward and Jane Judge arrived. Ian tried to introduce them to me but they weren't having any of it and spent most of the night sitting silently together, looking tense and out of it, possibly terrified that I'd descend on them and make a scene, poor things. Likewise, Tom Spilsbury smiled wanly in my general direction but we didn't speak. It was an odd evening. Michelle Collins arrived, a tiny figure in tight trousers and spiky heels, and was paraded around as the trophy guest and Ian asked people to make speeches about him, some of which were candid to say the least and very funny. Towards the end of the night I was cornered by a guy called Sheldon Collins, who used to write for *DWB*. He asked me if I felt 'guilty' about the JN-T book, but didn't specify exactly what he meant by this. So, like Zammo, I just said no.

20th July 2013 Richard Marson diary extract

My birthday party. Patrick gave me a T-shirt printed up with a picture of the pair of us in our 80s prime, labelled 'doable barkers'. Very droll.

2nd August 2013 Email from Roy Hawkesford [John's childhood friend] to Richard Marson

I have a terrible admission to make. I find your book hard to read. Not because of your writing and research – which are excellent – but because of the world you are describing. It is, frankly, a world populated by the kind of people I dreaded back in the 70s and 80s, in my prime. People I imagined as incompetent, but somehow acceptable to the establishment. Why? I was from the same background as John, but I developed differently. I was an academic, yes, but with close affinity with the arts and entertainment – and television. I was heavily involved in film, music and media education, and the highest role model was, I regret to say, the BBC. Of course I wasn't naive. I knew that those industries were imperfect, and I knew that nepotism was probably all. But the world your book portrays is even worse than I could have imagined... to think that I could have submitted scripts of my own, so optimistically, with virtually no chance of ever being read – well, I feel betrayed. Sorry, this is nothing to do with your writing; it's to do with the content, the world you are so expertly describing, and so well researched.

I'm not surprised at your portrayal of John. He is a logical development from the John I knew. Gary seems to have been a monster. The BBC a kind of Gormenghast!

I really do admire your research and your writing. I think I have more of a problem than I ever thought with the establishment. Sorry.

6th August 2013 *email from Robert Neill* (The Culture Show) *to Richard Marson*

I am writing from the *Culture Show* at BBC Scotland. As you know we are currently producing a special documentary to coincide with the 50th anniversary of the first episode of *Doctor Who*. I understand my colleagues may have approached you in the past about being interviewed for the programme.

We are now planning filming days during August and September to interview contributors. From what I understand you are interested in taking part and are available in August. We are keen to make this happen and I just wanted to confirm this was the case and also what days would be most suitable for you. We have no firm filming days at the moment so would look to film with you at the most suitable time possible.

It would be great to know your thoughts on this and I would be happy to answer any questions you may have about the programme. I look forward to hearing from you.

6th August 2013 *Email from Richard Marson to Robert Neill*

Thanks for getting in touch about the special.

The various conversations I've had with Jude were based around the biography I wrote about *Doctor Who*'s longest running producer, John Nathan-Turner, which, as you probably know, was published in May – and how the culture of the BBC in the 80s affected the show and led to its postponement in 1985 and then its demise in 1989. I'm assuming you have a copy?

26th August 2013 *Richard Marson diary extract*

Drove to the Media Centre for this *Culture Show* filming, where I was to be interviewed by Matthew Sweet, the man who wrote the rather sniffy Guardian review back in March. He was affable and didn't mention the book. Instead he was enjoyably indiscreet about the shenanigans going on in Cardiff. The kind of gossip that's the mark of the true *Doctor Who* fan – naturally, I lapped it up. He told me that Cardiff hadn't at all wanted this special to be made and had tried to insist upon total editorial control. Quite rightly, they'd lost that one as the Controller of BBC Two, Janice Hadlow, had dug in her heels. Having lost that one, they also tried to prevent the programme devoting any airtime to the book. I wondered whether perhaps this is why it had taken so many months for me to make my contribution, given that they first approached me at the start of the year. Sweet told me that this was the very last day of shooting on the project.

I was amazed to discover that they had a proper make-up person, two camera crews and a full lighting rig. Clearly thousands of pounds had been spent, so I felt the pressure to keep my teeth in and my eye on the ball. Jude, the director, was very friendly and efficient but clearly a 'not-we', bemused by the bizarre and labyrinthine detail of the *Doctor Who* world she was trying to engage with. There were a lot of questions to wade through, most of which I knew didn't have a cat in hell's chance of making their way into the final cut. It took over two hours; and was exhaustive – among many other things, I was asked for my thoughts about the casting of Peter Capaldi, the issue of violence in the show and even my opinion of the music composed for *The Talons of Weng-Chiang*. Not even I care what I think about that. Then, after a break, another set of questions appeared and now a slight tension was palpable. These were evidently the 'sex and scandal' questions. Jude explained that these had all been carefully vetted and stressed to Sweet that he must ask them exactly as they were written. I got a bit frosty at this point, given that I had made it perfectly clear during the various preparatory conversations that I didn't want this to be the focus of our discussion on John. Indeed, I'd been reassured that the main areas of interest were discussing John's genius for promotion and his foresight in recognising the power of the *Doctor Who* brand and what went wrong with the series during the 80s. Jude handled my concerns deftly, offering a guarantee that this wouldn't be the only aspect of the interview that was used in the finished programme. But it was the BBC's way of 'owning' the story so that no one could accuse them of any kind of cover up. I wasn't very happy with it but I agreed and made a mental note to be as precise as I possibly could, only too aware of the danger of my answers being edited so that the context was lost or the emphasis of what I was trying to say altered. We worked our way through the list and then there was another break while Jude conferred with her crew and tried to decide whether she wanted to take us all to the now empty offices on Shepherd's Bush Green where the drama department had been based in the 1980s. The idea was to shoot some 'GV's' (general views) of myself and Sweet walking round the abandoned corridors, presumably to illustrate the 'scandal' bit of the story. In the end, they decided against making the effort and so the GV's were shot with us wandering around the Media Centre instead; rather odd as I'd been working here only recently. As the shots were taken, Sweet asked me about my kids and I told him that my son had died when he was 14. "Oh, I didn't know that," he said lightly, as if he should.

I was finally cleared and free to go just before 3pm and drove home with the car windows wide open and the wind whipping up my hair, deep in thought about the whole more than slightly surreal experience.

17th September 2013 *Email from Jude Ho to Richard Marson*

Thanks so much for your strong contribution the other day.

22nd September 2013 *Richard Marson diary extract*

Peter Harness (writer of the British version of *Wallander* and various episodes of *Doctor Who*) has again been in touch to say he is re-reading JN-T and has anyone optioned the film and TV rights yet? No, but here's hoping, say I. Shortly afterwards, Matt calls to say that the book is about to go into its 6th impression.

2th November 2013 *Richard Marson diary extract*

To the NFT for the preview screening of *An Adventure in Time and Space*. A beautiful crisp winter night and a beautiful, moving film. I'd agreed to get there early because the BFI wanted me to sign some copies of *JN-T* for their shop. Then the lovely BFI chap, Justin, ferried me to the green room which was heaving with an odd medley of *Doctor Who* glitterati. Chatted to the very tiny Philip Hinchcliffe and his wife Dee, and he was immediately interested when I told him I was embarking on a biography of Verity Lambert. "She took no prisoners," he said, in admiring tones. He's a man with a fund of stories about the drama greats. Unfortunately, a tiresome actress called Sarah Douglas kept butting in, her eyes constantly swivelling the room in case she missed a better networking opportunity. This doesn't help the flow of conversation. "I want to meet Andy Pryor (long-term casting director on *Who*)," she announced, apropos of nothing. "I bet you do," said I, tartly but she wasn't listening – too busy swivelling again. I detach myself, bored by her neediness. Over in a corner by himself was Matthew Waterhouse, in a 1970s style leather jacket. As shy as the day I met him all those years ago in the crappy Marvel offices, but his sweet nature and intelligence shine through the awkwardness. Very different is the welcome I receive from Sophie Aldred and her husband Vince, whom I once directed in a children's game show for ITV. They are the definition of ebullient. Sophie has the great ability to make everyone she talks to feel as if they are the person she most wants to talk to at that moment, and I'm no exception, instantly under her spell. She is as much a fan as the rest of us and is so excited about the film. Louise Jameson is much in demand, ushered hither and yon by the charming Matt Evenden, who acts as a kind of 'companion to the companions' at many of these events. Edward Russell makes the effort to seem friendly, though I'm sure he wishes I'd just fuck off out of it. It's boring exchanging fake pleasantries in a room full of so many genuinely interesting people. Tom Spilsbury is there and this time we share a few words. He's a gentle, considered man, and it has been a difficult year for him, banging out the magazine with his skeleton team and navigating all the Cardiff control-freakery. Centre of attention, and rightly so, is Waris Hussein, who looks remarkably young and thrilled to be revered for a little job he did right at the start of his distinguished career. At one point he whispers to me, "My dear, how Verity would have loved all this," and I feel a pang for her, and Lis Sladen, for Jon Pertwee, and Nick Courtney, for Barry Letts and, of course, John – all of them giants of *Doctor Who*, all of whom would have 'loved all this'.

22nd November 2013 *Richard Marson diary extract*

The Culture Show Doctor Who anniversary special aired. Leaving aside my own agenda, I thought it was a right bloody mess, editorially all over the place. Clearly, they had shot far too much and the narrative meandered about, never truly delivering anything that felt satisfying or significant and, critically, the programme inspired no emotional impact whatsoever. Well, not on me anyway and I was willing it to make me cry, in celebration of such a wonderful series which has meant so much to me over the years. I find Matthew Sweet difficult enough to take in small doses, never mind on something of this scale – his manner seems so contrived, his approach creepily oleaginous, and always there is that aura of smugness and intellectual superiority. "I know something you don't but fear not, let me translate to those of you without a degree..." Not my cup of tea at all. They'd clearly wasted their cash on me; there was a brief, blink and you'll miss it, mention of John's skill in promoting the show overseas and then a half-hearted stab at the so-called scandal, a story which was so out of kilter with the rest of the programme it made me cringe at the lack of craft. Their very own behind-the-sofa moment. Predictable, I suppose, when I think back to the circumstances of the shooting, but disappointing still. They could so easily have run with a positive JN-T story instead; they certainly had all the material to do so.

After it went out, Matt emailed to report another surge in orders.

2014

The book has continued to sell. From time to time, it continues to cause arguments. It is frequently used to support the various contrary positions people take up when they start discussing John, his work, his personality, his impact and his legacy. There is plenty that I would approach differently if I were to write the book now. The writing could certainly have been more elegant and the editing more rigorous. I know that I was beset with the fear that if I didn't quote in full, people might assume I was making my own assumptions. The strive for balance became a slight burden and, as a result, there is undoubtedly repetition and this sometimes allows the narrative to sag or lose focus. The title was unhelpful and I wish I had held out for one of the others; it would have been less of a distraction and would have made no difference to sales. But I'm proud of the fact that the book was authentic to the workings of the BBC as both John and I knew it, and how that changed irrevocably over the years. I'm also glad that I stuck to the principle that this was a book for adults, which would place the fantasy world of Doctor Who *firmly within the reality of the world in which it was made and the people who made it. I continue to receive feedback and comments, and they are (mostly) always welcome. This is one of my favourites:*

20th July 2014 *Email from Kate Easteal to Richard Marson*

I just wanted you to know how much pleasure I got from reading your book and how I appreciate your asking for my contribution. Your research was incredible! I don't know how you found half those people – I'm still not quite sure how you found me – you must have access to state files or something.

The book was a mixture of two things for me. An absolutely brilliant trip down memory lane – we don't normally get a chance to re-live a period of our lives, but I felt I did that through reading your book. I took my time over it and savoured every page, not wanting it to be over too quickly.

I felt I was back in that Drama department 28 years ago – all the names and faces. I pictured everything as it was and the friends I had there, and remembered how exciting it all was for me. I was 21 then (I turned 50 this year).

The other impact the book had was the realisation of how little I knew of what was really going on! I had my suspicions but I was quite shocked at the scale of the propositioning of fans and all the stuff with *DWB*. I knew John hated *DWB* and that crowd, but never fully understood why. He either didn't trust me or felt I was too young/naive to know. I'm glad I didn't know at the time as it may have affected how I felt about him and Gary. I also hadn't realised how everyone hated Gary – to me he was just a camp, crude old dancer with nothing very interesting to say – I was ambivalent about him really.

But what a sad old story. I can't quite work out how a clever man like John couldn't get more of a grip on himself – both with his predatory approaches to fans, and his alcoholism. Steered off-course by his own ego I expect, and by Gary. He was such a contradictory character – such a doting, kind son to his elderly parents, while at the same time using his powerful position on *Doctor Who* to take advantage of young, vulnerable fans. There were some decent, good people around him at the time – Fiona, Ian and Colin for example – who must have all known what he was up to but still talk about him with such high praise and affection. I can't imagine accepting that kind of behaviour in a friend. Maybe the entertainment world was so bawdy at the time, that his behaviour was not so shocking. The more revelations that come out in the media, the more this appears to be the case.

I lost touch with John very quickly after leaving. I saw John's obituary in *The Guardian* one day and was shocked that he had died so young. I hadn't heard anything about him for such a long time but I didn't expect that. From your account of it, his funeral sounded a very positive tribute to him – he would so have loved all that flamboyance. When I read about the tap dancing, it really made me smile as he always wanted everyone involved to 'do a turn'.

I still love *Doctor Who* (how could I not?). I went with my 2 youngest sons to the cinema for the 50th anniversary, absorbed myself in all the programmes that weekend, and felt very proud. Working on *Doctor Who* is a small fact about me that few people know, but something I like to drop into conversation and surprise people with, from time to time.

It all happened such a long time ago... so thank you for taking me back.

About the Author

Richard Marson graduated from the University of Durham in 1987 and joined the BBC, progressing rapidly from floor assistant to producer/director. His credits include *The Movie Game, Disney Adventures* and *Disney Club, The Big Breakfast, Record Breakers* and *Tomorrow's World*. In 1997 he joined *Blue Peter*, where he remained for a decade, with four years as the programme's Editor. During this time, he won a BAFTA, and was nominated for another BAFTA and an RTS award. In 2007, he was Executive Producer of BBC Four's *Children's TV On Trial* and in 2009, wrote the script for the BBC's Darwin anniversary Prom. He also produced and directed *Tales of Television Centre* for BBC Four.

For the last few years, he has been an Executive Producer at TwoFour, where his credits include *The Holiday Makers* (Sky One), *I Know What You Weighed Last Summer* (BBC Three), and three series of the CBBC documentary series *Our School*.

He is the author of several books, including *Inside Updown: The Story of Upstairs, Downstairs, Blue Peter 50th Anniversary* and *Drama and Delight: The Life of Verity Lambert*.

He has contributed to many TV and radio programmes, including *Newsnight* (BBC), *The Culture Show* (BBC), *Archive on Four* (BBC Radio Four) *Doctor Who Confidential* (BBC Three), *The Media Show* (BBC Radio Four) and *The Richard Bacon Show* (BBC Five Live).

About the Cover Artist

Andrew Skilleter is an experienced and creatively versatile illustrator living in and working from, the Isle of Purbeck, Dorset, UK, with a track record spanning decades using both digital and traditional techniques.

He has provided artwork for over 70 *Doctor Who* book and video covers and in 1985 collaborated with John Nathan-Turner on the book *The TARDIS Inside Out*, selling over 45,000 copies worldwide.

www.andrewskilleter.com/

AVAILABLE FROM **MIWK PUBLISHING** BY THE SAME AUTHOR

Drama and Delight

THE LIFE AND LEGACY OF
VERITY LAMBERT

by Richard Marson

For five decades, the name Verity Lambert appeared on the end credits of many of Britain's most celebrated and talked about television dramas, among them *Adam Adamant Lives!, Budgie, The Naked Civil Servant, Minder, Edward and Mrs Simpson, Eldorado, G.B.H. and Jonathan Creek.* She was the very first producer of *Doctor Who*, which she nurtured through its formative years at a time when there were few women in positions of power in the television industry. Later, she worked within the troubled British film business and became a pioneering independent producer, founding her own highly-successful company, Cinema Verity.

Within her profession, she was hugely respected as an intensely driven, sometimes formidable but always stylish exponent of her craft, with the stamina and ability to combine quantity with quality. Many of her productions have had a lasting cultural and emotional impact on their audiences and continue to be enjoyed to this day.

But who was the woman behind all these television triumphs and what was the price she paid to achieve them?

Combining months of painstaking research and interviews with many of Lambert's closest friends and colleagues, *Drama and Delight* will capture the energy and spirit of this remarkable woman and explore her phenomenal and lasting legacy.

ISBN 978-1-908630-33-9

www.miwk.com/

www.facebook.com/MiwkPublishingLtd

www.instagram.com/miwkpublishing/

www.twitter.com/#!/MiwkPublishing